THE TIME WRITER AND THE NOTEBOOK
A HISTORICAL TIME TRAVEL ADVENTURE

THE TIME WRITER
BOOK ONE

ALEX R CRAWFORD

This book is a work of fiction. Names, characters, places, and incidents are the product of the author's overactive and squirrelly imagination or are used fictitiously. Any resemblance to actual events, locales, or persons, living or dead, is purely coincidental.

Copyright © 2022 Jodie Renee DeLeon

All Rights Reserved

Cover design and original illustration by Roland DeLeon.

Cover copyright © 2023, 2022 by Spilled Red Ink LLC

No part of this book may be reproduced, to include but not limited to, scanning, uploading, printing, distribution, or any other form of reproduction, without written permission from the publisher. If you would like permission to use material from the book, other than review purposes, please contact editor@spilledredink.com. Thank you for the support of the author's rights and intellectual property.

Spilled Red Ink is an imprint of Spilled Red Ink LLC. The Spilled Red Ink name and logo are trademarks of Spilled Red Ink LLC.

Spilled Red Ink
PO Box 731
Garrisonville, VA 22463-0731
spilledredink.com

Names: Crawford, Alex R. | The Time Writer and The Notebook.
Title: The Time Writer and The Notebook / Alex R Crawford.
Description: Spilled Red Ink trade paperback edition. | Virginia: Spilled Red Ink, 2022.
ISBN 9781953485007 (softcover)
Subjects: BISAC: FICTION / Fantasy / Historical. | FICTION / Historical / Colonial America & Revolution. | FICTION / Science Fiction / Time Travel.

Content Warnings: mild language, violence, attempted assault, death, war, secondhand embarrassment, and intentional misuse of the French language.

READING ORDER

The Time Writer Series:
Prequel: *The Time Writer and The Cloak*
ebook and audiobook available for FREE download to newsletter subscribers

https://bit.ly/CloakNB

Season 1: 1750s Virginia - French & Indian War
Book 1: *The Time Writer and The Notebook*
Book 2: *The Time Writer and The March*
Book 3: *The Time Writer and The Hunt*

Season 2: 1690s - The Golden Age of Piracy
Book 4: *The Time Writer and The Escape*
Book 5: *The Time Writer and The Chase*
Book 6: *The Time Writer and The Surrender*

Visit my website for early releases, special offers, and to purchase ebooks, audiobooks, signed paperbacks, and exclusive merchandise.

alexrcrawford.com

INTRODUCTION

Beware of doorways through time... and the French

While on a routine research trip, author Amelia Murray walks through a doorway at an old fort and slips back in time to 1754, leaving her friends and college-aged daughter behind.

Taken hostage by a French military unit, her confiscated notebook, with the dates and locations of battles for a young George Washington, could lead to his early death and the demise for the future United States.

Amelia must escape the French, retrieve her notebook, and save Washington without changing the course of history.
When the door she traveled through won't exist for another year, where will she find another doorway through time?

INTRODUCTION

How is a modern-day woman going to survive in Colonial America on the brink of war?

The Time Writer and The Notebook is a Historical Time Travel Adventure exploring the beginnings of the French and Indian War through the wit and mindset of a 21st century woman.

Dedication and Ramblings

*For my ayesayers and naysayers:
The anachronist has arrived.*

Content warnings *found on the Copyright page include, but are not limited to: my intentional ridiculous misuse of the beautiful French language, cringe-worthy secondhand embarrassment, and mild violence. There are a few more listed; however, I'm sure I missed something that someone will find troubling to their good senses. For instance, Amelia's brusque behavior and pushback to adapting to her new environment is possibly upsetting to someone. She's not perfect, and neither am I. Life is a learning process, and it is never my intent to offend anyone.*

If I missed a warning that someone finds disruptive to their reading enjoyment, I apologize in advance. I'm not blaming it on the fact that my crystal ball is in the shop, but I'm supposed to get it back next week.

Grab a drink, sit back, relax, and enjoy the adventure.

CHAPTER ONE

"I'm heading to Winchester for a week, not to the moon. It's not like you won't be able to reach me." My cell phone laid on the bed as I video chatted with my daughter Hannah. I had tried to prop it up on the side of my suitcase; however, an errant pair of jeans being thrown into the suitcase knocked it over and left her to stare at my ceiling. *Would my cell phone work on the moon? Focus, Murray!*

"Mom," Hannah said, exasperated, in a voice loud enough for me to hear her from across the room. She sounded irritated with me. I paid no attention to what she said. I walked back from the dresser with an arm full of bras, underwear, and socks. Should I bring a spare or two? "You're a forty-year-old woman who lives alone. It's easier for me to know if you're okay if you are at home writing. I don't know why you need to go on a week-long research trip a couple of hours away from home. You could just make a few day trips out there. Or just do the research on the Internet."

I swear there must be an old lady hiding in her body.

"Don't forget you said you would stop by the house to water the plants and bring in the mail," I said, as I ignored Hannah's comments. I continued to wander around my room, pulling out clothes from drawers, tossing some to the side, looking for just the right outfits to wander through historic battlefields—nothing fancy, just sturdy. The laundry basket was full of clothes that were clean and folded but hadn't made their way into the drawers and closet. I searched through it, looking for my favorite hoodie. I would put the rest away when I got back from my trip. "It's a research trip for my next book. It will be nice to visit the place where George Washington had his headquarters during the French and Indian War. I need to get a feel for the area, and I can't do that behind the computer."

Hannah lived in Williamsburg and was a freshman at the College of William and Mary, just far enough from home to move out, yet close enough to visit within a couple of hours' drive. And close enough to call and harass me for what she thought were frivolous pursuits for a story. We were close for as long as I could remember; however, after they killed her father, we bonded to the point of becoming nearly inseparable. She originally wanted to go to school at the University of Mary Washington in Fredericksburg and continue to live at home, but I had other plans for her. I insisted Hannah experience university life away from home, that it would be a fun adventure, an opportunity to meet new people, and get out of her dependence on me. She didn't need to become an old spinster with me. Maybe I wanted to break that dependence as well. I hoped she would look back on her college time with fondness in the years to come.

"Those research trips were fun to go on. Do you remember the one we went on to Scotland with dad?"

I stopped packing and sat down on the edge of the bed and spun my wedding ring around my finger. It was a simple gold band, but a reminder of the life I had once lived and wasn't ready to give up. "Of course, I do. It was nearly six years ago, but it seems like an eternity." I traced the edge of the phone with my finger. Nervous habit, I suppose.

Hannah faced the camera on her phone towards the ceiling. I don't think she realized I could see her chin and up her nose. Her blue eyes welled up with tears. She didn't want me to see her cry. When we would discuss Todd, it was always the same. She would cry. I would fight back the tears. I still held a love for him; however, after five years, I started to become numb to the pain. From the angle that Hannah was holding her phone, I could see that she wore her auburn hair down. We looked so much alike. The both of us had auburn hair and blue eyes. Sometimes, I felt as though I was looking at a younger version of myself, as if she were a clone. She had a blend of mine and Todd's nose. I guess, she wasn't entirely my clone. I wanted to hold my daughter and offer her comfort from the loss of her father, but that would require her to be at my home with me, instead of being one hundred miles away at her apartment in Williamsburg.

"It was our last trip as a family before... you know. It is the best memory I have of all of us together." Hannah's voice cracked as she gulped, wiping away the tear that rolled down her cheek and hung on the edge of her chin.

CHAPTER TWO

"Is Kyle going to meet you up there?"

"Oh goodness, no." I was quick with my sharp reply. I desperately wanted to move on with my life after five years as a widow and thought I'd give the dating pool a chance. That is when I stumbled on Kyle. That was a mistake. We had met while hiking in the Shenandoah. He had attempted to cross a stream and slipped on a mossy boulder. Hiking alone, I was not too far behind Kyle on the trail and had seen the complete debacle in his attempt to cross a stream. I tried to contain my laughter while his tall, lean body hopped from one rock to another and slipped on another mossy boulder. I traversed my way across the stream and gave him my hand while he gained his footing. He almost pulled me into the cool water with him. We finished the hike together, and he asked me out to dinner as a "thank you" for pulling him out of the stream. We had gone on a few dates over the past few months, but I realized he was not what I was looking for in a partner. He had been hiking that once and refused to go any other time. I had asked him to join me on an adventure. I wanted someone that would take a risk to explore something new, and he wasn't up for that excitement. The man was boring.

Kyle preferred to sit at home and surf the web or glued to the television. I tried hanging out with him and read while he sat in front of his computer, hardly paying any attention to me. Occasionally, he would ask me what I knew about Colonial Williamsburg or Blackbeard the Pirate. I couldn't offer much information other than I had visited a couple of the museums in Williamsburg when Hannah was young but hadn't been back in years. I offered to take a visit with him down there, if he was interested. He never took me up on the offer, and to be honest, I had lost any bit of interest in him. He was an odd cookie.

After losing Todd, I had realized that life is too short to sit still. I needed to get out there and experience all that life could offer. I surfed the web when I needed to do research for the book I was writing, but I didn't want to spend all my time in front of a computer screen. Even though I could take my work anywhere I needed to go, I preferred to keep my home base near Hannah, and explore all that history-rich Virginia offered.

My recent historical fiction series was based on the life of George Washington. His childhood home, Ferry Farm, near Fredericksburg, was just up the road from my house. During the winter, when the trees lost many of their leaves, I could see the house sitting above the Rappahannock River. George inherited the 600-acre Ferry Farm after his father died. It was small and simple, the opposite of his sister's house, Kenmore Plantation across the river.

Later in his life, when Washington would visit

Fredericksburg, he would visit The Kenmore Plantation. I went on a tour there to see how George's sister lived. Her home was the height of opulence during Colonial America. Fielding and Betty Washington Lewis, George's brother-in-law and sister, built it in 1770 and possessed 1200 acres. As I looked at the development of Fredericksburg today, filled with homes and buildings from the 18th century to modern-day, it didn't seem possible for there to be that much open land. The idea that I lived surrounded by history only fueled my imagination.

"I would rather not date someone who wouldn't know an adventure if it crawled up his ass and bit him."

"Oh, come on, Mom. Are you trying to tell me that there is nothing redeemable about the guy?"

"I made a list."

"Of course, you did," Hannah said as she rolled her eyes. I admit, I liked to write lists, especially when making decisions on important topics. "Let's hear what you have on your list." Her phone jostled as she plopped back on her bed.

I held up fingers in front of the screen on the phone, numbering my list of reasons that Kyle was not the guy for me. "He doesn't like to visit unknown places. Sure, he went on a hike once. One of his golf buddies suggested they go hiking one weekend. He went to test it out so he wouldn't look like a newbie when they went with the guys." There was something always off about him. I just couldn't figure out his angle. "He fell in the stream and refuses to go again. In fact, he complains that there were too many bugs trying to kill him."

"Doesn't like to hike and is afraid of bugs. Got it. It's not like you go hiking every weekend, and you don't have a bug collection. You don't like bugs, don't forget. You scream if you see a spider."

"I used the hike as an example," I said. "He doesn't like to try new things. He only did it to save face, and I can't say he was very successful." I rolled my eyes as I looked back at the circumstances of our meeting. It was ridiculous. He was ridiculous. I was ridiculous to agree to go out with the guy. I hadn't been having much luck in the dating scene, and I suppose I thought he might have differed from the rest. He didn't. "You might be correct about me and bugs. How is he supposed to protect me from the scary bugs if he is more afraid of them than I am?" I shuddered to think about an insect touching me. I am not sure where I got my fear, but I was afraid they would somehow crawl under my skin. It was a silly fear, but one that I couldn't shake.

"The way you would scream throughout the house for dad when you saw a spider. He would come running to save you. You know you are one of the independent and bravest people I know. However, when it comes to spiders, you are such a wimp." Her laugh radiated through the room. I peeked at my phone to see her smile. Her blue eyes lit up at my short-coming.

My whole body shivered. I needed to change the subject away from the spiders that now haunted my thoughts. I held up another finger. "Second, he asked too many questions about your dad. I wasn't sure if he was a conspiracy theorist or a stalker." I grabbed a pair of skinny jeans from the bottom drawer of my dresser, held them in front of me, inspecting them, and laid them on the bed. They were my favorite pairs of jeans, broken in and comfortable. Those jeans hugged my curves in all the right places and didn't make me feel like an overstuffed sausage, like my slightly too small clothes normally did. I was a healthy size twelve, give or take ten pounds.

"We were having drinks and watching a movie at his house. He kept asking me about your dad. What he did for work. What projects was he working on? If I knew who he was meeting with before they killed him. It was so strange, and it just didn't feel right." I stopped and twisted my ring around my finger. "Why would I want to continue reliving that day? With a man that wasn't your father nor my therapist? Then he kept asking about Williamsburg and if I had ever been there; it was all so strange." What number of reasons to not date Kyle was that? Two? Three? That covered twelve different reasons the guy made me feel uncomfortable. I stood up and propped the phone on the dresser. I needed to pace.

I held up another finger. "Third, when I wouldn't discuss your dad, he tried to kiss me and couldn't seem to take no for an answer. I didn't want to let him, but he forced one on me. To be quite honest with you, there were no sparks. Nothing. It was like kissing a soulless drone. The dense rock head was inappropriately forceful."

"You don't need to explain yourself." Hannah let out a snorted laugh. "In fact, I would like for you to never mention kissing anyone ever again."

"It isn't funny," I pouted, my arms across my chest. "I didn't know how to get myself out of that situation." I didn't want to add that his tongue darted in my mouth like he was a snake. It was gross, messy, uninvited, and I didn't want to do it again with anyone. The thought of Kyle made me want to consider celibacy. It seemed like a safer route.

"You sound like a child throwing a tantrum over a kiss." Hannah said as she laughed at me again.

"I sound like someone that was assaulted with a kiss." I plopped down on my bed. "Is it too much to ask for someone that will make me melt when we kiss? Maybe I just compare every other man to your father, and none come close to him." I spun my wedding ring around my finger. "What time is it?" My phone laid on the dresser and I didn't own a clock. "Oh! My boots!"

I jumped up and rummaged in my closet for my favorite boots. They were dark brown, had a zipper that went from ankle to knee, a one-inch heel, and were ab-so-freaking-lute-ly comfortable. A familiar friend.

"It's almost eight," she said with indifference in her voice. "You know, you don't have to replace dad. You can just grow old with me. I can see it now. We can be two old women with a bunch of cats that hang around in our bathrobes."

"I'm not trying to replace him." My shoulders sank at her comment of me trying to replace Todd. He would always hold a place in my heart. There was something missing in my life. I wasn't sure what it was, but a replacement husband was not it. I mused, "Ah. Yes. We know Old Widow Amelia Murray. I heard she used to write books and travel. Rumor has it, at one point, she used to be interesting. Now she feeds cats and cleans litter boxes all day."

Hannah joined in, "The daughter, Old Spinster Hannah Murray, finished college and brought home three cats with her. That started it all. I hear they won millions in the lottery but choose to live the simple life living off canned tuna and the vegetables they grow in their garden. The cats inherit it all when they die."

"Please, Hannah, don't bring home cats." The phone was still propped on the dresser. I walked over to it and gave her the mom glare. "That will be our downward spiral. Now, if you just so happen to win millions in the lottery, we can talk about becoming recluses and collecting cats."

"I'll get right on that," Hannah said with a laugh, as she tucked a lock of hair behind her ear. "What's your plan for the day?"

The sound of my zipped suitcase scratched through the air. "After breakfast, I'm heading to Winchester, scope out my hotel, then head north towards the site of Fort Cumberland. It was a pivotal rallying point for the British forces during the French and Indian War. Then up to Fort Necessity."

I changed out of my joggers and into the skinny jeans. "I'll be back at the hotel later." It was edging towards the beginning of May, and the weather in Virginia could still be on the chilly side. My favorite skinny jeans, a pair of knee-high brown leather boots, a white pullover cotton blouse, and topped off with a navy corduroy blazer–the outfit of champions. With a twist and a coil at the nape of my neck, I pulled my hair back and formed a chignon. I couldn't tolerate my hair on my face. I always considered myself a low maintenance woman, with my hair pulled back in a bun or in a braid. On the rare occasion I would wear makeup, but it required too much effort to wear it regularly. As a writer, when I was not out doing research for a book, attending a conference, meeting with agents and publishers, or running errands, I worked from my home office and found no need to put much effort into putting on makeup or dressing up. There was no one at home to impress, and Todd had preferred the more natural look, which suited me perfectly. Without makeup, he could see the freckles that crossed over my cheeks and nose. He loved my freckles.

"Sounds boring. Were you going to head to Pittsburgh?"

"Not today. Fort Duquesne will be on a day trip all on its own. I want to spend some time at the other two locations, and I cannot do it all in one day." I grabbed my phone before heading down the stairs to my office. "When are you coming up to spend some time with me?"

"Did you make sure you packed your toothbrush?" Hannah asked.

"Yes, mother," I said as I grabbed my brown leather crossbody satchel from under the desk. "Laptop–check. Power cord–check. Notebook with research notes–check. Pens–check. Phone charger–check. I'll grab some snacks and fill my bottle with water, and I think I'm good!" I said, stuffing everything into the satchel. "You still didn't answer me. When are you coming to visit?"

"I have classes every day of the week. I can't make it right now."

"Next semester, you should adjust your schedule. That way, you don't have to go every day." I knew she wouldn't spend every day off with me. I wanted to spend at least some days with her and to make sure she got out of her apartment and make friends. "What about this weekend?"

"You just want a travel buddy." A deep sigh came over

11

the phone. She was right. I didn't always want to be alone. "You should invite Beth on one of your excursions."

"Her teaching schedule and office hours keep her busy. You didn't answer me about this weekend."

"What about Maggie?"

"She has some event at the bookshop." I'll call her later to set up a time to come in and sign more books. "Again, what about you?"

"I, uh, well..." Hannah was hesitant in her answer. "I have a date on Friday."

"Why didn't you tell me?" I stopped what I was doing and stared at my daughter on the phone. It didn't disappoint me that Hannah had a date and was too busy to come hang out with me. It disappointed me she didn't feel as though she could tell me about the date or the guy.

"I didn't want you to get all weird about it. Last time I had a date, you practically threw a party for me." She was rattling through her answer. "And it's not like your love life is great. I didn't want you to think that I have it good and you don't."

"I just get excited for you and I'm okay with my love life, or the lack of a love life. Besides, if one thing leads to another, you won't have to become an old recluse with dozens of stray cats with me." I was happy for Hannah, but it made me more aware that I may end up spending the rest of my life alone. *Maybe I should think about getting a cat or two.* "So, who is the guy?"

"Mom." There was the sound of hesitation in Hannah's voice. There was more to this conversation than we could get into over the phone. I didn't understand why she would keep anything from me, but whatever it was, she didn't want me to know.

"Come up to Winchester on Saturday, after your date. You can tell me all about it and we'll go explore together." I checked the time on my phone before I slid it into my back pocket. "I'm meeting Beth. Gotta go."

8:05. Late again.

CHAPTER THREE

*B*eth waited for me in front of *Betsy's Biscuits*, located in an old building in the historic district of Fredericksburg. The history professor uniform, as I liked to call it, was on full display. I thought the outfit of a black pullover blouse, topped with a forest green, oversized, chunky cardigan, dark grey slacks, and a pair of black loafers made her look decades older than her forty-two years. The forest green played well with her green eyes and the floral pattern on the long silk scarf tied around her neck. Besides that, she wore her medium-brown hair twisted into a loose bun on top of her head, with a few escaped tendrils framing her face. She claimed it made her students take her seriously. I claimed I wouldn't borrow her clothes.

Betsy's was Beth's and my favorite place to grab a meal once a month. It was our guarantee to see each other and catch up on our current projects. Beth, a Colonial America history professor at the local college, University of Mary Washington, was my one of my few touches to the outside world. We had been friends for years. Shortly after Todd,

Hannah, and I moved to Virginia, I had contacted her for an interview for a book I had been writing about the American colonies pre-Revolutionary War. We could get lost in history discussion for hours. However, during this visit, there was no option of traveling too far down a rabbit hole. I had time for a quick breakfast and chat with my friend before heading to Winchester.

Opposite me, at a table along the wall, sat Beth. Along the white wall covered in black-and-white photos of the town and people stretched a long booth-styled bench, with small rectangular tables lined up down the length. Seven tables fit the length of the wall. Chairs sat opposite the bench. Small tables, which could comfortably fit a party of two, filled in the open space. I lifted my hand to shield the sun that blasted through the window. I thought about pulling my sunglasses out but opted to scoot to my left, a bit more out of the path of the sun.

Beth twisted to look at the room behind her. "We can try to move to another table." She pointed towards the back corridor that led to the back section of *Betsy's*.

"Nope." I smacked my menu closed, perhaps with a little too much force than I had intended. The morning crowd of tourists and locals poured into the restaurant and quickly gobbled up empty tables. I didn't have time to wait for another table as I had already packed too much into my morning and needed to get on the road. "I'll be fine."

I was thankful they didn't place us at a table in the middle of the room. I always felt as though I was sitting in the middle of a three-ring circus with the chaos swirling around me. Admittedly, living alone offered me a quiet solitude that I come to appreciate. The restaurant clamored with people. As the tourists continued to fill all available tables, they pushed together two-seater tables to make it a table for four or six. On any other Monday, it would have been a quiet breakfast downtown, but tourist season had settled into Fredericksburg. Senior snowbirds were on their way south, heading towards the hot and humid Florida summer and leaving the cold north behind them, crowding the establishments along the way. "I would like French toast, eggs over easy, sausage, and coffee."

"I'll take the ham and cheese breakfast biscuit and coffee." Beth said, as we handed our menus to the server, Olivia. "You should consider one of the smaller forts to visit."

"Oh, yeah? Which one?" I asked, raising my eyebrows. "My focus is the start of the French and Indian War skirmishes, which include Necessity, Duquesne, and Jumonville."

Olivia placed two empty mugs in front of us. The smell of coffee wafted through the air as she filled the mugs. "Your food will be out in a just a moment."

Beth nodded towards the young woman. "Fort Ashby."

I pulled out my notebook and made space for it on the table. "I don't have that one on my list." Only moments later, Olivia placed our plates in front of us. I snuck in a bite of the French toast before flipping through the pages like a madwoman on a mission.

"It doesn't come around for another year–or so–after the start, but Captain Ashby's wife was a bit of a troublemaker and quite the personality. Her brother was selling rum out of the fort, and–you're going to love this–she was the instigator for sedition among the men." Beth grabbed her breakfast sandwich and took a huge bite. Her cheek bulged out as she pushed the food to one side to finish her thought. I continued to make progress on my plate of food. The French toast was sweet and eggy. "From around here, somewhere. She is a little out of the time frame you are writing about; however, take the opportunity to see where it happened."

I leaned closer to Beth. "She sounds like she came from a family line of pirates."

"She was young, really young, married to a much older man, stuck out in the middle of... well, you'll see."

"He sounds like a pig, but she sounds intriguing. I might take a quick stop over there." I sat back in my chair, folding my arms over my stomach. A smile crept across my face. *Betsy's* was famous for a hearty breakfast and spending time with Beth made me content. I leaned back in my chair, closing my eyes, and began to plot a pirate series. "Ah! No time to think about another series." My eyes opened and my body shot upright. I grabbed my cup of coffee and took a swig. "I need to finish doing my site visits for this one. You do this to me every time. I don't need help to fall down another research rabbit hole."

"Ha! I knew she would intrigue you."

"How old is this building?" I asked, looking around. Something or someone caught my attention. It appeared a man ducked behind the corridor wall when I looked in his direction. It couldn't have been a ghost. Could it?

"I'm not sure. It seems old; minus the updates they've done over the years. Fredericksburg has buildings dating back to the mid-seventeen hundreds. I'm not an expert on buildings, but I would garner, this one must be one of the original town buildings."

A tingle crept down my body as if a spider raced down

my spine. The room was chilly. I shook it off as my imagination and took a quick glance around the room. "Don't look, but I think I saw Kyle duck behind a wall over by the kitchen." I looked over my shoulder in the kitchen's direction. The kitchen shared a wall with the corridor that led to the back of the restaurant. In the back, there was more seating, a long bar for evening drinks, and a door to the outdoor patio, which contained more tables.

Beth looked over her shoulder toward the mysterious shadow-man. "Did you tell him you were coming here?"

"No. And I told you not to look." I looked over her right shoulder towards the wall. "He has an uncanny ability to show up wherever I am. So, who knows?"

"That sounds like a bit of stalker material. You know, I've never met him." Beth turned around to look at me. "Do you want me to walk over there?"

"Please, don't go over there. I'm sure it was just my imagination. These old buildings can trap old spirits, and I'm sure that's what I must have seen." I waved her off as she moved to get out of her chair. "Let's finish our breakfast and not worry about my stalker." I sipped my lukewarm coffee and took the last bite of my French toast. "I was thinking this must have been one of the original buildings in the town. It just seems so old. I wonder if George Washington visited here. I can practically see Ferry Farm from the back door. He must have stopped by."

Beth finished her coffee. "What is your fascination with him?" She shoved the last bit of her sandwich in her mouth.

"I'm not sure I'm fascinated with him, but I find him interesting. He was tall, handsome, auburn hair, rich, and the first president. What's not to like?" I pulled out my phone from my back pocket, checked the time, and placed it face down on the table next to my plate.

"Well, he was..." Beth sat up, leaned her elbows on the table, apparently ready to give me an earful.

"Can I bring you ladies anything else?" Olivia asked, topping off my coffee. Beth waved her off from refilling her mug. Olivia shrugged her shoulders, laid the bill down on the table, and walked away before we could answer. We looked at each other and let out a laugh of disbelief. Some days, she acted as though we were more of a nuisance to her than paying customers there to enjoy a delicious breakfast.

"Was that her subtle way of telling us we finished breakfast?" I said, as I flipped over my phone and checked the time again. I grabbed my satchel from the seat next to me on the bench and pulled out my wallet.

"There was nothing subtle about that." Beth laughed and shook her head.

"He was what?" I pressed.

Beth put down the bill. "Hm? Oh, yeah. Washington. You've been to Mount Vernon and have seen his false teeth. He had bad teeth from a young age."

"Beth, I'm pretty sure many people had bad teeth during that time."

"You asked what there was not to like. I replied. You don't have to like it. I don't like it. But it's the truth. The man started having his teeth pulled while in his mid-twenties. Not exactly the hot young leader you hoped."

"Okay, bad teeth. Got it."

"It gets worse."

I let out a sigh. "How could it possibly get worse? You're not going to tell me he had a really young wife that we didn't know about, are you? You already told me how Ashby's wife was basically a child." It wasn't as though I was ever going to meet the man. He died two hundred thirty years ago.

Beth leaned closer to me and dropped the volume of her voice. "No, only one woman agreed to marry him, Washington, that is. However, don't forget enslaved people. He owned people, Mel."

"Well, there's the deal breaker." I threw up my hands in defeat. "There is no way any decent person could've enslaved people." Although I spent hours upon hours every day reading history, I had to admit, I focused more on other topics rather than the ugliness of slavery.

"Oh, come on. Stop being obtuse." Her hand caught the edge of her fork and sent it clanking against her plate. A few conversations halted and heads from the surrounding tables snapped in our direction. I snarled my nose at the busy bodies.

"Beth, how am I being obtuse? Seriously?" I shook my head. "That fact should disgust us."

"We are. There were a few that didn't believe in having enslaved people. Those that didn't believe in having enslaved people were mostly the Quakers and there were some abolitionists. Washington was neither." Beth leaned closer to me, tossing her napkin on the table next to her plate. "It was about economics and ego. Look, we can't change history as much as we would like to change it. Life was much different during that time. It was rougher and uglier, and people were more interested in their economic gain and the thought that even if they didn't enslave people, others were doing it, and it wouldn't make a difference. The generations that follow can only learn from their mistakes and we need to do better." She pulled her satchel that hung on the back of her chair to her lap. "I just don't want you to forget that with all that he did for the country, he still did some pretty heinous things."

"I suppose you are correct. Is this what you teach your students?" I grinned. Her students loved her. I loved her. "I have this romantic idea of what life was like back then. You know... simple. I think I gloss over the ugly parts of it."

Beth stared into her empty mug, then looked around the room. "You study history about as much as I do. Just so you know, there is a town in Northern Virginia, it was called the German Settlement, now it's called Lovettsville. Anyway, they were against slavery, so not everyone enslaved people. How could you even think life was simple back then?"

"Maybe I want it to be simple, because life is just so damn complicated now." I twisted my wedding ring around my finger. It was a simple thin band that I never stopped wearing after they killed Todd. It had been my connection and remembrance of my husband.

"Life was complicated then. You think we have conflict and war now? It was worse during Washington's time." Beth pulled out her wallet. "Oh! We didn't have the medical knowledge that we do now to help mend those injured in combat. And don't forget the amount of people that died of sickness and disease during the wars. They lost more men to consumption, dysentery, and syphilis than to wounds."

I shuddered. "I'm buying breakfast," I said as I pulled the check towards me. "It's the least I can do for today's history lesson." Olivia walked by and snatched up the bill and my card.

Beth hadn't finished with her morning lecture. "Let's not forget buying clothes and food. Supplies had to be shipped from England. No, thank you. I am happy to be alive in the twenty-first century. You should get your head out of the clouds." Beth looked at her watch. "I need to tell you something, Amelia. You might not like it."

I gulped down any emotions that erupted into my throat. "This sounds ominous."

"You might think it is, but I want you to be happy for me." She reached across the table and grabbed my hand and looked at me as though I were an injured puppy. Whatever was coming next was going to devastate me.

"Stop trying to tiptoe around my feelings and just tell me. It will be fine. I will be fine. We will all be fine." *Did that sound convincing?* Olivia placed the receipt and my card on the table. I looked up to thank her, but she was off to another table before the words left my mouth. I filled in the tip and signed the receipt. The distraction helped me gain my composure.

"I have some good news." Her attempt at sounding cheerful was anything but that. "I've accepted a new position. Starting the fall semester, I will teach at William and Mary. Hector, the dogs, and I will move to Williamsburg this summer."

I could feel the blood drain from my face. "Oh, geez, Beth. I thought you were going to tell me you were moving out of the country. You will not be too far." I squeezed her hand in a desperate attempt to reassure her I was okay with her news. I wasn't. I was being left alone. Again. Todd was dead. Hannah was away at school and would move on after graduation. Maggie was a good friend, but she was always too busy with her book shop and solving local mysteries to hang out. I didn't need anyone. "It will be great. Maybe Hannah will take one of your classes. It will give me time to get lost in writing more books." I knew I rambled on. It was my attempt to make it appear that I was going to be fine without her. I wasn't convincing myself, either.

I grabbed my satchel, slid off the bench, and walked up to the hostess stand near the door. "Did you walk here? I can give you a lift to the campus."

"Thanks," she said, opening the door for me. The cool morning breeze wafted in, bringing the sounds of the cars driving up Caroline Street with it. It was still early in the morning and the shops up and down the historic district began to open and come alive. "I'm going to enjoy the walk."

She wrapped her arm around my waist as we walked up the street to my SUV. I found a spot along the curb, a few buildings down from *Betsy's Biscuits*. We arrived at my black SUV, and I pulled my wallet and keys out of my bag and threw the bag on the passenger seat. I thought about stopping at *By the River Bookshop* to grab a book to wind down in the evenings. "Walk with me to Maggie's." I pulled my phone out of my pocket and checked the time again. *9:09. Behind schedule again! I should have been on the road.*

"You know what? Sometimes, I miss having Todd around. I miss the conversation." We arrived in front of the bookshop. Historic Fredericksburg comprised adjacent buildings that lined the quaint streets. The buildings were a mix of business and residential and mainly ranged in age from the mid-1700s to 1900s. *By the River Bookshop* was one of the older buildings that was originally built as a home and later converted into a business. The antique glass and wooden double doors were placed in the middle of the yellow painted bricked front and flanked by a large bay window on each side. They filled the windows with a display of books and an advertisement for an upcoming book signing. *Cathy Stevenson!* It took all the strength I could muster to ignore the display while I was with Beth. "With Hannah being away at the college in Williamsburg, the house is too quiet. And now, well, you will move away. It will be fine."

I grabbed the latched door handle before looking back towards Beth as she continued walking down Caroline Street. I raised my free hand to wave and called out to her, "Have fun at school today."

Beth waved back at me. "You should get a cat."

CHAPTER FOUR

"Cathy Stevenson!" I roared. The green door flew open with a bang and rattled the glass inset into the middle, as I burst into *By the River Bookshop*. "That is who you have coming in to do the book signing next week?"

Maggie stood at the counter, mouth agape. She was a petite woman—but a mouth of a Tyrannosaurus from the South, dark brown hair, mid-forties, and dark brown eyes that hid behind a pair of black round glasses. "Just sign with your finger." She handed the electronic pad to the customer at the counter. "Yes, Amelia, Cathy Stevenson."

"How could you invite my arch-nemesis into your shop?" I gestured towards the display in the window.

She put the stack of books in a green plastic bag with the white *By the River Bookshop* logo and handed it to the customer. The woman grabbed the sack and was at the door in four long and quick strides. Maggie waved to the woman as she left. "Thank you for stopping by," Maggie called out in a cheerful customer service voice. She turned and scowled at me. "She is not your arch-nemesis. And I can invite whoever I want to sign books in the store. I still own this place."

"But... Cathy?" More animated than the last time, I flailed my arms and pointed in the direction of the window display with the banner of Cathy Stevenson and her new book.

"Yes. Cathy." Maggie came out from behind the counter and walked over to me as I stood next to the window with the oversized sign with Cathy's oversized head, and her oversized blond hair, her oversized ego, and her oversized stuck-up look on her face with her oversized red lips. *I can't stand that color of lipstick. What was the name of that shade of lipstick? Cathy-is-the-devil-in-disguise red?* "Did you come in here to yell at me or was there something I can help my favorite author find?"

Humph! She tried to placate me and my temper with honey-dripped words. "I wanted to pick up a couple of books for my trip, but now... I can't even think straight." My ears burned. I couldn't fall for Maggie's sweet southern charm. Not while I seethed at the thought of Cathy-I-will-flirt-with-your-husband-and-sabotage-your-publishing-deal Stevenson being in my favorite bookshop. I was livid.

"Romance? Cozy mystery? Something for research?" Maggie put her arm around me and led me further into the shop. Shelves hugged the walls around the room. Books lined shelves on three stories in the historic building. We stood on the main floor, which held non-fiction, local interest, new arrivals, and historic books. In the basement, there were children's books, special interest books, and books in foreign languages. The next floor up had fiction, biographies, and another display of new arrivals. The next floor up from the fiction was out of limits to the public, as it was a private apartment. "Oh, I know what you need. How about a historical mystery?"

"As long as you're not suggesting one of Cathy's books." I couldn't stay angry with Maggie, but I wasn't willing to lower my standards as to read one of Cathy's books.

"Of course not. I'm going to grab a couple of books—not Cathy's—for you. While you stand here and pout," she said as she motioned to a table next to me, "you can sign that stack of books." She always had a display of my books by the front of the store. I grabbed a pen from behind the counter and signed a stack of ten books by the time she got back. Pom, the bookshop's tubby orange tabby cat, stretched and jumped down from her perch next to the window with a little grunt. She sauntered over to me; her purr vibrated my leg as she wove her body around me. I gave her a quick scratch; little orange hairs flew off her coat like a tornado. She needed a good brushing. Maybe I would tackle that when I got back from my trip.

"Pom adores you," Maggie said as I swiped at the stray cat hairs on my boots. "Maybe you should get a cat."

Why did everyone think I needed a cat? I paid for my books, gave Fritz—her very adorable red Dachshund, that has never said no to an extra treat—a rub on his belly, and headed out the door. I didn't forget to glare at the large poster of Cathy on my way out.

∾

I HATED driving on I-95 in Virginia. Especially this part of Virginia. The traffic was always congested, and it forced the memory of my husband's death down my throat. Todd died shortly before Hannah's thirteenth birthday, and both Hannah and I continued to mourn his death. He was running late from the office, on his way to the restaurant where we were going to celebrate his fortieth birthday. We moved many times around the world because of Todd's work with the State Department. Finding lasting friends was difficult, so birthdays centered on our family.

That day, he had been in the office longer than he wanted, with a last-minute meeting that dragged him nearly kicking-and-screaming to the White House—at least, that is how he told it to me. The traffic on the I-95 southbound freeway out of Washington, DC, was the typical heavy sludge. Stop. Go. Stop. Go. He hated that drive but living outside of the political chaos made it worth it.

Dinner would have been just the three of us at our favorite local restaurant, *Betsy's Biscuits*. Betsy made a special dinner that night for us, to include the dessert of a strawberry biscuit, topped with fresh strawberries and whipped cream. Hannah and I waited at a table near the front window in anticipation of his arrival. I watched the traffic travel down Caroline Street from my seat. I returned a half-smile to Betsy. Another refill of our peach tea. I checked my watch again.

He was in the far-left lane, speeding up to merge into the express lane, when a car clipped his bumper and sent him barreling into the rail. The other driver was illegally speeding down the left shoulder when it had clipped Todd's car. His car careened into the barrier, crumpled into a tangled mess, and left him nearly unrecognizable.

If the death of my husband on his birthday wasn't bad enough for me to deal with, it got worse. The coroner ruled it a homicide, as they had found that besides the accident, someone had shot him. They never traced the odd bullet they dug out of him, nor find the hit-and-run driver. All I was told was that it was a cold case and that we might never find out who killed my husband. I couldn't understand who would want him dead. There were no suspects. How could there be no suspects?

We were married for sixteen years, ever since my first year of college and his senior year. We met while I was in orientation, and I suppose it was love or infatuation at first sight. I spent almost half my life with him by the time he died. He had joined the foreign service shortly after he graduated. I got pregnant with Hannah and started writing travel books and blogs for whichever country they would assign him. We lived outside of Washington, DC, when I became a widow and single mother at thirty-four and left practically alone. Thankfully, I had our friends, Beth and Hector Bennedet, to help me navigate my new world living alone with a teenager.

∼

THE VIRGINIA COUNTRYSIDE WAS A WONDERLAND, with rolling green fields and farmhouses that dotted the landscape. For a woman from the city, I never tired of seeing the green openness and simplicity of farm country. The hustle and bustle of thousands of people and vehicles rushing by in massive quantities didn't exist in the farmland. The steady flow of cars, let me know there is civilization and people nearby; however, it was nothing like growing up in Los Angeles.

I tried to imagine what it would have been like during the mid-1700s, when there was conflict over the borders between the French and British forces in this quiet terrain. It was a tumultuous time in the colonial history that gave rise to George Washington. I wanted to use the trip to gain a better understanding of the locations where Washington developed his skills—to get a hands-on assessment of his early battlefields.

I arrived at my home base for the next couple of weeks, *The Winchester Inn*, a hotel in the historic downtown district of Winchester, Virginia. The historic site for George Washington's office was a short walk away and was on my list to visit the next day. My GPS screen on the dash of my SUV flashed a "P" to show there was parking at the hotel and the location of parking garages near the walking district. I wasn't staying long but wanted to figure out my game plan. Checking the clock, it was too early to check-in to the hotel. I made a mental note of the parking and pulled over to plug in the address to my next destination. Taking Beth's advice, I went to Fort Ashby instead of heading directly to Fort Necessity. I typed Fort Ashby's address into the GPS. It was just over the West Virginia border, a quick drive that should get me there within the hour.

A small, paved parking lot stretched between a log cabin and the Fort Ashby Museum. I could fit five cars and not much more in the lot. An empty lot didn't seem too promising and left me with the feeling that the museum was closed. I should have checked the operating hours, but I hadn't thought that far ahead. This fort, or what remained of it, was not on my original itinerary, and left me unprepared. I parked my SUV, pulled my laptop and twisted charging cables out of the satchel, and shoved it all under the passenger seat. I wouldn't need them inside or while exploring the grounds.

The actual fort was long gone. Instead, a brick path led me to a concrete footprint of where the fort had once stood. It seemed small for a fort, ninety feet on each side, with a bastion at each corner. At least, that is what the informational sign had printed on it. Part of the back corner of the fort's imprint was in someone's backyard. I could understand why Captain Ashby's wife would be discontent with having to live there in such tight quarters. *How many soldiers were to be quartered here?* To be honest, I wasn't sure what to expect regarding the size of a mid-18th century fort on the frontier of Colonial America, but if I had to live there, I would have wanted something more spacious.

To my left stood a log cabin with a double sized chimney sticking out in the middle. It appeared to be about thirty feet square, with dark brown logs and white chinking between the joints. I walked from the side around the dovetailed corner and to the front door. It was locked. I continued to make my way around to the other side of the cabin and peek in the window, only to find a curtain blocked my view. Three brown wooden doors, one on each side and one on the front, and I wasn't sure which one I was supposed to use. Fed up, I decided that the side entrance next to the parking lot was the main door. The sign next to the door showed it was open Friday, Saturday, and Sunday. "Son of a…" It was Monday and not open. I grabbed the door handle, in hopes someone would be inside and allow me to take a quick peek around, when I noticed a coin on the ground.

The long drive caused my knees to tighten—ah, the joys of

being forty–which left me with the need to use the door as a brace to bend down and pick up the coin. I felt all my forty years of life in that squat. "Find a penny and pick it up, and however else the saying goes." I noticed that the copper coin was about an inch wide and not a penny like I had expected. They engraved one side with a man that looked like he was Roman and the words "Georgius II Rex". "Is that King George the second?" I flipped it over. "Hello, beautiful. What's a coin like you doing in a place like this?" I said to the coin, half expecting it to answer me. The backside of the coin sported a woman, the word "Britannia," and the date 1754 at the bottom. I held it in my hand and would give it to one of the museum's employees. If I could find one.

As I used the door to help heave me from my squat, the latch moved, and it slid open slightly. "Hello? Anyone here?" I called out as I pushed the door open. An icy breeze poured out of the building, swirled around, and encompassed my body, as though a blast freezer had swallowed me whole. I could smell the sweet smoke from burning cherry wood. A low humming noise drowned in my ears, blocking out all other sounds. I squinted as I raised my arm over my eyes to block out the lights. It was as though the brightness from a thousand suns concentrated in the small building. There was an overpowering urge to continue to open the door and to look inside. I wasn't sure if it was my curiosity getting the best of me or something else, but I needed to get inside the building. The bright white light twisted around me. I squinted my eyes harder and struggled to see any of furnishings in the room. "Anyone here? I can't see what's going on. The light is too bright. Can you turn it off?" My eyes burned from the intensity. "Hello." I called out to the bright chasm in front of me.

The light continued to swirl, and the humming got louder as I crept into the room. I could feel the reverberation from the humming sink into my bones. My teeth ached. Head spun around in a dizzying abyss. When I stood up quickly, my blood pressure dropped. I grasped the door handle. Before I collapsed to the floor, I had to grab something–anything–to help me brace myself. I looked over my shoulder, away from the light, towards the parking lot. There was a car parked next to mine that looked like Kyle's car. *Could anyone else see what was going on?* With my other hand, that still held the coin, I grasped at my blazer that had blown open and allowed the freezing air to bite at my skin. I had regained some sense from being light-headed. My hands shook as I tried desperately to button up my blazer. The blazer only offered a little protection from the piercing cold. The door slammed shut behind me.

The bright light continued to burn my eyes. I needed to figure out where it was coming from, to turn it off. "This is so stupid. What is going on? I need to get out of here," I said. What kind of fool was I to continue to walk into this madness? My chest heaved as I panicked. I gasped for air. The cherry wood smoke filled my nostrils. Burning sensation from the smoke traveled down into my lungs. I felt like I'd choke on the sweet scent. My vision narrowed. The bright light continued to blind me, but the world around me seemed to get dark.

Overcome with the sensation of being pulled into a tunnel and the only thing I could see was what appeared to be the burning sun at the other end, I continued into the room. It called out to me, beckoning me to come closer. The overpowering scent of cherry wood smoke continued to permeate the surrounding air; it was intoxicating. I reached out in front of me and crept towards the light. I expected it to be warm, but it was frigid. None of what happened made any sense. My head spun. I was confused and lightheaded. The world felt unsteady under me as I swayed. The blood drained from my head and threatened me into unconsciousness. There was nothing I could do to stop it.

It all went quiet and dark.

CHAPTER FIVE

The breeze tickled through the towering stalks of grass. White pillowy clouds dotted the blue skies. Somehow, I must've been dropped into the middle of heaven. I propped up on my elbows, looked around, and planted my hands on the ground to get a better view of my surroundings. "What happened?" I said out loud, unsure who I thought would hear me. *How did I get to this field?* I sat up and ran my hands over my face. There was confusion and disbelief at what had just happened. I couldn't wipe it away.

My head spun, which left me lightheaded and confused. I was hungry and exhausted. My mind raced through a million thoughts all at once. A fly buzzed in my ear. *Not in the mood, fly.* I tried to remember what had happened to me. What felt like just moments ago could've been hours or days. I had no sense of time or location. As the dizziness passed, I stood up with caution, straightened my satchel across my body, and looked around the small field that had a few trees scattered throughout. There were heavier wooded areas on both sides of me. I know there hadn't been that many trees a few moments ago.

My surroundings were not familiar. What happened before I had passed out? I rubbed my forehead and searched for the answer. I blocked the midday sun from my eyes and looked around for my sunglasses that I had pushed on top of my head before I had walked into the building. "That's it! I had walked into a building. But now, the building is not here." I rubbed my neck. I continued to talk to myself. It wasn't as though anyone was around to question my sanity. "In fact, nothing was there. *Where in the hell am I?* None of it made sense. I could've sworn that I had seen Kyle when I entered the building." *Did he have something to do with me blacking out?*

I twisted around slowly in a circle to take in my surroundings. No sign of civilization. A building? Road? Cell phone tower? Sound of cars? Nothing. I held my breath and concentrated on the surrounding sounds. It was still too early in the year for the drowning noise of cicadas, so it didn't surprise me at the lack of their buzz. There was a slight rustle of the trees as the breeze blew through the branches. I felt the breeze slip across my face and the tall grass brushed up against my boots. I looked for a landmark or a sign to help me figure out where I was or how I got into that field. No clues. I remembered the scent of burning cherry wood had filled the room before I had passed out. I could no longer smell it. Someone parked next to my SUV, but I couldn't remember who I thought I had seen. I thought it could've been Kyle. But that made little sense to me. Nothing made sense. My brain was in a fog.

My stomach grumbled and begged for food.

I looked around again, my hand shielded my eyes from the bright sun. I had never felt more lost in my entire life than I had felt at that moment. When Todd died, I had Hannah and Beth to lean on for support. In the middle of this field, I had no one as I panicked. I had no sense of which direction to walk. It was all too quiet and empty. Had someone dragged me out into the middle of the woods? Kyle? Thousands of thoughts tossed around my head, and I couldn't make sense of them. They felt jumbled together. Lost. Confused. Alone. Afraid. The situation reminded me of Stephen King's story, Misery. The writer was in an accident and rescued–if you want to call it that–by a stalker. He ended up escaping. Even as crazy as that was, he had someone with him. I was alone.

I continued to turn around, looking for some sign of people. Groves of trees. Fields. Sky. What sounded like a creek babbling nearby? That was not what I had planned for my day.

Tears pricked, and the sting in my nose told me that a big cry was imminent. I fell to my knees and sat back on my heels. I was emotionally and physically drained and felt defeated. The last time I had felt this physical and mental exhaustion was when Todd had died. It had taken me weeks to recover. I sensed I couldn't afford that recovery time.

I laid down on in the tall grass and looked up at the sky. The sun was almost directly overhead. I covered my eyes with my forearm, blocking the sun, and gave myself a moment to pull my emotions back together and think this situation through.

"Get yourself together, Murray. Stop your bellyaching, it will not help. Think. Think. Think!" I sat up, wiped my tear-soaked cheeks with the sleeve of my navy corduroy jacket, and searched my satchel for something to wipe my nose. There was a travel size package of tissues at the bottom. I almost forgot I had packed a few protein bars and felt my stomach cramp in hunger. My fingers couldn't open the package fast enough. I was absolutely famished. It didn't feel like it could be enough to help re-energize me, but it offered me an opportunity to slow down my racing thoughts and focus on finding my way back to civilization. And to not think about all the ticks that were probably lurking in the field.

"Pull on your big girl panties and figure this out. What do you have available? Pens. Notebooks. Protein bars. Water bottle with some water left in it." I rocked the bottle back-and-forth to judge what was left. "Satchel. Car fob—obviously of no use without a car—and... my phone! No sunglasses. Must've dropped them at the fort." I searched my bag, pulling everything out to look for the phone, and couldn't find it. "Back pocket! Of course!"

I patted my back pocket and found the phone where I had put it when I got out of the car. I always carried my phone next to my body or else I wouldn't feel it vibrate when I got a text or call. It was a habit I had picked up after Todd had died. I didn't want to believe that he was dead; he was just on a trip, and he was going to call me when he had the opportunity. That phone call never came, but the phone was always nearby. I pulled the phone out and tapped the screen. Nothing. I pressed the power button. Nothing. "Are you kidding me? Come on!" Tap. Tap. Tap. It almost turned into slam, slam, slam.

I continued to tap the screen and push the buttons, with no success of getting it back on. Frustrated with what was going on, I shoved it into my satchel instead of hurling it into a nearby tree.

"No phone. No car. No people. No landmarks. No sense of direction. No sense of time. It just makes no damn sense." Frustrated again, I felt the tears welling up. I twisted my wedding ring around my finger. "Honestly, how can this day get any worse? Think, Murray, think. What would Todd do?" Todd always had a way of working through odd situations, and it didn't get any odder than waking up in the middle of a field in the middle of nowhere.

Still seated, I looked around again and looked up at the sky. "The sun! Okay. Okay. The sun is almost overhead, so it must be around noon. I walked into the building a little before noon. Unless it has been longer than a day, then it is shortly after I walked in. How did I get moved into the middle of nowhere so quickly? Was the cherry wood scent a poison or something to make me sleep? Have I been asleep for days? That makes little sense." I rubbed my temples to stave off the headache that threatened to make this day worse. "Who would do that? Who was there? Kyle? Was there anyone else? Why can't I remember? That part doesn't matter right now, Murray. You can worry about that later. You have got to figure out where you are and get to the police, hospital, home... anywhere but here." I slammed my fists onto the ground. A gritted growl burst from my lips.

I inhaled deeply. A shaky exhale escaped. Try again. Inhale deeply. Slow, controlled exhale. Rinse. Repeat. My panic subsided, and I could think with a logical mind. "Wherever I'm at, I couldn't have been taken far. There was not enough time in between me passing out and waking up. I could head north, I guess." I looked around again. Maybe I would come across a town or a road. "Maybe? Now, which way is north?" Talking to myself made me feel better. As if I was talking to someone else and not alone.

I stood up, looked around the vicinity, tried to figure out which way was north, and realized that I hadn't had to really think about directions before. My SUV's GPS would tell me which direction I was driving. My phone had a compass app. I always stayed on marked trails when I went hiking. And I was terrible at reading maps. I never needed to figure out direction by using the sun or a real compass. Besides, with the sun directly overhead, it was difficult to figure out the direction it was moving. I knew when it moved, I could tell which way was north. "Sun rises in the east and sets in the west. Move, sun, so I can figure out which way is which. Why does this even matter? I don't know where I am and what will be in any direction."

I took a deep breath in through my nose, using the deep inhales to fill my lungs with the clean air and long exhales to help center myself. The air was clean. No scent of car exhaust or dirty air lingered. The cool breeze was light and continued to blow now and then. A gust blew through and caused my blazer to flutter open. I could feel the cool breeze cross over me. I inhaled deeply, the faint scent of burning wood tickled up my nose. "Mm. I love the smell of a campfire. Campfire! Where there is smoke, there is fire. Where there is fire, hopefully, there are people." I had to admit, I danced a little and whooped.

I looked around above the tops of the nearby trees, looking for the telltale sign of a fire and people. There was a small amount of smoke above the trees, and I headed off in that direction. I couldn't tell you if it was north, south, or otherwise, but I didn't care.

CHAPTER SIX

*I*t was the middle of April, and the branches of the surrounding trees began to fill in their leaves. Sunlight dappled across the wooded ground. It took a moment for my eyes to adjust to the dimmed environment. Puddles of sunlight scattered about my feet. If I didn't know where I was or how I got there, it would have been a lovely walk through the woods. I appreciated having my tall boots on to protect my legs from the underbrush. Although, there wasn't as much as I thought there would be. Before the day was over, I would have to check for ticks. I could feel the temperature in the woods drop from the sun-drenched open field. The blazer was doing little to keep me warm.

I like to be prepared for whatever may come my way, but that was one of those times when I wouldn't have been able to foresee a kidnapping that dropped me off in the middle of nowhere. I thought my over-packed suitcase would have saved the day, but it sat in my missing car. *Where is that damned car?*

I crossed my arms and tucked my hands in my armpits, to

keep my fingers from getting too cold. Why would I need my gloves going into the log cabin? I regretted leaving them in the passenger seat of the SUV. The sound of a burbling stream was getting louder than the leaves that crunched under every footstep. I hoped my sense of direction was not too far off from the path towards the smoke. I weaved through the trees. It was highly likely I set off in the wrong direction.

When I would go hiking, I knew not to veer from the trail. That is how people get lost in the woods and a family member would end up reporting them missing. There would be a large rescue team to search in the last known area. If they were lucky, they found them alive and well, usually cold and hungry. I didn't even want to think of what would happen if I got lost in the woods and there was no rescue team. I hoped to not become a missing person statistic. The camp and whoever lit the fire that lingered in the distance was my salvation to get back home. I knew I was navigating purely on luck and not skill. If I survived, I was determined to take a land navigation or survival course. I wouldn't be a victim of terrible navigation skills again.

I weaved my way through the trees for about five minutes–I could only guess the time; my phone was dead, and I was terrible with guesstimating time–when the sound of the water dancing over rocks got louder. "Cheese and rice! How am I supposed to get across that?" I threw my hands on my hips. The stream looked to be at least ten feet across and deep enough to get me wet up to my thighs. Water bubbled and gurgled over rocks and mossy branches. The stream would have been lovely if I didn't have to figure out how to cross it. It didn't matter how wide nor deep it was, it was early spring in West Virginia. The water would be cold from the melting snow of the nearby mountaintops. I was not looking forward to getting wet in the icy water. I stood an inch over five feet and a shallow stream could be deep for me.

I walked back and forth along the stream, in search of a shallow location to cross. Further down appeared to be shallow, but the stream had widened to at least double in width. I wouldn't jump across a stream that wide. I would be in the water longer trying to cross it. It felt like a no-win situation. I walked down, which seemed to me to be about a quarter of a mile and back up, afraid that I would lose the path towards the campfire. The banks towered over the stream by about four feet. I needed to figure out how I was going to cross.

I looked from one bank to the other, sizing up the distance between the two locations. I scrunched my face, bit my lower lip, and spun my ring around my finger. The water was darker in the middle than it was at the shallower and wider location. Light filtered through the tree canopy and dotted the stream here and there. It was difficult to determine if the dark water was from being deeper than the other part of the stream or the lack of light. Would I go back and trudge across the stream about a quarter of a mile from here? Or would I take my chances at that location? In my most brilliant of ideas, I decided to jump across the stream and hope that I wouldn't fall in. It couldn't have been over four feet across to the other side. Five or six at the most. Maybe seven. Could I jump over eight feet with enough momentum? It couldn't be too deep. What was the worst that could happen? I would get wet to my knees instead of my waist. It didn't matter. I would find my way to people, get to my hotel, take a long warm bath, and sleep in a warm and soft bed. It would be worth it to get out of there.

I flung my satchel to the other side of the stream. The possibility of my body and clothes getting wet was forefront in my mind, but I would be damned if my notebook, dead cell phone, key fob, and everything else would get wet. I would need them in good shape by the time I got back to civilization.

I backed up to give myself a running start. Starting line was thirty feet away from the bank, hoping to pick up enough speed to launch myself over to the other side—in my desperate attempt at avoiding the stream and getting wet. "I'm athletic. I got this." I tried to convince myself of my athletic prowess. As I stretched my neck from side-to-side, I told myself that I needed to be limber, flexible, and move like a gazelle being chased by a pack of lions.

I ran for exercise occasionally. It helped clear my head and keep me in somewhat decent shape. I started after an eventful trip to Scotland. For some strange reason, Todd kept telling us we needed to run to the next location we were going to visit. We ended up running from one end of Edinburgh to the other. That was the determining factor for me to get in better shape. I hoped my ability to run would help me clear the stream. I was curvy and swayed between a size eight and ten, and currently wearing somewhere in between the two sizes, maybe I inched up to a twelve. However, I thought I would be light enough to launch myself over to the other side of the stream. Perhaps I was not fast, but I was certain I could gain the momentum needed. I readied myself and brought my arms up and tucked them close to my sides. "This is a stupid idea, Murray," I said to myself. I wasn't as convincing as I hoped.

I took a deep breath and set off for the bank of the stream. The leaves crunched beneath my boots. Closer and closer to the edge. My short legs went as fast as they could. I imagined myself as quick and graceful gazelle. The jeans I wore might have been comfortable for traipsing in and out of museums, but I could've used the extra movement and flexibility that my running pants would have given me.

Twenty feet.

My feet slipped a bit underneath me, but I caught myself before I took a tumble. The boots certainly were not helping for traction. They were designed for fashion, not running through the woods. I prepared my mind for the jump. "You got this. Gazelle. Gazelle."

Huff. Puff. Pant. Pant. Crunch of the leaves. Sound of my heavy breath filled my ears.

Ten feet.

I couldn't afford to hold back. I had to go full force if I was to make it across. Heart pounded in my chest. I picked up more speed.

Five.

Three.

Ready.

Go!

Screeched to a sliding halt. I nearly slid over the edge of the embankment into the stream below.

What was I thinking? Clearly, I had overestimated my athletic prowess. There would have been no way my short little legs could make it across that stream. I wouldn't have cleared it. Crashed and burned. There is no way I would have been able to get hold of the edge of the embankment. As I looked over the edge of the embankment and heaved for air, I realized I would have landed in the middle of the stream and possibly twisted my ankle or broke my leg. Safe and wet are better than broken and wet.

My lungs begged for air. I folded over, hands on knees, from exertion. Head above your heart. *You don't want to pass out in the middle of the woods with no one around.*

With a shrug and a deep sigh, I accepted my defeat and headed down the stream to cross at the shallow part. It would take a little longer and I would get at least a little wet, but I would make it across in one piece. The stream reached mid-calf; however, the larger rocks would offer a respite from getting too much water up my legs. The rocks wobbled under my feet and tested my balance. I knew it was a desperate attempt, but for the sake of staying out of the water as much as possible, I had to try.

The exhaustion from earlier, coupled with the run, didn't help me with my trek across the creek. My legs continued to shake under me. The icy water from the springtime thaw soaked into my socks.

The sun kept the temperature mild, and I was dry—except for my feet—and I wouldn't die of hypothermia. At least, I hoped I wouldn't die of hypothermia. *Would I get hypothermia?* The socks continued to act like sponges and soak up the icy water. I made it halfway across the creek. The next rock was not far away. I just needed to give a little jump. With whatever energy I had left, I jumped. My right foot landed on the rock. The moss-covered rock wobbled and offered no traction.

With a scream and a large splash, I landed on my back in

the frigid water. My head and shoulder hit a large rock below the surface of the water. My shoulder caught most of the impact and would be sore tomorrow. I gasped, sucked in as much air as I could before my body submerged under the slow-moving current. The exhaustion from passing out and the attempted jump over the stream left me drained of energy. I hit another rock with my hip. I grasped for anything to help stop my journey down the creek. I need to slow down and keep myself from being pulled further downstream. I came across a felled tree limb, pulled myself up, and walked across the rest of the stream, soaked to the core. My head and shoulder throbbed from the impact. I limped over to the side of the embankment. My hip ached from scraping up against the rock. I was sore, cold, wet, and exhausted, but I survived.

I climbed up the small embankment and headed back to grab my satchel. My teeth chattered and my body started to convulse from the cold that settled into my bones. I hoped to find that campfire sooner rather than later, or I might get hypothermia after all.

CHAPTER SEVEN

My skinny jeans were plastered to my wet body and felt two sizes too small. I pulled my hair out of the chignon and wrung out the excess water. I twisted my hair back into place in the attempt to keep cold water off my body. Ha! That was wishful thinking. My wet locks would have to wait.

I walked back about a quarter of a mile to where I had thrown my satchel and my unsuccessful attempt at jumping across the creek. I took off my blazer–weighed down with water–and twisted it in order to wring out any excess water. I did the same for my blouse. The entire time, I shivered. Teeth-breaking shivers. If I took off my jeans, there would be no way I could get them back on my sticky, wet body. I sat down, unzipped my boots, poured the water out of them, took off my socks, and wrung them out. I sat there in my soaked jeans and my bra, desperate for a hot bath and dry clothes. The wet clothes clung to all the wrong places as I struggled to put them back on. I needed to find a way into the sun or next to that fire. Finally dressed, I threw my satchel back on and headed towards my salvation.

The smell of burning wood grew stronger as I continued to walk in the smoke's direction. I kept my arms clenched around me, desperate to grasp onto any warmth. I needed to get out of the woods and find the strong sun before hypothermia set in or I broke all my teeth from shivering. Looking back, I'm sure neither one would have happened; however, at that point, no one could convince me otherwise.

I inhaled and drew the scent in through my nose and deep into my lungs. Someone was cooking meat. My stomach protested its emptiness and begged for me to find the food. A faint murmur of men talking and laughing emerged over the sound of the crunching leaves beneath my feet and the water squishing in my boots. My body trembled in pain from the cold, and I picked up my pace through the thick woods. The light was brighter, voices louder, and the scent of food let me know I was getting closer to my salvation.

I grabbed my growling stomach and picked up my pace. The protein bar I had earlier hadn't satiated me, and I was famished. The exhaustion had become more pronounced. I ached to sleep in a warm bed only to waken to eat for the next week. That would have to wait until I could figure out where I was and how to get back home.

As I emerged from the woods, in front of me was a desolate dirt road, barely wide enough for a car, but no sign of a car or person coming from either direction. I could see no one along the road, but I could hear the indistinct murmur of voices coming from somewhere in the woods on the other side of the road. I worked my way through another set of woods. Again, the shade dropped the temps and turned me into a teeth-chattering ice cube. Fortunately, the trip through the frozen tundra didn't last long, and a small clearing filled with the afternoon sun was ahead of me.

Small tents, barely large enough to fit two people, were set up in a somewhat orderly fashion–if not snug–of five or six tents in four rows throughout the field. Some tents comprised a cloth tarp with sticks. Others were half-sized lean-tos. It looked as though they were using what they were willing to make do with or lug.

After a quick assessment of the camp, I could see approximately thirty men, and they appeared to be war reenactors. There was a stark difference between these men than what I had seen before with the Civil War reenactors. I had never been to a Civil War reenactment, but I had seen plenty of them on documentaries, movies, and television shows. The uniforms these men wore were not the typical Civil War uniforms. What I remembered from the shows, the reenactors were supposed to be dressed in blue or gray uniforms. These men were wearing dark blue trousers with blue or white gaiters, some had blue vests or white jackets, others were in their white shirts. I couldn't place where I had seen the uniforms, but they were not what I had expected from any of the American uniforms of the past. I could, at the very least, discern that from the style.

Reenactments meant there was civilization nearby, or at least someone could give me a ride to the nearest town. Men milled around the encampment, cooked food, cleaned rifles, set up their living areas, and sat around chatting. Their voices grew from a murmur to a jovial roar. I couldn't make out what they were saying. There was too much commotion, and my teeth were chattering louder than their voices.

"Arrêt..." A soldier ran up to me, rifle pointed at my chest. I couldn't understand everything he said. "Arrêt" sounded French. I thought I had heard or read it before. There was a lull in the voices as the other men turned their heads in the soldier's direction, running towards me. "... vous?" He nudged at me with the tip of his rifle. He was young, early twenties, with light brown hair and eyes, lean, a delicate jawline, and ears that seemed a bit too small.

"Sorry?" I stopped, shook my head, and raised my hands up in surrender. "What is wrong with you? Stop pointing that damned thing at me." I pushed the muzzle away from my chest and took a step back.

Reenactors don't use real guns, at least I didn't think they did, but that didn't mean I wanted one pointed at me. I wasn't sure what the man was saying to me, although I was almost positive that he was speaking French. However, that he had a rifle pointed at me gave rise for concern. "Sorry. Need you to break character. I don't speak French."

Another soldier was upon me, rifle inches from my body. "Qui... vous? Que... vous...?" More soldiers ran up to me. A variety of ages and sizes; at that point, it was a blur. They joined the soldier and pointed more rifles and swords at me. The men continued to speak in French, which left me confused and able to decipher only a word here-and-there, nothing to make out a conversation.

"What in the hell is going on?" I looked around at the gathering crowd of reenactors. By the look of things, they took their reenactment seriously, and I was, unfortunately, at the other end of the game. "Take me to your leader?" I felt as though I landed on an alien planet and the old parody of being captured and requesting to be taken to whoever was in charge was the only thing I could think to say to them. These men were in full character, and I stuck out like a sore thumb, but I needed to speak to whoever was in charge so I could get home.

A man in full uniform, with fancy accoutrements on the chest of his uniform–that I didn't recognize–walked with a distinguishable limp, favoring his left leg, towards the gathering crowd. He looked to be close to my age, if not a bit older. "... moi ... moi passer!" The crowd parted, letting the man through. "Pardon, Madame. Qui ... vous?"

"I'm sorry. As I told this gentleman," I said as I motioned to the overly excitable, rifle-toting sentry, "I don't speak French. I had asked him to take me to whoever oversees your group here."

Another poke in the side with a musket. My head snapped towards the soldier. "Next time, if you want to poke me that much, take me to dinner first." I brushed the end of the gun away from me and turned back towards the man that had joined our group.

"Oui." He paused, looked at me down his long, pointed nose, and let out an audible breath. "English. What are you doing here?" The man said with a heavy French accent, raking his eyes over me from the top of my stream-soaked head down to my boots that hid my hypothermic toes. I wasn't sure if he was trying to size me up to decide if I was a threat or if he was looking at me with disgust. I wrapped my arms around myself. Intentions, whether good or bad, he made me uncomfortable, and I had no clue what was going on. My clothes hadn't dried. I continued to shiver. No doubt, I looked like a drowned rat.

"Hi! Oh! Great! You speak English. I'm Amelia and I'm

just trying to get home." *Be friendly, Murray, win them over with charm.* "I don't know how I got here. Well, I know how I got here from over there," I said, as I pointed behind me towards the woods. "I'm tired. I'm freezing. I'm hungry. Could you please take me to your commander, or whatever he is called, unless you are the commander? So, he, or you, can arrange for me to get a ride to the nearest town?" My teeth continued to chatter uncontrollably.

"... français?" He humphed and looked down his nose at me again. Jerk. This was not going as planned. "Oui. S'il vous plaît, Madame," the man said, gesturing to me to follow him. He leaned to the side and said something to a soldier.

"Oui, chef," the soldier said as he saluted. He turned around to bark instructions at the other men. They all continued to speak in French, which were hollow sounds in my English-understanding ears. I understood "oui", and a few other words here and there, but nothing made sense. I had gone to France twice when Todd was stationed in Europe but had never needed to learn more than a few words. If he was the chef, I hoped I could get some food from him. My stomach felt as though it was going to scream if I didn't eat.

CHAPTER EIGHT

That entire day confused me, and I didn't understand enough words to make out an actual sentence. Why did the reenactors insist on staying so deep in character? They could've made this so much easier on me if they would just speak English. I put the clues together and realized these were French military reenactors, but I didn't know from which war. Throughout various times in American history, the French took part in combat on American soil. They fought against the British and colonists during the French and Indian War, also known as the Seven Years War. The other significant time they took part on the battlefield was with the Colonists against the British during the American Revolution. There weren't any reenactments that I knew of during the French and Indian War. Maybe there were, and I never had heard of them, so they must be Revolutionary reenactors. However, the most I knew of reenactors during those times were at historical places, such as Colonial Williamsburg in Virginia, or at larger battlefield events. Whichever time they were reenacting would make a tremendous difference if they considered me friend or foe.

I understood with Revolutionary and Civil War reenactments, the men and women stayed in character throughout the entire event. When I visited Colonial Williamsburg, the employees stayed in character, even the man that played Lafayette. I found it amusing to watch. Their dedication to their characters was impressive. Like the other reenactments, they dressed these soldiers for their parts. Two of the men followed me, pointing their rifles at my back. I was quite aware of their presence and quite annoyed that they pointed their rifles at me, but I was more concerned about getting warm. I crossed my arms and pulled my jacket tight around me to maintain what little body heat I had left.

More soldiers gathered before they ran off to the woods where I had just emerged from, with their rifles pointed, as if they were on the hunt. I wondered if they thought I had come from the British or Colonial side. If they were nearby where I woke up, I hadn't seen or heard them. I couldn't imagine that they would be too far away if the French reenactors were in the field. I wasn't sure where I was, but I assumed there must have been a skirmish nearby, big enough to warrant a reenactment. The one at Fort Ashby wouldn't be the one for the reenactors. They must have moved me closer to Fort Necessity when I was knocked out. I had stopped at Fort Ashby to get an idea of the size of smaller frontier forts. My curiosity about where Jane Ashby, the spitfire wife of Captain Ashby, lived was what drew me to that particular fort.

The chef led me to the largest tent on the other side of

the encampment and stopped before entering. He turned around and said, "Wait here." He entered and left me outside with the armed guards. I sighed and shook my head. I should be used to the level of commitment this group had; however, all could think about was getting to back to my hotel and collapsing in a hot bath and indulging in plenty of food. If he was the chef, although he didn't seem to be dressed like any chef I had seen before, the least he could do was find me something to eat.

The chef came out of the tent and held open the flap. "S'il vous plaît, Madame." He motioned to me with his hand. "Enter."

"Thank you, Chef. If you could find me something to eat while I'm speaking to your commander. I'm famished." I said with conviction. The man tilted his head and looked at me for a moment longer than I was comfortable with, then looked over at the commander. "Please? It's been a long day and I haven't had enough to eat."

"Oui, Madame. I will have cook prepare you something." He said and turned back to the commander with a look of confusion. The commander nodded, and the chef left the tent.

The commander, a man in a decorated uniform that rivaled the chef's uniform, sat on a simple stool, not much more than a cut log, he was shuffling stacks of parchments, which were laid out on a cot he was using as a table in front of him, into a pile and flipped them over. I assumed he was trying to hide the maps and plans from me, but I had no desire to get involved with the reenactment. "If you please, Madame. Have a seat." He said to me, motioning me to another log that sat across from him. I sat down; thankful for the opportunity to sit and, since I was still soaking wet, that it was a piece of wood instead of the cushioned fabric chair. "You seem to have caused quite a perturbation in the camp today. Let's talk about who you are and how you came upon our camp."

I shifted on the stump. I was not sure if I was uncomfortable because I was wet, cold, and hungry, or if this man's line of questioning was too accusatory. Lord only knows where he gets his harsh tone. Ugh. I was not involved in the reenactment, and I would have thought that was quite apparent, given my attire. This whole charade became absurd to me, but I played along so I could get out of there.

"I'm Amelia Murray. They kidnapped me. I think... I'm not sure." My head spun as I shook my head in confusion. "I don't know how I got here or where here is." I hesitated. He continued to judge me. "I went to visit Fort Ashby, and they knocked me unconscious, or something. I don't know. And I woke up in a field that wasn't at the fort. I'm not sure how long they knocked me out for, so if you know what day it is, that would be great."

I continued to rattle on. The man just sat there with a confused look on his face. "My cell phone was dead. My car wasn't there. I had no clue how I got there. Then I smelled a fire and thought someone might be nearby, so I headed in this direction. I fell into a stream and am soaked to the bone, freezing cold, exhausted, and extremely hungry. I would love a ride to the nearest town or if you have a phone I could use, that would be great."

The man sat there for a moment, flipped over the

parchment, and ran his finger over a map. "Where is this... Fort Ashby? They garrisoned how many men?"

All that talking, and he only picked up Fort Ashby? Nothing about me being kidnapped? "Fort Ashby is in Fort Ashby, West Virginia. I'm not exactly sure where it is. I had plugged in the location into my GPS, and I just followed the directions and paid little attention to it," I said with a shrug.

"Virginia doesn't have a Fort Ashby. What is a G-P-S and what do you mean you..." He fluttered his hand with an arrogant wave, "Plugged your location?"

"Oh, for goodness' sake," I said as I threw my hands up in defeat. As ridiculous as I found the situation, I figured I needed to play along as though I was living in the 18th century, because the way this conversation veered was towards a dead end. "My carriage driver took me to what I thought was Fort Ashby. I'm uncertain where it is located. I was on my way to Fort Duquesne and thought I would make a stop at Fort Ashby. What more I can tell you? I just need to know where I am and get a ride to the nearest town."

"Oui, Madame. Why were you going to visit the Marquis Duquesne?"

"Not the Marquis Duquesne," I said, my frustration level increased with every minute passed. "Why is everyone making this so difficult?" This guy seemed to know his history. I was far from an expert and was in the middle of my research when I ended up in this encampment. Shortly prior to my trip, I had done research into the locations and importance of some forts erected during the French and Indian War. Fort Duquesne was originally a trading post on the confluence of the Allegheny and the Monongahela in modern day Pittsburgh, Pennsylvania. The fort would change hands between the French and the British throughout the conflict. "I'm talking about Fort Duquesne. Wait. What time period in the war are you supposed to be reenacting?"

"Pardon?"

I closed my eyes to focus on the deep breath I had to take in order to regain my fleeting patience. "What's today's date?"

"It is the twelfth day of April, in the year of our Lord seventeen fifty-four."

"Okay, cheese and rice!" I was scrambling through my thoughts, trying to place the date with the events. I remembered when I had researched battles for my book that the fort was supposed to be established in April and was currently being built as an English fort. French forces will confiscate it in six days. "You know, the English Fort Prince George being built at the Forks of the Ohio? Anyway, I was headed there to do a little research for my book, and I visited other forts along the way."

"I see," said the man, as he sat back on his stool, tree stump, whatever he wanted to call it. He looked at me. The weight of his stare hung heavy in the air. I thought it would be a simple conversation to get me on my way, but it became a confusing interrogation. At the very least, I knew the date they were basing the reenactment. "I do not believe you understand the predicament you seemed to have gotten yourself into. I believe you will stay with us longer and we will have more of these conversations. Oui?"

"I was really hoping to get to my hotel and not stick around here any longer. Oui?" I said, my words dripped with sarcasm. I lost my patience with the reenactment game played.

"I'm afraid you do not understand. You will remain with us, as my guest. Do not cause me to make you my prisoner, s'il vous plaît," he said as he stood up and straightened his white coat.

"I'm not sure you understand. I am going to have people looking for me if I don't get to my hotel tonight. My daughter will expect me to call her."

"S'il vous plaît, let's get you accommodations for your visit."

"Okay, so if you and nobody else are going to let me leave, could you at least tell me how long you expect me to stay? Mister? Commander? I don't know what to call you."

"Joseph Coulon de Villiers, Sieur de Jumonville, at your service, Madame." He gave a dramatic bow. "You may call me Sieur de Jumonville. I am in command. I will expect you to stay as required." He walked over to the tent flaps and spoke to one of the two men posted outside the tent. The man ran off, leaving one guard out front. "They are making suitable accommodations for you. The cook will provide you with a meal when you get to your tent. You can clean, eat, and rest. You'll join me for the evening meal."

I sat in silence. What more I could say to get me to my hotel that night? I was too hungry and exhausted to argue anymore. "Very well. Will you have your men show me to my tent? I'll need to dry my clothes; this is all I brought with me." I stood up and pulled down on my navy corduroy blazer, straightening it up. I knew I looked a mess, but I no longer cared how I looked. That man and his dismissive attitude didn't deserve for me to look decent. It took everything in my power to stay calm with his treatment towards me. When I came into the camp, I thought they would save me from my precarious predicament, but he only contributed to it and my frustration. I wondered if he was in on my kidnapping.

CHAPTER NINE

The soldier came back, along with the chef, and they escorted me to a tent in the middle of the encampment. The tents varied from small, enclosed tents, like this one, and tents that were a mere sheet of canvas held up with sticks. Easy to set up. Easy to take down. Chef opened the flap to the tent and motioned for me to enter. There was not much to the accommodations, as there was only a bedroll along the side of the tent, barely enough room for me. I stood there slack-jawed. "Seriously? This is what I get? This is pathetic and disgusting."

Chef stormed in the tent, yanking me by my arm and spun me around to face him. "You stupid woman." His eyes burned a hole through me. "You are the one that got yourself here. That soldier that was tasked with finding you a place to stay. He gave you his bed and tent. He will sleep outdoors without a blanket in this cold because of you." It was as though his brown eyes turned solid black and burned with rage. Aghast, I snapped my mouth closed. "I have a few options for you. We could tie you to a tree and let him back in his tent. You can sleep in the cold. I allow you to stay here," he motioned to the tent, "and he can stay here with you. He can take his liberties with you for payment for the use of his tent. Or you can stay in here by yourself with guards posted. You will need to show respect, sit down, and close that viperous mouth of yours. Your choice."

I was confused and terrified at what had just happened. No one had ever spoken to me like that, especially the blatant threat of being assaulted. I hadn't expected the rage from the reenactor. It was supposed to be fun and a way to learn more about the history of the war by participating in some actions. Some people, I supposed, get a bit too invested in the storytelling. As a writer, I could understand getting invested in a story. That's how I got into this predicament to begin with. If I stayed with the original plan, I wouldn't have gone to Fort Ashby. I wouldn't have ended up in an odd French reenactment encampment, being held as a prisoner to extract information that I knew about the upcoming war. *Damn my curiosity!*

"Please, tell him thank you." I knew I needed to remain calm—so he would know that I was smart and not easily intimidated—which was difficult to appear grateful, and not give him more fuel for his rage. In truth, I wanted to explode and could barely hold back my angry tears. If he was easy to rage and threaten me with being assaulted over my response to the accommodations, if he felt I challenged his authority, he wouldn't think twice about having me killed. He acted as though they were doing me the favor, and I doubted my intelligence for heading towards their camp. I should have scoped it out better before barging in. My life and safety were more important than his game, so I played along with the situation as best as I could, as absurd as it all seemed. They said they would let me go when they received the information they thought I hid from them. Screw the hotel. I was done. I wanted to go home, and I wanted these creeps in jail.

I would give the jerk who pretended to be Sieur de Jumonville all that he needed to know. I scrolled through my mental notes about from where I knew that name. My thoughts were in a fog, and I could barely tell up from down after everything that had gone on today. I would need to look at my notebook in my satchel when I was alone and out of the prying eyes of my captors. If seen, they might damage my notes or call me a spy or who knows what could happen to me.

"The cook will bring your food."

The small and sparse tent would suit my needs. "Thank you. My clothes are wet from falling into the stream." I turned around to face Chef. "Is there somewhere I can dry them? I'm supposed to have dinner this evening with Sieur de Jumonville and would like to be a bit more put together than I am now."

"I will have something brought for you to wear while your clothes dry." Chef's eyes burned a hole in me as he sized me up.

He left me sitting alone in the tent. I wanted to cry from pure exhaustion, frustration, and hunger, but it was not the time for tears. The smell of food lingered throughout the camp, and the cook couldn't get to me soon enough. What felt like only moments later, I could smell food inching its way towards the tent. The smell of cooked meat burst into the tent like an avalanche, as a soldier opened the flap to the tent and carried a bowl filled with a stew and a chunk of bread. "What kind of meat is this?"

"Pardon, madame?" He said, handing me the bowl and bread. He gave a quick bow of his head, turned around, and closed the flap.

I poked at the meat with my finger. It smelled delicious. I poked again, trying to assess the type of meat in the stew. I had expected a beef stew to be dark and stringy, but it wasn't that way. It seemed like it could be a chicken, although I didn't see or hear any chickens. It might not have been fresh, but I decided I was hungry enough not to care what kind of meat it was. All I needed was to get some food in my stomach and, hopefully, without food poisoning. The soldier hadn't brought a spoon, so it relegated me to use hands to pick up the larger chunks. The meat tasted like chicken, but there was something off about it. There was a bit of a nutty flavor to it, which seemed odd for chicken. The rest of the stew was quite bland and not well seasoned. My taste buds might have cared what it tasted like on any other day, but my stomach was happy for the nourishment. I made my way through the chunks of meat and vegetables, then attempted to eat the stale bread. The broth helped reconstitute the bread and made it more palatable. Finally, after what seemed like an eternity, my stomach stopped screaming at me.

"Madame?"

"Yes?"

"... pour vous." A soldier ducked as he reached in, holding a white folded piece of fabric.

"Merci." I gathered he had told me that the fabric was for me. My French was extremely limited, but I figured I would use the few words I knew.

I took the fabric from him, and it unfolded as I held it up. It was a white woolen shirt, long enough to be a mid-thigh dress. It was softer than I had expected and seemed well worn. I stripped down and pulled the shirt on over my head. Even though wool would cause me to scratch my skin raw, I appreciated having something dry.

I popped my head out of the tent and the soldier that was guarding jumped back and pointed his rifle at me. "Oh, for the love of..." The longer this went on, the less I felt like a guest and more like a prisoner. It didn't matter what Chef or Sieur de Jumonville wanted to call me. The constant pointing of rifles and the threats of my wellbeing told me I was, without a doubt, their prisoner. "I need somewhere to hang my clothes to dry."

The soldier didn't understand—or chose not to understand—what I said in English and my limited French had been exhausted. I struggled to figure out their angle. He said something to me I didn't understand, but he gestured his rifle back to the tent. I held out the wet clothes, hoping he would understand that I was not trying to escape, but to hang my clothes. He snatched my clothes out of my extended arms and immediately dropped them.

"Hey, don't drop those! Those are my clothes and they're just wet. I need to hang them up to dry." I gulped back the tears that were ready to burst out. The soldier pointed to the top of the tent. I feared the weight of the wet clothes would pull down the fabric precariously held up by sticks. It appeared I had no other choice. I spread out the clothes on the section that had the wood braces, hoping it wouldn't decide to collapse on me while I rested.

The clothes had dried a bit since my unfortunate dip in

the stream but getting them off and fully dried would help soften the blow of the shit-show day I had so far. I stretched up to reach the top of the tent, although not that tall, everything seemed high to me. I went inside, spread out my bra and underwear on the small piece of cloth that was on the floor. I might have to put my clothes outside for the sun to dry and the camp to see, but I wouldn't allow those men that threatened to assault me the opportunity to see my undergarments. They didn't need any additional motivation.

I tugged my hair out of the chignon and spread it out, along with the blanket on the floor, to give it the opportunity to dry while I slept. Exhaustion took over, and I would look at my notes after a quick nap. I laid my head down and instantly fell into a deep and exhausted sleep.

CHAPTER TEN

My heavy eyelids struggled to open. Something stirred me awake. I clenched my eyes tight before I could focus on the room. *How long was I asleep?* I wasn't sure, but exhaustion lingered throughout my body. I closed my eyes again. Rest, that I had hoped to get with a nap eluded me. I must have tossed and turned throughout the night. The dream of being kidnapped, the distinct smell of burning cherry wood ending up in the middle of nowhere, exhausted, famished, and fell into a stream seemed so real. It continued with me stumbling into a French and Indian War reenactment where the reenactors insisted it was the year 1754. I laughed at the thought of the story I would write about it. Certainly, my editor would laugh me out of the pitch meeting if I tried to sell that as the story for my next novel. "Not believable," she would say. She would laugh. I would laugh. We would get on with our day.

I must have been daydreaming and went on autopilot to get to the hotel. The cold sank down into my bones. With my arm thrown over my eyes, I could see the sun poking through my eyelids. I wanted more sleep. My body ached. I needed to contact the front desk about the quality of the bed. It was hard, as if I had laid directly on the ground, and the wool blanket, although it was meant to keep me warm, felt like a scouring pad. To top it off, I was still cold. "Are they doing construction outside?" I grumbled. The sound of men's voices surrounded me. I could hear them, but the words they were speaking made little sense to my tired body. I was certain they were speaking a foreign language. "They aren't speaking Spanish. They couldn't be speaking French, could they?"

"No." I bolted up and, with great effort, forced my eyes open. "Son of a... are you kidding me?" That wasn't just a vivid and weird dream? I wanted to cry a river. There was no time to cry. I needed to figure out what was going on and how to get home.

I looked around what I had hoped would be my hotel room, with all the amenities of modern-day living, only to discover I was laying down in a small tent being illuminated by a setting sun. A dark brown woven wool blanket covered my body and was doing a terrible job of keeping me warm. The cold had settled too deep in my bones and the only thing that was going to break me of the frigid curse was a soak in a hot bath. The blanket was rough to the touch. My sensitive skin found most wool blankets and garments rough. The scratch of the wool gave me the sensation of bugs ripping at my flesh. I had a fear of bugs crawling under my skin. The sensation I experienced from wool didn't help contain my fears. I had considered my situation, and it was quite possible that lice could crawl throughout the blanket and over me while I slept. I wondered if the day could get worse. At that rate, it probably would. I was ready to break down and cry. I had been fighting it off all day and it made me emotionally exhausted. Even after the nap, I couldn't shake the physical exhaustion.

I studied the weave of the wool shirt I wore and recalled Todd loved to wear wool shirts as a base layer to his everyday wear. He would wear them in the summer and winter, no matter the season. He insisted I try a wool shirt of my own. "It will change your idea of comfort," he said. Sure, it did. It made me appreciate a soft cotton or slippery silk, even more than I had before. My skin was sensitive to every fiber of the wool shirt and constantly scratched my body while wearing it, much like the blanket. Todd told me it needed to be washed and broken in. I didn't want to suffer to that point and refused to wear it again. I could throw on a sweater or coat, or easily buy something else from the department store, but I refuse to wear wool again.

Reality came crashing into me. It stopped the pleasant thoughts of soft cotton and silk and Todd's wool shirts and his clean scent when he slipped on his shirt after his morning shower. The tent and the men that surrounded it stunk. They needed a shower and deodorant. I was being held against my will by war reenactors, who refused to tell me where I was or to take me to the nearest town to find my way home. By that point in time, I had believed they may have been involved in my kidnapping but couldn't figure out why they had dragged me into it.

I pulled out my satchel and checked my cell phone. Dead. My finger repeatedly pressed the key fob alarm button. I hoped to set off the alarm in the car and hear it in the distance. The red light on the key fob didn't flash. Dead. I pulled out my notebook and a pen. I opened the book, looked at the list of battles and forts that George Washington fought in or visited. Some I had planned to visit; others noted for reference. I recalled Joseph Coulon de Villiers, Sieur de Jumonville, had mentioned the date being April 12, 1754. "Jumonville." I repeated the name. "Why is that name familiar?" I flipped through the pages of the notes and pounded my finger onto an entry. "George Washington will lead a skirmish at Jumonville Glen at the end of May. This couldn't be the same Jumonville as that incident. This reenactment cannot possibly go on for that long. Why doesn't any of this make sense?" I threw the book down on to the floor. The words, my notes, the book, these men–no part of the situation made sense.

"Madame Murray." Chef's voice came from the other side of the tent flaps. "Sieur de Jumonville requests your attendance at the evening meal." He threw my clothes in the tent, without opening the flap more than it took to wedge my clothes inside. They landed on the floor next to me. The shirt was dry. The denim and corduroy had dried enough to not make me miserable.

"Thank you," I said, loud enough for him to hear me. "Asshole," I added under my breath.

"I will return to escort you." A sound of irritation oozed from his voice. "Be ready."

That man infuriated me with every breath that he took. He was curt with me, and I didn't understand why. I didn't ask to be here and held against my will. I looked forward to the moment I could get away from this group, especially that insufferable jerk. I was ready to end my entire trip and go to the safety, warmth, and comfort of my home in Fredericksburg. At the first chance, I would call the police. There would be no way these men could do this to anyone else by the time I was done with them. The world had yet to feel my wrath.

My clothes were stiff from being draped outside on the tent and the dirt that was embedded in the fibers. They needed a proper wash, but I was thankful they were mostly dry. My boots, still damp, would keep my feet cold throughout the evening. Cold feet can make a bad day worse. I'm miserable with cold feet. It would be a miserable evening for me.

I ran my fingers through my slightly damp hair to calm my wild, wavy locks. It was no use. Like my clothes, I needed a proper hair wash and a brush. Flyaway strands of hair were slicked down with the hand cream I had found in my satchel. A pull and a twist, and my hair was back in the chignon. I hoped it would hide the fact that my hair was a tangled mess. Blazer buttoned, satchel pulled over my head and slung across my body, I waited for my irritating escort to arrive.

No sooner had I stood up and stepped towards the flaps of the tent, than Chef called for me. "Were you just waiting outside for me to finish getting dressed?" I asked with a snark in my voice that told him I was tired of his attitude.

"Oui." Direct. Sure, I could deal with direct.

I followed him down the row of tents. "Am I going to leave here to tonight and go home?"

"Non." Okay, the direct answers sounded more venomous than I expected.

With a bite in my voice, I asked, "Will you say more than one word to me?" I could tell he wouldn't warm up to me, but I thought I could try to smooth things over. Was I more irritated with his abrupt attitude or with the fact that I couldn't win him over? He continued to walk on. He left me behind, reluctant to catch up with his pace. His lack of reply answered my question.

CHAPTER ELEVEN

We arrived at Jumonville's tent without additional conversation. Silence was better than hearing his grating voice. Chef opened one side of the tent flap. No sooner than I started to walk in, the flap hit me on the head. "Asshole," I said, as I rubbed my head. That time loud enough for anyone to hear, without a care if he heard me.

They used a piece of wood as a makeshift table, set for what I hoped to be a delicious dinner. A couple of low-rimmed metal bowls, two mugs, and spoons set on either side of the slab of wood. Two logs that we had sat on earlier were to be used as chairs. A single candle sat in the middle of the table and lit the small tent. After the bland lunch, I could use some food with a bit of flavor to it. A meal with the commander should garner some privilege on the gastronomical front.

"S'il vous plaît, Madame Murray." Jumonville motioned for me to sit. I approached my log to sit. A quick jerk back of the strap of my satchel yanked at my neck. He had grabbed the strap as I had walked in front of him. I yanked my shoulder forward in the attempt to dislodge his grip. That was not how I had imagined the dinner would be.

"S'il vous plaît, Sieur de Jumonville," I said with a sharp sting to my voice. "I would prefer to keep my satchel on my person."

"Évidemment. You would be comfortable without it during dinner, I would think." His false sense of concern oozed like snot out of his every word. It surprised me he hadn't forced it off me at that point.

"I will keep it with me," I said as I sat down on the log, pulling the pouch to my front, and draped my arm over it with a grip that made my knuckles turn white. I was not sure what was going to happen, but I knew I needed to keep whatever I had in my satchel away from him. It was my only leverage to get out of there in one piece.

"May I offer you wine?" He poured the dark red wine into the metal mug in front of me without waiting for a reply.

I was not much of a drinker. If I was going to pour a glass, I preferred the light, sweet wines. I despised the name "girly-drinks", but that was what I would order when going out. Friends would make fun of me when we went out and told me I lacked a refined palate. Why would I drink something that I didn't like until I liked it? I'm sure people didn't like the taste of cigarettes when they started smoking, but they kept at it until they would crave it, and no one is telling a non-smoker that they don't smoke because they aren't refined. My friends refused to see it my way, but they eventually stopped giving me a difficult time about my wine choices. I thought about the choices he offered me. Drink it or don't. That was not the time that I should refuse a mug of wine.

"I would have preferred a margarita." I couldn't help myself. As much as I wanted to play into this absurd situation, my mouth had a mind of its own.

Jumonville stopped mid-sip. "I'm not familiar with margarita. What region is it from?" He looked at his mug and tilted it back.

My mouth was going to get me in trouble. "The Mexican region. Sort of. I guess. You know, tequila, lime juice, some triple sec. A little shaky-shaky." I mimed shaking a drink like I could rival Tom Cruise in the movie *Cocktail*. "Serve it over ice with salt on the rim. A margarita!" I closed my eyes and sunk into my seat and thought about the sweet concoction to help sweep me away from that place. To my great disappointment, when I opened my eyes, Jumonville sat across from me, and stared at me, unable to decide how he should respond to the ramblings of a madwoman, to the wine, or the mention of a margarita. My response had nothing to do with the wine, but the thought of drinking a cold margarita on the deck in my backyard.

I could tell he was trying to get me to let my guard down in order to extract information from me. I've watched enough crime dramas to figure out his angle. Good cop-bad cop. I wondered if the bad cop stood outside the tent, ready to rough me up. Honestly, I couldn't figure out what was with this drama? It wasn't like the war was really happening. This had all occurred over two hundred sixty-five years ago, and he couldn't possibly learn anything new about it now. I needed to wake up from this nightmare. I must have hit my head harder than I thought when I was at Fort Ashby.

"Let us drink to margaritas, honest and enlightened conversation, and getting to know each other better." Jumonville held his mug up to me, and I returned the toast and took a sip of the wine. I was not sure what to make of him. He was highly invested in the role he played, but deep down, the whole situation didn't sit right in my gut. I couldn't place it. There was no logical reason for my being in the middle of a war reenactment. One thing I noticed, he knew more English than he let on when I first met him. The deception thickened.

"I could really go for a hot bath and a drink," I said as I took another sip. There went my mouth again. "I had the stew earlier today; I couldn't identify the meat. What was it? Chicken? Rabbit? Pork?" That was my attempt at enlightened conversation.

"The stew today was squirrel," he said as he studied me. I did my best to not react to his mention of squirrel stew. I wasn't sure if he tried to upset me or if it was a common meal for them. He looked down his long nose at me. "You dress like a man and the garments you wear are nothing I have seen before. Why do you dress like that?" He asked, waving his hand up and down at me. I could've sworn he exaggerated the tilt of his head in order to further look down his nose at me.

Was this part of the honest and enlightened conversation we had toasted?

I raised my eyebrows at him in disbelief at his audacity.

"This is just a couple of items I pulled out of my closet. Where I'm from, you know, the real world, women can wear whatever type of clothes they want, and I choose this to wear." I looked down at my clothes and straightened up my jacket. I was fond of this outfit. It was comfortable, and easy to dress up or down, depending on the occasion. Besides all of that, I liked to keep things simple. That location, the situation, and his arrogance left me to feel self-conscious about my choice in attire. I didn't want to give him any more fuel to deepen the divide between us. I didn't keep up with trends or consider myself fashion-forward, but I was not used to people commenting on my clothing with such obvious disdain. The day left me and my clothes in need of a good cleaning. However, he was a judgmental jerk, and I shouldn't give a rat's ass what he thought of my clothes. He looked for ways to get under my skin. I tucked a stray lock of hair behind my ear.

"And exactly where is that? Where you are from?" He continued his line of questioning as he relaxed into his seat. He took a sip of his wine. "You do not speak like the English, the Colonists, or the savages." I had to think about how to answer his questions. He obviously was going to stay in character, and I was not sure how much I would reveal to this man. If he held me hostage, was he going to blackmail or ransom me? The only family I had left was Hannah, and she couldn't come up with any money for a ransom. I had to be careful as to not give him too much information, but true enough to help keep my story straight. If I lied to him, he could find out or I would misspeak, and that would make matters worse for me.

"Fredericksburg, Virginia." I kept my answers honest and succinct, not to give him more than I needed to in order to get through the night and get home. "I am offended that you would refer to the Native Americans as savage, regardless of you staying in character or not. It is offensive on so many levels, and I will not be a part of that." I crossed my arms in protest.

"They are savages." He emphasized are with a wave of his hand. He took another sip of his wine.

My blood boiled. This must be the part where we get to know each other. I knew I didn't want to know any more about him.

"Where are you from?" If he ended up releasing me, like he said he would when I arrived, then I would need to provide the police with as much information as I could get in order to arrest him and the chef. I was certain they, or someone they knew, were behind my arrival at that place... wherever that was. I was still confused and unsure of my location.

"I was born in the seigneury of Verchères, New France," he said. Jumonville understood the tactics I played. It became a game of chess. Too bad I only knew how to play checkers. He needed to remain in control. He knew I had critical information. I had mentioned the French and Indian War many times, so I must have information regarding the details of an attack on the French, which he clearly was, or was reenacting the part of a Frenchman during the Colonial period. *New France. Where exactly is New France? Canada?* I provided little information, and, in return, he did the same.

The sound of a man clearing his throat outside of the tent, paused our conversation. "Entrer," said Jumonville with a tone in his voice that told me he held himself in high regard. A man dressed in a simple uniform entered with a tray of food and placed it on a small side table made from a log. He returned to the tent entrance and grabbed another tray of food from someone lingering outside of the tent. I couldn't see how many men stood outside the tent, since the night had taken over. The glow of campfires in the surrounding area peeked through the flaps and lit up the sides of the tent. The man placed the additional food on the side log and served the dinner. *More mystery meat.*

Throughout the conversation, I focused on my exhaustion and tried to keep my wits about me. I hadn't realized how hungry I was until the smell of dinner crept up my nose. My stomach growled loud enough that I was certain the entire encampment could hear it. My cheeks tingled as my face flushed from the embarrassment. Jumonville tried to hide a smile; he found my weakness–food. "I beg your pardon." I grabbed my stomach as it growled again. "It has been quite an eventful day for me, and it has caused me to have quite the appetite."

"Oui. Let's talk about your day. Shall we?" Jumonville looked up from his plate with the telling look that my presence was an inconvenience. He preferred to get me and my story out of the way and enjoy his meal in solitude. "You had said you were on your way to a Fort Duquesne and not the Marquis Duquesne. I am familiar with the French forts; however, that one eludes me. Where is that located?"

I closed my eyes and racked my brain to go through my notes in the attempt to remember where it was located. Exhaustion kept me from remembering the details. Evidently, I had relied on my notes more than I should have.

I didn't pull out my notes, as I didn't want Jumonville to know of the existence of my notebook, which contained more detailed information than I could remember. He would confiscate it, and I would have lost my research notes. It was not like I couldn't pull the information again when I got to my computer, but that would set me back, and I didn't want to share any information with him. I kept it hidden in my satchel. I laughed at the thought. As a leader of the reenactment troupe, he should know the history of what happened. He could Google everything he needed to know. His continued line of questioning about some of the basic information from the war was leading me to believe he didn't study up on the events of the war. I took a few more bites of the food, stalling my answer. The meat was more tender than the squirrel stew from lunch. I enjoyed the meal, but not the company.

I put down my spoon. "Listen here, Sieur de Jumonville. I'm tired of playing this game." Deep inhale through my nostrils and release the breath slow. Calm your emotions, Murray. There was no way I was going to return to the conversation. I hoped he would realize that I was not part of the reenactment, but at this moment I was not sure what was going on but felt as though I was stuck in some sort of alternate universe. "I was kidnapped and now lost. I just want to get home. Until I get more information from you, I'm not answering more questions." My eyes stung from the tears welling up. I didn't want to cry, but I was exhausted, hungry, and scared of my situation. I picked up my spoon and took a bite, as I tried to appear as though I was not phased.

"Oui. Comprends," he said with a calm demeanor. He

touched the corners of his mouth with a linen cloth and placed it next to his plate. He stood up and walked over to me. The pressure from a firm placement of his hand on my back told me I may have pushed my limits with him.

"I suppose you cancelled dinner." I put down my spoon, letting it clank with a bit of dramatic flair, wiped my mouth with the napkin, and prepared to stand. Jumonville shoved me forward and slammed my ribs into the makeshift table. The force of the shove caused my body to lurch forward over the plates. Wine flowed from the mugs that fell over from the abrupt impact, staining the white linen napkins. I gasped in pain when his other hand grabbed my hair and yanked my head back. With quick force, he shoved my face into the plate of half-eaten food. I tried to pull my face out of the smashed peas. He pushed harder in response. My nose throbbed. I thought he might have broken my nose. The metallic taste of blood filled my mouth. I had bit my tongue. I gasped for air and spit out a mouthful of blood.

My body was flung back, and my neck was being strained from the force Jumonville used to yank me back. If he had a knife, he could've slit my throat. The situation took a turn for the worse.

I couldn't catch my balance as my log teetered backwards. The grip he had maintained on the back of my hair kept me from falling to the ground. My stomach muscles ached and strained to pull myself upright. I gasped for air and reached out towards his arms. He released the grip on my hair. I tumbled backwards onto the floor. Pain seared through my shoulder from the impact of taking the brunt of the fall on the edge of another log. I was sore from my fall on the rock earlier in the day. This tirade of his didn't help my already injured body. I gasped for air again and searched for the breath that eluded me.

"Stand up," He yelled at me as he leaned over my pathetic body. I couldn't move. I didn't want to move. It hurt to move. It hurt to breathe. Admittedly, I wanted to be defiant. I needed to fight back.

"Bouchard," He bellowed as he looked over his shoulder. He looked back down at me with hate-filled eyes.

Chef came running in the room. Chef's name was Bouchard. Why did they call him chef? I looked into Bouchard's eyes. A plea for help. Panic struck me when I could see his brown eyes light up with pleasure from seeing me on the ground in pain. My whole body surged with pain. Bouchard brought his foot back. Pain pierced through my body as his black boot landed a solid kick in my ribs. My face was drenched with sweat and tears. I couldn't breathe. I grabbed my side and rolled away from him. The earthy scent of dirt and grass, along with the metallic smell and taste of the blood I spit out, filled my nose. My muscles failed me when I needed to get up. They refused to listen. With the impact of another boot on my stomach, I lost my breath again. I struggled to sit up. I coughed. The air burned my lungs as I tried to fill them. I held my hands up and gasped out, "Stop! Just stop!"

Bouchard reached down, grabbed me by the hair and pulled me to my feet. Jumonville's voice filled with venom as he turned to Bouchard. "... vue ... attachez... arbre.... dormir...!"

I heard a few words through the hard thumps of blood surging through my veins. Bouchard gripped my arm with such force, I could feel the bruises as they formed.

Before we could get to the flaps of the tent, Bouchard stopped and pulled my limping body to a stop. "Arrêt," Jumonville said as he walked over to us, opened my satchel, and pulled out my notebook. It was my brown leather notebook with the list of battles that George Washington took part in and a few other notes. He flipped through a few pages and glanced at what I had written. It was not much, but it was enough that I knew it would cause trouble for me. "I knew you were lying to me. I will find out the truth about you." With a strong and painful thwack, he hit me across the face with the book. My legs buckled. Bouchard held my sinking body up by my arm with a tight grip that would leave more bruises.

"You can't have that." I choked the words out through the tears and gasps for breath that ached at every inhale. "It is mine."

Jumonville flipped his hand in a gesture Bouchard understood as to remove me. Outside, he pulled me by my arm and forced me to walk. I could barely catch my breath, and every bone and muscle in my body ached. I turned at the end of the row of tents to head back to my tent. Bouchard pulled me in the opposite direction.

"My tent is over there," my voice squeaked out. He remained silent and dragged me to the side of the encampment to a grove of trees. Nearby, a group of soldiers sat around a campfire enjoying their dinner and each other's company. Some had mats rolled out, ready to settle in for the evening. They fixated their eyes on the scene unfolding before them. We limped away from the tent. Bouchard led me over to a tree and yelled back to the group, "Corde!"

He shoved me against the tree and held me in place with

a tight grip at my throat. I watched through swollen eyes and tears as one man ran off and swiftly returned with a length of rope. I was not sure if they were going to tie me or hang me up. *This can't be real! Wake up, Murray!* The pain that throbbed throughout my body told me I was awake, and it was real.

CHAPTER TWELVE

Every muscle and bone in my body ached. My nose was swollen two sizes too big. Whichever passageway that was not swollen shut was clogged with congealed blood. I tried opening my eyes. My left eyelid and cheek were enlarged to where I couldn't open my left eye. It hurt too much to force it open. It didn't feel as though Jumonville had broken the skin when he had hit me with the leather-bound book, but the thwack across my face was going to take some time to heal.

My shoulders ached. My wrist burned from Bouchard's ropes that bound me to the tree. He tied me in a position that caused my shoulders to be awkwardly twisted behind me and around the tree, making it impossible to find any comfort. I couldn't shift my position throughout the night, where my bottom had been spared the torture from Jumonville and Bouchard. It didn't survive the torture of the cold ground all night. I shifted my weight to check what else they injured and if I had any broken ribs. Bruised not broken. My tongue was swollen. I wasn't sure if I could speak or eat.

If they are going to give me breakfast. *What the hell was all the madness from last night about?*

The early morning fog gave me an eerie feeling as I looked towards the camp. The dawn was upon me to celebrate a new day. Or to remind me I lived through the night and would have the pleasure of having the bajeesus kicked out of me. I hoped the darkness would keep me out of sight of my captors. Out of sight, out of mind. The fog that lingered across the field glowed a hue of faded blue. It was peaceful and wouldn't last for long. I wanted to scream out for help. I hoped there would be someone that would be sympathetic to my pleas. There was always the hope that a search team was out looking for me and all I had to do was wait for them to arrive and let them know I was there, in the fog, tied to a tree, battered and ready to go home. If I screamed out, they wouldn't hesitate to kill me. I needed to remain quiet. It was not a game, and clearly, I was not dreaming.

I thought back to when Jumonville had taken my notebook with my chicken scratched notes and dates of George Washington's battles at the beginning of the French and Indian War. Why would anyone want my notes and information? I was 100 percent sure the info was available through Google. I talked through what I knew and tried to make sense of it. "Okay, Murray. Think. What are the details? You went to Fort Ashby. There was a penny. No, not a penny. A coin from 1754. Did it have George II on it? Yes. Things got blurry. I smelled cherry wood. Kyle? Was he there? Maybe. He wasn't in the building. A bright light. Then, I wake up in a field. Coin no longer in my hand." I questioned my reality. Was I in the past? There must be another solution. That didn't make any logical sense. I questioned my bright idea of talking out loud to myself. That could be a dangerous habit.

Orders were barked out, and men roused. Morning meal had come early, and tents torn down and packed up. There were no questions and beatings for me that morning.

Bouchard stood outside his tent with his hands on his hips as he surveyed the commotion in front of him. One of the younger soldiers ran over to Bouchard and they spoke for a few moments while I strained to hear what they said. It didn't matter. It was all in French. The young soldier untied me from the tree. "Thank you," I mumbled through swollen lips. Last night's beating included a hit to my mouth that I didn't remember. Maybe it was when I was hit with the notebook? It was a painful blur. I ran my tongue across my lips, bottom lip swollen and split. I thought I would lose a tooth. Not that I needed teeth with the broth and mushy, overcooked peas the soldier brought me for breakfast. He stood nearby while I sipped my breakfast.

He took my bowl from me before I could finish. "Please, let me go. If I get caught, I won't tell them it was you that set me free."

I was not sure how much energy I would have to run. The time travel–*do I dare to call it that?*–lack of a decent meal, and the abuse over the past day left me weak. I was ready to pool all the energy I could muster and run as far away from there as my wobbly legs would take me, if he would just set me free. The young soldier looked at me and cocked his head to the side. He didn't understand what I said. I took his offered hand, thankful for the first bit of decency I had received since they had held me captive. I stood up, ready to run; however, he didn't let go of my hand. I tugged. He refused to release it. I tugged again. He gripped my wrist. He motioned to me to give him my other hand, tossed the bowl to the side, and tied my hands together with the rope. A tear slipped down my cheek. My hopes of escape had disappeared within seconds. If anyone looked for me, they would never find me now.

I couldn't believe that no one noticed my car at the old fort sitting there since yesterday and that I hadn't checked into my hotel. Hannah and Beth knew where I was supposed to be and would have expected a phone call. Yet, there was no sign of anyone trying to find me. There were no search parties or helicopters overhead. There was no one who called out my name. No sounds of cars in the distance. No one was looking for me. They abandoned me. Could this really be 1754? It didn't seem logical. I shook off the absurd thought. Survival. That's what I needed to think about. I needed to survive.

As they led me over to the group, the soldiers finished packing up camp and prepared to leave. They tied the end of my rope around the soldier's waist. We would walk as a unit to wherever Jumonville and Bouchard led us. He was stuck with me, and I was stuck with him.

I hoped my body and my boots could handle the walk. My boots were comfortable but intended more for fashion rather than going on a hike, and I couldn't afford to get blisters in addition to their interrogation technique. I looked down at my blood-stained shirt. If someone was to come upon us, they couldn't ignore my swollen face and bloody shirt. They would know I was in distress. My blazer had blood on it, but the navy color hid the stains. I was thankful for my nearly empty satchel. As it continued to hang across my body, I wouldn't have to worry about the weight of my notebook. I needed to figure out how to hide or dispose of my phone and keys. If my notebook, and not providing more information to Jumonville, got me beaten and tied to a tree. What would happen if they found my phone?

With the men together, I could get a better look at the party and assess my situation through my swollen eyes. Thirty-five men. Rifles. Swords. Packs filled with who-knows-what. And me. I trailed at the end, tied to my guard. If someone would have asked me a day ago, I would say with confidence that the rifles and swords were props. I no longer believed that to be true.

CHAPTER THIRTEEN

The crack of a rifle echoed in the distance and sent a flock of birds squawking into flight. My silent pleas were heard, and I didn't end up with a splat of bird poop on me. I can't say the same for Bouchard. A snort of laughter through my swollen nose caused a bit of pain, but to see his anger as he wiped the plop off his shoulder made it worth it. My sentry dragged me off the path and into the tree line. The men held their weapons at the ready. Having been pushed to the ground on my stomach, I reached into my satchel. The men continued to scan the area. They were intent on listening for more weapons fire. My tied hands found my phone, and I pulled it out and shoved it under a root I had fallen on. Next, I tried for my keys. Without warning, they jerked me up and pulled me along. Keys would have to wait for another time. They must've believed it was safe to continue. After the past night of torture and humiliation, I was shocked they hadn't already shot me and left me for dead. It would have been easier for them to leave me behind.

I didn't recognize most of the men, not that I could see much out of one eye. My left eye was still swollen shut. They stayed away from me while they tied me to the tree, and all refused to speak to me. Not that I could understand French, but they seemed to avoid me at all costs. All I could see were their backs and the empty road in front and behind us. Escape from the group proved to be more difficult than I had expected, but I figured there was plenty of time to plot this out. If they rescued me, I couldn't identify these men. I laughed at the thought of giving a witness statement. "Yes, officer. The men that kidnapped me were faceless French soldiers from seventeen fifty-four. Maybe I can recognize the back of their heads." That wouldn't go over well.

The hours passed by, and we continued to walk north. Mile after mile, we moved through a narrow footpath through the wooded countryside. With every sound of a potential passerby, they pulled me into the tree line with a dirty hand clamped over my mouth. The constant movement off the path provided ample opportunity for me to hide my keys under some debris. I might not have a phone to make a call and will have to pay to replace keys, but at least I won't get beaten for contraband. It was a slow ten miles, but I was certain that was the most we could've gone. By the time we stopped for the day, I couldn't have walked much further. I ran half marathons in the past, but I trained for the runs, wore proper shoes, and was not tied to someone. I felt all ten miles of the walk through my forty-year-old body. Bouchard's limp grew heavier by the end of the day, as did mine. We stopped in a wooded area close to the road. I wondered if we would have company along the way. Every morning was a disappointment of no nighttime rescue.

The next few days were repeats of the day before. Going to the bathroom behind a bush or tree was my time for comfort and privacy. Every evening was the same routine. Jumonville would have Bouchard bring me to his tent for questioning. I would give an answer. I would refuse to answer. It didn't matter if I answered or not; Bouchard would beat me. Jumonville would pretend he didn't see or hear the beatings. His presumed innocence infuriated me. He could stop it, yet he didn't. In fact, if anything, I would say that he encouraged it. They would bring me back to a tree, provided with a few bits of whatever food was leftover, and I would spend the night in the cold. The next morning, we continue our trek north.

The night brought on another summons to Jumonville's tent. I didn't have the energy for another beating; however, food always came after the ritual torture, and I was hungry. A black eye or more bruised ribs would be worth it to get sustenance. In typical nighttime fashion, they escorted me to the tent. My entire body ached as I hobbled into the room. They left me alone with Jumonville. Focusing on the prize of food helped me walk into the tent and take the kneeling position they had forced me into each night. Jumonville liked me in the submissive position. I liked not having to fall too far when Bouchard hit me with enough force to knock me over. That night, I was alone with Jumonville.

Stretched over the hard week, my skinny jeans had gone from hugging my curves, to me being thankful I had put on a belt before I left my house. The belt buckle was in the last hole. I lost weight as quick as I lost my last bit of sanity. That was all I could think about. The weight loss was my distraction.

"Tell me, woman, why did you cross out the entry of Fort Duquesne on seventeen April? They have summoned us to march on a British fort. I need to know if we need to focus our efforts elsewhere."

My tired brain searched to place the name and date. I was running on empty. I closed my eyes to focus on the question and what I remembered of the fort. Under stress and exhaustion, my brain didn't work well. "The British are building a fort in Pittsburgh at the fork of the Allegheny and Monongahela Rivers. That is where I was headed before all of this happened."

"You said you were going to Fort Duquesne." He flipped through a few pages in the notebook. He grabbed my chin and forced me to look up at his face. "Are you lying to me again?"

"No! That fort will be Fort Duquesne," I said as I tried to gulp back the tears.

"How do you know this?"

"What do you mean 'how do I know this'?" I was half-tempted to imitate his accent and thought better of that and just kept to a snarky response. "I read about it. The novel I am writing is about George Washington. I wanted to make sure I knew where he had his battles so I could go visit the forts and locations. You know, I wanted to get a feel for what the man endured and where it happened." My body shook from frustration, hunger, and exhaustion. "That is what you are reading in my book. Nothing more. I don't know of any secrets; you can Google it or find it in history books. I can recommend a few to you, if you'd like."

Jumonville stood up and walked over to the opening of the tent and whispered to the guard. I wondered what type of torture device Bouchard was going to bring with him for this evening's entertainment. The tent was silent while we waited, his eyes heavy on me. I snorted up the snot that dripped from my nose. A wipe on my shoulder cleaned up the rest. Jumonville flipped through the worn pages of the notebook. I continued to kneel in the middle of the tent.

When a soldier arrived, thankfully not Bouchard, he grabbed me by the arm and led me out. He pulled me until we got to a tent in the middle of the camp and thrust me inside. It was much like the first one that they gave me when I first joined the group, sparse and small. I didn't care; the blanket would keep me warm for the first time in a week. Food arrived. Thank goodness! It was a serving befit a human being, and not the table scraps for a dog they had given me for the past week. I was not sure what I had done differently this time than any of the other evenings, but I was going to relish in the comfort of not being tied to a tree. I was going to sleep well.

CHAPTER FOURTEEN

"Get up," Bouchard barked at me as he gave a kick to my ribs. I gasped, grabbed my side, and rolled away. I thought we had moved beyond the kicks. My sleep hadn't been this good in a week. Sleep had been restless; being tied to a tree would do that to a person. I almost forgot that I was being held captive, but my aching body and a kick to the ribs ensured they reminded me they had turned my life upside down. By then, I figured out their routine and was ready to go after my morning rations, albeit small rations. I ran the edge of my dirty shirt over my teeth and pried my fingers through my tangled hair. It was the closest I could muster as a morning hygiene routine. When we trailed along the stream, they allowed me to splash cold water and clean up. That morning, they didn't afford me that luxury.

The unit packed up, and we headed out, with me in tow at the back of the group. I didn't understand what caused the big change in my treatment last night, but I couldn't understand most of what happened to me. Daily, a few scouts left earlier than the group, returning by the end of the day. They would often come back with what looked like bloodstains on their clothes. When they would return with a cow, pig, or chickens, the entire camp feasted, and they would give me something solid to eat.

I remained observant, that's all I could do. Other than being interrogated by Jumonville or the abuse from Bouchard, I remained untouched and ignored. For that, I was grateful. I realized the situation could've been worse for me. They barely tolerated my presence. At least there was not a vicious hate for me or the use of their sexual gratification. They always posted a guard nearby to prevent my escape. Not that I could muster enough energy or know which way to go. They wouldn't speak to me except for the occasional grunt of something in French, which I could only pick up a word here and there and was meaningless to me. What good was "vous" when I didn't understand the five hundred words before or after it? I was certain the need to watch over me didn't thrill any of them, and they would rather be with the rest of the soldiers.

I walked along with the soldiers; it was uneventful, except for the occasional stream crossing. We had crossed the Potomac, at least I believed it to be, days ago and through mountainous terrain. Those crossings had slowed our progress and left me exhausted. That day was like most days; however, there was an uneasiness amongst the men. I could see Bouchard speak to Jumonville and glanced back at me. Bouchard limped over to me. "You will stay hidden in the woods with LaRue. You will not make a sound or try to run. If you do either, it will bring me pleasure to slice your throat. Comprends?"

THE TIME WRITER AND THE NOTEBOOK

"Stay over there and be silent, or you will enjoy killing me. I understand." My voice was direct. If they wanted me dead, they would have killed me days ago. I knew this was a scare tactic. "Where are we?"

I hoped he would share more information, to give me something to go on. Bouchard remained silent and picked up his pace to get to the head of the detachment. I knew he wouldn't answer me—he never did—but I thought it couldn't hurt to try to get some answers.

The rumble of voices, the neigh of horses, and the crackle of wheels as they rolled over rocks and dirt sounded in the not-too-far distance. My mind was refreshed by getting rest by sleeping on the ground and not freezing while being tied to a tree. My body still ached from the abuse, but at least I didn't have the exhaustion of lack of sleep while tied to a tree. If I could get someone's attention, that would be my opportunity to be rescued. I took a deep breath and relaxed. The end of my torture would be soon. I could sense it. It was what kept me going.

The roar of the men grew louder. I peeked from behind a tree to see a congregation of hundreds of men dressed in uniforms, horses, and other equipment. This must be the end of the reenactment, and it would be over soon. I still wasn't convinced that I had, somehow, wound up in the year 1754–that would be illogical.

The groups made camp, and they hid me in my usual tent. Later in the night–later than I had found to be typical–they summoned me to Jumonville's tent. "We are going to take the British fort tomorrow. Why is this date not in your book?" He held the book in my face, as if I didn't know which book.

"I don't even know the date." I shook my head in confusion. "Where are we? Which fort are you talking about?"

"Today is the seventeenth of April. We are taking the new fort on the Ohio being built by the British."

"New fort on the Ohio? April seventeenth. Are we still acting as though it's seventeen fifty-four?" For the love of all that is good. "Fort Prince George? It will end up becoming Fort Duquesne." I searched through my mental notes, since he kept my notebook at a distance from me. My book surrounded the battles that involved George Washington, but I had done preliminary research involving the forts and locations. I didn't include those in my notebook and couldn't remember all the details. "I believe I already told you about it."

"Yes, and I do not understand why you continue to act confused. Perhaps Bouchard has hit you too hard in the head." He patted me on the head as if I was a child. "It is seventeen hundred fifty-four, and it is you that doesn't seem to understand the situation."

"Right. Well. Then, there's your problem. George Washington is not here. I told you I was writing a story about him, so if he wasn't in the battle, then the battle is not in my notebook." It exhausted me to repeat what I felt was the same information, night after night. This time, the line of questioning was more intense. I could tell there was a sense of urgency. "Why are you so obsessed with my notebook and George Washington? You already know what is going to happen—French and Indian War, the War of Independence, first President—none of this is new information. You are acting obtuse with this charade."

"This is no charade," Jumonville struggled to maintain his voice in a low tone. His face flushed, and the nostrils of his long-pointed nose flared with every exasperated breath. He clenched his fists. He wanted to scream at me and hit something. I hoped I was not the something he wanted to hit. My body felt as though it was in a constant state of being bloodied and bruised. I needed to escape tonight. I knew I needed to be sent back to the tent and not tied to another tree if I was to sneak away from my captors.

"Of course, my sincerest apologies," I said. I was desperate to diffuse the situation and to get out without being hit. "You know war is coming, and I am quite certain that I am not a part of it. I am assuming you are going into battle soon, since we have joined a larger group." I looked over my shoulder, as if I could see the commotion outside of the tent. He knew I wasn't a fool. "What is the plan? Just so I know what I should do during that time."

"Tomorrow, we will take the new fort that is being built. There is a small British force. Our mission will be complete before the day is through. You will stay in your tent, out of the way. There are more dates and locations in this book." He pounded his thick finger on the cover. "I will need to know more about them."

"Of course, until tomorrow." I held my breath, turned on my heel, and headed out of the tent. I faked my confidence, and he gave his villain monologue. Why do they always tell their prisoner the details of the attack? My ever-present escort waited for me. I let out the breath I held and inhaled a shaky breath. I finally felt as though I could maintain a sense of control. As I walked back to my tent, my head spun with information and confusion. I thought back to our conversation. He said something about a glen of Jumonville. There was a sound of concern in his voice. Urgency. I shook the thought out of my head again. *It can't be possible. Or is it?* He was determined that it was the year 1754 and he didn't know dates of the battles. *Time travel? Is it true? Was I really in 1754?*

CHAPTER FIFTEEN

Back in my tent, I sat on my bedroll, and waited for the meal that had never arrived. The time to sneak away was tonight. The dark night sky would cover my escape before the soldiers awoke in the morning. I led them to believe I was compliant most of the time that I was with them, but I was biding my time for the opportunity to escape. I hadn't known exactly where we were before. The terrain was unfamiliar. But I knew for the first time I knew where to go. I visited Pittsburgh, Pennsylvania once before and had an idea where on the fork of the rivers the fort sat. If the men were to attack it in the morning, we had to be nearby the fort. My plan was to sneak out of the tent, head there, and get the help that I desperately needed. I needed to get to the British to save them from trying to be heroes and defend the fort against the amassed French army. Most of all, I needed to save myself.

I grabbed my satchel and listened for movement outside of the tent. My heart raced. If they didn't hear my movement, surely, they heard my heart pound. There would be a guard at the front, so I couldn't escape that way. I knew there should be no one on the backside of the tent. My tent was at the furthest edge of the encampment, instead of the usual middle, surrounded by everyone. They had put me as far away from the additional men they joined in order to keep my presence unknown. If they hadn't hidden me away, my plan wouldn't have worked. Fortunately for me, the tent was near a heavily wooded area, which would give me the opportunity to slip out unseen. If I could get out unheard by the guard. *Quiet, heart.*

    I laid on my stomach and lifted the edge of the tent and pried out a couple of stakes from the ground. My plan to belly crawl to freedom sounded so much easier in my head. As I pulled myself out of the tent, my satchel caught on the edge. Lose the satchel or bring down the tent? I wasn't willing to take either option. I slowed down, untangled the satchel, and wiggled my way out of the tent.

    The dark night would hide me, but it would add a minor complication to my escape plan. If I could see no one, surely, they couldn't see me. I slid underneath the edge and moved towards the trees. Leaves crunched under my feet. If I ran, it would be loud and draw more attention to the noise. I took tender steps and tried to minimize the loudness of the crackle and crunch of the dried leaves. At first, the moon didn't provide as much light as I would have liked to see where I was going, but I knew the darkness would help keep me hidden from the soldiers. My eyes adjusted to the dark as I made my way away from the camp north through the woods and followed the river towards the fort.

The woods had thinned along the river. The moon came out from hiding behind clouds, making my trek north slightly easier. I stopped by the river. Moonlight reflected off the river. "This isn't right. Where are all the buildings?" I asked the man in the moon, as if I expected him to answer. The concrete? The asphalt? The cars? The people? "This isn't Pittsburgh." My chest heaved, and my breath shortened. I panicked. "This doesn't make sense." I paced back and forth as I twisted the wedding ring around my finger and searched for a plausible answer. I didn't want to ask the question that lingered in the back of my mind. The question I had tried to keep hidden. *Did that incident at Fort Ashby pull me through some sort of time portal? Was it possible?*

As I regained my head and continued to pace, I noticed a light in the far distance. I ran towards the light, towards what must be the fort. If this was 1754, then I really needed to warn the soldiers of the French coming to claim the outpost. I remembered it was a trading post before the Virginians built it up as a fort. I didn't know how much of the fort would've been built when the French took it, but I knew something should be at that location. Governor Dinwiddie requested the fort, but I couldn't remember who was supposed to build it or the exact dates, only that the French would come and take it by force tomorrow. If I could save the lives of the colonists, then I had to try.

The walls of the fort were still being constructed, and I followed my way around to find the entrance. The lack of guards and gate surprised me, but figured they probably had no expectations that a large French force was making their way to their location. Fools. A soldier leaned against the entrance and didn't move as I approached. As I got closer, I could see that he had fallen asleep while on guard. I shook my head. *If this is what I'm working with, how did the British win?*

"Pardon me," I said as I cleared my throat. No movement from the sentry. "Hello." I said louder.

The man startled and pointed his rifle at me. "Who are you? What are you doing here?" His voice cracked. Although it was too dark to get a proper look at him, he sounded young. I could tell he was younger than my eighteen-year-old daughter, Hannah.

"My name is Amelia Murray. I escaped from a French detachment. I need to speak to whoever is in charge here." The young man hesitated. He stood there and continued to look at me with no movement. "Now," I commanded, folding my arms across my chest.

He cracked out, "Stay here." Turned heel and went inside.

The young soldier returned and asked me to follow him inside the area that would eventually become the fort. We approached the man that I assumed was in charge. He appeared to be in his mid-thirties. "Ensign Edward Ward, at your service," he said, with a slight look of surprise. After a brief pause, I assume he was sizing me up. He continued, "We'll go inside, warm you up, and talk. Please, follow me."

"Amelia Murray. Thank you, Ensign." Our introduction was brief and to the point. I appreciated the brevity and hospitality.

Ward led me to a small outpost building that was used as a headquarters. The log cabin couldn't have been more than fifteen-foot squared. I was thankful for the small fire warming up the room. It had been a chilly night and the breeze coming off the river had only made the cold sink deep into my bones. He held out a chair. I hesitated. The last time a soldier held a chair–I suppose it was a stump–for me, was Jumonville, and he had slammed me into my dinner, knocked the air out of me, and threatened to kill me. If I didn't have trust issues before, I had trust issues then. I found it difficult to trust anyone, even my own eyes. It felt as though my loved ones abandoned me, and the people I thought would rescue me tortured me. I could only hope that I wouldn't add Ward to my growing list of reasons to fear the world around me.

"I will stand for now, if you don't mind." Ensign Ward looked at me, tilted his head with confusion, and walked around to the other side of the table and sat down. The fire lit up the plain room and as he sat across from me, I could get a better look at him. He hadn't fully dressed from being woken up with the top of his shirt missing a cravat and his waist coat haphazardly worn. His disheveled brown hair fell just below his shoulders. I sat there, looked at him, and tried to size him up. I needed to know if I could trust him.

"Private MacDonald says you have information for me." He held out his hand in a gesture for me to continue the conversation. "Please." I was not sure if he was going to believe me or not, but I had to place my safety in the hands of this man. I had no choice.

"Around a week ago, Ensign Joseph Coulon de Villiers, Sieur de Jumonville, kidnapped me, while I was in West Virginia, in, um, western Virginia. They have held me captive and have beaten me daily." I touched my face and the lip that struggled to heal. The tender lip reminded me I must look like Frankenstein's monster. *Oh, that's why he looked at me strange. I must look horrible.* "They brought me with the detachment of thirty-five soldiers, which has now been grouped with many more French soldiers. It could be five hundred, six hundred, or more. I'm not sure. You're all I have for safety. Believe me when I tell you they are going to attack this fort tomorrow."

"Lieutenant Colonel Washington and more of his troops are to arrive here to help us defend the fort while we finish building it."

Washington headed towards the fort was news to me. "I understand that may be true," I said, knowing no one would get there before the morning. I moved to sit down in the chair, completely exhausted from the recent events. There was something about this man that allowed me to put my guard down. I collapsed in the chair. He watched me with concern, not with the vitriol that I had seen with my French captors. "However, Lieutenant Colonel Washington, nor any of his troops, are going to get here by tomorrow. The French forces will be here, and neither you nor I can stop them. You and your men are outnumbered and outgunned. If you want to live to fight another day, you need to give up the fort."

"This fort cannot fall into the hands of the French. We must defend it." Ward slammed his fist on the desk. He sounded confused at the turn of events. I should know. I was the queen of being confused, especially after the past week. "Captain Spencer was supposed to arrive and take command while Captain Trent and Lieutenant Fraser were away. We were to wait until Lieutenant Colonel Washington arrived."

"This fort will fall into the hands of the French tomorrow. If you don't believe me, send a scout south of here along the river to confirm that there are at least five hundred soldiers camped and getting ready for an attack. You cannot defend this fort against that many men. You need to leave here by tomorrow. Please, you must believe me." I stretched my hands out in front of me in a plea of asking for him to trust me.

He sat back, closed his eyes, and contemplated his choices. He opened his eyes, leaned forward and stared into my eyes as if he searched for the answer and truth in them. It should have made me uncomfortable, but there was comfort in knowing that he looked to me for the answer. He was nothing like Jumonville, and I knew deep down that it was the correct choice that I had escaped to the fort.

Ward slammed both of his palms on the table. "When do they plan on attacking?"

"I don't know." My voice squeaked. The bangs on the table made me uncomfortable and jumpy. "They wouldn't have told me." I gulped down hard.

He stood up with a jerk, ready to pounce. "Why should I trust you? For all I know, you could be a French spy, sent here to infiltrate."

"I am not a spy." I clenched my fists. "You have no reason to trust me," I said through gritted teeth. I could feel the tears pricking in my eyes. "Send a scout and keep me within your sight. You'll see that I am not lying. I need you to believe me." I kept telling him he needed to believe me, hoping he would get it through his thick skull.

"I will send a scout and you will stay in here," Ward said. He pointed a sharp finger in my direction. "Stay here." He said over his shoulder as he shot out of his chair. The walls shook as he slammed the door shut.

I looked around the sparse room. There was a table, two chairs, and a small rope bed. In front of the fireplace, to my right, was a large, cushioned chair. I assumed they had left the chair when it was a trading post. I couldn't imagine anyone dragging it out here for luxury to build a military fort. But what did I know? The cot looked inviting and had to be more comfortable than anything that I been sleeping on since I arrived in the year 1754.

It still didn't seem probable to me. I had trouble wrapping my head around the possibility that was real and was not a dream. Perhaps I hallucinated all of it or dreamt while in a coma. That was the only logical explanation. The bang of the door being flung open interrupted my thoughts of the wild possibility of being thrust back in time. I shot straight up, ready to run.

"The men are preparing the camp for our departure. I've sent a scout to confirm what you have claimed about the French. I pray you are wrong."

"I'm not." I shook my head and plopped back down. A sigh of relief washed over me. We were finally getting somewhere instead of idly sitting by.

"You'll stay in here while we prepare." Ward ran his fingers through his hair, attempting to comb it and tie it back. He straightened up his clothes and ran outside to help the camp get ready.

I sat up to survey the room and wondered if I should lie down or if I should help pack up his room. There was not much to pack up. A couple of books and a stack of papers on his desk. I wandered over to the desk to snoop at the contents. The papers were maps and building plans, nothing of use to me. Since my last meal was in the morning, and without the opportunity to have dinner after my interrogation, I searched for food. I was used to the lack of food by then, but I had hoped for a tiny bite. There really was no place to hide any food, which made my search quick and unfruitful. I crawled on the bed and ignored the protests from an empty stomach and fell asleep.

CHAPTER SIXTEEN

"Wake up, mistress." A familiar young man's voice filled my ears as I slowly opened my eyes. Private MacDonald stood over me. In the light, he looked younger than he had sounded the night before. He was lean and looked to be around fifteen. His smooth face showed no signs of needing to shave soon. His brown hair was pulled back out of his face and tied at the nape of his neck with a thin leather strip. Stray hairs escaped. He looked frazzled. So incredibly young to be a soldier. "Ensign Ward sent me in here to wake you and to tell you to get ready to leave."

I looked around the room and noticed the papers and books were missing, along with every other packable item. Somehow, I slept through the commotion. I stood up and straightened up my clothes. While I pulled my hair out of the chignon and attempted to smooth down the flyaway hairs, Private MacDonald rolled up the bedding. No sooner had I twisted my hair back up, MacDonald shoved the bedding into my arms. "You are to go to the stable and await Ensign Ward. Please, follow me."

The early morning sun spilled over the landscape and into my groggy eyes. I squinted as I left the building and held the bed roll tighter in my arms. I yawned while I stumbled behind MacDonald as he led me across the fort and to a small stable. He took the bedroll from me and tied it to the back of a saddled horse. "Remain here." Of course, I would remain there. *Where was I going to go?*

I sat down on an overturned bucket near the stable, rested my chin in my hands, and closed my eyes. I would need to find somewhere to relieve myself. Although I slept well enough in a bed instead of the ground, I felt lethargic from the lack of food. I had just closed my eyes when I was woken up by Ensign Ward. "You will go with Private MacDonald. You need to leave now before the French arrive. I'll surrender the fort over to them and we'll meet you along the way to Wills Creek."

He brought the horse out from the stall and into the courtyard. He checked the side bags and latched on a rifle. "Mistress Murray, please, we must leave now," Private MacDonald said. He mounted the horse and held out his hand. I walked over and Ward began helping me mount the horse in front of MacDonald.

"You're going to ride behind me?" I was confused. My thoughts were being clouded with exhaustion, hunger, and a full bladder. Surely, the two of us would be too heavy for the horse to travel. I suppose MacDonald couldn't have weighed much, probably less than I weighed.

"Yes, behind you. I need to make sure you do not fall off the horse, and I cannot do that if you are behind me. Now, please, move forward." I complied, and MacDonald started walking us out towards the opening to the fort. Apparently, the gate would have been installed soon if they were not about to be evicted. "I need you to hold on tight; we need to keep you safe from the French."

A sudden burst of energy flowed through my body as my head shot back and forth, looking around the perimeter of the half-built fort. "Jumonville! Where is he? Please, don't let him take me again." I panicked. Jumonville would kill me if he found me. I clamped my hand on Private MacDonald's forearm. That caused him to nearly jump out of the saddle. Poor kid.

"I will keep you safe, but we have got to leave. Apologies, but I need use of my arm." I released his arm and grabbed hold of the saddle in front of me. We rode out of the fort, and MacDonald nudged the horse to run. Shouts near the river and the sound of a rifle being shot pierced through the morning sky. I ducked my head out of instinct, certain that Jumonville or Bouchard must have meant that bullet for me. MacDonald leaned into the horse's stride, pressing his chest against my back, giving me the sensation of being pushed forward. With what little energy I had left, I held on tight to the saddle. Without stirrups, I bounced around with every hoof landing. It wouldn't be a gentle ride and my bladder didn't appreciate the jostle.

"Use your legs," MacDonald shouted next to my ear, as my head bounced up and hit him in the chin.

"For what?" I hadn't been on a horse for years and when I last was on one, it was a gentle trail ride in the Shenandoah, not the ride of my life.

"To hold on to the horse," he grunted. "With your thighs."

I tried to brace myself by squeezing my thighs. I was not sure how effective it was to keep me from bouncing around. At that point, I would have run over cut glass while barefoot, if it meant getting away from Jumonville.

MacDonald slowed the horse down, and I let out a deep breath. "We should be well enough ahead of anyone that could follow us," he said as he sat back in the saddle.

My eyes closed and head lolled as the adrenaline rush subsided. "When do you think the other soldiers and Ensign Ward will catch up?" That was the limit of what I could squeeze out of my thoughts. That and, "I have to pee."

"They will be along after the surrender." His voice trailed off. Something caught his attention.

I looked up and saw a soldier on horseback approaching our location. It was another British soldier. If I were religious, I would have said a prayer in gratitude that it was not Jumonville, but this man could be trouble for me as well.

"Tanaghrisson, the Seneca Half-King, told me that there was trouble at the fort." He looked at the both of us, sizing me up. "Why are you leaving with this woman? Where is the rest of your unit?"

"Private MacDonald, sir. The French arrived. Ensign Ward is surrendering the fort. This is Mistress Murray. I was told to get her to safety and the rest will meet up with us on our way to Wills Creek."

"Is that so?" The man sat tall in his saddle, raised an eyebrow, and looked me over. He sounded arrogant, and it didn't impress me. We wouldn't get along.

"Yes, it is so," I replied in a matter-of-fact kind of way.

"There are at least five hundred French soldiers arriving to take the fort."

"How do you know this?" He lifted his chin in my direction. He wore the uniform of an officer: red coat, white breeches, brass gorget hung around his neck, and tall black boots. His cocked hat–or what I would incorrectly refer to as a tricorne hat–cast a shadow down his face.

Why would I lie about it? I tried to save their asses and grew tired of repeating the same story. "I was kidnapped by a group of them a week ago and could finally escape last night." MacDonald should have told the man what happened and let me keep my mouth shut. The instant I said that I was with the French, I could tell he was ready to send me back to them. "I found my way to the fort and warned Ensign Ward of the impending attack."

"I was on my way to take command while Captain Trent and Lieutenant Fraser were away. Lieutenant Colonel Washington is on his way with a larger command. Mayhap I could..."

I cut him off with a wave of my hand before he could finish saying he would try to stop the surrender. "He won't get here in time. They lost the fort to the French. Ensign Ward and the rest of the troops will be on their way, and Washington or someone else can take it back later. Live to fight another day, and all that." I knew there was nothing that could be done. The addition of one more man against five hundred would still end in failure. I needed to make him aware of it and have him stop trying to play the arrogant hero.

The soldier sat quiet for a moment, inhaled and exhaled deep enough I could see his chest rise and fall. He looked at me sternly. "Who are you, and why do you have this information?"

"My name is Amelia Murray. Ensign Joseph Coulon de Villiers, Sieur de Jumonville," I sighed. I was really tiring of saying his name, "and his team took me hostage. I escaped last night."

"I haven't heard of him."

"You wouldn't have. He isn't notable." I suppose he was notable enough to have a glen named after him. It was on my list of places to visit. I couldn't remember all the details from my research, but I relayed what I could to the soldier. "And who are you?"

"Captain Henry Spencer, at your service, Mistress Murray," he said as he gave a slight bow with his head. "You mentioned something about an escape?"

"Yeah. Escape. I know this is going to sound like I'm crazy. I'm not. Really. But I got lost and stumbled across an encampment and it was Jumonville, Bouchard, and about thirty other French soldiers. They held me hostage and beat the crap out of me for about a week. We marched north and joined at least five hundred other soldiers. I really couldn't tell how many there were at the meeting point. It was dark when I escaped. I knew someone would be at the fort that was being built, so I went to warn them about the attack," I belted out in one breath. He raised an eyebrow in response to my story. *How do people raise one eyebrow?* He was going to believe me or not. I was too tired, too hungry, and too sore to care anymore. Private MacDonald remained quiet on the saddle behind me. I had hoped that he would speak up and offer some validation to my story, but he was young, inexperienced, and—apparently at this point—mute.

"Listen, if Bouchard or Jumonville get their hands on me, they *will* kill me."

"Right then. Tanaghrisson warned me about the French and told me not to go to the fort. I thought I could get there before the French. I should have listened to him." Captain Spencer looked me over. I'm not sure why he believed what I told him. "Private MacDonald, I'll travel with the two of you to meet up with your unit and head to the rendezvous at Wills Creek."

They kept the conversation to a minimum as we rode further away from the fort. Spencer and MacDonald chatted about the progress of the build. The fort was far from finished. Weather delays and a lack of support stalled progress. They would have installed a gate in the upcoming days, if they had built it. Captain Spencer grunted in disapproval.

We headed towards wherever this meeting point was located. Wills Creek was not on my list of places to visit. We had traveled for a good part of the day, stopping only for bathroom breaks—which I desperately needed—and a drink of water from the occasional stream that we crossed. It surprised me I hadn't got dysentery with the number of streams I drank out of while on the road. One thing that I don't like about camping is the lack of a proper toilet. That past week or so took "roughing it" to a whole new level.

"I hate to bother you," I interrupted the conversation about whether the spring rains have been too heavy for the young seedlings that had recently been planted. Thinking about the crops made me think of food even more. I don't know how people do those fasting diets. "Will we be able to get something to eat soon? I think I ate yesterday morning."

My stomach made an audible protest and drew the attention of the men. We left in such a rush from the fort that there was no time to pack anything to eat. Earlier in the day, Captain Spencer mentioned he had no more rations, as he had expected to have been able to eat at the fort when he would have arrived. Neither man had food for our journey. I would have to ignore the hunger for a while longer.

The slow rock of the horse reminded me of when my late husband Todd would take me on a road trip, and the vibration of the car allowed me to relax my mind and easily fall asleep. My blinks got longer. The push of adrenaline from the morning's escape, minimal rations of food for the past week, constant abuse to my body from Bouchard, and the lack of sleep took its toll on me. A long blink turned into my head bobbing down. I felt my body shutting down. I pressed my back into Private MacDonald's chest for support.

"When we stop, we can," Captain Spencer spoke before I couldn't focus on what he said, and everything went black.

CHAPTER SEVENTEEN

"Mistress Murray," a woman's voice beckoned me to awaken. Her voice was soft and familiar, although I couldn't give a name to the voice. A gentle hand touched my arm. I struggled to open my eyes. My eyelids felt as though they placed steel weights over them.

"Hm... where am I?" I tried to sit up in the bed but lacked the strength and collapsed back down on the soft pillow. My unfocused eyes shifted around the unfamiliar room. I rubbed my eyes to beg them to focus. The room was about the size of my room at home, with a small dressing table and a smaller side table next to the four-poster bed with a canopy. There were a couple of paintings that hung on the white painted walls, portraits of a man and woman. Nothing too spectacular. There were two windows with the curtains pulled open to let in the light. The curtains, canopy, and bedspread matched in a simple indigo cotton. I didn't recognize the woman that stood next to my bed. She wore a simple, long brown dress, and looked as though she had come from a play or a reenactment. It was not clothing from the 21st century, which meant I was still in 1754. *This was not a dream.* Her light brown skin and the realization that I was in 1754 told me she was an enslaved woman. I had hoped that I would have gone through my time in Colonial America without crossing the path of slavery. I was not sure how I would react. Do I help her escape to somewhere safe? Stand on a soapbox and preach about people being equals no matter the color of their skin? Or the atrocities of treating people as chattel? Start the Underground Railroad? I ran through different scenarios of how I thought this could play out. Then, I realized I was not up to starting a revolution while lying in bed. I needed help to sit. How could I help an entire population? Surely, I couldn't do it on my own. I would have to figure how to help, even though I wasn't sure where to begin. I took a deep breath of defeat. "How long have I been asleep?"

She bowed her head. "Three days, mistress."

I shook my head in disbelief. "Who are you? Where are Captain Spencer and Private MacDonald?"

"Ruth, mistress. I will get Mistress Lovett." The young woman fled the room and left me alone and confused. By this point, 1754 didn't impress me. I was exhausted, hungry, and confused. If I had been there for three days, I didn't remember any of it. However, Ruth's familiar voice told me she spoke to me those three days.

Ruth opened the door and a stout woman with a heavy step walked in. "I am Mistress Lovett. You are at my house." She sat down on the side of the bed. "Your man brought you here three days ago. You were delirious with fever. He has stayed by your side day and night, fraught with worry about you. You gave him a good scare." Mistress Lovett wiped her hands down the front of her apron.

"I was traveling with two men, Captain Spencer and Private MacDonald. Where are they?"

She patted down her greying brown hair. "I don't know about a Private MacDonald. Captain Spencer brought you here," she said as she grabbed my hand. Her hand was soft, cold, and showed her years, which I guessed to be around sixty. "You gave us all quite a fright."

My eyes shot around the room. There was not much in the room. "Where is Captain Spencer?"

"He has gone into town to pick up a package. He will be back soon. Are you hungry? We couldn't wake you to eat proper. Ruth has been feeding you a stew. I was afraid you would choke on anything solid."

"Oh, goodness, yes," I said with enthusiasm that seemed to startle Mistress Lovett. "Please, I could eat a horse."

"We are not serving horse, but we have some turtle soup," Mistress Lovett said with a laugh and a look of confusion on her face. "I've added a bit of sherry to it. It will make you feel better." She gave a coy smile and patted my hand again.

"Turtle soup sounds wonderful," I said, trying not to seem hesitant to try turtle soup. After the scraps of food over the past week, a proper meal–even if it was turtle soup–sounded like heaven. "Thank you."

Ruth returned, helped me sit in bed, and handed me a warm bowl of soup and a spoon. "You will want to sip it slowly, since you haven't eaten properly in days. You will make yourself sick if you try to eat it too quick."

Mistress Lovett sent Ruth away with a flick of her head. I

felt an interrogation about to happen. Avoiding eye contact to stave off the interrogation, I blew on the soup to cool it down. All I accomplished was to make myself lightheaded.

"Now, now. It will cool, you must be patient. No one is going to take the food from you." She looked me up and down. "You don't look like you could eat much. You are too thin."

I snorted. No one had ever called me thin. In fact, thin wouldn't have been in any of my descriptions, as I was always on the curvy side. I blew on a spoonful of thick soup and took a sip. I took another spoonful filled with chunks of meat. The meat was delicious. It felt good to chew food. The strange combination of flavor tasted like chicken, pork, and clam all rolled into a chewy morsel. The sherry helped bring together the flavors of the turtle meat with the stewed vegetables.

"Is that not the best turtle soup you have ever tasted?" Mistress Lovett's brown eyes beamed with pride. "Ruth does a wonderful job in the kitchen."

"I have never had turtle soup before," I confessed. "But this is delicious."

"Never had turtle soup," Mistress Lovett exclaimed. "Where exactly are you from?"

My face flushed with embarrassment. By her reaction to my comment, I must have committed the biggest mistake of the eighteenth century, or she must think of me as a simpleton. "What I meant to say, my late husband didn't care for the taste of it. I didn't serve it in our house." Not that anyone would serve me in my house. I tried to wrap my head around the thought that Ruth must be enslaved. It was one thing to read about the atrocities of slavery, it was another to sit in the middle of it and witness it firsthand. I hoped that statement recovered my faux pas. I reminded myself to avoid going off on her about Ruth. *Be mindful of your words, Murray.* Things were not the same, and I needed to play the part of a typical 18th century woman. I couldn't let this woman know I was from the future. They would brand me a witch. Although the witch trials were a thing of the past, with the luck I had, I was sure they would bring them back just to persecute me.

"You finish eating." She patted my leg and stood up. "I will send Ruth in later to take your bowl. There is a chamber pot over there, if you need it. Ruth has been helping you with that, but I think you can do it on your own now."

"Thank you." I smiled and continued eating my soup. She left me alone in the room with my soup, chamber pot, and my thoughts. It was a hearty soup and, after the past week of being given very little to eat, my stomach could only handle a small portion at a time.

I needed to relieve myself but hadn't used a chamber pot before. If Ruth helped me use it, I had no recollection. When I was at the encampment, they had taken me to a spot in the woods and I would squat. I convinced myself it was like camping or when had to go while out on a long hike. *No big deal. Right?* A chamber pot was a unique experience altogether. My aim had better be good or else I would be on my hands and knees cleaning up a mess. I tossed the blankets back and padded over to the pot in the corner. "Well, I can't sit on it. How in the... oh! This is going to be interesting." At some point, they removed my clothes and dressed me in a long white gown. I lifted my shift with my right hand, held on to the back of a chair, and squatted down. "Come on,

Murray, it's just like camping." I thought the stream would never stop flowing. That was not nearly as bad as I had expected. Although, I would have preferred to use a toilet.

The knock on the door startled me. I stood up quick and almost tipped the chamber pot over. That would have been an embarrassing mess. Before my brief excursion to the chamber pot, I paid no mind to the fact that the only item of clothing I wore was the linen shift. I looked around and find my clothes. I stumbled over my feet, weak from all that had happened, missed the chair that I reached for, and fell hard on the ground with a loud bang and an equally loud "humph."

The door flew open. I looked up. Captain Spencer ran in, dropped a package at the door. "Mistress Murray, please, let me help you," he said, reaching out to me to help me up. He lifted me into his arms and carried me to the bed.

"Really, I could walk," I said as I wrapped my arms around his neck for support. I felt embarrassed about the whole situation and was sure my cheeks had flushed to crimson. I laughed at the absurdity of the scene. *Could this day get worse?* I decided not to tempt fate, or whatever powers or being brought me here, and not ask that question out loud.

"And I can help you," he said, as he sat me on the bed and covered me up with the quilt I had tossed to the side when I got out of bed. He moved a lock of wavy auburn hair out of my face and tucked it behind her ear. *That was cheeky of him.* I grabbed my hair and pulled it back, out of the way. "I'm sorry, I didn't mean..." He darted towards the door.

"Wait, don't leave." I reached out to Captain Spencer as if to pull him back. Sitting up in the bed, I pulled the quilt up to cover my chest, quite aware that the shift hid little. I was nude under it and felt uncomfortable with the lack of support from a good bra. The pull on forty-year-old breasts was something that I was painfully aware of. "Jumonville and Bouchard are cruel men. They did some, um, terrible things to me. I need to work through it all, I guess. It's going to take me some time." I shook my head and tried to shake off the thoughts of my recent past. "You don't need to leave. I was just a bit startled, is all."

"Of course. Would you like me to come back later? I'm not sure what I was interrupting when you fell, but I will let you get back to it." His blue eyes glanced over to the chamber pot that was near the spot on the floor where he found me. He knew what I had done but was too polite to acknowledge it.

"Interrupting?" My eyes widened, and I could feel my face flush again. "Please, don't worry about that."

"Are you feeling well enough to get out of bed today?"

"I think so." I stopped to think about how I felt, having only recently awoken. "Besides the fact that I'm still weak, I mean."

Captain Spencer continued to stand next to the door. He was tall and filled the space quite nicely with his broad shoulders. "I'll send Ruth in to help you get dressed." He differed from what I remembered when I met him a few days prior. Although he still seemed proper in his presentation, he was more approachable.

"I was wondering where my clothes went. I didn't see them in here." My eyes darted around the room to look for the missing clothes.

"I am not sure what she has done with those clothes that

you were wearing. I brought you this to wear." Captain Spencer held out the package he had retrieved from the floor and placed it on the nearby table. He realized I wouldn't stand up and come retrieve it from him and he would not get near the bed again. "The men's clothes you were wearing were filthy and falling off you. I thought you would be more comfortable in women's clothing."

"Men's clothing? That was my favorite..." I stopped mid-sentence. I thought about the clothes I wore when this had all started. My favorite blue corduroy blazer had seen better days. My skinny jeans had become saggy and loose. I assumed it was from the constant wear of the pants and I hadn't realized the minimum amount of food and the long walks had caused me to drop a significant amount of weight. *Too thin? Ha!* The belt I had worn ended up being moved to the tightest hole. I regretted not using it to wrap around Jumonville or Bouchard's neck. "You bought me clothes? Who undressed me?" I threw my hand over my chest and looked down at my covered body and felt exposed.

"Mistress Lovett and Ruth took care of all of that. She had some of her daughter's old clothes stored away. They were in good condition, but you are much smaller than her. Ruth has been busy taking care of you, so I took them to a local woman to get them altered to fit you. You needed new shoes," he said as he pulled a pair of shoes out of the package. "And I know these are not new. We didn't have time to order you a new pair. We found a pair that should be suitable." He held up pieces of clothes pulled from their wrappings.

"This is a bit surreal for me, you see. I am afraid with everything that has happened and me being so weak, I may need some assistance getting dressed." I hadn't expected help from the captain, but I was not sure how to put together all the different dressing layers that women wore in 1754. There would be multiple layers of clothing. In order to not look like a fool, I decided it was best to ask for help and use my weakness as an excuse.

"Of course, Mistress Murray. I will send Ruth in." He turned around and held the doorknob. His hesitation told me he wanted to say more. He would have questions about Jumonville. Maybe he expected more gratitude for delivering me to safety or providing clothes.

"Thank you," I shouted to him as he left. His ears raised when he smiled and closed the door behind him.

CHAPTER EIGHTEEN

"Well now," said Mistress Lovett as she entered the room, flattened down her apron, and looked ready to set upon a mission. "Captain Spencer says you're ready to get dressed." Ruth followed behind. I smiled at the women. The older woman reminded me a bit of my mother. I smiled at the thought of days back in my time, to the people I knew and loved. Days when I was in my own time and when everything made sense. Perhaps, it didn't all make sense—Todd's death, Beth moving, Hannah starting college, the constant wars of the 21st Century, my editor's changes to my last manuscript—but I understood the world around me. I didn't know what I was doing there or how—or if—to get back home.

"I am, and I could really use your help. I'm afraid my head is in a bit of a fog," I said as I rubbed my forehead. "And cannot remember how all the clothing goes together."

"You were wearing some interesting clothes. I had never seen those types of clothes worn by a woman." She raised an eyebrow and pursed her lips. "Your undergarments were quite puzzling to me. What would you call them?" She flattened down her apron again.

"They are a new fashion. They're called a brassiere and bloomers," I said. I remembered women didn't wear the same type of undergarments in 1754 that we did in my time, if any. I couldn't remember the entire history of when women wore bloomers, panties, underwear, or drawers and went with terms that I could remember. When I got back to my time–or I should say, if I got back to my time–I needed to remember to study historical women's fashion. "They're French? Perhaps?" *Ugh! Why did I say they were French?*

"Hmm. I hope you weren't too attached to your fashionable undergarments. They were not salvageable, just like the rest of your clothing." Mistress Lovett looked down her nose at me and gave a disapproving look. I thought she liked me, but my fashion choice had apparently offended her. "Why you would have dressed like a man with trousers?"

Why did people keep asking me that same question? "A French detachment kidnapped me for a couple of weeks." I said, as if that was some type of excuse for the way I dressed. "What did Captain Spencer tell you about me? I wouldn't want to tell you something he already had mentioned." Truth be told, I didn't want to give away more information than necessary.

"He didn't say. He brought you here when you were burning with fever and unconscious. We could get you to eat and drink a bit, but you were in a fever sleep the entire three days you were here. I was not sure if you were ever going to come out of it." She had a genuine look of concern written across her face. "Last night, your fever broke and then Ruth said you awoke this morn." Mistress Lovett laid out the garments Captain Spencer had brought back from the tailor. "You were speaking about things in your dream that I couldn't understand."

My heart sank into my stomach. Ever since I realized that I had traveled back in time, I had tried to make sure not to give away my secret. I couldn't control what I said when I was delirious with fever. I gulped and forced out, "What exactly was I saying?" Not sure if I wanted to hear the answer.

"You had mentioned Jumonville, Bouchard, Washington, war, and escape. And what was it?" I was not sure if Mistress Lovett was pausing for effect or if she really had to think about what I had said in while I was in my delirium. "You had said that you needed to get home, that you didn't belong here."

"Well, of course." I searched my mind for an excuse of why I would say that and decided that I needed to stick as close to the truth as possible. "Jumonville and Bouchard had kidnapped me. They had asked questions about Washington. I need to get home, so, you know, I didn't belong there or here. Did I mention I was being held hostage?" I panicked. I was terrible at making excuses on the fly. Another good reason to stick as close to the truth as possible.

"Hmm..." I could tell that Mistress Lovett was not buying my excuse, but what choice did I really have? It was all true and it would be easier to keep my story straight if I stuck to the truth. They held me hostage. I didn't belong there, in that time, by about two hundred sixty-five years' worth of not belonging. "That's not how it sounded; however, I don't know how it was supposed to sound. You were saying a lot of words, with only a few making any sense. I know it had been a terrible experience with the French, but you are safe now." She came over and patted my hand. The pat comforted me. "Let's get you dressed, so you can join Captain Spencer downstairs and mayhap go for a walk. I know he has been eager to get to Lieutenant Colonel Washington, and you have held him up."

"I see. I didn't mean to be such a burden." Embarrassed at the disruption I caused, I threw my feet over the edge of the bed, stood, and held the edge for balance. The sooner I could function, the sooner I would be out of Mistress Lovett's graying hair. Ruth came in and hurried to my side. Mistress Lovett handed Ruth a pair of white linen stockings that had embroidered decorations at the ankle, and two pieces of ribbon. I sat down on the chair and looked over the ribbon, unsure what I was supposed to do with them, and placed them on the table while Ruth helped me put on my stockings. With one foot in a stocking, Ruth pulled it up over my knee and did the same with the other. "I am not sure they will stay up my leg."

"That's what the ribbons are for, my dear. Ruth will tie them around your leg here," Mistress Lovett said, while Ruth wrapped the ribbon just below my knee and tied a bow. "I am not sure how you were keeping your other stockings in place; they were missing the ribbon. You really had a difficult time about you." She tsked and shook her head in disappointment–or was it pity?

Stockings on and ribbons used as garters in place, the shoes that Captain Spencer had bought for me were a little tight on my feet, they were on and buckled.

The stays were next. I looked at them with concern. In movies, women would have them laced up with vigor. I thought they were going to be tightened to where I could barely breathe. I hesitated. An underwire bra digging into my armpit or threatening to stab me in the heart sounded more desirable than being bound to the point of not being able to breathe with stays. I no longer had a choice in the matter. Mistress Lovett started lacing and cinching up the back of the indigo stays, detailed with white piping. I took a deep breath, ready for my ribs to crack under the pressure. That was not the case. I found they offered support to my breasts and back. All the while, I could breathe and didn't feel like a stuffed sausage. Thank goodness the cinching down to 6-inch waist was not in fashion yet.

I held onto the back of the chair to regain my stability. After being bedridden for days, the muscles in my legs were weak. Mistress Lovett brought over a linen petticoat and handed it to Ruth. She slipped it over my head and tied the strings around my waist. "What are these pouches for?" I asked as two pouches hung on my sides with the ties secured around my waist.

Lovett cocked her head. "Have you not had pockets before?"

"Pockets? I love pockets. Not enough women's clothing has pockets," I said with excitement. I put my hands in the pockets and felt around inside of them. "Do you realize how much stuff I could fit in these bad boys? I could fit all my snacks. Who needs a purse?"

Mistress Lovett stood still and stared at me. "I think your fever might come back."

I giggled like a child. It was such a simple thing that made me so happy. Two hundred and sixty years of devolution in women's pocket fashion. Large pockets that I could hide my notebook. My notebook. I needed to figure out how I was going to get that back. Later. I would think about it later. "Please, continue. I just love having a fabulous set of pockets."

Ruth placed a white linen kerchief over my shoulders and the ends brought to the front over my breasts.

"The busk goes down the front," Mistress Lovett said to me, when she noticed I stood there holding the piece of wood.

"What is that for?" My eyes lit up with curiosity at the sight of what appeared to be a tubular pillow with strings at both ends. Ruth tied it to my waist with the pillow at my backside. It reminded me of the travel neck pillows, only larger and not worn at my neck.

"It's to give you a bit more shape to your backside. You will move easier with your upcoming travel using it, rather than the hoops."

"Of course, much better than those hoops. I never cared for the hoops. Too cumbersome." I tried to play off the fact that I knew what she was talking about with wearing hoops under skirts or petticoats. I had never worn a hoop in my life and was happy to know that I was not about to start.

"Oh, Captain Spencer picked out a lovely stomacher for you. It goes well with your eyes and the embroidery is lovely. My daughter's stomacher had been destroyed. We were not sure if he was going to find a suitable one for a replacement on such short notice." The embroidered stomacher had a floral motif of large blue flowers and smaller red flowers on a white background. "You are a smaller than my daughter and the clothes needed to be adjusted. With you being ill, I couldn't have Ruth take time out of her duties to alter the dress. Captain Spencer said he would ensure you had proper clothing. He bought the clothes from me. I didn't have matching pieces, but we did the best we could. He had to take them to town and get a rush on the alterations. I am sure he has spent more coin on dressing you."

"Oh! Well, he is very kind." I could feel my face flush. She seemed to be quite concerned with the amount of attention Captain Spencer had given me. "I will make sure I tell him thanks."

With the stomacher pinned into place, an indigo petticoat, which matched the stays, slid over my head and tied. Ruth helped me put on a crimson gown and pinned it into place. I looked at myself in the mirror and noticed that I was much thinner than I was a couple of weeks prior. "It's lovely. I would like to brush my hair before I head downstairs." I brought my hands up to my hair and ran my fingers through it. Someone—I'm sure it was Ruth—took the time to brush out my tangled hair while I was asleep.

"Ruth can help you with that. She does my hair." She primped her hair with her hand.

"No. Thank you. Ruth has done more than her share of taking care of me. I can do this on my own." At least I thought I could. Ruth had been doing a lot and I couldn't have her do more. I sat at the dressing table and attempted to brush my hair. During the time being held hostage, the most I could do was run my fingers through my tangles. With my wavy hair that fell past my shoulders, I struggled to manage it. With my fingers, I would try to work through my tangled hair whenever I had my hands freed from being tied up. As I removed any remaining tangles, it gave me a way to bring myself back to some sort of normalcy—when the world didn't appear turned upside down. My hair band that I had, somehow, kept in my hair the entire couple of weeks went missing. I brushed my hair—which ended up looking like a frizzy mess from all the brushing, yanking, and picking—and twisted into a low cinnamon roll bun at the base of my neck. I found a hair stick on the dressing table, poked it through the bun, and secured it in place. "Well, that's as good as it gets," I said as I stood up. I immediately felt lightheaded and braced myself with the chair.

"Sit back down, Mistress Murray. I will help you put on your cap." Ruth had come back into the room, no doubt to check on my pathetic attempt at doing my hair.

She pinned a simple linen cap trimmed in lace to my hair. A half-attempt to stand ended in failure. "I believe I need to take it slowly. I am still a bit wobbly and lightheaded." Deep breath. "I hate to ask, but I think I need your help." I reached out a hand towards Ruth. "Would you help me downstairs to meet with Captain Spencer?"

We slowly descended the narrow stairs, barely wide enough for the two of us. Ruth was on my left and I gave the stair rail on my right a tight grip. The stairs groaned with every step. When we left the room, I noticed the house was not at all what I had expected. I had let my romantic imagination of the past and Georgian-styled mansions cloud my image of what I thought the house would have looked like. My carried away imagination had it as a grand house on a large estate, with servants running around and opulent furnishings. Instead, I was in a simple home with Mistress Lovett and Ruth. Mistress Lovett stood at the bottom of the stairs. "You have a lovely home, Mistress Lovett," I said as we continued at a snail's pace down the stairs. "Is there a Mister Lovett?"

"Sergeant Lovett is in the Virginia Regiment under Lieutenant Colonel Washington and Captain Spencer," she said as we reached the bottom of the stairs. "He will be headed to help protect the new fort they are building. That is how Captain Spencer knew to bring you here."

"Mistress Murray," Captain Spencer said, smiled, and stood up from his seat in the armchair in front of the fireplace as we walked into the room. "Would you like to have a seat?"

"Thank you, Ruth." I turned to look at Captain Spencer. "I thought we could take a walk to the garden, if you don't mind. The fresh air is something I could use."

"Thank you, Mistress Lovett," Captain Spencer said with a bow of his head, and opened the door for me. Ruth placed a brimmed hat on my head, and I headed outside for the first time in days. The sun and fresh air felt wonderful.

CHAPTER NINETEEN

I insisted on walking on my own, unaided, down the two steps. The kitchen garden was in the early stages of growth and hadn't fruited for the season. There were neat rows of what appeared to be cucumber and cauliflower. Their leaves gave their identity away. Cabbages were in tight balls with large leaves tucked away to one side. Asparagus tips protruded from mounds. The earthy smell of a compost pile brought my attention to the steaming pile off to the side. It looked as though it was ready to be turned.

The previous year, I kept a small garden where I grew tomatoes, cucumbers, peppers, various herbs, and a pumpkin vine that seemed to take over the entire yard, but only produced four pumpkins. My tomatoes would grow taller than I could reach and produced more than I knew what to do with. Sometimes, I would dry them in my oven for my version of sun-dried tomatoes, or give them to neighbors, toss them in salads, or make a delicious sauce. Squash bugs continued to decimate my zucchini plants year-after-year, but I continued to grow them. I transplanted seedlings into the garden before my trip, set up the timer to water the plants, and now I was not sure if I was ever going to see my plants or the fruits of my labor.

I laughed. "This was not the type of garden I had expected. It's lovely and reminds me of home, but it was definitely not what I had expected."

He walked with his hands clasped behind his back. "Where is home?" Spencer glanced down at me.

Six-foot tall, I thought as I looked up to meet his glance. I was not sure how to answer. I had a husband and a daughter; they were my home no matter where in the world we had lived. With my husband dead and daughter away at college, all I had left was myself and a house. I had to make it my home again, even without them. My house was near Fredericksburg, Virginia, but that was two hundred sixty-five years in the future. My house didn't exist in 1754. I shouldn't exist in 1754. That was one of those times where telling the truth would be difficult, but I needed to tell him something. "I am not sure how to answer that question."

"With the truth would be sufficient. I thought it was quite simple. If you knew where your home was, mayhap we can get you back to it." His eyes searched my face for the truth. Or was it the lies?

"I do not believe you could get me home. My husband is dead, my daughter is away, and my house doesn't exist. I have nowhere to go. Even if I had a home to go to, Jumonville would ensure my capture or death." I twisted my wedding ring around my finger. It was loose and spun easily around. I looked off into the distance, as if I could look hard enough and see my house–two hundred sixty-five years in the future. "Look, I know my circumstances are unusual. I cannot go into too many details, but I am telling the truth." The feeling of doubt hung heavy in the air between us.

"What do you have that Jumonville finds so valuable that he cannot risk it getting into someone else's hands? The only thing we found on you that could've been of any value was your ring and the empty satchel." Captain Spencer stopped and stared at me. Sweat trickled down my back. It was from the warm sun or the level of interrogation. Perhaps a combination of sun and the heated interrogation. The way my body told me to run away from there, it was the interrogation that made me sweat. "Neither one of those items would seem to be a reason for him to kill you over. Did you get that ring from him?"

I looked down at my wedding ring–a thin, simple gold band. Of course, he would think that I was in bed with the enemy. We had walked around the perimeter of the garden, down over to the stable. A tornado of flies swirled around a pile of horse dung. I turned to walk towards the house before they picked me up and carried me away.

"No. My late husband gave it to me. It was my wedding ring. The only thing Jumonville ever gave was orders to Bouchard to give me bruises and split lips." I huffed through my nose. "Listen, I'm feeling tired. I really should go back to bed." I wanted to cry but was unwilling to do it in front of Captain Spencer. What I really wanted was to go home. *1754 was turning out to be a miserable adventure.*

"I know there is more that you are not telling me. You may be under my watch, and I have no intention of abusing you in the same way as Sieur de Jumonville…"

I interrupted. "He doesn't deserve your respect. He certainly doesn't have mine. Call him Jumonville or whatever you want. I'll call him a narcissistic jerk." Captain Spencer had continued to use the "Sieur", which seemed to give Jumonville a level of respect he didn't deserve. It irritated me to the end of the earth and back. My stomached clenched when I thought of Jumonville or Bouchard.

"Very well." He nodded towards me. "I have no intention of abusing you like Jumonville and Bouchard, but do not confuse my kindness with weakness." He waved his hand out in an "after you" gesture. "We will continue our conversation later, after you've rested."

We made our way back into the house in silence. I wanted to run away from there, but I hadn't the energy to walk more than a half hour on my own, let alone escape. It didn't seem to matter who I was with; I was in a constant state of looking for ways to escape. No one could know I was from the future. I was not sure if I had already impacted the past—butterfly effect, and all that—but whatever happened, I needed to make sure that Jumonville couldn't use the information in my notebook and kill Washington. He kept the information a secret from everyone, including Bouchard. At least, Bouchard never let on that he knew anything about the notebook. He was the muscle between the two of them. Jumonville didn't want to get his hands dirty. Bouchard was more than happy to raise his fists to me. I was unsure of Jumonville's game plan. I knew I needed to think through the information that was in the book and what was coming next. He had to be stopped. My mission was to save George Washington.

"What happened to Private MacDonald? I haven't seen or heard from him since I woke up." My measured steps kept the pace slow.

"I had him meet up with the Ensign Ward and the detachment. The day I met up with you and MacDonald leaving the fort, I was to arrive and take temporary command. You'll have to tell me what had happened to you and how you came to know about the impending attack."

"We'll save that sob story for another time. For now, I just want to know where we're headed from here?" Save Washington from your mistake at all costs.

Captain Spencer stopped in his tracks. "Are you sure you're not a spy?"

"I'm certainly not a spy." I looked back at Captain Spencer and gave him a smile. I wasn't sure if he thought I was flirting, lying, telling the truth, or some version in between. Unfortunately, I needed his help to get my notebook back, so if I needed to play the flirt-game, then that is what I would have to do. Flirting was not my style, but if it was the means to my desired end, then I would have to do it. It made me feel cheap. I straightened up my back and looked ahead, insistent that I had to maintain my senses and not let down my defense. My emotions needed to stay hardened for the couple of weeks, and as much as I tried to keep the truth from Captain Spencer, he seemed like he could be an ally. I had to figure out how to manipulate him in order to get what I needed. *Get ahold of yourself, Murray.*

"I hear you say that, but it seems you are holding back the truth," he said as we approached the house. My battered and bruised body had enough excitement for the day, and it was only mid-afternoon.

The smell of food cooking filled the air as we entered the house. My stomach insisted I find my way to the kitchen. "How long will it take us to get to Wills Creek?"

"It will take a week, give or take. Will you be able to travel for that distance?"

"If you knew the distance I have traveled to be here," I had to stop myself from saying more. I began to come to terms with the idea of traveling two hundred sixty-five years into the past, but surely no one else could understand. If it hadn't happened to me, I would have never believed it to be possible. I had to figure out why I was sent back to 1754 and how I was going to get back to my time. But the first item on my agenda: get the notebook out of Jumonville's clutches.

CHAPTER TWENTY

The next couple of days were a repeat of the day prior. When Captain Spencer asked too many questions regarding my past and what I was doing when kidnapped, I feigned exhaustion. It was insulting to treat him that way, but I figured I would rather lie about the exhaustion—although I really did struggle with tiring easily—than to tell him the whole truth. I knew my time for convalescing would eventually come to an end. He met my pathetic attempts at flirting to win him over with dismissive comments, so I gave up that route. I despised the fake flirt to manipulate, which made it easy to move away from that tactic.

Along with casual conversation about the weather, crops, and my health, Captain Spencer continued to interrogate and demand more information from me on every walk. Self-doubt took over my thoughts. I was not sure I would be physically strong enough to escape.

One night, I tried to sneak out of the house, only to be stopped by a vigilant Captain Spencer, who slept in the room at the bottom of the stairs. I used the excuse of not wanting to use a chamber pot in the middle of the night, and he happily escorted me to the privy. He waited nearby and escorted me back to the house. I hoped it was because he was being a gentleman, but I was sure that he knew I had tried to escape.

"Are you a spy for the French?" Captain Spencer asked while on our daily walk about the garden.

"No."

"Are you telling me the truth?"

"I have never lied to you," I said. I stopped and looked up at Captain Spencer's blue eyes. He was tall, nearly six-foot, which towered over my five-foot one-inch frame, but I wouldn't let his size intimidate me. I also hadn't told him the whole truth, but I figured that was the reason for the constant interrogation and mindful eye. "I have always told you the truth."

"You might not have lied to me, but you haven't told me the complete truth." *Son-of-a... was he reading my thoughts?*

"You wouldn't understand the complete truth. I don't understand the complete truth and I am not sure I am comfortable saying all of what I know or believe to be true." And there it was—my admission to telling half-truths. He had a way of getting under my skin right when I thought we were getting along.

He let out a huff. "Are you well enough to travel? We need to meet up with the rest of the troops." He didn't seem pleased with my half-truth admission and was ready to get back to the fight or to turn me over to someone else. "The group from the fort should have arrived at Wills Creek and reported to Lieutenant Colonel Washington. He will not be pleased with the vacating of the fort, but your warning saved us from losing the men in a battle, where we were outnumbered. Thank you for that."

"You're meeting with Colonel Washington at Wills Creek? I need to meet with him."

He grabbed my arm and spun me around to face him. "You will not try to kill him, will you? How do I know you aren't an assassin?"

"I'm not an assassin. Do I really look like an assassin?" My eyes rolled at the thought he could've been mistaken me as an assassin. I pulled my arm out of his grip and stomped my way towards the stables. I hadn't given him much to trust me but telling him the truth about coming from the future was not part of the plan. If the gods of time travel sent me back to the future, I wanted to meet George Washington before I left 1754. "No. I'm trying to prevent his assassination. I wish you would just trust me," I called over my shoulder.

"You have not been telling me the truth. You admitted to that not moments ago. I need you to trust me and tell me what you know, Mistress Murray. You are safe, fed, and dressed by me. I believe you can see I am honorable." He said as he quickened his pace to catch up to me.

"In order for me to trust you, I think we need to take a break from the formalities. It is driving me crazy being on guard about every little thing you or I say. Am I going to use the wrong title? Should I curtsy? All that madness is just not me. Let's start by you calling me Amelia. At least, while we are we are out on our walks," I said, as I gave him a quick smile. Although he interrogated me throughout our time at the Lovett's home, he had been kind. I desired to move beyond the feeling of the roles of prisoner and interrogator.

"Pleased to make your acquaintance, Amelia," Captain Spencer said with a smile, bowing to me. "You may call me Henry." He paused for a moment before he continued. "However, only in private."

I curtsied in response. It felt like a minor victory. In my own time, I would have thought adults giving permission to use first names would have been ridiculous. Now, I was curtsying and gaining permissions to use first names after spending day and night with Henry for the past week. I could tell it made him uncomfortable using my first name, but I needed to move on from the constant state of formality. The formality drove me crazy. It always kept me on high alert.

"I will need the rest of the day to make sure we have enough supplies, and we can leave in the morn." He said as we entered the house.

The next morning, Henry saddled his horse, bags packed with rations and supplies. I turned to Ruth, gave her a hug, and whispered in her ear. "Thank you for all that you have done for me. I know it doesn't mean much to you now but know that one day your people will no longer be enslaved." Ruth stood there arms straight by her side, gave me an odd look, curtsied, and took five steps back, away from me. I say the wrong things at the wrong times. I hadn't meant it to be insensitive, but I didn't know what to say or do. By the look on her face, I would say it was one of those times. *I felt like an ass–a big old, braying ass. Hee-haw!*

Standing beside the only horse prepared to travel, I asked, "Who do I have the pleasure of riding today?" I hope that didn't sound wrong.

Henry said as he rubbed the horse's neck, "Oh, this is Louis. I think it is a fit name for a horse." Not Brownie? Or Buttercup? Knowing that Washington had named at least one of his horses Nelson, I figured Louis sounds like a typical 18th century horse's name.

"I hope you don't expect me to ride sidesaddle." I looked up at the saddle and down at my dress.

"Not at all," Henry said with a laugh. He helped me into the saddle, tucked my skirts in to prevent chaffing, and mounted the horse behind me. "I cannot have you falling ill again and slipping off Louis. You can ride in front of me." Mistress Lovett didn't have a horse or wagon to spare, and the one she had looked as though it wouldn't make it a mile down the road before it would keel over. If I had to live forever in 1754, I needed to get my horse and a carriage. Without one, it was too much like being an unlicensed teenager and having to bum rides from my friends.

The first part day we rode in silence. I enjoyed the time out of the house and all that springtime offered. April was ending. Tree buds opened, and the branches started to fill in with leaves. Birds chirped and sang their morning salutations. The fresh scent of the green canopy was a reminder of a new start. The bruises that riddled my body had faded. A light-yellow tinge to my skin remained. The muscles around my ribs had mended. I had regained most of my strength.

We took our midday break from riding to let the three of us rest and refuel. I relished in the opportunity to eat and stretch my sore legs. To say that I would walk funny for a week was not an understatement. I had never been on a horse for that long in one sitting. I was not sure I could muster enough intestinal fortitude to get back on it.

We spent days with each other and now that we were on our way, Henry seemed to let off the interrogation for a bit. This met with some awkward silence for part of our journey.

"I have a son, George. He is eight years old. I thought you would like to know," Henry blurted out as we headed back to get on the horse to continue our ride towards Wills Creek. That was a bit strange. I wondered if he searched for a conversation starter and that was all he could muster.

"Oh." I stammered. "Do you have a wife?" I hadn't thought about him having a life outside of His Majesty's Grand Interrogator.

"She died in childbirth, giving birth to a girl. They both died. Six years this November." His voice trailed off.

We needed that awkward moment to get the conversation flowing. I didn't realize how grateful I would be for the conversation until then. He must have thought about me with disdain, because I hid something from him. I withheld information from him. Not only about me coming from the future, but about the upcoming war. Silence would have made for a long ride, but I wouldn't have divulged any information that needed to remain a secret from Henry. Parts of history needed to happen. I didn't want to go back and have a planet ruled by apes—again, butterflies and all that—and a changed future wouldn't rest easy on my shoulders.

He told the story about being the second son and not inheriting his father's title. He had moved to the colonies after his wife's death, with not much more than his name. His brother, Charles, insisted on naming Henry's son as his heir and raise him to be the next Duke of Marlborough.

"And here I thought you were just one of Lieutenant Colonel Washington's captains. Should I have been calling you Lord Henry this entire time?" I said with a smile, nudging my elbow at him. The flirtatious nudge caught him off guard. Me as well. I must admit, he was handsome, but I needed to remind myself that I must stay mission focused and not get distracted by a pretty face and pleasant conversation.

"No one calls me Lord Henry outside of the estates or at court. Washington knows of my family, and of course Dinwiddie. My men only need to know that I am their captain."

"I hope you don't think this too forward of me, but I know Washington is young, early twenties and you are..."

"Older than that?" He snorted a laugh. "Yes, I am six and thirty."

"Is it odd to have someone so much younger than you in charge? I mean, he isn't much older than my daughter." *Hannah must be worried about me.*

"Washington has been involved with the Virginia Regiment for longer than I have. I only recently joined. He has the passion to lead soldiers. I... I..."

"It sounds to me as though you were running away from something." I thought about my life before and now. *Was I running away from something?*

"Or, mayhap, I was running towards something. I just didn't know what it was."

I shook my head. "No one should want to run towards war."

"We are not at war. There is but conflict along the bordering territories. If I would have joined the British Army while I was in England, I could've been sent here, or they may have sent me elsewhere. I wanted to be in Virginia, hence the reason I moved here. Then, joined the Virginia Regiment on the request of Lieutenant Governor Dinwiddie."

"Why the colonies?" I genuinely wanted to know. It would be a wonderful insight for my book.

"I think it is the new opportunity the colonies offer to those that have the courage to seek it. I can come here and build a new life and tame a wild new land, with new experiences." He looked longingly towards the woods on the horizon. "Besides, you may never understand living in the shadow of my brother." There was disappointment in his voice in that last statement.

I thought about what he said about the colonies being a new opportunity. It was idealistic in my mind and the reason I thought it would be a simple life. Worry about the basics. That was what sent me down the path of writing the book about a young George Washington. However, I knew what that would mean for the indigenous people that would have their lands taken from them as they were killed or relocated. I also had to face the ugly truth about what would happen to the enslaved people. Both situations would negatively impact the people for many years. I wanted this man and his dreams to come true and those of the millions that would come after him, but it would come at the expense of those that were here before them and those that came without consent. I wanted to scream.

He continued, "Why did you come to Virginia? Or is your family from Virginia?"

Ha! Those are good questions, Lord Henry.

I adjusted in the saddle and stretched my back. "You wouldn't believe me if I told you. Let's just say it took a lot of time to get here. I moved to Virginia with my husband about eight years ago. We bought a house, we worked, and raised our daughter. A few years ago, he died in a terrible accident on his birthday. It was really a tough time for me and Hannah. We were mending our broken hearts. She went to college, and I ended up here. I still don't know how I got here, but here I am."

"You didn't offer any information before, and now, when you spoke, you really leave so many questions unanswered. Where did you move from? Do you have a family to return to? What happened to your house? Your daughter is at college? Married to someone in the faculty? If your daughter is married, how old is she? I thought you were close to my age."

"Slow down there, Tex. No, she's studying..." I had to stop myself mid-sentence. I almost forgot that women didn't attend university during this time in history but saying that she was married to someone in the faculty would be a lie. *Keep it simple, Murray.* I couldn't lie to him. I told him I wouldn't lie. "We have quite a long journey ahead of us and we have plenty of time to get to your questions." Overwhelmed and cautious, I needed time to sort through how best to answer. "It is getting dark. We should stop and let the horse rest and I could use food and to stretch out."

CHAPTER TWENTY-ONE

We found an area close to one of the many streams that curved their way through Pennsylvania—*or were we in Virginia?*—and set up camp for the night. Louis, the horse, was grateful for the water and the field of grass to refuel its belly. I was grateful for the stream to wash my face; I ached for a refresh from the travel. A layer of road dust on my face an inch thick was gratefully deposited into the stream. I filled the canteens up with water and headed back towards the camp. In my previous life, I would have hesitated at filling water from the stream. I was too much of a city girl that. I preferred filtered water from the fridge. It was not quite the same in 1754. I questioned the cleanliness of the water. Isn't that how people got cholera or dysentery? I had to learn to adapt to my new environment, including filling the goat skin canteens from a stream. Henry had gathered some wood and prepared a fire. The springtime nights were cool, and a fire would help keep the cold from sinking into my bones. Throughout my time with the French, they kept me on the outskirts of the encampment and prevented the opportunity to warm up near a fire. The cold would sink deep to my core, which only exaggerated the torture.

I thought about his questions and tried to decide which one would be the safest to answer. I nibbled on a chunk of the bread we had brought in the satchel from Mistress Lovett's home. With the sun going down, the air began to cool. Frogs sang a nighttime chorus to each other. Rustled leaves and snapped twigs sent a shiver down my spine. The woods were alive, and I wasn't sure I wanted to know what lurked in the dark shadows.

"You look as though you are trying to solve all the problems in heaven and earth," Henry said. He tore a piece of his bread and shoved it into his mouth.

"I'm trying to remember your questions." Truth was, I was stalling to give my answers. "My daughter, Hannah, is eighteen and lives in Williamsburg." I hoped to gain honesty points, even if I was the only one keeping score. When I told him she lived in Williamsburg and didn't mention she went to college two hundred sixty-five years in the future was close enough to the truth as I could get. He would never know if I told the truth or not, but I had to tell the truth for my peace of mind.

"Oh, I see." He rubbed his hand on his face in contemplation of my statement. "Is she married or a governess?"

I wasn't sure how to respond. If he stopped digging into my story that I couldn't tell him, it would be easier for me to keep it simple. I wanted to leave it there, but my mouth had different plans. "She might be a governess." That lie squeaked out. "I'm not sure if she is doing that. I haven't spoken with her recently."

"Mayhap, I know her employer. I own a house in Williamsburg and am acquainted with the notable families."

You should have kept your mouth closed. "I'm not sure. Maybe it was Smith? Or Jones? Or Windsor? I don't remember." Great. All I did was make myself sound like an uncaring mother by not knowing my only child's employer.

As I finished the bread and a chunk of dried meat we had brought with us, I took a swig of the water. A cup of tea, coffee, something with a bit more flavor to finish the meal would have been nice, but I was happy with just being able to take a moment and indulge. I leaned back on my hands. The muscles in my legs strained from the stretch as I flexed my toes and ankle in a melodic movement. My back muscles finally gave in to the stretch. I sat there with a stupid grin on my face. "You know, you act as though women are powerless and not intelligent enough to be accomplished. In the future, women will have the opportunity to have a higher education. They will get college degrees, become doctors and lawyers, teach at universities, become officers in the army, run businesses, become politicians, and will vote. Women will be more than just wives and mothers."

"In a way, women already do all those professions. They are not just wives and mothers. A child scrapes their knee or has a sniffle, the mother knows how to clean the dirt out and bandage up the wound. Mothers and governesses are the first educators of our children. A houseful of children can be more difficult than running a regiment of men; yet women are masters of bringing them all in line. Households require budgeting and managing supplies and clothing and food, none of which can be run properly without women. One day, I would hope that women would have the opportunities that you had mentioned. Unfortunately, that is not a possibility today," Henry said, full of fiery passion that took me aback. "Just so you know, I don't think you are weak or incapable. You have shown great strength and determination." His gaze pierced me. "Determined to keep your secrets."

I was ready to defend feminism to a man that I assumed was so deep in the patriarchy that he could never find his way out. He was a man of noble birth, able to do whatever he wanted, including moving to another country and joining the military as an officer, because his power, money, and gender gave him that opportunity to succeed however he wanted. I might have been too quick to judge him, but it was 1754. What else was I supposed to believe? Regardless of what I thought of his modern thinking, he continued to pry into my past, and I needed to be careful, or my secret would slip out.

"That is not what I was expecting to hear you or any man say in seventeen fifty-four. You are a rare man." I was flabbergasted. In my time, we were still dealing with many men that want women subservient and no body autonomy. It was absurd. "You're correct. I have secrets. We all do. Some we keep. Some we eventually share. Others will eat at us until the day we die." I wasn't finished putting him on the spot. "Change of subject. What about slavery? Do you own people?" It fired me up. Ready to fight the world and find fault with him.

"There must be more like me out there." He took a drink from his canteen. "And, to answer your questions, I do not. I have renters and own 400 acres and indentured and bond servants work the fields until they earn their contracts."

"Good. Don't. Just don't. Find some other way to run your property. Hire help. Collect rent. Do anything else, but don't buy into the notion of slavery." I had to fight back the tears. *Why couldn't I have been this fired up when I was around Ruth? I was such an ass.*

I took a deep breath and paused while I swallowed down my emotions. "Um, what are your thoughts about traveling through time?" I nervously bit my lip while waiting for a response.

"From women's capabilities, to slavery, and now to time travel. Quizzical topics." He pulled his hair out from the tie and let down his brown, shoulder length hair. He ran his fingers through it, massaging his scalp. "I believe it is something that comes from tales for the fanciful, stories we tell children. Fairies and all that." Henry laid back on his bedroll, his arm tucked behind his head, and stared up into the night sky.

"So, you don't think it is possible to travel through time?" I was not sure he would understand but had hoped he was opened minded enough. "If you could travel through time, when in time would you like to go?"

"I would have to think about that notion. Do you go to the past and try to right the wrongs? Marry the woman? Don't marry her? Or do you go to the future? See how your actions today impact the world of tomorrow? Or do you realize your life is insignificant and should have stayed in your time? Time doesn't wait for us. There is never enough of it when you are with the ones you love." It was getting late, and Henry threw another log on the fire before laying back down to sleep. "I will be the first to inform you when I discover the secret to time travel. We have an early morning. Sleep well, Amelia."

"I look forward to hearing if you marry her or not. Or if you decide that whatever time you have with the ones you love, you cherish every beautiful second of it." Stars filled the sky like millions of lightning bugs out for a party. Unbeknownst to Henry, he saved me from divulging my secret. I was ready to spill it all out. "Good night, Henry."

CHAPTER TWENTY-TWO

*H*enry bolted out of his make-shift bed. It was morning, and I was nowhere to be seen. Last night, he had finally let his guard down, out of pure exhaustion, and I had crept away from the camp in the early morning. He was upset with himself. He knew I hid something and assumed I would take the first opportunity to go back to the French. Perhaps he thought I had lied to him about the treatment. He gathered up the bedrolls and let out a loud and frustrated grunt. He wanted to yell at something... he wanted to yell at me. "Damn you, woman," he blurted out. His outburst carried through the surrounding area and alerted the early morning birds into flight. He questioned his every move and conversation with me. "At least she didn't take you. Did you see where she went?" He asked Louis as he stroked the horse's neck. He looked around. "Let's get you ready and we'll go find that insufferable woman." He was upset with me, but he wouldn't dare take it out on Louis.

He finished putting the saddle on Louis and loaded up when the sound of crunching leaves, swishing fabric, and heavy breathing came out of the trees behind him. He grabbed his pistol out of the side pack and spun around, ready to shoot.

"Cheese and rice! Don't point that at me, asshole." I threw my hands up in a surrender and dropped the fish I had been carrying on the ground. It flopped on the ground as I waited for Henry to lower the pistol. My body trembled, afraid that he would shoot me. His eyes blazed with fire, and he continued to point it directly towards my center. "Henry, please, don't shoot me," I pleaded.

He looked around and lowered the pistol after he realized I stood alone. "I thought you had run off to find the French to lead them to me and Washington."

I stood there in disbelief, unsure of what to say. I had tried leaving before when we were at the Lovett's home, but I knew that there was nowhere to go. At that point, my only chance of survival was in the hands of Captain Lord Henry Spencer. I had no intention of trying to escape him. Jumonville had my notebook with the dates and locations of Washington's upcoming battles. My new goal was to make sure Lieutenant Colonel George Washington didn't get ambushed. I could feel the tears prick at my eyes and my nose tingled. It overcame me with emotions–scared and angry at the same time. "Well, I didn't run anywhere, you... you... pretentious jerk," I said. My entire body trembled, and tears streamed down my cheeks.

He slid the pistol back into the bag and ran to me. "Oh, Amelia," he said as he approached, grabbing hold of my shoulders so I would look at him. "My humblest apologies. Please, don't cry. I didn't mean to frighten you."

"You were pointing a pistol at me," I sobbed. I wiped the

tears off my cheeks. "You were going to shoot me, Henry. You wanted to shoot me. Of course, I was frightened."

"No, Amelia, please stop crying." He grabbed and held me. "You were gone. I thought you ran. I heard a noise and thought the French were attacking."

I pushed away from him. "I was scared and upset. But now," I paused mid-sentence to wipe a tear away. "Now, I'm ticked off." I could feel my nostrils flair, like staring down the barrel of a shotgun. "Why would you think I ran off? I could've been injured or kidnapped again. I'm sure that asshole has a bounty on me by now. And the first thing you think of is that I ran away, and you were going to shoot me? You're an asshole."

I picked up the fish that stopped flopping, its gills fluttered as it tried to breathe. I plopped down where my bed roll had been and stabbed at the smoldering logs with a stick I found on the ground. "And another thing, you didn't even bother to look for me." I pointed the stick at him and swung it around like it was a sword looking for its target. "You were going to take off and leave me here. Oh? How do I know? You packed everything up and were getting the horse ready."

"Correct. I am a complete and total arse," Henry said, coming over to the campsite and sat across from me, out of reach of the stick I flailed about. "In my defense, you had tried leaving when we were at Mistress Lovett's home, and you weren't here this morning." Busted. Did he have to remember that?

"I woke up and had to relieve myself and I was washing up in the creek when I saw a bunch of fish. I didn't mean to be gone for so long. Are they edible?" I said, as my anxiety and sobs subsided. I had seen live trout only twice and was hoping my memory was correct in the identification and that I wasn't trying to feed us a toxic fish. "Anyway, there were a bunch of them, and I don't know how I could do it, but it was like a voice told me to try. I grabbed one. I thought we could have it for breakfast and I came back as quickly as I could, and you pointed your pistol at me."

"You grabbed a fish? Out of the water?" He shook his head. The look of confusion shifted to anger. "I have already explained my reasoning and I will not continue," he said as he stood up and stormed off through the woods towards the creek.

"Whatever. Throw your tantrum. Jerk." I took a moment to gather my thoughts as I watched him stomp into the woods. A few deep inhales, and the adrenaline stopped coursing through my veins a million miles an hour. I grabbed a log and put it on the smoldering embers. If I was going to cook this fish, I needed fire. After a few minutes, orange flames licked the log. I found a knife in one of the side bags on the horse and tried to clean the guts out of the fish. I didn't frequently find fish on my menu but was determined to make this work. When I had purchased it in the grocery store, I found them cleaned and usually frozen. Catching and cleaning a fish right out of the stream proved to be a task that I had wished I never had to endure. It was a messy business. "Come on, Murray, you've watched enough tv shows and movies. You can do this!" I tilted my head from side-to-side, rolled my shoulders back, and let out a deep breath in mental preparation for the task at hand. I was not prepared for the mess that I created, but if I wanted to eat, I needed to get over the having fish blood and guts on my hands.

With the fish sufficiently cleaned without me gouging a

hole in my hand. My makeshift sword-stick shoved through the fish, I held it over the weak flames of the fire. My hands were sticky and slimy, but hunger won over cleaning them. The flames intensified. I wasn't sure how long it would take to cook—it was a complete guess—I had hoped it cooked it long enough so we wouldn't get sick. The skin had blackened. I removed it from the heat and carefully picked at it to check if it had cooked through and was flaky. *Ah, white flaky flesh.* Breakfast was a success.

I picked at the flesh. Salt and pepper and a squirt of lemon, that would have helped. In the end, it didn't matter. I caught, prepared, and cooked a fish on my own. I ate half the fish before I sat back, leaned on my elbows, soaked in the morning sun, and basked in my glory of accomplishment. *Woman hunt. Woman cook. Woman provide.* I wanted to pound my chest in victory, but my hands were gross from the slaughter. I would take my victory lap after I cleaned up.

Henry walked up as I savored my victory and growing independence. I handed him the stick with the other half of the fish, without saying a word to him, my hands still disgusting with dried fish blood and guts. He grunted a thanks. I could tell that was a strain for him.

"I don't know why you are angry with me," I said as I rubbed my hands together to remove the grass and dirt that was stuck to my hands still caked with fish guts. I still fumed at the thought of him pointing a pistol at me, but I tried to maintain a sense of control. "Do you feel better after taking a walk? I'm assuming that is where you stormed off to go do."

"Mayhap." He sat there, focused heavily on the fish, and refused to look at me.

"I've eaten. The rest is yours." I looked at my filthy hands. My nose scrunched up as I smelled the fish guts.

"Why didn't you do the cleaning at the stream?" He still didn't make eye contact. "You wouldn't have made a terrible mess near the camp, and you could've washed your hands."

I sat there, mouth agape. I had no answer for him. He was correct. I should have cleaned the fish at the stream, but I wouldn't give him the satisfaction of telling him he was right. Or maybe I didn't want the other fish to know that I murdered their friend. I looked at my hands. They looked and smelled disgusting. I almost wanted to keep them that way, out of spite. "And where, mayhap, would I have gotten a knife if not from your bag?" I huffed.

Trudging off to the stream to clean up, I stayed longer than required. The other fish found another area to swim. Word must have got out that I was on a killing spree. Ha! I let my emotions get the better of me. The extra time needed to wash my hands and face brought down the heat of my anger.

Henry helped me mount Louis, with him saddled behind, and we headed toward Wills Creek in silence.

"Amelia, please forgive me," he said in a soft voice. I gasped at the feeling of his soft and warm breath on the back of my neck. He was close. I could almost feel the touch of his lips brush on my neck. A shiver slid down my spine and into my toes.

I leaned back into his firm body; it was warm and inviting. I turned my head to look back at him. He looked down at me, his face close to my face. "Forgiven," I whispered. The emotions of the morning had me spent. Misunderstandings would make for a very long ride, and I wasn't up to the emotional exhaustion to prove that I was correct. Our eyes locked a moment longer than I expected. I took a deep breath and turned to face the path ahead, unable to focus on anything around me.

Henry cleared his throat. "I wanted to thank you for catching breakfast for us. They are a bit more difficult to catch than I gave you credit for."

"Is that where you stormed off to this morning?" I stifled a snorted laugh.

"I didn't storm off." I huffed in disbelief at his statement. He continued, "I went to wash up and saw them swimming around, like you did. I thought if you could catch one, then surely, I could catch one. They are quick and slippery. I must admit to defeat."

"Don't underestimate me Lord Henry, there's more to me than you can ever imagine." I nudged him in the stomach with my elbow. "And, by the way, you did storm off in a big, grumpy pout."

"Mayhap, I stormed off." His voice was low and close to me. I felt the small hairs on my neck and arms react to his breath on my neck. *Get ahold of yourself, Murray.*

CHAPTER TWENTY-THREE

We rode south towards Wills Creek. Neither one of us wanted to speak much. The obvious attraction we had earlier that morning left me unsure where this was headed. My stomach twisted in knots at the excitement and heartbreak I would endure if I let myself get emotionally invested in him. I would find my way home and leave him behind.

The sun's heat had disappeared by the afternoon and storm clouds had rolled in. A drop of water landed on my cheek. "It's going to rain. I'm not sure this dress can hold up to too much water. Do you know anyone around here? We need... I need shelter." I looked down at the red coat and blue petticoat. They would become a heavy sponge if I was caught in the rain.

"I see smoke coming from the base of the mountain. It looks to be someone's home. Let's see if we can find a dry place to stay until the storm passes."

"Do you know who lives there?" I flicked my head in the

plume's direction that wafted above the trees against the dark sky.

"No," he laughed.

"So, you think they are going to let some stranger into their home because you ask?"

"If they won't do it for a soldier, they might be obliged to assist my wife that is with child."

I scoffed. "You're going to lie to them for sympathy?"

"If it means keeping you dry and safe? Then, yes."

I looked down at my stomach. *Did I look pregnant? Nope.* "I'm too old to be with child," I squeaked out. I didn't want to add that I had a hysterectomy eight years ago, making it impossible for me to get pregnant. That was none of his business.

We had taken the trip easy for Louis, since he carried the both of us, but it was not the time for a peaceful walk through the countryside. We needed to move before the rain poured out of the dark sky. Black clouds continued to roll in as a few large drops continued to threaten our ride. Henry gave encouragement to Louis to quicken his pace. We hoped to find a friendly host at the base of the rising smoke. As we approached the small cabin in the woods, we could see that there was smoke billowing out of the chimney, but there was no person or animal in the yard. The house was still. Eerily still.

"This doesn't feel right," Henry said as he pulled his pistol out from the side satchel and held it between our bodies. My breath skipped from the pressure of the pistol next to my back. I understood what was happening, and this was a risky situation that we didn't expect to encounter when we went looking for a place to escape the rain. I tried to look as calm as possible, as to not draw any attention to Henry loading the pistol.

I swallowed and let out a barely audible voice. "Shouldn't there be some sort of activity? Chickens? Goats? People? Something?"

"Aye. Are you well to handle this?" Henry leaned over, speaking in a low tone to ensure I was the only one that could hear him.

"Absolutely," I lied. My stomach tightened and felt as though it was going to turn in on itself and make me lose any food I might have left in my stomach.

"Are you telling me the truth?"

I gritted my teeth. "Absolutely not, but let's do this." I wanted to throw up.

Henry took a deep breath to calm his nerves. My jaw clenched. If he was worried, that meant the outlook must be grim, and I certainly should be worried.

"Stay on Louis. If something happens to me, I need you to get out of here as quick as possible." Henry slid off Louis and cautiously walked towards the cabin. He scanned the area. His head moved left to right. Pistol in his hand at the ready. Each step was smooth, sure, and silent.

I gulped, closed my eyes, and took a deep breath to calm my nerves. I exhaled slowly and controlled, and listened for footsteps, voices, the cocking of a gun, anything that might let me know if someone was going to sneak upon us through the surrounding woods or out of the cabin. The breeze passed through the branches on the trees as it picked up from the rain heading our way. The smell of rain was close. Leaves that had fallen during the autumn still carpeted parts of the ground nearby spun in little cyclones as the breeze picked up.

Agitated, Louis snorted with impatience from standing there and stomped his hoof on the ground. I knew to trust the instinct of an animal. If he was worried, then I was worried. Henry was worried. All of us were worried. Louis had taken good care of us so far; I wasn't about to doubt him. No sounds of livestock snorting, neighing, or clucking came from the barn or coop. There was only an unnerving silence for a house and barn that looked like they should be occupied. Louis stomped his foot again. My anxiety shot through the atmosphere like a ball of lightning. I stroked his neck. It helped calm us.

Henry walked up to the side window of the small cabin, pistol in his hand and ready to fire. He peered through the window, looked back at me, and shook his head. He walked along the side, close to the wall, to the corner, and popped his head around the back. Once. Twice. He disappeared around the back and left me alone. I again gulped down my anxiety and spun my ring around my finger. I shifted in the saddle, uneasy at not knowing what was going on and concerned for our safety. Louis stomped his right foot and huffed his nostrils. Henry came back around to the front of the cabin, pistol still in hand. He walked up to the front door and tapped, using the muzzle of the pistol. No answer. He tapped again. No answer. He tried the latch and found the door unlocked. He slowly opened the door.

He called out, "Is anyone inside?" No response.

Henry looked over at me–still mounted on the horse and ready to bolt if I needed–he shrugged his shoulders and waved me over. I rode the horse closer to the cabin, still looking around for any sign of the occupants or anyone else that may have been lurking about. Henry grabbed the reins and tied Louis to a post on the porch. He helped ease me to the ground and ensured I had my footing. After the long days of riding and not being used to sitting in a saddle, my legs wobbled under me. I wondered if I was ever going to get used to sitting in a saddle all day. I put my hands on his chest until I could stand and nodded when ready to move. We spoke using our eyes, hand signals, and jerks of our heads. My stomach twisted in knots.

There was an uneasiness in the air and neither one of us wanted to make any more noise than required. Henry squeezed my hand, and I followed him to the front door. He didn't want to leave me outside and unguarded. With gentle steps, he led the way to the front door, pistol still in hand and at the ready, and pushed it open. He looked inside and took a step past the threshold. I followed behind, with my hands on his back as if to use him as a shield. I held my breath. The last time I entered a vacant cabin, I slipped to 1754. Another step in and Henry stopped and turned around, almost knocking me over.

"You don't want to go in there." His voice trembled, no longer whispered.

"Why not?" I tried to look past the threshold as he blocked my view and entry.

"There was a reason that no one answered the door."

I tried looking around him. "Stop being so damn cryptic. Tell me what is going on."

"Dead, Amelia. They're dead."

"Are you sure? What if they're just sick?" I asked, as I tried to look around Henry. I didn't want to believe that we walked into a house with dead people in it. How did they die? Were we in danger? During that time, many people died of illness due to lack of medical treatment, as medicine was still evolving. I thought if they had an illness that I could use my limited knowledge of first aid and save them.

Henry continued to block my entry. "Amelia, I don't want you to see them."

"What makes you think I can't handle sick people that may or may not be dead?"

"Someone has butchered them. They are not sick. Considering the fire is still going, whoever did this could still be around." He looked around the yard and into the woods.

I pushed my way past Henry and saw the body of a woman and a man lying in a pool of blood and human waste on the wooden floor. The smell of the blood and waste hit me like a ton of bricks. The smell was going to make me sick more than the sight of the slaughter. I gasped and covered my mouth and nose. My stomach lurched, and I and begged for it to calm down. I didn't need to get sick and add to the stench. "We cannot leave them here." *Who would do that to them?* I moved to the door to get fresh air. My eyes watered. "We must bury them. What if they have family and friends nearby? Should we leave a note? Who did this?" Rapid breaths coupled with anxiety caused my chest to heave.

Henry moved outside to gain his composure and take in the fresh air. "We don't have time..."

"We need to make time," I yelled out in anger and disgust at the evil. "I will help dig the graves if I need to, but we cannot leave them here like... like... like this." I motioned towards the cabin.

Henry let out an exhausted breath. He knew he couldn't win this argument with me.

"I will see if they have a shovel in the barn." His shoulders sank as he headed to the small barn.

On the front porch, I was alone with my thoughts. I took a deep breath and held it, covered my nose and mouth with my scarf, and headed back inside. I wanted to get a better look at what happened to them. They both laid on their stomachs, the man halfway on top of the woman. It appeared they had been shot in the back as if they were running away from their attacker. Curiosity and sadness drew me closer to them. I needed to understand why someone wanted them dead. They didn't seem to have any neighbors nearby, so for them to be in a dispute seemed unlikely to me.

I lifted my skirt and petticoats and walked closer to the couple, careful not to step in the pool of blood that soaked into the wood and through the floorboards. I thought I heard a sound come from one of them. One of them made a noise. I ran out of the house towards the barn, my adrenaline spiked, and shouted, "Henry! Henry! Come quick!"

Henry ran out of the barn, pistol in hand, and looked around. He crossed the yard in a few strides, pulled me into him to shield me from whatever had startled me. He looked around for the danger. Stifled with my face pressed against his chest, I pushed myself out of his arms. It wasn't time for him to be my protector. "One of them made a sound. I think they are alive."

"What?" His eyes narrowed in disbelief. Henry looked around, saw no one coming, and lowered his pistol. "Bodies sometimes make noises after they died."

"I know what I..."

Henry grabbed me by the shoulders. "Amelia, they're dead."

"Listen to me. I know I heard one of them made a noise, and it didn't sound like a dead person's noise to me. I'm not stupid."

"How many dead people have you been around?"

"My husband, for one." I stepped back further away from him and looked away. Whereas I had seen Todd after he died, it was from behind a glass panel at the mortuary. They covered him and wouldn't let me near him. My parents were declared dead when I was in my twenties, and I remembered little from their funeral. Their bodies were never found. In fact, it didn't matter how many bodies I had seen and their condition, I knew what I heard, and I was furious that he would try to brush me off like that.

"I'll go check the bodies. Do you want to stay out here?"

"No. I don't want to be left alone." I wrapped my arms around myself. "There is something not right about this place."

I looked over my shoulder and my eyes darted into the woods around me as we walked back to the cabin. A feeling of doom hung overhead like the storm clouds that approached us. It was if someone was out there watching us. The thud of Henry's boots on the wood floor echoed onto the porch. He flipped the man off the woman.

The rain that threatened our ride to Wills Creek finally arrived. I wanted the rain to wash away the blood. It was everywhere.

The rust-colored blood on the man's shirt had a hole in it caused by a bullet. He flopped over with his eyes wide open. I hoped his death was quick. The bullet had gone through the body, and he bled out onto the woman. "His blood is covering her. There is just so much blood everywhere." My voice trembled with every word.

Henry looked over his shoulder at me as I stood in the doorway. "Amelia, you don't have to stay in here. I can take care of this."

I twisted my loose ring around my finger. "No. We are in this together," I said as I walked closer to the couple. "Do you see where the bullet entered her?"

"Does it matter where the bullet entered?" He sounded irritated with me. Maybe, I asked too much of him. Perhaps, he was the one that couldn't handle being around dead people.

"I suppose not. What happened to them? I'm just trying to make sense of it all. Will you turn her over?"

Henry reached to pull her over and she let out a faint groan through her pale and slightly parted lips.

"Amelia, she's alive. Help me with her."

CHAPTER TWENTY-FOUR

"This isn't happening!" I ran over to help move the woman. We flipped her over and discovered she had been laying on top of a blood-soaked blanket. If I didn't know better, I could've sworn it was an infant's blanket. "What's your name? Who did this to you? Where is the baby?" There wasn't much time left for the woman and I needed to know who to blame and who to help. I closed my eyes and hoped that it wasn't Jumonville and his men. I thought they might have come across this couple on their way to look for me. If they would do this to this couple, I knew my days were numbered.

"Janet," the woman said with an accent I believed to be Scottish. Her dark hair plastered to her scalp with blood. "Savages." Janet whispered. Her pale lips barely moved. "Tamhas."

"Tamhas? Is that your husband?" I looked at Henry with a confused look on my face. Henry shook his head and shrugged his shoulders. I grabbed Janet's hand.

"Bairn, Tamhas..." Janet's voice trailed off. She could hardly breathe, let alone speak.

"Your baby will be fine. We will care for it. You need to rest so you can get better." I stifled my emotions.

"Aye," said Janet, her voice faded as she closed her eyes. Her head slumped over, and she fell silent and still. I placed her fingers on Janet's neck, desperate to find the pulse. I knew I wouldn't find it. *No pulse.*

"Henry, she said savages killed them. There is no baby here." I searched around the room. "What happened to it?"

"I don't believe it. I can't believe it. This is Haudenosaunee land, Tanaghrisson." He looked at me to confirm that I remembered the name. I did. "He wouldn't have this family killed."

My ears burned hot with the anger of a thousand suns all going supernova at the same time and in the same space. "I don't think a dying woman would lie about who killed her. If the Haudenosaunee or Tanaghrisson didn't kill them, who did?"

Henry stood next to me and looked down at the bloody mess. "The French have the Shawnee in the area fighting for them. It could've been them."

"What can we do?" I reached down and held Janet's lifeless hand.

"We do nothing besides bury them, like you had requested. I would leave them where they lay, and we could move on." He sounded defeated and annoyed at my request to bury the couple.

He knew that would be a losing argument with me. I couldn't leave the couple laying here in a pool of their own blood. I broke free from the hold I had on Janet's hand and stood next to Henry. "If she was alive... whoever did this to them... well, they can't be very far away. They could come back here, and we could have the same fate as them." My heart ached as I looked down at the couple. "I suppose we need to find a place to bury them after it stops raining. I don't know what to do. Should we go to the barn? Should we move them outside? Should I go look for the baby? I can't sit here and stare at them."

"We could leave them here. Remain on the porch. I found a shovel in the barn. I don't want you wandering off into the woods alone, looking for a baby that isn't there."

"Do you think whoever did this took the baby with them?" I no longer held my breath. As terrible as the smell of blood and body fluids was in there, my senses began to dull to the stench.

Henry walked across the room and looked out the small back window. "Mayhap they did. I haven't seen or heard a baby since we arrived. Have you?"

"No." I sucked my bottom lip. I had listened for the men that could've done this, not a baby's cry. We walked outside. The smell of rain tumbled through the trees and refreshed my senses. I closed my eyes and drew in a lungful of clean air.

Henry stripped off his jacket and waistcoat and startled me out of my trance when he shoved them in hands. I stood on the porch out of the rain and listened for a baby's cry. He went to the side of the house and started digging a large hole with the shovel he found in the barn. I focused my ears on the surrounding sounds. I heard the raindrops slap the leaves. *Thwap. Thwap. No baby.*

I watched him and kept an eye out on the surrounding woods. What else could I do? I felt silly about not being able to be in the room alone with them. After taking a deep breath, I headed inside to clean the crime scene. I found a bucket and scrap pieces of cloth. Stripped out of my gown and petticoats, bum roll, and pockets. I left my stays and shift as my only clothing and tied a piece of found rope around my waist and made a belt. I pulled the front bottom of my shift through my legs and tucked it into the back waist, using the belt. The makeshift shorts gave me the ability to clean without the extra fabric getting in the way and kept my outer clothes free from the deceased's bodily fluids that had pooled in a sticky puddle. I placed my clothes and hat on the small table near the kitchen area.

Outside on the front porch, I shouted to Henry, who had dug down about two feet, "I will need buckets of water. Where did these people get their water from?"

"A well out back." He grunted as he shoveled the dirt. He stopped digging. "I can fill it for you."

"You're digging. You don't want me to search for the baby, but I need to do something productive. I will let you know if I need any help." I waved him off and went to the back of the house to look for the well.

Henry stood in awed silence as he watched me round the back of the house. I was barefoot and my shift became transparent in the rain. If I hadn't been wearing stays, my breasts would have been on a full wet tee shirt contest display. The bucket full of water splashed back and forth as I struggled to carry it. I made a mental note to go back to the gym when I get back to the future.

"Amelia, what are you wearing?" Henry gave me a

disapproving look. "What I mean to say, why are you indecently dressed?"

"Why do you give two shakes of a lamb's tail at what I'm wearing?" I sat the bucket down and pressed my hands firmly on my hips. "If we are going to stay the night here, I would prefer to clean up as much of the mess as I can. I'm not getting down on my hands and knees scrubbing in that dress. I swear, I don't know how the women did it."

"Pardon?" He did that raised one eyebrow thing. How do people do that one eyebrow lift? "What do you mean you don't know how women did it? You *are* a woman."

"Yes. I am a woman with work to do and the longer you stand here questioning my choice of work clothes, the wetter and colder I am getting by standing out here in the rain. So, if you don't mind." Grabbing the bucket, I turned on my heel and headed inside. Of all the things that we had going on, he was concerned with what I was or was not wearing in the middle of the woods, in a cabin that contained people that were murdered.

I cleaned the bodies as best as I could. Wet the cloth, wipe them down, rinse, and repeat. I threw the bloody water out the door, retrieved clean water, and repeated the process. I wiped up the floor around the bodies the best I could. We had to move them outside and bury them before I could finish. I was on my hands and knees, wiping up what I could, and sat back to take a breath. Henry walked in and stood a moment in the doorway. "We can bury them now if you'd like."

"Yeah. Good idea. I'm tired and I can't rest until I know they are at rest." My heart ached for Janet, her husband, and their missing baby. Who could do such a thing to these people? It was beyond my comprehension.

Henry put his hands under the man's arms to drag him outside. I ran over and grabbed the feet. "We do this together." I struggled to carry the weight of the man. We took Janet and laid her next to her husband in the grave. They almost looked like they were sleeping. Peaceful. Henry tossed the dirt over them. "What if we find the baby?" I asked, mindlessly watching the dirt cover the bodies.

He didn't look up from his task. "We will be concerned about that if it happens." He continued shoveling dirt into the grave.

His answer didn't satisfy me, but he was correct. There was no sense in worrying about burying a child that we may or may not find. "I'm going to finish cleaning while you do that. Unless you need me here."

"I would like you to stay here with me, and them," he said with a flick of his head towards the couple. "Until they're properly buried. It was your idea to bury them." More dirt in the grave. Even with the rain, I could see the sweat pouring out of him. Every muscle in his body flexed with the weight of the wet dirt. "When I'm done, you can go back to cleaning, and I will check in on Louis." I hadn't expected him to want me to stay. He was more sensitive to their death than I gave him credit. The couple in their grave with dirt being thrown on top of them made me realize they were, in fact, dead and not just sleeping. The weight of reality hit me hard. This would be their ultimate resting place, and no one would know. No family would come and visit them. I wondered if I could find my way back here when I returned to my own time. Would someone find the bodies in two hundred years? Would they build a shopping mall or parking lot there? They would be lost in time, and no one would ever know what happened to them, except for me and Henry.

Henry tossed the last bit of dirt and covered the mounds with the rocks that he had dug up and others he had found nearby. I stood there, soaked and shivering, with my arms crossed, trying to keep in what little heat I had left in my body. I stayed throughout the time to finish burying them in their grave, even if I felt like I would never get warm again. It is strange how many times I had been cold and wet in 1754.

Henry placed the last rock and put his arm around my shoulder. "Thank you for staying out here with me. Why don't you finish up inside while I take care of Louis?" His voice was deep and comforting.

I nodded. My teeth chattered so hard I couldn't speak, only nod.

Henry walked into the cabin, having finished stabling and feeding Louis to find the blood cleaned up off the floor. He looked over at me soaked with blood, sweat, and rain, and he put a couple of logs on the fire. I focused my mind on cleaning, that I hadn't noticed how much I was shivering with cold from the fire becoming nothing more than a smolder.

"Let me do that." He took the rag and bucket from me and set them on the porch. "You are nearly frozen. You should get out of those wet clothes."

"I... I... I... can't get the stays off... fffff.. off." My teeth chattered to the point I could only stutter. I turned around with my back was towards him, "Ties in ba... a... ack."

He loosened the stays, his own hands trembled from the icy rain. He got in front of me and untied the rope I had used as a belt. "I'm going to get clean water in the bucket. The fire should start picking up soon. Stay close to it."

I nodded, and when Henry left the room, I peeled off my wet clothes. I pulled a blanket that was on the bed, wrapped it around me, and stood with my hands outstretched towards the fire. A hot bath would have been perfect, but in the middle of the woods and in an unwelcoming time, I wouldn't find a bathtub or hot running water.

"I'm going to fill the kettle and pot with water. I'll be back with more water to rinse out our clothes." Henry's voice carried over my chattering teeth. When I realized I was not alone, I closed the blanket. My exposed flesh to the fire felt good, but I didn't need Henry to see me in this state of undress. He had called me indecent when I had my shift and stays on to work. I might have given him a heart attack if he had seen me naked. That type of reaction would have done nothing for my ego.

"Thank you," I stuttered through chattered teeth.

He came back and searched through the cabinets, bringing over day old bread and butter. "They must have more food in this house."

"Whoever killed them might have taken it," I said as I gnawed on a chunk of the buttered bread.

Henry grabbed my shift—that I had thrown over a chair by the fire — and rinsed it out in the bucket. He dipped and squeezed it, and rubbed the cloth together, trying to get out one of the bigger spots of blood. He pulled off his shirt and repeated the process. With another fresh bucket of water, he gave them a good rinse and hung the clothes by the fire. On the bed was another blanket, which he wrapped himself in it, and pulled off his trousers, socks and boots and hung them next to the fire to dry.

Henry sat down on the floor next to me and held his hands out to warm them. He knew his plans of moving on were changed and we would have to stay the night. We hoped the person or people that had killed Janet and her husband wouldn't return before we left.

CHAPTER TWENTY-FIVE

"How did you know to check how if she was alive?"

My body defrosted a bit, and my teeth stopped chattering, but the cold sunk deep into my bones. "You mean when I checked her pulse on her neck pulse point? Sometimes it is easier to check on the neck than the wrist." I looked away from the fire towards Henry and noticed the dumbfounded look on his face. It didn't matter to me if he thought I was a crazy old woman or if I knew what I was talking about. I had taken a first aid class when I was younger, and I had watched enough movies to feel confident in how I checked Janet out. "I suppose I could've checked her wrist instead, but I figured it would have been more difficult finding her pulse there. Either way, it was going to be faint. Pale lips and skin told me she had lost a lot of blood. Her breathing was pretty much non-existent." The fire in the hearth crackled. My toes crept from under the blanket towards the fiery flames. "I knew there was not much we could do for her but offer comfort."

Henry went to the cabinets, pulled out two cups. Steam drifted out of the cups as he poured hot water from the kettle into each one. "There is no tea, but the hot water should help warm you up."

"Thank you," I said, as I took the hot cup of water from him. I gripped the hot cup, warming my hands. I blew over the cup before I took a sip. The hot water warmed my insides. "It's going to get dark soon. Do you think whoever did this is going to come back?"

"Not tonight, mayhap in the morn."

"Thanks for rinsing out my clothes. How did you know how to do that? I thought Lords had servants to do that for them," I said as I gave him a smile. I enjoyed poking fun at his title, especially since he tried to hide it from me. Being born in the United States in the 20th century, I had never met someone that had a title. I had expected someone with a title to act as though they were better than everyone else, but Henry proved me wrong.

"As you can see, I have no servants here to care for my every request. Unless you want to apply for the position." He waved his hand around as if to have me look around the small cabin. "Do you really find me incapable of caring for myself?" He asked as he looked over at me.

"No, not at all." I scooted closer to him. "Where I'm from, we don't have royalty. I mean, there is royalty, just not in my country."

"I'm not royalty." He scrunched his eyebrows together. "The colonies are under the English crown and..."

I needed to change the subject before he asked more questions that I didn't want to answer. "I'm not sure I'll ever be warm again. My feet feel frozen." *Nice pivot, Murray.*

"Give me your foot," he said, holding out a hand. "It helps to rub it and my hands are not as cold."

He rubbed my right foot, bringing the circulation back to it. My face flushed at the intimacy and my eyes rolled to the back of my head with the enjoyment. I closed my eyes and tried to get the thought of him out of my mind. He stopped rubbing my foot. I sat up. "You haven't finished." I put out my left foot for him to grab and laid back in front of the fire. I opened my eyes and saw him looking at me.

"Amelia, I..." Whatever he had to say at that moment was no longer important to me.

"Shhhhh." I strained to listen for the noise I thought I heard come from outside.

He dropped my foot. "What is it?"

I bolted up. "Be quiet and give me a minute." I closed my eyes to focus on the sound. "Do you hear that?"

"Hear what?"

"I'm not sure if I'm imagining it." I stood up, walked to the door, and gently opened it, afraid to scare away the sound. The rain had stopped, dusk approached, and whatever animals lurked in the woods were quiet. "I could've sworn that I heard a baby cry. Come here. Can you hear it?"

Henry stood next to me, the both of us wrapped up in blankets, as we listened to what could've been my imagination. "Jesus, I think you are right."

"It must be Tamhas. We've got to find him." I turned around and Henry was already getting dressed. I ran over and threw on my shift, still slightly damp. My stays were wet, so I left them and wrapped myself in the blanket.

"You're not going out there dressed like that." Henry scowled.

"Yes, I am. If we can hear him, he must not be that far, and you're going to need my help."

I ran outside barefoot, to the back of the cabin, in the direction of the cry. Every stick and rock pierced their announcement under my feet. A baby's faint cry lingered somewhere in front of me in the darkening woods. I stopped to listen. Twigs snapped as Henry searched to my left. The faint cry started again. The sound echoed near a fallen tree. I ran over and found the newborn under the brush next to the tree. His lips were blue from the cold. I scooped him up, looked around for Henry or the person who put the baby there, and found myself alone with the baby.

"Hello, sweetheart. Let's get you safe and warm." I bundled him next to me, wrapped the blanket around both of us, and headed back towards the cabin. His hoarse wail began to fade.

"Amelia," Henry shouted. "Where are you, woman?"

"I'm over here," I shouted back, hoping that I wouldn't upset little Tamhas any more than he already was. He needed his diaper changed, food, and warmth. Diaper–I could figure out. Food–we were out of luck; my breasts were all show, no go. Warmth–I would work on that.

The cabin was warm. I held Tamhas close to me, while Henry searched for a clean cloth through the few cabinets they had in the small cabin. I looked down at the crying baby, who wanted nothing more than to be attached to his mother's breast. His cry was faint, and he wouldn't have made it through the night if we didn't find him when we did. I didn't want to think about what could've happened, so I held him closer and gave him my pinkie to suck on. He cried in disappointment. "I'm not sure how we are going to feed him. I am certainly not equipped."

Henry handed me a linen cloth. I had no clue what I was going to do with it. When Hannah was a baby, I used disposable diapers. "Can you get me a wet cloth to wipe him down?" I studied how the one he was wearing was put together in order to figure out how to put the clean one on.

"Don't you know how to change a baby's clout?" Henry stood over me and watched me fumble with it. I wrapped it and unwrapped it a half dozen times, all the while little Tamhas cried himself hoarse.

"No," I sighed. Tears pricked my eyes. I traveled two hundred sixty-five years into the past. Escaped from kidnappers that beat me regularly. Figured out how to relieve myself in the woods. Figured out how to use a chamber pot. Caught and cooked fish. Slept in the rough. Dealt with the death, clean-up, and buried Janet and her husband. Now, I was being completely defeated by a baby's diaper.

Henry bent down and wrapped Tamhas in the clean cloth and tied the lacings around his waist to secure it. He picked up the baby and held him close to soothe him. "Why don't you finish getting dressed and we will head on our way? We need to find him a nurse."

After I dressed, he left to ready Louis for our ride to this baby's next meal, while I was desperate to get the little guy to sleep. If I couldn't feed him, I hoped that if he slept, he wouldn't realize how hungry he was and that his mother's breast would never soothe him again. Henry packed the rest of the bread and butter, additional cloths and clothes for Tamhas, and a blanket. I used a sheet from the bed to make a baby wrap to hold him close to me while we rode.

"Do you know if there is someone nearby?"

"There must be."

"But how do you know? Have you been around here before?"

"No one lives completely on their own. There should be someone not too far from here. We will head back to the road and follow it."

The sun had set, and the aura was fading to black. I hoped the moon would provide enough light for us to find our way through the night. We had traveled for about a half hour when we came upon a house with lights in the windows. Thank goodness someone was home. We approached with caution. They could've been the ones that killed Janet and her husband and left little Tamhas in the woods for dead.

I stayed on the horse with Tamhas, while Henry approached the house and spoke with the man that answered the door. He peeked around Henry and looked at me. I tipped my head down in greeting. I had no clue what Henry had told him, but I hoped we could get Tamhas fed and someone to care for him.

He offered us a place to sleep in the barn, food for us, and goat's milk for Tamhas. I dipped a cloth in the milk and let him suckle on it. We continued the process until he had his fill, and the color returned to his sweet little cheeks and lips.

Mister Lewis lived alone, and the house was not much bigger than Janet's cabin, but it had a small bedroom off the main room, whereas Janet's home was just the one room. We were grateful for a full meal and a place to sleep. There was plenty of room in the cabin next to the fireplace. I don't know why we were relegated to the barn. Tamhas wasn't the baby Jesus. Henry wasn't Joseph. I certainly wasn't the Virgin Mary. He seemed a bit put out with our appearance on his doorstep. Would the three wise men visit us?

Mister Lewis told us that Janet and her husband, Graham, had moved to the area a year ago. He and a few of the locals had helped them build their cabin and barn. He wasn't sure if they had family back in Scotland, so we were out of luck in finding relations for little Tamhas.

"Maybe a local can take on Tamhas," I said to Henry as we were settling in for the night in a pile of hay in the barn.

"No." He was firm and direct. No explanation.

"What do you mean? We cannot care for him. We are not equipped to care for an infant." I looked down at my breasts. "You know it. I know it."

"We will pack some goat's milk and take it with us, but we do not have time to go off to search for other families."

"What are you not telling me, Henry?" He was adamant about taking Tamhas with us. "Your son is in England, so do you think Tamhas is a replacement for him? Come on, you can't possibly want to take on that responsibility. I know I don't."

"We need to get to Tanaghrisson's people."

I looked down at the sleeping baby bundled next to me. His sweet lips slightly parted. "I thought we were going to Wills Creek to meet with Washington and the rest of the troops."

He blew out the candle on the small stool near the door. "Change of plans. Get some rest." Hay rustled as he adjusted into his make-shift bed. "We will leave early."

CHAPTER TWENTY-SIX

I hadn't worried about midnight feedings and diaper changes in nearly eighteen years. The memories came flooding back, like a nightmare. Tamhas woke up every couple of hours throughout the night, wanting to be fed and changed. We wouldn't have enough linen cloths to get us through more than a day at this rate. I felt like a zombie. My eyes felt as though steel weights hung from my lashes. I was forty years old and too old for that madness.

Henry was up early and prepared Louis for our ride to Tanaghrisson and the Haudensaunee. The appetizing smell of cooked food wafted through the air. I could also smell the stench of the barnyard, which was much less appetizing. I longed to slip into a booth at *Betsy's Biscuits* with Beth and indulge in a stack of french toast drenched in maple syrup, a glass of orange juice, and mug of piping hot coffee, while we chat about the subject of one her upcoming classes or one of my research projects. Afterwards, a stroll over to *By the River Bookshop*, sign a few copies of my latest novel, chat with

Maggie, and pet her tabby cat, Pom, and her Dachshund, Fritz, before I headed home to work. Instead, I get to wake up to the smell of horseshit. Also, a crying baby that wants food–which was a constant struggle to provide–and a diaper change. All of that prior to spending the day on a horse. Poor Louis. The remarkable horse was a good boy, and put up with all that madness with grace. I thought I would get used to riding after a couple of days. When I dismounted, I walked bow-legged, like I was one of those cartoon cowboys. I was a hot mess. All of us were a mess.

We had breakfast in the house, replenished a couple of canteens with goat's milk for Tamhas, cleaned the cloths that were soiled throughout the night and tied them to the saddlebags to dry as we rode. Then we stocked up with food for us to get through the day. Henry offered our host a payment, which he graciously accepted.

The warm morning sun, combined with yesterday's rain, left the air thick with humidity. The multiple layers of clothes hung heavy with sweat by the time we were out of sight of the cabin.

"Are you going to tell me why we need to bring him with us?" Cranky from the lack of sleep and too warm with my clothes, sun, the baby strapped next to me, Henry's warm body behind me, and Louis' overworked body between my legs, I was not in the mood to deal with an infant or Henry, for that matter. Henry didn't say a word. "Listen, I thought we were beyond this whole keeping secrets and not talking to each other."

"It is not that I do not want to tell you. I am not sure if I should or how to say it without sounding as though I am a lunatic."

"Well, I'm going to have to walk for a bit. I'm overheating. That should give you time to figure yourself out." I snapped at him. I was too hot, too tired, and too old to dance around whatever he was trying to decide to tell me.

We both dismounted, allowing Louis to cool down without the extra weight and heat of our bodies. "Do you remember when I told you that Tanaghrisson visited me while I was on my way to the fort?"

I wiped the sweat away from my forehead with my kerchief. "Yes, he said that it was going to be attacked. He must have seen the French encampment, which I escaped from."

Henry fidgeted with the reins in his hands. "He also told me of a dream that he had. He said that in his dream, I would meet the woman that walked through time and that I should bring his people the child."

"He said what?" I felt the blood drain from my face. I repeatedly gulped until I buried my fear of what he would ask or say next.

His pace continued. "Listen, I know it sounds strange. There's more. Well, then I met you, but you didn't have a child with you. I thought nothing of our meeting." His voice was quick and jagged. I had never seen him this uneasy.

My breath shortened. "Right." I was about to hyperventilate.

"Then you asked me if I believed in time travel. Mayhap that was just a coincidence," he continued his story, looking straight ahead. "But then, you found Tamhas. I'm not sure what the walking through time has to do with anything, but here you are and..."

"And here we are." I swallowed. "Headed to see

Tanaghrisson to bring me and this child to him. Okay." I couldn't tell him about me walking through time, but he had believed what Tanaghrisson had told him. He might believe me.

"Cheese and rice, Henry. I need to tell you something and I'm not sure how or if you will believe me."

His paced slowed. He cocked an eyebrow at me. If I wasn't about to explode in a nervous bundle, I might find that utterly charming.

"If it will make you feel better, I don't understand what I'm about to tell you, but the truth is... the truth is..." deep breath, "ugh... the truth is, I am from the future. One minute I am in the twenty-first century walking into Fort Ashby, the next minute I am passed out and waking up in the year seventeen fifty-four."

"Do you hear what you are saying? This is absurd." Henry turned away from me and quickened his pace. "Why would you say that? After everything we have been through, why would you lie to me? Why would you play on what I just told you about what Tanaghrisson told me?"

Why in the world would he get worked up over that, after what he had told me? "I told you," I got angry at being called a liar. "I told you from the very beginning that I wouldn't lie to you. You need to know why I can't always tell you everything. Why would you believe me when I tell you I came here from two hundred sixty-five years in the future?"

"*If* I believe you came from the future," Henry said, he emphasized the word "if" in a way that crushed my hope that he would believe me. "Why would you come here? Why would you go with the French?" His arms flailed about. Louis snorted in disapproval.

Tamhas stirred in his wrap. I patted his bottom to soothe him. "There is a lot to unpack here, and I will try to explain it all as best as I can. If it becomes too much for you, let me know and I will stop." I rubbed my forehead.

He drew in a long, deep breath. "Continue."

Slowly, I explained I was conducting research on a book about George Washington's involvement in the French and Indian War. I had gone to Fort Ashby, which doesn't exist in seventeen fifty-four, but would be built in the next year. It was there that I had stumbled upon a French detachment headed by Jumonville and Bouchard, thinking they were a reenactment troop. The explanation as I thought they were a group of men that liked to dress up and pretend they were living in the past. I sounded like a knucklehead. Instead of helping me, they abducted and beat me, all for the information that I had in my notebook.

"Exactly what is contained in this notebook?"

"Dates and locations of conflicts where George Washington will be for the next few years."

Silence hung in the air, except for the birds and the bugs. The bugs were always around, ready to feast on my blood. They nipped, gnawed, and bit at me, which irritated me further. Why wouldn't the birds swoop down and have a nice, tasty, buggy lunch? I smacked a freeloader bug before it made a meal out of my sweaty neck.

"Why? How?" Henry's mind clearly raced all over the place with this information. His eyes searched my face for the truth. He turned away from me and looked down the path in front of us.

"I was, or is it will be?" I said, confused with the idea of past and future and present and where we currently fit.

"Basically, I am writing a book and I wanted to visit the places he had gone in order to make the story more accurate and to get a feel of where things happened. Jumonville Glen is coming up, but I only remember a few items on the list. There will be a skirmish that will help launch the French and Indian War."

"The French and Indian War? We are not at war with the French in the colonies." Henry pulled Louis to a stop.

"War is coming. Until now, it has been just border disputes and the occasional skirmish. There will be a long war you will have with the French, and this is only the beginning." I continued to pat Tamhas. "We need to meet with Washington, and I need to get my notebook back from Jumonville."

"Where is this Jumonville Glen? I am familiar with areas around here and the only Jumonville I have heard of is the insufferable Jumonville you had mentioned." We started walking down the path again. My legs cramped. They just couldn't get a break from the constant riding. "If he had land nearby, I would know about it."

"Yes, I remember him telling me something about New France." I pulled a sweaty Tamhas out of the wrap. We both needed to be cooled down. "Well, maybe it's his family's land or something. I don't know. I had some of my notes in the notebook and other notes on my laptop. Neither one is available to me. My notebook is with Jumonville, and my laptop is in the twenty-first century."

"What's a laptop?"

"It's complicated for me to explain, but it contains my research and is safely two hundred sixty-five years in the future, out of the hands of Jumonville, and also out of my hands."

"Your notebook is not as safe."

"No," I said as I tucked a tendril of hair that had stuck to the sweat on my face back behind my ear. "And I don't know how to get it, but we need to secure it from that bastard."

"I do not believe he is a bastard. However, you are correct. We need to secure it."

"Are you beginning to believe me?"

"About being from the future?"

"Yes, about me being from the future."

"There is what Tanaghrisson told me. I don't believe you lied to me previously." He seemed to think through the evidence laid in front of him. "I may not understand how it could've happened, but it would explain your odd clothes and some of the strange things you say and your lack of understanding of how women do things here. I've seen things I couldn't explain." He huffed a laugh and trailed off into a memory he kept to himself. "Are things really that different in the future?"

I fought the urge for a good kick to his shin, or really could yell at him for the lack of understanding of 'how to be a woman' comment. *Sigh.* "The future is so completely different. I don't know what I'm doing here. I feel so completely and totally lost."

"We need to get to Tanaghrisson's people."

"We need to get my notebook." At that moment, Tamhas cried. I rubbed his little back in order to soothe the little bundle against my chest. Notebook aside, I felt a tremendous weight lifted from my shoulders.

"What we need to do is feed the baby."

The smell of a full diaper hit my nose as I moved little Tamhas over to my left shoulder. "What we need to do is change the little guy. Whoa. I'm not sure goat's milk agrees with him. He needs a wet nurse." That was going to be a long trip to find Tanaghrisson.

CHAPTER TWENTY-SEVEN

"First, I'm not too old to have a baby," I said, pointed finger ready to impale the young barmaid. "Second, just serve the food and drinks."

"She is going to spit in your cider." Henry said to me with a chuckle as he crossed his arms in front of chest and sat back in his chair.

"And you best keep your spit in your damned mouth. I'm watching you," I yelled across the tavern. A hush fell over the crowd and all eyes shot towards me. The old witch in me wanted to hiss at the nosey men. I turned towards Henry and said through gritted teeth, "If it wasn't for the baby strapped to my chest, I would have grabbed her by the throat."

"Are women from your time always this violent and outspoken?" Henry leaned closer to me. "I don't believe anyone here thought a lady of your standing would be full of vinegar. Mayhap, you could smolder the fire." He rubbed Tamhas' back, still strapped to my chest.

"Oh? Really, I wouldn't have laid a hand on her. She just made me so angry. She just didn't need to tell me I was too old to have a baby." My nostrils flared. "I think she was hoping to get her claws in you. The way she looked at you when you walked in the door was obvious to me." I wiggled my eyebrows at him. "And the disappointment at me following behind you with the baby. I can't believe you didn't notice."

Henry looked back towards the barmaid loaded up with tankards to bring to the patrons and raised an eyebrow at the man behind the counter. The young woman appeared to be around the age of my daughter, Hannah, eighteen, light brown hair and eyes, short, slim build, and a plain face sprinkled with a few freckles across her nose and cheeks. The barman looked old enough to be her father. Perhaps it was her husband. In 1754, you could never tell if a young woman was married to a man that was old enough to be her father or if he was her father. It really wasn't any of my business, but she seemed to think that my fertility and Henry were her business.

"Do you think the owner's first name or last name is Allan?" I asked, sinking back into the chair.

"Why would I know?" Henry looked around the room at the lively bunch of diners that filled the room's ten or eleven tables.

The barman filled a few tankards and placed them on the barmaid's tray. "The sign outside, the one that hung by the door, it said Allan's Tavern on it. So, which do you think it is? First or last name?" I asked.

A loud roar of laughter came from the handful of men that stood that at the bar, drinking and enjoying each other's company. Plates of food and tankards of beer, cider, and other concoctions covered the available space on every dark-colored table. Apparently, we stumbled into the hottest club this side of the Potomac. The room had a few lanterns lit, but no roaring fire. With the number of bodies occupying the room, it would have been too hot. The town was small, a couple dozen buildings that offered various businesses dotted the road. Henry paid the stable to care for Louis for the night. We needed to find the inn after dinner.

"Shall we wager on it?" Henry gave a mischievous smile. "The lady shall make her guess and I will take the other. Whoever loses shall wake up and tend to Tamhas throughout the night."

"You're on, sucker!" I stuck my hand out to give a hearty handshake to seal the deal.

Henry took it and laughed. "When you get up with him, pay mind as to not wake me."

"So, it's a deal?" I scowled. "I'm saying it's his first name. Gotta be. And it will be you that will need to not wake me."

Henry folded his arms and leaned back in his chair. He looked across the room to size up the barman. "It is a deal. I shall take the surname."

The young barmaid handed a few drinks to other patrons before cautiously approaching our table. The barman, with our food on plates, arrived behind her. My eyes narrowed at her approach. I didn't know what sort of secret sauce–or spit–she would add to my food or drink.

"I must apologize for my daughter's indiscretion, my lord." From the way he looked down in embarrassment, I would have guessed this was not the first time he had to apologize for her behavior.

Henry sat tall in his chair. "Your daughter's comments were inappropriate, and she spoke above her station. You should put a rein on that before my wife truly loses her patience with her."

I almost snorted out my cider but contained my laughter, as to not wake little Tamhas. He had slept through my yelling and the commotion, but the jostle made him stir.

"Of course, my lord, my lady." He bowed his head in each of our direction. "Please, accept this meal and drinks as an apology for her wayward behavior and to celebrate your good fortune on the birth of your child."

I took a victorious swig of the cider. Henry nodded a thank you to the barkeep. "Thank you for your hospitality... I offer my humblest apologies. I am afraid we haven't been introduced. I am Henry Spencer, and this is my wife, Amelia Spencer. And you are?"

"Daniel Allan, my lord," the barman said. My soul crushed into a disappointed little ball at the loss of the bet. "The girl is my daughter, Eloise."

"Pleased." Henry responded. I swear I could hear the absolute elation in his voice. "My family will need a place to sleep tonight. Do you have any available rooms?"

"I will have Eloise prepare a room for you." With a nod of his head, the barman took his leave from us.

Henry turned to me. "It will not trouble you to stay here? We can continue and find an inn elsewhere."

At the rear of the room, I noticed a set of stairs that led to the second floor. I leaned into Henry so only he could hear me. "We can stay here. But I will have you know, that will mean only one bed. Things might be different where I'm from, or should I say, when I'm from, but I don't want to intrude too much on your delicate gentleman sensibilities."

Henry snorted a laugh. "We've slept plenty of times with

the two or three of us. I think we can figure out one bed. Besides, I already called you my wife. No one will think it odd for us to stay in the same room." Henry took a bite of chicken and a gulp of cider. "I will be more than happy to sleep on the floor. You and little Tamhas can take the bed. It will be easier for you to tend to him throughout the night so I can sleep."

"You won't make this easy on me, will you?"

Henry took my hand and brought my knuckles to his lips. "Certainly not." My entire body flushed.

We finished dinner, and Eloise showed us to our room. It was small, not much bigger than the single bed that was provided. There was a chair, washstand, small bed, and a small oil-skinned window which let a sliver of the evening light through. Henry dropped our bags on the floor. The roar from the tavern's evening shenanigans crept through the floorboards. I fed and changed Tamhas, who had been quite content bundled up next to my chest. "We will need to get more goat's milk before we leave tomorrow."

"I'll make the necessary arrangements." Henry turned to leave.

"Oh, and before you go down... I need to wash his diapers and the wrap. Can you find some sort of bucket and clean water?"

He stopped with his hand on the handle. "You don't have to change him all the time." He sounded frustrated. Each time I had to change a diaper, it lengthened our travel time.

"Says who? You? How many times have you dealt with diaper rash?" I raised a feisty eyebrow at Henry. Maybe it was two eyebrows. I didn't have Henry's single eyebrow lifting skills. "I have, and once is more than enough. There is no way I will leave a stinky, soiled diaper on a baby. Especially when I have the little nugget attached to my chest."

"As you wish. Anything else, Lady Amelia?" He asked with an exaggerated bow.

"Ask for another room if you keep that up."

Breakfast and goat's milk arrangements made, cloth diapers cleaned and hung to dry, Tamhas fed and settled in for the next couple of hours, and it was time for my exhausted head to hit the pillow. It wasn't the most comfortable of beds, but it wasn't the ground or a pile of hay. I hoped there wouldn't be any bedbugs or lice to keep me up through the night. Those were some of the last things on the planet that I wanted to deal with in my exhaustion.

CHAPTER TWENTY-EIGHT

We left the next morning with Louis raring to get a move on, Tamhas bundled to my chest, and Henry behind me. "We should be at Tanaghrisson's by the afternoon."

"How do you know where we're headed?"

"It's close to one of my tobacco plantations. That is how we met."

"Plantation? I thought you said you didn't enslave people." My blood boiled. *Had he lied to me?*

"I do not."

"Then how do you run a plantation?" *Did I hope to catch him in a lie?*

"I told you, indentured servants. Most are on contract for transportation to the colonies. They can either stay or leave when their contract is completed." He said matter-of-factly. "The others are renters."

I supposed he hadn't lied to me. "Do you spend much of your time at the plantation, or are you always out running around with Washington?"

Henry laughed at my question. I didn't find it funny. Perhaps he found me naïve. "I don't run around with Washington. I joined the Virginia Regiment only of recent, at the request of Lieutenant Governor Dinwiddie."

"But you're a captain. I don't understand." I knew a bit about the military and knew there were the officer ranks lieutenant to general and that the men worked their way up through the ranks. Washington had been serving with the Virginia Regiment for a few years and had quickly worked his way to lieutenant colonel, but he was still so young and Henry, well, he wasn't that young.

"I served for a couple of years and was a lieutenant when I left His Majesty's service and eventually moved to Virginia after Caroline died. Governor Dinwiddie asked me to offer my services and here I am."

I pulled my hat a little further over my eyes. The sun beamed over our heads. "How long have you been working with Washington?"

"Two months. Taking command of the Fort Prince George while Captain Trent was off taking care of other business was going to be my first assignment. That was not the greatest start to my illustrious career with the French taking the fort before I could arrive."

"You've only been in the Regiment for two months? You could've fooled me." Tamhas stirred in his wrap. Our bodies were producing enough heat to cook an egg. "These past couple of weeks we've spent together, you've known where to go and who to speak with. I thought you had been doing this forever."

"I've lived in Virginia for nearly six years." He laughed. "Hardly a newcomer to the colonies or the people. In fact, I am not in full-time service. I am called up when needed. I spend the rest of my time managing my businesses and estates."

By my hunger calculations, and the sun beaming down on our heads, it was a little past noon when four of Tanaghrisson's men approached us. They sat on their horses at the edge of the woods. The Haudenosaunee men led us to the encampment to speak with Tanaghrisson. Women and men worked outside of longhouses, young children played, older children tended to the gardens, and all turned to look at us when we approached.

"Are you sure we are supposed to be here?" I whispered to Henry.

"Yes, Tanaghrisson told me to bring you and the child to him. It will be fine. I won't allow any harm to come to you."

I gulped hard. "But did he specifically ask for me?" My pulse quickened. "How did he know to ask for me? Are you sure he doesn't want me dead?" My voice shook.

"I'm not sure of anything right about now." I could sense Henry felt the same uneasiness I experienced as we approached.

Tanaghrisson, the Half-King, stood at the doorway of a hut, flanked by two people. One was an older woman, who I later found out was the clan mother; the other was a man that appeared to be close to my age. Tanaghrisson appeared to be mid-fifties; his skin weathered. His gray hair laid down his back in two long braids. "Thank you for welcoming us," Henry began. Our hosts welcomed us into the shelter they had exited and sat down. Tamhas squirmed. After these few days with him, I knew if we didn't feed him and change his diaper, we would experience an epic meltdown in three-month-old proportions.

"I must apologize," I interrupted the stare down I had received by the three hosts. Either they were sizing me up or offended by the interruption. "I need to get Tamhas, the baby, fed and changed." I motioned towards the child wrapped at my chest. "The goat's milk, that is what I've been using to feed him, is in a bag on our horse, along with clean cloths. I... uh..." I looked over towards Henry, desperate for acknowledgement or help.

After some negotiation, I agreed to follow the woman outside to meet with a group of women working next to one of the other longhouses. As I understood it, one woman had agreed to care for Tamhas while I sat in the discussion with Tanaghrisson and Henry.

I hesitated as I handed Tamhas to her. I didn't want to care for a baby, but at this moment, I found it difficult to part with him. Where did those maternal instincts come from? I knew it wouldn't be for long. She would care for him while we discussed the situation with the French. Perhaps I felt guilty for passing the responsibility on to someone else.

Tanaghrisson nodded to us as we returned. I tried hard to hide my anxiety. I twisted my ring around my finger. Henry had mentioned that Tanaghrisson wanted the woman who walked through time and the child. I closed my eyes and hoped that they wouldn't throw me on a pyre, having deemed as some terrible spirit.

Our hosts stared at me. My eyes shifted from one to the other. Tanaghrisson broke the tension and told a story that I didn't understand. My recollection of the story doesn't matter, it is not my story to tell. Only everyone laughed at it, except for me. Henry said he would explain it to me later, but he never did. Without notice, the mood changed and hung heavy in the room, when Tanaghrisson stated I was the woman that walked through time. It wasn't a question, and I couldn't deny it.

"I, uh, well, I suppose that's me." I looked towards Henry. He grabbed hold of my hand and gave it a squeeze.

He told me the story of how they watched the area and saw the French pour in like a flood. They were curious about me when they saw me escape and run to the fort.

"You were watching me?" I was taken aback. They saw I was in danger with the French, but they chose to not get involved. "Well, yes. I escaped the French. I had to warn the British that they were going to be attacked and they had no chance against the French."

They encouraged me to continue my story about the French and the British. "There will be many deaths and battles over the boundary of the land, but the British will win in the end." Henry's head snapped at me. His eyes bore a hole deep into my soul. I looked over at him and my shoulders sank. What could I do? I had told him about the notebook with some of Washington's upcoming battles, but I hadn't told him too much about the future of the war. "At least, that is the way it is supposed to be. Jumonville, the guy that had held me captive, has my notebook. If he can get to Washington, I'm referring to Lieutenant Colonel George Washington, he will try to kill him. I don't know where the future of the country will end up."

The Haudenosaunee spoke among themselves and asked if I knew the dates and locations of the battles and who would win.

"Well, some. I don't know them all by heart. There's Jumonville Glen, Fort Necessity, and sometime next year will be a march to Fort Duquesne. I'm not sure of dates or exact locations."

Henry looked towards me. "Why haven't you mentioned this to me?"

"I mean, I mentioned some of it. I told you I needed to get the notebook back." Henry's face dropped in disappointment. I mouthed, "I'm sorry," to him. My heart ached. *Add this to the growing list of the times that I felt like a complete ass.*

Henry sat up straight and looked at Tanaghrisson. "We are to join with Lieutenant Colonel Washington at Wills Creek." Henry said, avoiding looking at me. I really screwed things up with him.

"Listen, I'm not sure how much you knew or if I had over-shared and will cause some time catastrophe, but whatever happens, I need to get the notebook from Jumonville."

Tanaghrisson told me they would find Jumonville and see that I get the notebook back. Tamhas and the murder of his parents were next on the docket. As Henry expected, they were not responsible for their deaths. The woman sitting next to Tanaghrisson said they would adopt him into her clan. It was her decision. I admired the respect she held with her people. The walls expanded as I let out the enormous sigh of relief from the weight of caring for the infant was taken off my shoulders.

They offered us food and a place to sleep in the longhouse, which we gladly took. I tossed and turned. Henry slept nearby, with his back towards me. He hadn't made eye contact or spoken to me since our meeting with Tanaghrisson. I could hear Tamhas cry a few times throughout the night, but whoever was caring for him soothed him. I didn't need to worry about him anymore.

I was excited about our journey tomorrow. I would get to meet the young George Washington. Sure, he was young enough to be my child—if I had a child at eighteen, but that didn't matter, he would be the first president of our new country. Meet George Washington and save his life? No problem, just a day in the life of Amelia Murray. Who am I kidding? I was terrified that we would fail, and Virginia would become a colony of France. *Jumonville mustn't use my notes and change the course of American history.*

CHAPTER TWENTY-NINE

"Are you still refusing to talk to me?" I huffed out. Henry, stubborn as a mule, hadn't said a word to me since the night before and all throughout the morning. I contemplated returning the silent treatment to him, but I thought he would be more annoyed if I talked to him. To be fair, I was the one that kept information from him, but I didn't think it was as critical as he made it out. "I told you that a war was coming. I told you that Jumonville had my notebook." Excuses, Murray. That's all you're giving. Excuses.

He grumbled. "You held back so much information from me. I took care of you for the past two weeks. You just met Tanaghrisson, you informed him of critical events. You trusted someone you had only met before you trusted me."

"He already knew about me. You told me yourself, and you failed to mention that you were to take me to him. He can help me get back the notebook."

"Not only that," he continued, making no response to what I said. "You easily gave Tamhas away. You didn't know that woman and you just handed him over, like he meant nothing to you."

"Tamhas didn't know us, either. He wasn't mine or yours to begin with." I could feel my face flush with anger. My neck burned hot as the fire spread throughout my body. "I'm not equipped to take care of an infant. Are you? If we meet up with Washington. If we find out where Jumonville and Bouchard are. If we get the book back from Jumonville. That's a lot of ifs, and none involves carting an infant into the middle of this... this... madness." My arms flailed about. Louis huffed with agitation.

"Damn you, woman." That stopped me and Louis in our tracks. I was taken aback. I held my breath as I waited for his next outburst. Louis jerked from Henry's nudge and started walking. He took a deep breath. I could feel the exhale on the back of my neck. Apparently, Henry had better anger management skills than I. "What more can I do to gain your trust? What is it going to take to get you to show a bit more compassion?"

"You have it," I said as I half-turned to look at him. "I just didn't know how much you could handle knowing. Besides, I still don't know why I'm here. I would have thought if the power-that-be wanted me here, I would at least know why. All I was just supposed to do was to do some research. That was it. I didn't ask for any of this." Tears threatened to erupt. "As far as Tamhas is concerned, well, that was a coincidence. I took care of him until we found someone better equipped to care for an infant."

"That is what I mean." Henry's voice was louder and angrier than I had heard from him before. Apparently, I tested his power over his emotions. I cowered. *Would he strike me?* "I'm not sure if you have noticed, but you weren't the only person taking care of Tamhas. It's not all about you." We weren't the happy little family he dreamt up.

That stopped my breath. My blood and frustration surged up my neck. "You're right. It's not all about me. If *you* haven't noticed," I said with a decided emphasizes on "you." My frustration rose to meet Henry's level and volume. "I am trying to save the future of the United States and get my notebook back from Jumonville, so he doesn't kill the future President Washington. All the while, we kept getting sidetracked by side quests. Mistress Lovett's, Tamhas, Tanaghrisson, and that little floozy at the tavern." I rubbed my forehead. "I don't belong here and just want to go home. To my time. To my quiet and lonely house. To Hannah and my friends. To running water and showers. To flushable toilets and toilet paper. To cars. To electricity. To grocery stores on every damned corner. To my bed. This... this..." I flailed my arms around to emphasize everything around us. "This is stupid."

Frustration, anger, and lack of understanding the world around me it all crashed to a head at that moment. My face burned hot with anger. Tears pricked at my eyes and there was no way I was going to swallow it down. I cried. I wanted to cry forever.

Henry was quiet. I didn't want him to say anything. At that point, there was nothing he could say that could make the situation better. The tears and snot flowed. I looked down at the sleeve of my dress and contemplated to use it to wipe my nose. I pulled my scarf out from around my shoulders to use that instead. Before I could remove it, Henry handed me one of Tamhas's clean cloth diapers that had been tucked away in the bag. My face ached from the crying. I knew I was going to end up with a headache that I wouldn't be able to get rid of without a pill or two from my medicine cabinet. *Damn this place and the lack of a bottle of aspirin.* My nose was raw from the blowing. I felt stupid for crying. I felt emotionally weak. The time travel and all that surrounded it took its emotional and physical toll on me.

Henry pulled Louis close to a stream. We were always close to one, as they spread throughout the area. We dismounted in silence. I left him to tend to the horse, while I meandered to the stream. The water was cool and allowed respite for my face that was hot from tears and the midday sun. If I stayed there much longer, I would have to invent air conditioning. The multiple layers of clothing didn't help keep my body temp down. I wanted to strip down, lay in the stream, and just cool down. That would have been another distraction to my mission—a distraction that I couldn't afford.

"Feeling better?" Henry asked as I walked over to where he sat in the shade while Louis nibbled on some grass. He sat on the ground, leaned against a tree, with his eyes closed as if he was taking a nap. I joined him against the tree.

I threw a stone towards the stream. Thud. Missed. "I'm sorry for my outburst earlier. It's all been... it's been..."

"Overwhelming," he finished my sentence for me.

"Yeah," I said as I scrunched my face up to hold back the tears that threatened to make their reappearance. A deep shuddered sigh escaped. I picked up another small stone, tossed in my hand a few times and lobbed it towards the stream again. Plop.

"You know," he began. He placed his hand on top of

mine. "You are not doing this alone. We are partners in this adventure."

"Ah, yes. If I remember correctly," I sat up, looked at him, and gave a smile. My anxiety and tears were disappearing. "It was you that told the floozy's dad that I was your wife. You're stuck with me now, buddy."

"I need to ask. You've used the word floozy twice to describe the barmaid, and by the tone in your voice, am I to assume that is not a compliment to her?"

I snorted out a laugh. The term might have been old-fashioned for me, but I had to assume that it wasn't even a word used in the 18th century. "Harlot?"

"Ah, I see." He looked down at my hand firmly placed in his.

"Well, she called me old, and she looked as though she wanted to eat you alive." I had to pause for a moment. I wasn't sure my 21st century colloquialisms would translate very well to an 18th century man. Turning towards Henry, I sat up straight. "Not really eat you, but she wanted to devour you. With passion. Nibble on your bits." *Open mouth, insert foot.* "Oh, geez. I'm not as tactful as the women from this time. I don't think I'm saying it correctly." I sank back into the tree.

"Oh, I think you're doing well." I could feel his shoulders shake from trying to stifle his laughter from me. "Are you well enough to continue to Wills Creek? We will need to stop tonight, but if we leave early, we will arrive midday."

"Right. No more distractions. Let's do this." I smacked my hands on my thighs. Henry offered a hand to help me up. "Thank you. I know this couldn't have been on your schedule of things to do for the Regiment. Is this going to cause problems for you? Am I going to cause problems?"

Henry took Louis by the reins. "No need to concern yourself. I'm sure Lieutenant Colonel Washington will understand."

"Man, I hope so." Skirts tucked in to prevent chaffing, and we were on our way. I leaned forward in the saddle and stroked Louis's neck. I hoped Washington's ambition to make a name for himself wouldn't clash with Henry's help. The last thing I wanted to be around was a struggle for power.

As we approached Wills Creek the next morning, I felt uneasy. I shifted in the saddle. I shifted again. My stomach clenched tight on itself. I twisted my ring around my finger. Another shift in the saddle. The camp comprised rows of tents and a couple of small buildings. There must have been at least a hundred men milling about.

"What is it?" Henry placed a hand on my shoulder. "You're making Louis want to jump out of his skin."

"I want to jump out of my skin. So sorry, Louis," I stroked his neck in a pathetic attempt to calm us both down. "I know this place."

"Future or present?"

"Present, well, sort of. I walked through here with Jumonville's unit. Off in those woods over there." I pointed beyond our rallying point. "Fort Ashby is a couple day's walk from here. Well, when Fort Ashby will exist, it will be not too far from here. Over those hills, somewhere." I took in a deep breath. "We need to meet with Washington."

"*I need* to meet with Washington. *You* need to be patient." He rubbed my arm to reassure me he had a plan.

I snorted. "When have you known me to be patient?"

Henry belly laughed at my comment, which caused heads to turn in our direction.

"You might want to stifle your laugh, my lord. You don't want to bring too much attention to us."

"Your being here is going to be more attention than either of us can manage. We need to find Lovett before I find Washington."

Sergeant Lovett was a man in his early sixties, with stocky build, gray hair, and seemed like a perfect fit for Mistress Lovett. He took care of Louis and offered us a bucket of clean water to wash up before heading to find Lieutenant Colonel Washington.

"If I thought I was nervous about anything before, I certainly am now." I spun my ring around my finger. I wanted to throw up. We walked through the camp to find the young man that would, one day, become the first President of the United States. If I could keep him safe from Jumonville and Bouchard. "What are we going to tell him? We can't tell him I'm some woman from the future you picked up on the side of the road."

"Right. We'll tell him the abridged truth. Simple. Yes?"

"Yeah. Simple." I didn't believe him or myself.

The first thing I noticed about George Washington was that he stood a little over six feet tall. The second was he was young. I couldn't imagine Hannah or any of her friends leading that many men into battle. He was attractive and had a charming presence about him. Our introduction was quite formal. He bowed to me, and I wasn't sure what I was supposed to do. The 21st century version of Amelia had to think about customs and courtesies that were out of my realm of working knowledge. *Curtsy, Murray!* I grabbed the sides of my red coat and my indigo petticoat and gave a curtsy that I was sure would make the queen of England proud. Well, she probably couldn't care less what my curtsy looked like. It wasn't like I was going to meet her. We hadn't discussed what I was supposed to tell him. I obviously couldn't tell him I came from two hundred sixty-five years in the future and that my notebook could end up being his demise.

Thankfully, Henry spoke up and explained that a French detachment had captured me, escaped, and warned the soldiers at Fort Prince George of the impending danger.

"The rest of the troops from the fort arrived over a week ago. Why have you taken so long to join us?"

"We ran into a few complications along the way," Henry said. Washington gave him a look, contemplating how much he believed what he had to say.

"You've been with the Regiment for a couple of months. Do not let this reflect the rest of your career," Washington was direct. *This arrogant kid is going to be our first president?*

"Are you…" I burst out. Henry raised his hand to silence me. He was right. That was not my fight, and it could've been disastrous for him and me.

"Does the lady have something to add?"

"No. I mean. Yes." Henry shot me a look. I had to fix my outburst. "Lieutenant Colonel Washington, I unwillingly spent a great deal of time with a French detachment in and around this area. They took me from nearby, on their way to the fort. They moved through the woods around this area to avoid being seen. Captain Spencer graciously helped me recover from the immense abuse." I shifted my weight and twisted my ring. "Are you, I mean, do you have any plans to take back the fort?" I didn't want to meet up with Jumonville soon and hoped that we wouldn't trek to Fort Duquesne.

"Madame, I appreciate your candor and your willingness to help. Please note that I cannot discuss our troop movements with you." Washington looked down at his papers. "Captain Spencer, when you have the opportunity, you may escort Mistress Murray to safety."

"Lieutenant Colonel Washington, sir, if I may," I began. "Jumonville has in his possession something that it is very near and dear to my heart. We must retrieve it from him. I suspect my departure from him will not be the last time I see him. I would like to accompany you, Captain Spencer, and the rest of the troops until I can get it back."

Washington turned to Henry. "Captain, you have already taken on responsibility for this woman. If I allow this to happen, she will be under your charge." Washington looked at me. "Do I make myself clear?"

With that, a couple of bows, curtsy, and a thank you later, Henry escorted me back to the tents where we had met up with Lovett. "Is he what you thought he would be?"

"Well, sort of, I guess. I wasn't expecting him to have an accent like that."

Henry laughed. "Whatsoever do you mean?"

"Well, you have a little bit of an English accent. Do I know what part of England? Nope. I guess you've lived in the colonies long enough to lose your accent." I looked over at him. He looked bewildered. "I live near Fredericksburg, the same Fredericksburg that Washington is from." I leaned in close to whisper, "just a couple of hundred years in the future."

"So, you expected his accent to be the same as your accent?"

"I don't have an accent." Bewildered, I looked at him.

"You have an accent."

"Uh, I suppose I do." I shrugged. *Did I have an accent?* I hadn't thought of me having an accent. I just thought I sounded American. That was an absurd and egotistical way of looking at it. "I just didn't expect it to sound the way it does. It's like part English, but not. It's close to my accent. I don't know what I was expecting, it just wasn't that."

"You truly are a fascinating woman, Mistress Amelia Murray." Henry smiled and shook his head. "And it seems you are even more so my responsibility."

"I'm beginning to think I'm just weird and that I will be your demise." I twisted a smile.

CHAPTER THIRTY

"Back towards the fort? I can't seem to get away from this area, can I?" I exclaimed to Henry one evening.

It was mid-May as we headed north to a place called the Great Meadows. Washington's troops were expanding the road over the Allegheny Mountains and each day brought us closer. Most of the days I had spent helping where I could and stayed out of the way when I couldn't. Henry and I kept our conversations in the present for fear that someone may overhear us. Social decorum kept us from being alone together. It didn't matter that we had spent weeks together traveling alone. When it came time to be in front of the men and his commanding officer, Henry fulfilled the expectations of his position. I found it charming and annoying at the same time. I knew the closer we got to the Great Meadows, the closer we got to the conflict that started the war.

Great Meadows was a favorite of Washington's. It had a fairly open area, surrounded by the mountains, with a stream that ran through the middle of it. The surrounding woods would offer the opportunity for hunting and pasture for the horses, cows, and goats we brought with us. We set up our tents and planned to make it a base for the next couple of weeks while trees were felled, and the road widened.

"This is our current mission. The road will make it easier to move troops north." Henry plopped down next to the fire I used for cooking.

"I know it's just been, well, boring. Believe it or not, I got used to our adventures, our side quests." I slid the sewing basket into my tent. "Now, all I do is cook, clean, mend clothes, and really, that is the least exciting thing I could do." I will not confirm that I might have stuck my lower lip out in a childish pout.

"I thought you said all of this was... what was your turn of phrase? Stupid and that you didn't like all the distractions." Henry laughed at me while he poked at the fire. It was early evening, and we finally had the opportunity to sit down and relax.

"I'm thinking I prefer the distractions." I sat back against a log. The long day had finally ended, and I was spent.

"I can take you away from here." Henry looked away from the fire towards me. "Would you like to go back to Fredericksburg? I have a home in Williamsburg if you would like to go there instead."

"My home outside of Fredericksburg won't exist for another two hundred years." I picked up the stick Henry used to poke the fire and poked holes into the ground with it. What I needed was a distraction, and stabbing the ground seemed to be an excellent distraction. "I would like to see your plantation or your home in Williamsburg."

"My plantation is not the safest of places with the

ongoing quarrels with the French. Mistress Lovett currently occupies the other."

"You own the Lovett's house? They're your tenants? Why didn't you mention that before?" My eyes could burn a hole through him. "Besides, before I go anywhere, you know I need to get my notebook back." I wouldn't dwell on the Lovetts. "So, I can't leave here. I just get to pack up camp, set up camp, mend, wash clothes, and cook, biding my time until we meet up with Jumonville. I feel so domesticated. Blah." Stab. Poke. Stab. Poke. Poor ground, it took the abuse.

"We'll figure out how to get your notebook back. Yesterday, Lieutenant Colonel Washington sent seventy-five men with Gist to search the area for the French."

I perked up. "Well, that's great. Why didn't we go with him?"

"Captain Spencer," Private Brown came running over to us. "Lieutenant Colonel Washington requires your presence at his tent."

Henry and I looked at each other. Men stirred around the camp. Something was amiss. He ran over to the tent. I was hot on his trail. Henry entered a tent filled with men. An arm blocked my entry. They wouldn't allow me in. I stomped my foot in protest, but stood outside, hoping to find out what was with all the racket.

I could hear the excitement in all their voices. Haudenosaunee scouts had come across French soldiers about six miles from where we were located. This sounded familiar to me. I wondered if Jumonville would be with them. It felt as though they took forever debating if they would advance. Tanaghrisson's men had spotted them and reported their findings to our group. Jumonville and

Bouchard must be with the group. Tanaghrisson told me they would find him. If they were going to scout the group, I had to go with them. I needed to get the notebook back before Jumonville could cause damage with the information in it or it could reveal my secret to the masses. They would label me a witch and in 1754, that wouldn't go over well at all.

Henry pulled me by the arm as he rushed out of the tent. "Jumonville has been spotted." We headed back towards his company tents.

"I knew it!" I exclaimed, louder than I had expected. "You know I'm coming with you." Elated, I was ready to conquer that mission.

"You need to stay here," he said as he leaned close to my ear. "I will get your notebook for you. I cannot allow you to go with us."

"You can and you will." I stopped in my tracks like a stubborn child. "I know what it looks like, and I want him to know that I am the one taking it back."

"Amelia, I don't want you hurt." He turned to face me. "We are taking weapons, and I don't want you in the middle of it."

"Listen, I need to look him in the eye and let him know he has not won. I need to do this, Henry." I grabbed his hand and pleaded.

He looked down at my hand that held his. "You are going to be the death of me, woman." He let out a huff.

"I hope not." I snorted a laugh. "I can't do this without you."

He took a deep breath and pinched between his eyes with his free hand. "Come on," he said, defeated. We gathered a few items and met up with the group of soldiers.

 We walked throughout the night. Forty of us. Six miles through the rainy Allegheny Mountains. My clothes didn't appreciate the rain, and neither did I. Dawn approached, the rain subsided, and we met with Tanaghrisson and a group of his men. To say that I was excited to be going into battle with George Washington would be an understatement. No one else understood the significance of this event. I did. I wanted to pee my pants... well... dress. My stomach felt as though it was going to turn upside down.

 Tanaghrisson and his men were going to approach the French encampment from behind in the glen. We would approach from above. I would stay behind the frontline. Surprise engagement. That's what Washington had planned. A low dimmed sun took over the woods in the early morning hours. We could hear men rouse. A deep yawn. Clank of a pan to fix breakfast. Rustle of fabric to get dressed. I remember what it was like traveling with this group. They seemed to take their time in the morning to get started.

 Smoke rose from down below in the glen as we approached, weapons ready. They were sitting ducks. They thought the edge of the hill would provide them cover. It only provided us with the perfect vantage point. Trees filled the area, but the French had found a spot next to the twenty-foot rocked wall. They were easy to look down on from our high ground position.

 I could hear my pulse pounding through my ears like a big drum. *Breathe.* I tried to steady my breathing, but it was no use. Every breath trembled out. I was about to face my bullies and I was bringing my forty overprotective brothers with me. I had one thought and one thought only: get the notebook. To hell with Jumonville and the asshole Bouchard. I didn't care what happened to them.

The sound of gunfire popped through the quiet morning woods. Nesting birds squawked and took flight above the canopy of trees. They scattered in every direction in the sky. Men yelled in French. Outnumbered, outgunned, and outmaneuvered, the French returned fire. I stayed out of range, just beyond the crest of the small cliff. I was determined not to get shot two hundred years before I was supposed to be born. The yelling continued, both in English and French. A scream from below. Another scream. More yelling. More pops from the muskets and pistols. One of the Virginians fell. He laid there in pain, bleeding. Reload. I couldn't save him. He died before he could take his next breath. Men reloaded pistols and rifles. Shots volleyed back-and-forth. Fifteen minutes later, it stopped. Moans, cries, and barked orders joined the smoke from the gunfire that lingered low in the heavy, humid air.

I wanted to see if Jumonville was alive. I silently wished to see Bouchard laying on the ground squirming in pain to his death. *Where did that come from?* It was unlike me to think with such hatred. But there I was, wanting him to suffer. I needed to get to the bottom of the glen and retrieve my notebook. Henry looked back towards me and nodded for me to come over to him. I wanted to throw up. A deep breath and a twist of the ring around my finger, I walked over to the edge and looked down. Someone had hit Jumonville with a bullet. Under my breath, I had hoped it would have been Henry that shot him. Shot him for me. Bouchard was alive, dirty, and not wounded. Damn. On the ground laid

227

thirteen French soldiers dead or on the brink of death. Twenty-one had surrendered. Tanaghrisson's men had kept all but one of the French from retreating. We could see the man running away. Private Davies chased after him. Washington stopped him, "Leave him. He can go tell his command that we are not to be challenged." *That was a bit arrogant, Washington.*

The rest of us worked our way down to the bottom of the glen. Looking up, I could see why Jumonville thought it hid him from view. He thought it hid him behind the wall. It was a good thing we had Tanaghrisson on our side or else we would have never seen their approach. Jumonville spoke in French. Apparently, his ability to speak English must have left him while his blood was spilling from his wound. He approached, carrying documents in his hand, along with my notebook. I gave a panicked look towards Henry and Tanaghrisson. There was my notebook and, possibly, my demise. Jumonville held out the papers decorated with his bloody fingerprints.

Tanaghrisson stopped the approach of Jumonville. "You are not yet dead," Tanaghrisson said. I thought he was going to get my notebook for me. Instead, he pulled out an axe, striking Jumonville in the skull. I gasped and covered my mouth. I couldn't believe what I had witnessed. Yes, I wanted to be rid of him. He held me captive and allowed Bouchard to beat me. What I hadn't expected was to see him killed before my eyes. Tanaghrisson grabbed Jumonville's dead body and scalped him. The rest of his group scalped the rest of the dead. Trophies.

I walked over to Tanaghrisson, shaking with every step I took. I had to see if it was true. Jumonville was dead. His body laid on the ground in a slump. My notebook laid next to him in his outstretched hand. I tried to bend down. My legs shook uncontrollably. I couldn't. I just stood there. Shaking. I felt a hand touch my back. It startled me. I couldn't take my eyes off Jumonville. Tanaghrisson picked up my notebook with his hand covered in Jumonville's blood. The owner of the hand on my back took it from him and pulled me away from the glen. That was not a movie. It really happened. In front of me. Death. Murder. Blood. Flesh sliced away. I cannot get the look of Jumonville out of my mind.

CHAPTER THIRTY-ONE

I could hear talking around me. The sound was a blur. Everything was a blur. My eyes only focused on the vision of Jumonville. "Amelia," Henry's voice finally broke through the spell Jumonville's death held on me. "We need to get you out of here." His hand wrapped around my upper arm; he tugged me. "Now." His voice was firm and controlled.

I looked around. Everyone looked at me. Bouchard stood there, glaring at me as Henry pulled me away. He wanted me dead. Why couldn't he have died as well? I couldn't believe that I was now wishing for his death. I felt terrible. *Did I cause Jumonville to be killed?* Tanaghrisson wouldn't have looked for him if it wasn't for me.

"Henry," I somehow found a whisper in my voice. "He's dead."

"Isn't that what you wanted?" His voice was sharp. "What did you think Tanaghrisson was going to do? You made it clear that Jumonville was dangerous."

"No. I." I stopped walking and talking. I didn't know

what I wanted or expected. Henry pulled me towards the path we took down to get into the glen. "I don't know what I wanted," I choked on my whispered response.

The mountains were hard to traverse in my wet dress. I no longer had the excitement of the battle to help move me along. My feet and emotions were heavy weights. I wished we could've brought Louis, so I could collapse on him and have him carry me away from there. The day had only begun, and I had spent my emotional energy. I walked solely with the motivation from Henry. He spoke to me to ease my nerves. I could only replay Jumonville being killed over-and-over. His scream as the axe fell through his head. All the blood. The smell of iron. A bite of gunpowder. The sound of the knife cutting through the flesh. Wet, squishy, red flesh being pulled away from his head as he was being scalped. There were gasps and cries from the survivors. I grabbed the nearest tree to brace myself from falling over. It finally happened; I threw up. When nothing remained in my stomach, painful dry heaves decided I was not done suffering.

Henry glanced back and made eye contact with Washington. If Washington had said anything, I couldn't hear it above my body's self-inflicted torture.

"I need you to pull yourself together so we can get back to camp." Henry leaned close to my ear.

I looked up at Henry. "Are you kidding me? Did you see what happened?" I pointed toward the glen. "That was my fault."

"It was his fault." Henry was firm in his speech. "I cannot carry you. I need for you to walk." He took me by my elbow and pulled me away from the tree.

He was right. I needed to get away from the glen. Away

from the death. I needed to not be a burden. We walked down the small path to towards the camp. It would take us hours to walk the six miles back. My mind focused on the look on Jumonville's face. Then, my memories shot to the death glare from Bouchard. For as long as Bouchard lived, I would have to remain alert. I was sure he would stop at nothing to see me dead. All of that for my notebook. "My notebook," I exclaimed, and turned around to walk back to the glen. "I need to go back. My notebook. He had my notebook. I can't let anyone find out what was in it."

Henry grabbed my arm and turned me back around to head towards the camp. "I have it right here." I hadn't noticed that he had been carrying it the entire time.

"Thank you," I said as I took it from him and opened the pages. They were all there. My notes of the upcoming battles were all there. I hugged the book and slipped it in my pocket, even though it had smeared blood covering it. "Did you read my notes?"

"No." Henry's voice was direct. "When would I have the opportunity? I've been focused on you. Not that wretched book."

Finally, I found my voice. "I just thought you would be curious about what this was about."

"I've been curious about many things that you haven't told me." That stabbed me in the heart. The look on his face in the Haudonsauee camp when he found out I knew about upcoming battles pierced into my memory. "I figured you would tell me when you were ready."

"Oh." I sucked on my bottom lip and thought about what I haven't told him, which was nearly everything besides what happened when they captured me. "What do you want to know?" I knew I was about to open the floodgates to information that I wasn't sure if I was supposed to keep secret. Were their rules about time travel?

"I haven't been able to get you traveling through time out of my head. What happened? What was it like?"

I let out a relieved sigh. He started off with the simple questions. "Well, I told you about going to Fort Ashby in the twenty-first century and then, bam! I was in seventeen fifty-four. Well, I had found a coin on the ground when I was walking into a building. I thought it was odd, it said seventeen fifty-four on it. I thought someone had just dropped it and it should have been in a museum or a collection."

We continued to walk through the mountains on a small trail. I couldn't hear Washington and the rest of the soldiers behind us, or if they were still behind us.

"I walked into a building and there was a bright light. I could smell the burning of cherry wood. The smell was inviting, but the light was blinding. I turned back and thought I saw someone I knew, but I felt compelled to enter."

Henry helped me step over a log. "Do you think that person had something to do with your time travel?"

"No. I just didn't know why I saw him." I looked towards the sun peeking through the canopy of the trees.

A deer ran across our path. I watched as it leapt over a fallen log and disappeared into the heavy woods. "Was it your husband?"

"Hm? No. I told you he is dead. Killed." I shook my head. The muscles in my neck were still tense. I grabbed my shoulder and massaged it. "The strange part of it was it was this guy I had gone out with on a couple of dates. He was weird, and I felt uneasy around him. I thought he had showed up at a restaurant I was at that morning. So, I thought he might have been following me."

"Curious."

"Right? Anyway, everything went black. Or I blacked out. It was such an odd feeling. Then, I woke up in a field. I was exhausted and hungry. My phone didn't work. My key fob was dead. It was like all the energy was drained."

"Phone? Key fob?" Henry looked at me. I realized I was using terms of things that he just wouldn't understand. They didn't even have electricity, let alone batteries, phones, cars, key fobs, and the list would go on, but I didn't need to confuse him anymore than I already had.

"Yeah, it's one of those future things that wouldn't make sense." I shrugged. I didn't know how else to explain the difference in our technology. "When I woke up, I was confused and couldn't think straight. I didn't know how I got there or where I even was. The area looked so different."

We continued to crunch our way through the leaves along the narrow path. "There is a John Ashby that has some land not too far from Wills Creek. I wonder if that is the same person?"

"Maybe? I think so." I remembered Jane Ashby's name, but couldn't recall her husband, other than Captain Ashby. "Do you mean I was near other people? I mean, other than the French?"

"It's possible."

I let out a loud, annoyed laugh. "I guess that is my terrible luck."

"Why did you visit Fort Ashby? Is there going to be a battle there?"

"No, my friend Beth told me to check it out. His wife, apparently, was supposed to be interesting. I speculated that her family were pirates."

"Pirates? Are you sure?" That seemed to get his attention.

"No, but one of my books that I'm writing involves pirates, so I thought the museum might have something interesting about her."

We continued down the narrow path towards the fort, avoiding the occasional downed tree. "Did it?"

"It was closed." I knew I should have checked the Friends of Fort Ashby website before heading there.

"I thought you said that you went inside?" Henry gave me a strange look. I couldn't say that I blamed him. I had told him I went into a building that I had no business going in doing research on something that didn't pertain to my book on Washington. Then I was whisked away to the past. It was strange, and I didn't understand it.

"Maybe if I hadn't gone to find out more about her, I wouldn't have ended up here with you."

"Well, if that's the case, I'm pleased that you set out to find about this pirate woman."

"Alleged pirate woman," I giggled. "And that was only in my imagination."

We walked down the hill and came upon our camp. It was a sight for my tired and sore eyes and my sore feet. Riding Louis had spoiled me for the past couple of weeks that I hadn't needed to break in the shoes as much as I had since last night. My feet ached.

Two soldiers ran up to us. I suppose it looked ominous, with just the two of us coming back when we had left with the large group of around forty. Henry assured them all was well and tasked a private to find us food. I wanted to sneak away and look at my notebook, but was afraid my eyes would betray me, and I would instantly fall asleep.

"Thank you," I said to Henry as I sat down while we waited for breakfast.

He sat hip-to-hip next to me. "My pleasure, but I am unsure what you are thanking me for."

"For this." I slid my hand around his biceps next to me. "I need the conversation. You didn't leave me."

"I believe you told me I was stuck with you." He slid his arm around my back when I loosened my grip. I sunk into his embrace and rested my head on his chest. "This is me sticking with you."

CHAPTER THIRTY-TWO

To say that George Washington was upset about the killing of Jumonville would be an understatement. The biggest understatement of the century. We heard the troops arrive a couple of hours after we did, taking the time to bury the fallen soldier and gather the prisoners and the supplies. The commotion startled me awake.

It was after noontime and Henry rushed to Washington's tent to have a meeting with the officers. I wasn't sure if I should tell them that was the incident that would lead to the start of war? My stomach clenched again. I knew what would happen next and I wouldn't be able to leave to find safety elsewhere.

"Listen, I'm pretty sure he was going to die, anyway. Tanaghrisson only helped him die a little sooner." I tried to calm down Henry. He had come back from his meeting agitated and paced around me like a caged tiger while I prepared my cooking area for our evening meal.

"He wants to blame you and Tanaghrisson for the debacle."

I rolled my eyes. Blame anyone but himself. Figures. "What is today's date?"

"What?"

I huffed out a breath. "The date."

"The twenty-eighth of May."

I grabbed my notebook that had remained in my pocket. After what I had gone through to get it back, I wouldn't let it out of my reach. I flipped through the pages and found the well-worn page I looked for.

"Read this entry here and tell me what it says." He hesitated. I shoved the book towards him. "Go on. Read it." Henry tried to take the book out of my hand. I wasn't giving it up that easily and made him look over my shoulder.

"Jumonville Glen, May twenty-eight, seventeen fifty-four." Henry turned to walk away. "You knew what was going to happen this morning, and you said nothing." The venom in his voice stung.

I grabbed him by the arm. He wouldn't walk away from me before he understood where I was coming from. "Listen, I didn't even know what today's date was until you told me. I only have a few dates and locations marked in my book. If anyone knew what was going to happen, it was Jumonville. I didn't have the book until we took it back only hours ago. He knew when and where Washington's battles were going to happen."

"That place we went is not called Jumonville Glen. It is a place..." his voice trailed off as he pieced together what had happened.

"Right." I put the book back in my pocket. "It didn't have a name before, but it will now."

"It was a minor skirmish. We're not at war." Henry spun around and looked in the glen's direction.

"Yet." I stood next to him and looked in the same direction. "We are not at war, yet. What happened to the rest of the French?"

"We will move them." Henry looked towards Washington's tent. "Winchester."

"The escaped soldier is going to go to Fort Prince George, which we both know is now under the control of the French. Jumonville's brother is going to head this way with more men. We can't run. We need to build a fort in order to show our presence and maintain our borders."

"You keep using the word 'we'." Henry finally looked at me. "You don't have any business being here. You're going to get hurt or killed."

"Stop being an ass." I let out a small laugh. "We know you are stuck with me. You need to talk to Washington and tell him he needs to build a fort."

"We will both meet with him in the morning."

The morning came too soon. I dreaded the meeting that I knew we were going to have with Washington. I knew he didn't want me there, and he blamed me for the death of Jumonville and the backlash that would come from it.

I cleaned up as best I could, considering I had been roughing it in a tent, traveling over mountains, through woods, and into a skirmish. My shift dried from the washing the night before. I slipped it on and got dressed in my small tent. I was grateful for the privacy. Washington insisted his troops looked the part of being a proper English regiment

239

and I figured that would fall to me as well. When they were not stripped down to the shirts and breeches, the men wore their uniforms. I thought my red coat, blue petticoat, and red, white, and blue stomacher made me look quite patriotic and fit in with the rest of the troops.

Henry started a fire that would go full force for me to cook breakfast. I missed my kitchen. And takeout. And *Betsy's*. The rest of the camp stirred and came alive with the early morning sun.

They made arrangements for us to meet with Washington and the other officers. It took everything I had to keep my breakfast down. I knew the absolute worst thing they would do was send me away, but that didn't help calm my nerves. Henry would take me to his home in Williamsburg and I would be safe until his return. I couldn't leave him. To put it a little more precisely, I didn't want to leave him.

I tried to think of things to distract myself from the meeting. My wedding ring was getting bigger. That or I had continued to lose more weight. I would have to figure out a way to supplement my food allotment. We brought cows, goats, and chickens with us to supplement our milk and eggs. When I could get enough milk, I made butter–boy, that was an upper body workout–and cheese. I learned to trap small game. To me, that sounded like a reasonable task for a twenty-first century city woman to undertake.

"Are you ready?" Henry turned to me before we headed into Washington's command tent. I gulped down my nerves and walked in with my head held high. *You got this, Amelia.*

"Mistress Murray, please, join us. Captain Spencer said you wanted to apologize to the group about the killing of

Jumonville. You know you put us in quite the precarious situation." Washington's voice was calm and collected. He was well spoken, beyond his years, or what I would expect of a twenty-two-year-old man.

"Thank you, Lieutenant Colonel Washington, for allowing me to address you and your distinguished group of officers." I curtsied as I laid it on thick. I hadn't expected that I was to apologize for anything, but I knew I needed to in order to get past yesterday's event. "Gentlemen, I apologize for not knowing that Joseph Coulon, Sieur de Jumonville, was prepared to infiltrate and attack us. Thank you, all of you, for your support in bringing the scoundrel to his end. As some of you may know, he held me captive for some time. I cannot say with honesty that I'm saddened by his death."

Henry raised an eye at me but kept silent as some men mumbled to each other. Some in agreement, others appeared to scowl at me. They didn't trust me; I knew that, but I had to convince them I was not privy to Jumonville's plans, but that they needed to prepare for the next attack.

"Gentlemen, please, allow me to continue." I raised my voice to regain their attention. "From my time with the French, I know that was not the last we will hear from them. In fact, I believe the man that escaped is on his way back to the Fort Prince George to inform the others of yesterday's event."

"We will attack them before they attack us." Shouted Lieutenant Hector Bennet. I looked at Lieutenant Bennet. He not only had the same name but looked identical to my friend Beth's husband, Hector Bennedet, from my time, except this Hector was around twenty years old. I kept looking at him. He glanced at me, uneasy. The resemblance was uncanny. I shook it off. Focus.

"Mayhap," Henry finally spoke up. "We should fortify ourselves for the impending attack. If we leave the area, the French will continue to claim more land as their own. Let them spend their energy coming to us while we prepare. We should build a fort out of necessity for our safety."

"Yay! Yay!" the group of men shouted.

"A fort built out of necessity. To guard against the French. A fort... fort... Fort Necessity," Washington pondered that name. "We can build it here, at the Great Meadows."

"I mean," I hesitated for a moment to gain their attention. "Is this the best place for it?" I interjected. I couldn't help it. My mouth had a mind of its own. A hush fell over the group. The group of officers looked at me. "We seem to be in a bit of a valley surrounded by lots of trees and it's a bit bogged and marshy. Don't you agree?"

"It is cleared, and we have a water supply. If we look for another location, it will take us all that much longer to clear a spot large enough to facilitate a fort. The open area will provide the opportunity to engage in conflict. Removing trees for a new fort would be a hindrance and excessive use of our precious time." Washington countered my recommendation. "We will build it here." He pounded his fist down on his desk. The men cheered. *Well, Fort Necessity in a boggy marsh it is.*

He was correct. Clearing enough trees would make the project take longer, and I knew we didn't have the time for it. The French would be there soon enough and although I knew the battle would be lost, we could save as many lives as possible. In a month's time, life, as these men knew it, would take a rough turn.

"Well, gentlemen," I curtsied. "I will leave you to it and take my leave."

I headed back to my tent alone. Not sure if I was going to leave to somewhere safer before the month was out, I had nowhere to go. Jumonville's brother would use the attack as an excuse to avenge his brother and make Washington responsible for his death. I couldn't stop the attack, but I might keep Washington from taking that responsibility. I just wasn't sure how I was going to do that, considering he didn't want to listen to my advice, and I couldn't do it alone.

Henry was gone most of the day, knee deep in planning meetings. Finally, he came back late that night after I had gone to bed. They began making plans for the fort, which would require trees to be felled and more land to be cleared. The original mission was not abandoned, as they continued to widen the road to the Gist's plantation. I hoped they would take enough of the surrounding trees to give a better view of the attackers, but I was not a military expert, nor did they want the input from a woman. I just knew that we sat there like sitting ducks, waiting for the slaughter.

They formed Fort Necessity into a circular shaped stockade, with logs standing upright as the main walls. It was smaller–perhaps thirty feet in diameter–than I had expected, but it would have to do. A small storage building sat in the middle. We would store food rations and ammunition within the stockade. Men dug a trench around the perimeter. I told them it looked like a moat. They laughed at me and kept digging.

We set rows of tents up behind the stockade. I helped

maintain the camp while the men felled trees and dug ditches. On the ninth of June, commotion broke out in our camp as we received more troops and supplies from Fry's regiment. I was happy to see more supplies and rations, as we were running low. I had supplemented Henry's company's meat supply by trapping small game. Clearly, I learned something on that trip. It was pure dumb luck that I had caught anything in my traps. After the incident with the scalping of Jumonville, I couldn't skin and butcher the animals and left that duty to one of the soldiers. I traded meat for mending and washing of clothes with some soldiers. Those domestic duties, I could handle without getting sick to my stomach.

CHAPTER THIRTY-THREE

"Why did we receive more soldiers?" I asked Henry, as he sat down to enjoy a midday meal with me.

"Colonel Fry is dead." His voice was flat.

"Wait. What? How?" I asked as I dished out a bowl of soup. I served a few of Henry's soldiers earlier, grabbed a bowl for myself, and maintained a slow simmer to keep Henry's meal warm and ready. "What does that mean?"

"Colonel Fry fell off his horse, broke his neck. Died. It happened a little over a week ago." He said with a slight laugh, disbelief that it happened like that. He blew across the spoon of squirrel soup before taking a bite. I mended his shirt he had ripped when helping men move logs into place. "They have promoted him."

"Who was promoted?" I looked up from my work. "Colonel Fry?" I knotted and bit off the end of the thread.

Henry shot a look in my direction and snorted. "Washington. He's now Colonel Washington."

"Oh. He seems so young." I examined my stitch work.

Over the past month, I was proud of myself for my improvement. "Will they promote you as well?" I glanced up at Henry as I tried to judge his reaction to my question.

"Mayhap. Mayhap not." By the tone of his voice, I concluded that wasn't the way it worked. What did I know about the inner workings of the eighteenth-century military? "He will be the Commander-in-Chief of the Virginia forces."

"The additional men should be helpful to get the fort ready." I interjected. Henry made a noise of agreement. Since his promotion wasn't a guarantee–and I felt as though I was the reason for it–I wanted to change the subject. It appeared something else was on his mind. "And the extra supplies are really going to help around here."

"Aye." He peered into the pot for any remaining soup. He caught the chunk of bread I tossed to him.

"I saw them bring in nine small cannons. That will be great for defenses." I studied his face. "Hey, what's going on?"

"Why do you ask?"

"You have barely said two words to me since you told me the Fry died. I made you food, mended your shirt, and attempted to have a conversation with you." My temper was getting as heated as the noonday sun. I wasn't sure if it was from the layers of clothes in the June midday sun, or if it was my temper from his lack of concern of what I said. "You're just blowing me off."

"Amelia." His tone was short.

"Henry," I replied with a curt attitude.

He sighed. "My humblest apologies."

"What troubles you, my lord?" That got a half smile from him.

"Tanaghrisson's men left, and they won't return. I'm not sure why." He picked at his bread. "It has been troubling me."

"It's difficult for them. To be honest, I think Tanaghrisson is trying to start the war and see which side will win. He knows I must know something, or else he wouldn't have asked for me. I told him the British will win. That is why he stuck around as much as he did. And since I have said nothing more to add–than what I did–I'm guessing he isn't too pleased with me."

"Well, neither am I. Why won't you tell me what is going to happen?" He stood up and paced. I continued to sit on the log, mending a rip in my coat. "I can prepare for it. Make sure we win."

I looked up at him, shielding my eyes from the sun. "I'm not sure we're supposed to win this next battle."

"What the devil do you mean, woman?" He looked around our tents to see who was nearby and could hear our conversation. He stood up, offered me his hand to pull me up from the log where I sat, and invited me to go on a walk. "We are going to lose, and you're going to let that happen?"

"Yes. It's going to happen. I don't think I can stop that. I'm not sure I want to stop it." We walked toward the edge of the encampment, away from any prying ears. "I'm trying to make sure you're best prepared for when it happens."

"Why wouldn't you want to stop it? What is wrong with you?"

"Butterfly effect and all that," I said matter-of-factly. Henry looked at me as if I had two heads. "If I had information that would stop this next battle, then perhaps we don't go to war with the French. If we don't go to war with the French, then the future of the United States, our independence, and Washington as the nation's first president could be in jeopardy. I mean, if I screw this up, the country that I know, and love, may never come to be. Then what?" I paused for a moment to give him the opportunity to respond. He stood there and stared at my two heads. A third must have sprouted while we were speaking. "Then I could've really screwed things up."

"I do not understand what butterflies have to do with this." He shook his head. "What if that was the reason that it, whatever of whoever it is, sent you here? To change history."

"My historical knowledge of Jumonville was he was to die, and he did. That is why we will have Jumonville Glen. It is where he died. However, Jumonville died because of me, and I must live with that knowledge. I was not mentioned in the history books, but they mentioned Tanaghrisson killing Jumonville. And that happened, my intervention or not."

Henry let out an audible humph and continued to walk the perimeter of the meadow with me.

"We need to consider that I might have been the reason that he died. I mean, I suppose I was the reason. Maybe?" I shook my head. "I know some things that are supposed to happen and I'm here to make sure they happen according to history or future or whatever."

"What do your history books say about me?" He paused in front of me.

"I don't know. Nothing. They say nothing about me, either." I shrugged. "I just knew the death of Jumonville would start the conflict. We are going to lose this upcoming battle."

"We've got to try." Henry said with urgency. "If we're not in the history books, then what?"

"Of course we do. If we don't try, there could be many more deaths and it could change the course that they have set us on." We walked past the meadow where horses grazed. "However, we can't change the ultimate outcome. We are going to lose."

He stopped to look at Louis as he stood next to a couple of mares. "You're going to be the death of me."

"I hope not." He might have meant it as s turn of phrase, but I was serious about that. I wasn't sure what the plan was for Captain Henry Spencer, but I could only hope that I wouldn't cause his death. The knowledge that Jumonville's death was because of me I could live with. He was a jerk. I couldn't handle losing Henry because of my intervention. "I have one nagging worry."

We continued our walk around the perimeter of the meadow. There were a few cows and the more horses grazing nearby. "How to get home to your time?"

"Okay." I put my hands on my hips. "Make that two nagging worries." Anyone that looked at us thought he was getting an earful from me. "I had completely forgotten about trying to get home. No. What I'm worried about is Bouchard. He did Jumonville's dirty work. He was the one that inflicted the torture. When we left the glen, he was still alive."

"Do you think he is going to come after you?"

"Of course, I do." I scoffed. "You didn't see the way he looked at me when Jumonville was scalped. I could tell he blames me for all of that."

"Mayhap." Henry pondered what to do next. He ran his

hand over his chin. He seemed to think out his actions, whereas I was ready to pounce. "The prisoners are on the way to Winchester. Unless he escapes, he cannot harm you."

"Exactly." I wiped the sweat from my brow with a square of linen I had in my pocket. "I don't need to be his target."

Henry looked back towards the men. "I need to get back to my duties." We walked back towards the rest of the group of soldiers. "We will think of a way to keep you safe with this upcoming battle. Can you tell me anything about it?"

I pulled out my notebook to confirm the date that was etched in my memory. "The morning of the third of July. We will suffer casualties, but so will the French. I'm not sure how many. I didn't write that down."

"That gives us a month to get more men. Mayhap we can win, despite your prediction." Henry took a long step to cross the stream to get back to the side with the tents. He held out his hand, and I took it.

"Maybe." With a little help from Henry and a leap with my short legs, I made it over the stream. "You don't suppose someone could accidentally kill Bouchard on the way to Winchester, do you?"

"Ha," Henry exclaimed. "You can be vengeful. You are not a meek woman."

"What led you to believe that I was meek?"

CHAPTER THIRTY-FOUR

Four hundred men. We were going to battle with four hundred men. That was going to be difficult.

Captain James MacKay, from South Carolina, and his company of approximately one hundred British Regulars, joined us. We now had four hundred troops stacked on top of each other in that marshy field to prepare for our impending battle. Tents packed behind the fort slept six men and made for very close quarters. The name of the area was Great Meadows, but to me, there was nothing great about it. It was going to be a great disaster and I couldn't stop it from happening. We were packed tight. June in Virginia brought the summer rains. Most soldiers slept under the stars instead of stuffing in up to six soldiers to a tent. Officers and a few others, and I was one of those few others, had their own tents.

Work halted during the downpours. We huddled into the tents, packed like sardines. I can't say the smell of the close quartered bodies was any better than a pack of sardines. The rains would let up and we would all go outside, searching for fresh air and sun. The ground was thick with water, and the bottom of my dress was brown and heavy from the mud. My foot sank in the mud with every step. The humidity was hell on my hair. The rains made trapping small game difficult and if we weren't quick enough, we would lose part of our rations to the rain. I kept much of our group's rations in my small tent. Since I was the only one sleeping in it, I could stack as much as possible, and included the space under my small makeshift cot that Private Johnson had built for me. They built a storage room inside the stockade to house food and the supply of wine. Gun powder and weapons could be stored in there, as well. At least, that was the plan.

Wet, cold, hungry, and a constant fight for my life and sanity. Three months in 1754 and I spent a good part of it miserable with the lack of proper shelter. I was cold, except for when the sun would come out after a rain, and it would heat the ground. Then I would drip with sweat from the humidity. Food was always in low supply. Not that I ate much, but I always seemed hungry. As a woman, I received half-rations, and I caught small game, but what I wouldn't give for a grocery store or takeout. If it wasn't for Jumonville, Bouchard, or pneumonia—which I was thankful that I hadn't caught yet — I wouldn't feel like I was always fighting for my life or to survive. I would have been just cold and wet. Still miserable.

Henry made me feel quite safe, which I was fortunate for, although he had no obligation to do so. After Todd died, I had become skeptical of men and their goals. It seemed like they always had an ulterior motive or were hiding something from me–like my stalker, Kyle. That's why I despised the whole dating scene and resolved myself to be a reclusive cat lady in my old age. This wasn't the adventure that I wanted. I laid on my cot, arm draped over my eyes, as I reflected on the past couple of months. I remember the morning that I slipped through time at Fort Ashby and having breakfast with Beth. She laughed at me when I said it would have been much simpler during this time. She knew what I romanticized in the past was a bunch of bullshit.

"Can you put in a request for ink and quill for me?" I asked Henry as he was taking inventory of our supplies. "How long do you think it will take to get here?"

"Mayhap a month."

"Ugh." I kicked an imaginary rock. The mud was too thick for me to find a real one. "Forget about it."

"Are you certain? I had them already on the list. You have mentioned more than once that you wanted to write more in your notebook."

"I'll just continue using whatever you can scrounge. We won't be here by the time the supplies would get here." It was the twenty-eighth of June, just five days away from the attack. If we had caught the French soldier from escaping the ambush at the glen, we might have avoided this fight. He made it to French controlled Fort Duquesne—the former Fort Prince George—where I had found refuge with the British. They moved Bouchard and the rest of the prisoners to Wills Creek after the incident, and then onward to Winchester. I always felt as though I had to look over my shoulder, afraid that Bouchard was going to sneak up behind me. Perhaps I overreacted.

MacKay's men continued to reinforce the fort as much as they could in between the rains. They refused to help

253

Washington's men work on the path to Gist's plantation. MacKay seemed to take his orders from himself, and they were there only for the upcoming action.

I continued to wash clothes, cook, clean, and mend clothes. On the occasion, Henry would borrow Washington's ink and quill for part of the evening. I would sit by the fire, take notes, get frustrated at the constant dipping of the quill, and since I could see the page in front of me, I gave up. Finally, I resigned myself to remember the events when I got back to the 21st century.

"Unless you plan on giving me a pistol, I shouldn't be here tomorrow morning." I told Henry while we were out for a late walk. The glow from the sun hung in the last few minutes of light. Campfires lit up the fields like a reflection of the stars above or a beacon for the French to find us.

"What time will they begin?"

"I don't know. In the morning." I shrugged my shoulders. I knew they would be here in the morning. There was nowhere for me to go. The French and their indigenous allies would surround us. Henry needed to be here to fight and couldn't take me to safety.

"You will not need a pistol and can take Louis and ride away from here."

"It wouldn't surprise me if someone has already scouted our area." I studied the darkness that surrounded the encampment. "I wouldn't get too far before they would attack me and Louis."

"They wouldn't harm a woman." Henry seemed surprised that I would even suggest that they would attack an unarmed woman.

"Oh? You don't think so? What do you think happened

to me while I was with them?" My voice got louder as I my anxiety raised. I don't think they understood what their enemy could do to either a man or a woman. "What do you think happened to Janet and her family? Henry, this is about to become a long war. It will be called the Seven Years War. They wouldn't last long if they didn't fight dirty. I can guarantee that they wouldn't think twice about eliminating me. Especially if Bouchard is with them."

"We sent him to Winchester."

"How do we know Bouchard is not out there in the wood line?" I pointed towards the ink black woods that surrounded us. "He could be out there waiting for his chance to kill me." I looked again. It was pitch black in the trees, except for the occasional lightning bug.

"You will stay within the stockade tonight. None of the men will harm you. There is room next to the storage for you to set up your tent. I will stay next to you to keep you safe."

"I'm less worried about our men. They wouldn't dare touch me. Between you and Colonel Washington, these guys know better than to look twice at me." I smiled. Washington and I started off with our differences, but I think he had realized that I wasn't there to be their downfall. "Make sure Colonel Washington and the men know to be on alert. I wish he would have listened to me about the attack."

"War differs from books than reality. This will be a test for all of us." Henry had served in the British military before coming to the colonies. He knew that warfare was an ever-evolving beast. New country, new tactics.

"He needs this defeat." I sighed and put my hands on my hips. I rubbed my palm against the fabric across my stomach. He needed to learn about warfare in America. Washington studied from the old tactics, determined that the French would meet us on the battlefield. Volleys of gunfire would tear through the field and bodies. I tried to explain to him that there wasn't the field to do this, he wouldn't listen. I was a woman and not an officer. All I could do was shake my head in disappointment. He would have to learn on his own. "This will be a lesson for him to grow and learn to lead an army. He's smart. He would be smarter if he would listen to me. I know. I know." I raised my hands in surrender. "I'm just a woman."

"You and I both know that you are more than *just* a woman. When I tell him the same thing, he just assumes that I take my advice from you." We were almost back at our tents. "We both know you are an extraordinary woman, Mistress Amelia Murray. Now, let's go get you settled inside."

Before our evening meal, we packed up my tent and supplies. We made a spot for us in the stockade to settle in for the night. We lacked space, but I knew Virginia's weather could be unpredictable and insisted that we set up a small tent for our provisions. I hoped that Henry, Louis, and I survived tomorrow. If anything, I hoped to survive this and return to my own time. I started thinking of ways to send a message to Hannah. It was one thing for me to get pulled to 1754; it was another for me to die here and she never knowing what happened to me. I couldn't let anyone get hold of my notebook. The little bit of information inside could destroy the future if it fell into the wrong hands.

CHAPTER THIRTY-FIVE

The sound of gunfire burst through the early morning air. It was the morning of July 3, 1754. It was the day that I dreaded. All I could do was wish for it to be over and that I would live to see tomorrow. The men on patrol returned fire to a wooded abyss. They had no target to return their fire. The French and their indigenous allies maneuvered their way around us, using the trees as a protection from our gunfire. Trenches dug out around the stockade filled with men, and with the constant rain, it filled with water. We were sitting ducks in the water, unable to defend our pond. I heard the shouts of instructions. Louis neighed and reared. The both of us were agitated. I tried to comfort him, but Henry was the one he sought. If able, I was supposed to ride Louis to Winchester, then on to Fredericksburg, then to his house in Williamsburg. That was fine that Henry thought that would be the plan. However, without my GPS, I had no clue how to get there and would probably end up back in the clutches of the French.

Sporadic gunfire continued throughout the day. More

shouts. More shots. When I thought things couldn't get worse, they did. Mid-afternoon, the clouds burst open, and a torrential downpour made it difficult for us to return fire. The rain soaked the gunpowder and made it impossible to shoot anything. The French were protected from most of the rain under the canopy of the trees they hid behind. We were out in this godforsaken marsh, exposed to water both coming down on top of us and knee deep in mud. It doomed us before we started.

 I continued to hunker down in the stockade. I kept Louis with me, in the event I would have to make for a quick escape. They continually agitated him with the bangs and whistle of the bullets as they flew the air. I would duck as the occasional one broke its way through to the interior. I ducked, hoping to avoid catching a slug and the splintered wood. *How could I think I could duck a bullet?*

 The rain didn't let up throughout the rest of day and left me drenched. My dress was heavy from the constant deluge. The water had nowhere to go. The earth, already saturated, couldn't take in anymore water. We trudged through the mud to repair what we could and provide reinforcements.

 They brought casualties to the stockade. Our men fell one-by-one. My heart broke piece-by-piece. They were friends and brothers-in-arms. I attempted to provide whatever care I could under some guidance from Doctor Craik. It was not much. I lost count of how many came in wounded and left for dead. A bloody, undistinguishable face would come in, and I would swallow down in hopes it wouldn't be Henry. Every wounded man brought my emotions closer to a breaking point. A private. A sergeant. A corporal. A lieutenant. Patch him up. Pile up the dead outside of the fort for someone else to tend to him. Duck from a bullet. We patched and sent the injured ones back to the lines or to their tents. This continued into the early evening. Then there was silence. No more gunfire. No more yells of orders. Injured and dead continued to be brought in. I leaned over Sergeant Lovett as I attempted to wrap up his leg. A superficial wound. If we could prevent infection, he would live long enough to get home to Mistress Lovett.

There was a hand on my back. I pulled the wet twists of hair out of my face with my blood-covered hands. I turned around and had to focus my exhausted eyes. It was Henry. There was blood on him. "Cheese and rice, Henry. You're bleeding. Where?" I shouted as I opened his jacket to look for the wound.

"I'm well. Not shot." He looked down at his jacket. He seemed half in a daze. "I carried in Corporal Jenkins. It's his blood. I believe." He wiped at the blood.

My vision spun. I grabbed hold of his arm to brace myself. I could feel myself losing my balance. There was nothing I could do to stop me from blacking out. Henry grabbed me around my waist and helped me to sit on the ground. The rain continued to fall from the sky.

"Where have they shot you?" I could hear the panic in Henry's voice.

I regained consciousness and looked up at Henry. Water dripped down his nose. He was soaked. "Me? They haven't shot me. I don't think I have," I said as I looked down at my dress. The sting of iron from the blood pierced into my nose. It was not my blood, but there was a lot. So much blood. "Just got lightheaded from not eating and this damned heat and humidity." I stopped and listened to the silence. "What's going on? I don't hear the guns."

"I must go. I'm headed out with Van Braam and Bennet to begin negotiations with the French to offer the conditions of surrender."

"Who?" My thought processing slowed. I was confused. Words jumbled in my head, and I shook it to straighten them out. It only half-way worked.

"The French, Van Braam the translator, Bennet, and I are supposed to start the negotiations," he said slowly so I could take it in. I shook my head again in response. "Amelia, I need to get out there. I just needed to make sure you were alive and well."

"Who is the French officer?" I grabbed hold of Henry as he tried to leave me. He helped me stand up. I grabbed hold of both his arms and forced him to look at me. "I need to know who."

"It's a Captain Louis Coulon de Villiers."

"That's Jumonville's brother. We're screwed." I walked with Henry towards the command tent. "And he is ticked off."

"Where do you think you're going?" Henry stopped and looked at me.

"To the tent, of course. Colonel Washington needs to hear what I have to say about the terms of surrender that are going to be offered to him." I looked up at Henry and kept trudging through the mud.

"You know he will not allow you to be in there to discuss anything about the negotiations." Henry pulled on my arm to stop me. "Amelia, have you not learned anything while you've been here? You don't have the authority to do as you please. The colonel can send you away. Permanently."

"Listen, you go do whatever it is you need to do, but the French are going to blame Colonel Washington for the death of Jumonville. I don't trust Van Braam's translations."

"He's Dutch, and the only one that here that knows enough French." Henry let out a loud sigh. "I'll do what I can, but you need to know that we will do what it takes to get out of here alive and in one piece. We've had an abundance of casualties today. I'm not willing to have more before the night is done."

"Stay safe and come back to me. I cannot do any of this without you." I pleaded with him. He had been my protector and friend. I didn't want to lose him to what should be simple negotiations with the French.

Henry left me standing there as he met with Captain Jacob Van Braam and Lieutenant Hector Bennet before heading out to their meeting. I turned heel and went to meet with Colonel Washington, whether or not he wanted me to speak with him.

"Colonel Washington, may I speak with you?" I stood outside his tent. He was going to be in a foul mood, but I hoped he would grant me the curtesy of my wisdom.

"Mistress Murray, please make it quick." His voice dripped with stress and annoyance at my presence. Arrogant.

I needed to ensure that I didn't make this worse. I entered and fell into a curtsy. "Colonel Washington, I wanted to give you a few updates on the health of the men." I figured I better not jump into the "I told you so" lecture that I wanted to give him. "I've assisted Doctor Craik with the injured men as best I could, but we had some that succumbed to their injuries. Others, I'm not sure if they will make it through the night or if they will be overcome with fever."

"We will have to worry about that later." He turned to Captain MacKay, who had been in the tent when I had entered, to continue their discussion on our retreat. He looked up from the papers they were looking at. "Is that all, Mistress Murray?"

"No, Colonel, I'm not sure what the surrender terms are going to be, but whatever comes back, you need to reconsider it." I held my hands behind my back and twisted my ring to the point I was sure my finger would fall off. "The French are not to be trusted. Captain Coulon de Villiers is Ensign Jumonville's brother. He is most displeased with the death of his brother and wants to hold you accountable for his death."

"Mistress Murray," Colonel Washington stood up, towering over me. "If you please." He waved his hand towards the opening of the tent. I was no longer welcomed in there. I had to think of a way to make sure he didn't sign the agreement. They would blame him for the death of Jumonville.

It was almost midnight when Henry, Van Braam, and Bennet returned to the fort. They made terms of the agreement over the past four hours. The men made a beeline it to the command tent. Henry glanced over at me, shook his head, and waved me off. I had to know what they discussed. He should've known that I wouldn't stand by and allow Jumonville to win from beyond the grave.

I ran over and stood next to the tent, attempted to look busy, and listened the best I could—with ears that still rang from being strained from all the nearby musket fire—to the discussion. We were to surrender the garrison, supplies, and leave unarmed. Expected. All of us wanted to leave there, anyway. It would be difficult to leave without our rations, but we were to leave with our lives. I looked forward to civilization and a legitimate roof over my head instead of a tent or the open night sky. The part about being unarmed and without supplies bothered me a bit, but we would make do. Some men had brought their personal muskets. That would be a financial burden on them, but they were alive.

We, the British, were not to build another fort on the Ohio for a year. Of course, they were going to push the boundary of their territory into ours. Fine. We had plenty to do within that year to prepare for engagement and make a better plan to take back Fort Duquesne. I wanted to see the look on their face when it was taken back. I then realized that I would probably not be here for that, as I would hopefully find my way back to my time before that occurred.

I heard a noise behind me. It was Sergeant Lovett. "Mistress Murray, we have a stew made. Would you care to join us?"

I threw my finger over my lips to shush him. The command tent was not where I needed to be found eavesdropping. I stepped away and in a low voice, "I can't leave here just yet. Will you bring me something?" He nodded, and I stopped him before he limped off. "Do tell the men to eat and drink up. We are losing our supplies to the French in the morning. I don't want to leave anything to those bastards."

"What's this part?" Washington seemed concerned about the term of the surrender.

"The terms state you attacked Sieur Jumonville." Captain Van Braam said in his heavy accent.

I burst into the tent. I had to let Colonel Washington know what he was signing. "It doesn't state that you attacked. It says you assassinated him. Read it."

"Mistress Murray," Washington shouted as he stood up. He looked tired and angry. "Captain Spencer, remove this woman."

"Do you speak French?" Van Braam said, with a smirk, knowing full well that I didn't.

I shook my head. "No, but I know what that says."

"You do not understand the interpretation of this document. That is why I'm here." Van Braam was smug. He didn't want me there from the beginning, I knew that. His disdain for me was apparent.

Henry grabbed me by the elbow. "Amelia, please. You need to leave now."

"I'm leaving." I jerked my elbow away from Henry. "He needs to know what he is signing. It says assassinate." I lunged towards the document to point out the word.

"If we don't sign this document, they will kill us all and scalp us. Is that what you want? It doesn't matter what it says. If we want to leave here alive, Colonel Washington signs it." Henry turned around to the men that were staring at our quarrel. "Gentlemen, if it pleases you, Mistress Murray will take her leave."

I turned on my heel and left the tent. My blood boiled. This was not how I planned it to turn out. I thought they would be pleased with my knowledge and want to protect Colonel Washington from making a mistake. I wanted to find a dark corner to cower and cry. Private MacDonald stumbled over to me. "Mistress Murray," he said, as he shoved a bottle of wine in my hand. "Celebrate our defeat with us." He was drunk. I looked around at the men. The sound of singing, laughter, arguments, and chatter were all being enhanced by the raid on the supply locker's wine, ale, and whisky.

I took the bottle from my young bartender and tossed back a hearty swig. It didn't matter at that point, we either get drunk or we give it to the French. I had every intention of getting drunk with the rest of my brothers-in-arms. I took MacDonald's offered arm, carried my bottle with me, and joined the troops drinking by the fire.

CHAPTER THIRTY-SIX

"I think I'm going to throw up," I coughed out and gasped. My lungs and throat burned from tobacco smoke. I handed Sergeant Lovett his pipe. "That tasted and felt like shit."

The men burst out in laughter. Drunk and laughing his head off, MacDonald fell backwards off the log he used as a chair. That only caused the men to laugh harder.

"Mayhap the lady would like another puff?" Sergeant Lovett offered his pipe to me, followed by a laugh that sent his rotund belly in to a fit of spastic jiggles.

I stood up, attempted to curtsy, and hacked up a lung instead. My unstable legs caused me to sway. I finished the bottle of wine and never found a bowl of stew. "Mayhap, the lady thinks you should take the pipe and shove it up your arse." The men bellowed in laughter. "I've got to pee."

I looked around for a privy or a dark corner, somewhere to relieve the pressure. My eyes lit up when I spotted a location near the storeroom and where we had set up my tent the previous night, which offered a dark corner to give me a little privacy. To say that it was a corner is a bit of a stretch. They had built the stockade in a circular footprint, but it was a corner none the less. I crossed over our makeshift bridge and entered the stockade. *Left foot. Right foot. Left foot. Come on, Amelia. Left foot. Or was it supposed to be my right?*

It reminded me of Mardi Gras in New Orleans when I had turned twenty-one. Todd was in training for his new position with the State Department. It was my senior year of college and a couple of friends thought it would be fun to party it up in the overcrowded streets of NOLA. We carried yard-length tubes filled with boozy concoctions everywhere we went. By the end of the parade, I was drunk off my ass and my bladder felt as though it would burst. Of course, I couldn't find a bathroom. I stumbled behind a bank and peed next to the dumpster. By the smell of it, I wasn't the only one that found refuge behind it. I remember looking over as I balanced myself with a hand on the filthy dumpster and noticed someone had left a Victoria's Secret bra just lying there. What an odd place to leave a bra. I was young, drunk, and stupid. Fun times. I got pregnant with Hannah shortly after that trip. It was my first and last foray into the wild world of Mardi Gras.

The corner would have to do as my makeshift bathroom. As I wandered over to the dark corner, I could barely put one foot in front of the other. To say I was hammered would be an understatement. Leaning against the logs that made up the wall of the stockade, I lifted my dress off the ground, squatted, peed, and almost fell over in my attempt to stand up. I was certain I would be drunk for the next week. As I gained what little footing I could to walk across the muddy yard back to my drinking partners, a group of about five men approached me. I didn't recognize them. They might have come with Fry's or MacKay's group. They weren't any of Washington's or Henry's men. "Gentlemen," I clumsily curtsied. "There is a suitable spot to relieve yourselves back there. It should provide you with enough..."

"Aye, yes, mistress. It's a dark spot." said the soldier who I assumed was the leader of their group. It was too dark to see his face, but he was not much taller than me. His voice sounded like he smoked like a chimney. "Would you care to join us back there?" His voice scratched at my ears.

The nerve! "Absolutely not." I quickly retorted as I tried to push and elbow myself past the wall of men.

The leader flicked his head and one of the other men grabbed me, spun me around, and clasped his calloused hand hard across my mouth. My screams were muffled. The roar of drunken celebration occupied the night and drowned out my calls for help.

"We fought hard today. Friends died. We deserve a bit of recompense." He growled in my ear. I kicked back. I twisted and turned. The hand slipped from my mouth.

"Not from me, you bastard," I screamed out. "Go fu...."

The leader slapped me across the face. My attacker grasped me with more force. "This one's got a fighting spirit." They lifted me by the waist and dragged me back into the dark corner I had just flooded with urine. "You think you're better than us? You're just a harlot out here, drunk with all these men. That captain gets it from you. You can give it up to us."

Two men grabbed my arms. They forced me onto my knees and shoved face first into the ground. The sting of the urine pierced my nose and feel the urine-soaked mud caked on my face squishing its way into my nostrils. I tried to twist my way out of their grasp. I screamed. Only the mud could hear my call for help. Metal and leather scratched together as he removed his belt. The sound of laughter and conversation that surrounded the fort drowned out the commotion of my attackers. *Couldn't anyone see what was happening?* Of course not, I chose this location for the privacy and now it was a place where they would hide while they violated me. I clenched down on my teeth. Someone pinned my legs to the ground while I tried to kick them. I had to resist as much as possible, even as these men outnumbered and overpowered me.

Even Bouchard wouldn't dare to do the thing I braced myself for. Too tired to fight any more, I wanted to give up and just get it over with. The entire weight of my unsupported body crashed into the mud as they released me from their grasp. I heard a grunt. There was a crack of a fist hitting a jaw. I pulled myself up, weighed down by the mud that covered me. I looked behind me at the melee. Sergeant Lovett, Private MacDonald, Henry, Private Davies, Corporal Cooper, and Lieutenant Collins were engaged in repelling my attackers. They pressed my back against the wall.

Within two strides, Henry was in front of me, hands on my shoulders. "Did they violate you?"

I couldn't answer. I stood there staring at him, unable to speak from shock. The tears had already flowed down my mud-caked cheeks.

Henry grabbed my face and forced me to look at him and away from the fight. "Amelia, did they violate you?"

I shook my head. I couldn't tell him they almost did. He saved me before it happened, but I couldn't tell him. All I could do was stand there. My body trembled. My knees were weak. Henry grabbed me by the waist and lead me away. The rest of the men continued the beat down of my attackers.

I reached up to wipe the tears away. My hand was covered in mud. My face was caked thick with the urine-soaked mud. I needed to sit down. We crossed the walkway to the colony of tents and continued our walk over to the command tent. My feet and dress were heavy with mud. I wanted to collapse into a hot shower and cry.

They poured buckets of cold water over my head. I sat there, sobbing, unable to care for myself. The world around me was out of focus, but I could sense Henry's presence. I closed my eyes. Another bucket of cold water. Someone wiped my face with a linen cloth.

"Hm?" I thought I heard someone say something to me. "What?" I shook my head.

"I said, we need to get you cleaned up." Henry was within inches of my face.

In a daze, I looked down at my hands and dress. "I'm filthy."

"Are you drunk?" His voice rang with disappointment.

"I was earlier." The trauma of the attack had sobered me up. The shock of it kept me in a daze. "I need to get clean." The mud wouldn't wipe off my dress. "I don't have any clean clothes."

"Sergeant Lovett, find clothes for her. I don't care from where or who." He turned back and looked at me, then to Lovett. "Hasten man." Lovett limped away, determined.

Henry stood me up and walked me to the command tent. I shivered. "What is going on here, Captain?" Washington stood up from behind his desk and crossed the tent to us. He braced me on my left, Henry on my right, and they led me to a chair.

"It appears the men got into the storage and helped themselves to the alcohol. A group of MacKay's men thought they would take their liberties with Mistress Murray." Henry shot a glance at MacKay, who stood next to Washington. "We stopped them from harming her virtue, but they did rough her about before we found her."

"Mayhap the lady should not be on the battlefield." MacKay didn't care what his men did.

Washington interrupted, "You were to be with Captain Van Braam and Lieutenant Bennet meeting with the French."

"Captain Stobo went in my stead." Henry turned his attention back to me. "I have one of my men finding clothing for Mistress Murray. We will get her cleaned up."

"You don't intend on doing that in here, do you?" I could hear the annoyance in Washington's voice. He was not happy with my outburst earlier this evening, but why couldn't he show any sympathy for my plight?

"She has a small tent that we set up for her last night. If it's still standing, we can try to get her in there."

"Captain Spencer," Lovett's voice came from the other side of the tent. "We have what you asked for."

"I'll be fine. Thanks for asking." I glared at Washington as I gave a curtsy. "Captain Spencer, please take me to my tent. I need to get cleaned up for our departure tomorrow."

We headed towards where my tent was supposed to be near the storage room. "It's not here. It's supposed to be here. Why? Why would they steal my tent?" That seemed to be my last straw. My previous sobs went into a complete

271

meltdown. "My notebook," I exclaimed. I could lose everything else, but not that notebook. Not again.

"Are you sure you don't have it in your pocket?" Henry asked. "You never let it out of your sight."

"I, uh." I felt around my pocket. It wasn't there. "So much has happened today. I don't know. It must have dropped out somewhere." My hands shook.

"We will look for it, Mistress." Sergeant Lovett had been by our side as we walked over to the storage room. My eyes darted to the corner next to it. Not moments earlier, those men tried to assault me there. Suddenly, that place was supposed to be my refuge? I shook my head at the irony.

"It's not much, but you can use the storage room to clean and change your clothes." Henry handed me the stack of clothes. They weren't clean, but they were cleaner than my dress. It was going to be nice to put on pants again.

I walked into the storage room, looked around, and realized I was going to have to figure out how to get my clothes off with my trembling hands. It couldn't be easy for me, of course not. I stuck my head out the door, "I need clean water and a linen to clean myself."

"I'll send Private MacDonald, if I can find him in all of this, to bring you buckets of water. Sergeant Lovett and I will look for your notebook."

I continued to fight back my tears, nodded, and shut the door. I couldn't see anything around me. The room was pitch black. I felt around and found a crate to sit on and fumbled with the pins and ties to my clothing. The dexterity in my fingers disappeared as they trembled. I sloughed the mud- and water-heavy clothes and finally got down to my shift. I shivered. There was a knock at the door. "Yeah," I called out through chattered teeth. Private MacDonald opened the door, the glow from the fires still burning in the rows of tents dimly lit the room. He entered with two buckets of water and sat them down next to me. "Will you find a candle or a torch or something so I can see what the hell I'm doing in here?"

"Yes, Mistress Murray." Initially shocked, when he entered, he kept his eyes on the floor. Private MacDonald didn't want to look at me standing there in my shift. Can't say that I blame him for not wanting to look. I was probably older than his mother. "I haven't seen you eat since this morning before the attack. Would you like me to find you something?"

"Yes, please," I said. "Sergeant Lovett was supposed to bring me something earlier, but I think he forgot."

"Aye, mistress." His foot shifted around and continued not to look at me. "He had a bowl of stew for you, but Linden looked like he needed it. He was quite pale from being shot; you know."

"I think I knew that." My mind raced around the faces and injuries from earlier in the day. I could see the young private's face. He had to be only sixteen at the most. There were too many baby-faced soldiers. They should be at home, goofing off and finding wives. "In the shoulder. He bled. I think I pulled the ball out washed the wound as best I could. Sewed it with a dull needle and thread. If he makes it through the night without dying from infection, it would surprise me." It was well past midnight, and my body and brain were exhausted. The wine had kept me going earlier in the evening. It's probably why I didn't miss the stew earlier, but the wine no longer did its job, and I was hungry and tired.

"I'm not sure if there is anything left, but I will find what I can."

"And a light of some sort, please. Don't forget." I didn't shut the door completely behind him. The fires provided a small sliver of light. I didn't want to be left in the dark. I had wiped my face and hands when another knock came on the door. "Grand Central," I called out, exacerbated.

"Pardon?" Henry's voice called from the other side of the door.

"Come in, but fair warning, I'm wearing only my shift." I figured I would warn him before I received the same look of embarrassment that I received from Private MacDonald.

"Sergeant Lovett found your notebook." He cautiously opened the door and slowly entered. His outstretched arm had my notebook being delivered as though it was a sacrifice to the Minotaur.

"Oh, thank goodness," I said as I snatched it out of his hand and hugged the book. It was covered in mud and stunk to high heaven of piss. "Where on earth did he find it?"

"Where we found you. It must have fallen out of your pocket when..." his voice trailed off. He knew he didn't need to remind of the events from earlier that evening. "Yes." Henry said to whoever was on the other side of the door. Private MacDonald handed Henry a nub of a candle. It should give me a half hour of light. That is all I thought I would need. Long enough to get cleaned up and dressed in the clothes that Sergeant Lovett could scrounge up for me.

This time MacDonald addressed me from the other side of the door. I'm sure he didn't wish to see me undressed again. "There was no more stew, but I found this bread. I'm afraid it's hard and not much."

"That's more than I could ask for. Thank you, MacDonald." I called out over Henry's shoulder and through the door. I would have to make do.

The candle was lit and placed on one of the nearby crates. I turned to Henry. "Unless you plan on helping get this caked-on mud off my naked body, I suggest you give me a few minutes."

"Oh? Oh, but of course," Henry exclaimed in embarrassment. "I'll be right outside your door. Let me know when you've completed."

"I must be a VIP. Like, a queen or something."

"Pardon?"

"Well, who else would have a handsome lord standing guard outside her door to protect her honor while she bathed and dressed?" Exhaustion made me silly. If I didn't have to look at the place in the stockade's corner or the men that tried to assault me, I would be fine. At least, that is what I told myself over and over.

He smiled and gave an exaggerated bow. "Your grace, with your permission." He closed the door behind him and stood guard outside. I smiled. I felt as though I hadn't smiled in days. How could I flirt in those circumstances? I didn't handle stress very well and making light of the situation was all I knew to do. It gave me a sense of "maybe I would be okay and forget what happened."

Cleaned and dressed in pieces of uniform, I gnawed on the bread that had dried nearly rock hard. I picked up my notebook, looked at it, hoping I could salvage it. The candlelight had faded into a faint glow. I stared at it until it faded into nothing a minute later. When I opened the door to the storage room, I found Henry asleep and leaning against the wall. I wiped the notebook off with the water and linen cloth. I was without my pockets, since I piled them with the rest of my muddy and wet clothes. My worn-out satchel had been in my missing tent, so I dropped the notebook down my shirt. It was cold and wet as it rested next to my belly. I had to keep it safe. In a few hours we would be mount Louis and leave this place behind forever.

CHAPTER THIRTY-SEVEN

The sun crept up over the horizon. A soft glow lit the far side of the ravaged stockade. It was quite peaceful, considering all the mayhem that had occurred. The storage room in the middle of the circle of logs had a west facing door, which kept it cool in the early morning haze. The sound of men shuffling around outside of the raided storage room crept into the place I had spent a few hours tossing and turning on empty crates. I bolted up at the knock on the door. The time to leave Fort Necessity was upon us.

"Amelia, we need to leave," Henry called from the other side of the door. I collected my muddy clothes, tapped my stomach where the notebook had settled, and hopped off the crate. The bright morning sun was intense for my hangover. Henry greeted me with a gingerly smile, and all became right in my world.

"What do you think of my outfit?" I spun around in jest to show off my threads. "Actually, I've been looking forward to not wearing this dress and slipping into a pair of pants. I'm not sure I would have picked this outfit. Not really me."

"You look like one of my soldiers," he said with a frown. "The clothes are quite like what you were wearing the day I met you. The dress is filthy, and you're dressed like a man. It's a bit..." His voice trailed off.

Excuse me? "It's a bit? What?" I put my hands on my hips, ready to argue with him.

"Oh, bother. Never you mind." Henry held the door open. "Let's get Louis packed and ready to go."

As I left the storage room, I refused to look at the corner. It made my stomach clench. My attackers' faces were hidden from me, and I wasn't sure where or who they were. I took a deep breath and walked away with my head held high. I refused to let that corner defeat me.

Louis was agitated when we approached. He always seemed to know when something was going to happen. He neighed and stomped his hoof onto the muddy ground.

"Easy, buddy," I said as I rubbed his neck. "We're going to get out of here. Would my good boy like that? Are you ready to take me away from this place?" I was ready to leave.

Louis calmed down as Henry loaded up the saddlebags. I folded the layers of fabric into a bundle and tied it behind the saddle. I would have to figure out how to get it cleaned later. Besides the found uniform pieces that I was wearing, the dress was the only clothing I had left. Henry climbed in the saddle and pulled me up, while Private MacDonald gave me a knee to use as a step. I looked around at the men. There were significantly fewer men than we had started with. And the ones that remained were shells of what they once were. We would leave there and head towards Wills Creek on the path the soldiers had widened. At least we knew the trip back would take less time than our trip there.

We left Fort Necessity with little more than the clothes on our back. Whatever the men could carry, minus the weapons the French could confiscate and supplies we left behind, was all we had for our journey. Colonel George Washington led the way. Captain MacKay, from South Carolina, rode next to him. We followed up the rear. Heads hung low from disappointment. Half the men were hungover, while the other half were still drunk. We left Doctor Craik to tend to the wounded that couldn't travel with us. The French would ensure their care back at Fort Duquesne, as it was now called. I heard shouting from behind us. Cheers. Jubilation. Excitement. I turned to see what caused the commotion. The French piled the equipment and weapons we left behind in the field, and Fort Necessity smoked. The flames danced their way up the walls. I turned to look at the road ahead of us. I refused to look back.

It took us three days to get back to Wills Creek. The trek through the mountains was rough on our tired and defeated bodies. They said we left the field with military distinction, but the defeat was a colossal hit to our ego. I knew we would lose the fight and somehow thought it wouldn't be this bad. Damn that butterfly effect. I should have stopped the attack. When we left, thirty men laid dead, and another seventy wounded. I wasn't sure how many of that seventy would see many more days.

I stayed as close to Henry as I could throughout the trip. Not knowing who had attacked me the last night at Necessity, I refused to be caught alone with the guilty party.

"I haven't seen Captain Van Braam." I paused and looked around at the camp we had set up for the night. "Or Captain

Stobo. I know I saw them the night before we left." Normally, I wouldn't have noticed the coming or going of the men. I knew Henry's men and the officers, as we were in frequent contact with them.

Henry dropped a few logs next to the fire. "You haven't heard?"

"Of course not. No one would dare talk to me. After that last night, word got around, and they won't look or talk to me without your approval." I stared at the fire and ached for a pot of stew. "And we all know that will not happen. Which is fine with me. So, no. I haven't heard." My voice was sharp in response to his question.

"The night of the negotiations, I was supposed to go with Van Braam to deliver the signed agreement." Henry poked at the fire with a stick. "On my way out, I looked for you to let you know what was happening and couldn't find you. Private MacDonald said you went to relieve yourself. He could barely stand up from the amount of wine he had consumed."

"So was I. Drunk, that is." I refused to look at anything but the fire. It humiliated me at what had happened.

"I figured as much. There was a group of men huddled where you were supposed to be. I got a bad feeling deep inside me and knew you were in danger. I quickly mustered my men nearby and, well, you recall the rest." He paused for a moment. He looked at me and I could sense it. I continued to look at the fire and spun my ring. "There is nothing to repeat. I can see it still distresses you."

"The thing is," I began. "They acted as though they had the right to violate me. I never once gave anyone any sign that I was here for their pleasure. I have worked just as hard as any other man here. Shouldn't they have seen me as one of the men? An equal."

"Have you seen yourself?" Henry's voice lowered. "You are not one of the men. Even my men don't see you as a man. You have worked and fought with them, but you are not a man. You are a remarkable woman, and Lovett, Davies, Bennet, Johnson, MacDonald, they all know it. It was MacKay's men that attacked you."

My nostrils flared and lips pursed. "I could shoot those bastards." I said through gritted teeth.

"You will not shoot them, because they are not to get anywhere near you ever again. If they do, I will shoot them."

I sat there for a moment. Quiet. I thought about how much Henry had protected me. "You didn't tell me what happened to Van Braam and Stobo." I picked up a stick and poke at the fire. It reminded me of Necessity being burned to the ground. It was cathartic.

"The French took Van Braam and Stobo as political prisoners. If I hadn't stayed behind to assist you and sent Stobo in my stead, it would have been me and not Stobo."

My eyes widened. "They are war prisoners?"

"We're not officially at war with the French."

"Yet." I looked up from the fire and met Henry's eyes.

Wills Creek looked the same as we left it. We were to regroup, gather any supplies we could, and head to Winchester. I was ready to get further away from the forks of the Ohio with Henry. That place had brought me nothing but bad memories. There were a few wonderful memories, but the bad stayed at the forefront of my mind.

We left Wills Creek the following morning. I remembered crossing the river near there with Jumonville.

My stomach clenched. I thought I might hyperventilate and throw up at the same time. Memories of my capture flooded back to me and occupied my every thought and breath. We continued down the familiar path. My throat felt as though it was going to close.

I leaned back to speak to Henry in a hushed tone. "I know this place."

"In your time or now?" Henry spoke softly near my ear so no one else could hear. His soft breath sent a shiver down my spine.

I pointed to our right. "This is where I met up with Jumonville and Bouchard."

Henry sat tall in the saddle. "Are you certain?"

"Really? Do you think I would get this wrong? If one thing sticks with me, it's trauma. And... well... it was traumatic."

"Ashby owns nearby land."

"I told you I was visiting Fort Ashby when it happened. Didn't you think that this could've been where?"

"There's also Ashby's Gap, Ashby's Ferry. Both are quite a distance from here." He huffed. "No. I didn't know this is where it happened."

"Oh." I stopped. I hadn't considered that there could've been more places named after Ashby. "Well, it is. Right over there. In that small field." We crossed the stream near the location I had arrived at a couple of months ago. "I need to go over there." I pointed to the field to our left.

We separated from the group and headed over to the field where I woke up after I slipped through time. Henry helped me dismount from Louis. I rubbed Louis' neck. He snorted in protest; I couldn't blame him. I looked around the area to see if I could find any sign of my arrival or my way back. There was nothing. I closed my eyes, hoping I could feel something. Could I feel the rip to slide back to the 21st century? I stood in that spot and listened for the wind of time. I took a deep inhale, desperate for the scent of the cherry wood smoke. There were no bright lights or swirling winds. No coin or door. No exhaustion or insatiable hunger. Nothing.

I opened my eyes in disappointment. Henry remained quiet, standing next to Louis, twenty feet away from me. I'm not sure how he would have reacted if I were swept back to the future. I'm not sure if I even thought it would be possible. It broke my heart and hopes into a million pieces. Getting back to that spot and being whisked back to my time was my only plan of return. I felt lost all over again.

Without saying a word, I walked back to Henry and Louis, ready to leave. If I was going to be stuck in 1754, I better get used to it.

CHAPTER THIRTY-EIGHT

We rejoined our fellow band of weary travelers. Upon our return to the group, we received the odd look from MacDonald, Lovett, and Bennet, but the rest paid us no mind. Henry just shook his head to let them know not to worry, and that all was well. All wasn't well for me, but there was nothing more I could do. I looked around, took a deep breath to swallow my disappointment, and vowed to learn to appreciate my new life. It wouldn't be easy. I was still a 21st century woman, with a 21st century outlook in life, a love of modern conveniences like hot showers and flushing toilets, and the very bold opinion of feminism and equality stuck in the 18th century.

Within the next hour, we passed a homestead. It was small and people tended to their crops in the nearby fields. I stared off to the side as I looked at the activity, with my mouth wide open in disbelief.

Henry laughed. "You'll catch a fly in your mouth if you keep it wide open like that."

Tears pricked at the corners of my eyes. "Are you kidding me?"

"No. One might take advantage of it and fly in." Coincidently, I waved off a pesky fly as it buzzed near my ear.

"No. Not that." I shook my head. "If I would have walked in the opposite direction, I would have seen this," I dramatically waved my hands around. As if I was showing him an entirely new world. "Instead, I had to go the other way and get taken hostage by the French."

"Yes, it appears so." He chuckled. "However, if you had, then I wouldn't have met you."

I huffed and crossed my arms. "As charming as you are, that was not the rom com meet-cute I was hoping for."

"Rom com? Meet-cute? I need an Amelia translator." He shook his head. "You say the oddest things."

I laughed. "You're right." I took a deep breath in my attempt to stop giggling. "Rom com is a romantic comedy. It's a type of book I like to read. What I should have said was that there could've been a better way, a cute way, for us to meet. Instead, well... you know. There was nothing cute about all the malarkey I had to wade through to meet you."

He made a quick exhale. I recognized it as the sound he makes when he thinks about whatever crazy words have come out of my mouth and how he will respond. I called it his "thinking snort." He was less amused by my observation and the naming of his snort. "Do you think that was why you were sent here?"

"What do you mean?" I think I knew what he meant. I wanted to hear him say it.

"That the reason you are here is to meet me."

Romance couldn't have been the reason that it sent me

there. I thought there might have been the occasional spark from both of us. But I was more focused on staying alive and getting home than having a relationship. Romance, even a short one, was not on my bingo card. *Was I even going to consider it?* If I was going to be stuck in 1754 for quite a while longer, perhaps I could consider it. Hannah would be proud that I would throw myself into the world of dating and romance. I wouldn't have to be the lonely old woman wearing a housecoat and feeding her 34 cats.

"I mean, maybe the reason you were sent to Fort Prince George was to meet me. Have you ever thought of that?" I nudged him with my elbow.

"Mayhap."

I could feel his breath on the back of my neck. Shivers ran down my spine to my toes. *Did he always sit this close to me?*

I cleared my throat. "So, when should we get to Winchester? In my time, it is a decent sized city. And I know our illustrious leader used it as a base while he was working as a land surveyor. That is part of the reason I had used it as my base camp while I was doing my research."

"We will be there in a couple of days."

"You can tell me no if you would like, but can I ask a huge favor of you?" I didn't give him the opportunity to answer me. "I could really use a good night's sleep in a bed, a bath, and—if it's not too much trouble—some clean clothes."

"The bed and bath we might find. Our stay will be too short and may not find any clothes."

My shoulders sank. I had hoped to get out of a dead man's uniform. "I will take whatever I can get. Promise me that at some point I can get out of this," I said as I tugged at my clothes.

"I promise," he paused. "At some point, I will get you out of those clothes."

Wait! What did he say? "Captain Lord Henry Spencer, you, sir, are a bit too forward." I joked and put my hands on my hips. I might as well enjoy myself. The further away from the battle lines we rode, the lighter the weight on my shoulders.

"Hush, my lady." His breath was close to my ear. "I told you I wanted to keep the lord title unknown to my men."

I mimed zipping up my mouth. That stupid joke was lost on someone that had no clue what a zipper was. I would have to get better jokes.

We stopped for the night. I helped the men set up our meager campsite while Henry met with Washington and the other officers. I swear they couldn't go a day without having a meeting.

"I think you might like to hear where we're headed." Henry said to me as we left for the next leg of our trip.

"We're headed to Winchester, then to Williamsburg, right?"

"Yes, we are. I thought you would like to know we are stopping in Fredericksburg along the way."

It overcame me with emotion. Fredericksburg. My home. Many historical buildings still exist in the 21st century. I wondered if I would recognize my hometown. I longed to jump in my car and drive there, instead of the multiple days of travel that I was doomed to endure. My drive to Winchester took me two hours but would take us a few days to walk there. I had thought about the beautiful countryside and wondered what it would have been like to pass through the area in the 18th century. I was about to find out.

The well-traveled path was much flatter than the Allegheny and Blue Ridge Mountains that we had traveled through. The Virginia countryside comprised rolling hills, pasture lands, crops, wooded areas, rivers, and the smell of being home. I would like to say that the area looked familiar, but so much had changed over the past two hundred sixty-five years. Towns and cities popped up with shopping malls, movie theaters, suburban neighborhoods, cars that zoomed from one place to another, and hundreds of thousands of people. Virginia in 1754 was sparse, small towns with a few hundred people. No one was zooming anywhere in 1754. Except for that fly, which continued to buzz near my ear. I wanted to zoom it into smithereens.

We pushed our way into Winchester late on the third day of our trek and arrived on the tenth of July. I spent little time here before being whisked back in time, but I remember the urban sprawl of 21st century. Winchester of 1754 was much more compact.

My dress. My filthy, muddy, worn-out dress. I tried cleaning it the best I could throughout the travels, but I couldn't get it dried before it had to be folded up again and thrown on the back of Louis. It attracted the road dust to its wet cloth, like bugs to a light. I didn't mind the clothes that were found for me, and it made sitting on the back of Louis much easier and less of a struggle to prevent chaffing. Sergeant Lovett didn't mention where he found the clothes, and I'm not sure I wanted to know. I pushed the thought that they came from our fallen soldiers out of my mind. It was the only place that they could've come from, but it was that or the dress that would be too impractical at this point.

We met up with two companies from North Carolina while we were in Winchester. They were to head to Wills Creek to establish a permanent post. The groups of soldiers camped at the future site of Fort Loudon. Well, not all of us. Henry, ever the gentleman, was true to his word and found me lodging at an inn. I wasn't sure how I was ever going to pay back the money he had spent on me. He never once mentioned the cost, but I know he had bought me my now ruined dress and paid for food and lodging when we found taverns or guest houses. Unfortunately, we had arrived late and would leave too early to find me suitable clothing for a gentlewoman in 1754.

Cleaned, fed, better rested than normal, and ready to go home, I was up and ready to leave in the early morning. Captain MacKay and his company from South Carolina remained at Winchester. The weights continued to be lifted off my shoulders. I no longer had to endure his holier-than-thou attitude, nor worry about which of his men had attacked me. I know Henry had said they wouldn't be a concern for me, but that didn't mean I didn't look at each one trying to figure out who it was. *Would they wear a scarlet letter A for asshole?* None of Mackay's men would look back at me, so it could've been any of them. I was happy to leave them in Louis' dust.

CHAPTER THIRTY-NINE

"Where are they going?" I asked Henry later that morning as our group then split into two.

"Alexandria, to restock supplies. If you are correct and this is only the beginning, then they need to be ready for the next battle with the French and to build more forts."

"Well, I am correct." I teased him. "You should know that by now." I have given him and Washington enough information during my time with them they should know to listen to me. Washington was hesitant to listen to what I had to say, even after all this time. He thought he would learn the military tactics from English books, but I think he understood that the fighting style that was taught in England didn't apply here. War tactics were different in the colonies. There was more wild land here. More mountains. More trees. He needed to pay more attention to the fighting style of the indigenous people. It was their land, and it behooved our militia to pay attention and adapt.

The closer to the coast we got, the more homesteads and

small towns we found. Every day felt as though I was getting closer to civilization and further away from my torment. Whether it was generosity, obligation, or IOUs, we stayed at farms on the outskirts of towns along the way. I was waiting for Henry's money to run out. It wasn't like he carried around debit cards. He always found a way to take care of my needs. The way I dressed, in bits and pieces of a soldier's uniform, would bring me strange looks. Throughout the time I had been traveling with the Virginia Regiment, I didn't feel more out of place than I did when finally made it to Fredericksburg.

We crossed the Rappahannock using the ferry at Washington's home. I wanted to clap my hands together and jump up and down like I won a prize on a game show. It was home... sort of. At least it felt somewhat familiar.

Ships docked along the Fredericksburg side. I hadn't seen ships this far inland during my time. I knew Fredericksburg was one of the major ports in the thirteen colonies, but it was something else to see it in action. "We called this area Ferry Farm." I said, motioning towards Washington's family home. "They finished the reconstruction of Washington's home a couple of years ago. Well, a couple of years in my time."

"What happened to it? Did it get destroyed during the war? Do the French make it all the way here?"

"Oh, no, it's not that," I exclaimed. "I'm not sure when it gets destroyed. I think after the Revolution, and then it just got lost to time. As you can see, it wasn't like it was a grand house or anything. His sister's house becomes a tourist attraction."

"The house by the Lewis store?"

"No, the Kenmore." I looked at Henry with his

scrunched-up and confused face. Two years ago, I went to the Kenmore Plantation for a tour. I remembered Betty Washington Lewis had married Fielding Lewis, and they had built a large house. They wouldn't build that house for a few more years. "War will eventually make it here, during the Civil War, which won't happen for another hundred years."

"We are staying the night here before heading to Williamsburg. Colonel Washington said he planned for you to stay with one of his childhood acquaintances."

We crossed the Rappahannock River on the ferry from Washington's farm to the bank in Fredericksburg. Of course, there were not as many buildings in 1754 as there were in 21st century, but this was home.

Henry looked around the busy port. "Is your home here?" Henry led Louis from the ferry as we walked up the steep hill from the river to the main road. Carts traveled up and down the hill, past the tavern, carrying goods to and from warehouses. We mounted Louis at the top of the hill.

"No. It will be built in that area over there," I said, pointing beyond the main street of Fredericksburg. We followed Colonel Washington up Caroline Street. He rode his horse twenty feet in front of us. Old neighbors and friends greeted him along the way. He tipped his head in response to their accolades.

Henry looked around the area, taking it all in as though it were new to him. He had visited Fredericksburg many times, but he was trying to see it through my 21st century eyes. "Do you still take a ferry to cross the river?"

The hustle and bustle of the city was a lot to take in. "No, there are a few bridges. I usually cross the one that they will build somewhere to our right. The historical district, this area," I pointed to Caroline Street as we followed Colonel Washington to his friend's house. "There will be more houses and buildings crammed in here. Some of these buildings will still be here."

Henry studied a few of the buildings as we passed them. "Do any of these buildings look familiar?"

"That one." I was excited to see a building I had been to hundreds of times before. "My friend Maggie will own a bookstore there. It's called *By the River Bookshop*. She has a cute little tabby cat named Pom and a Dachshund name Fritz. She is always dragging me and our friend Beth into some craziness. Oh, my friend Beth, she is a professor at the university. She is one of the country's experts in Colonial America. She is brilliant."

Henry laughed. "I don't think I've ever seen you this alive."

"This is my home. Or will be my home?" I continued to look at the building that would be *By the River Bookshop*. "Over there will be *Betsy's Biscuits*. I love her French toast. I miss my friends and Hannah. Although, it makes me sad knowing that they are not here with me."

"Here we are." Washington dismounted his horse in front of a large white house on the street that I knew as Charles Street. I recognized the Georgian-styled house. I had driven past it what felt like a million times. "Miss Elizabeth Woods is expecting us."

A well dressed, older enslaved man invited us inside the home. The house was beautiful and well maintained, but not over the top decorated. A painted oil cloth, with the typical black and white checks, adorned the floor of the foyer. He showed us to a sitting room to the left. Miss Woods came bounding down the stairs. My jaw dropped. She looked exactly how Beth did, except she couldn't be older than nineteen or twenty. She pulled her medium brown hair back into a chignon, a few loose tendrils framed her delicate face. Her green eyes were full of life at the sight of her friend Washington.

"Beth?" I blurted out. I wanted to run over and hug her. *How could a younger version of my friend be standing in front of me?* Henry held my arm to keep me from darting over to her. She looked at me with a mixture of confusion and amusement.

"Captain Lord Henry Spencer and Mistress Amelia Murray, I would like to introduce you to Miss Elizabeth Woods," Washington said.

Miss Woods fell into a curtsy, and I returned the honor, albeit a clumsy attempt in my pants. I felt there should have been a dress for me to hold on to. Henry gave a slight bow. Etiquette of the 18th century differed completely from what I was used to. Curtsy. Bow. Miss. Mistress. Lord. *Oh lord, is right. I would have to get a book on etiquette.*

"It is my honor to invite you into my home," she said as she gave a smile to Washington. I could see that he was the reason she welcomed us with such open arms. "Supper is being prepared. Will you be joining me?"

"I promised Mother I would join her. Betty will stop by," Washington said as he took Miss Woods' hand and brushed her knuckles with his lips. "Captain, I will see you in the morn." His eyes didn't leave hers.

"George, must you leave?" They walked to the door, leaving me and Henry in the sitting room. I looked at Henry and mouthed "George", in a bit of disbelief that anyone would call Washington by that name. I only heard anyone call him Lieutenant Colonel and Colonel Washington. Not Mister Washington, and certainly never George. Well, at least not to his face.

"Mistress Murray," Miss Woods came through the parlor door, less enthusiastic than she was when we had arrived, but still as sweet. "Would you like to change and clean up before we sup?"

"I would love to, but..." I began, unsure how to tell her I was a scroungy looking mess and that was the best I could do. "Well, my dress was destroyed. This is all I have. If you don't want me at your table dressed like this, I can eat in my room." I looked at her and Henry. "Or something like that."

"Nonsense. There are plenty of clothes that you can wear." I looked at her, although taller than me. Her waist was small. I wasn't sure she would have anything that would fit me, but if she thought she did, I wouldn't argue with getting out of this uniform. She turned to Henry. "Captain Spencer, will you be staying here with Mistress Murray? George only mentioned the lady and I..."

I interrupted her. "We're not married. We would need separate rooms." Sure, we have slept near each other for the past couple of months, including a shared room, but I knew that during this time it would be highly inappropriate for us to share a room at the home of a friend of George Washington. It could've had a negative impact on Washington's reputation, and I knew he had an important future and a reputation to maintain.

"I will make arrangements at the inn and return to dine with you two ladies." He said with a bow and left.

CHAPTER FORTY

"*L*et's get you cleaned up," Miss Woods smiled and took me by the arm and led me upstairs, like we were college friends. "Anna, please bring clean water for Mistress Murray," she called down the stairs.

"This is your room. Anna will bring you up some hot water to clean." She opened the door wide for me to enter. It had a four-poster bed with matching floral curtains and bedspread, a dressing table, a chair that sat next to the fireplace, and a wool rug on the floor. "While you clean, I will find something for you to wear. It looks as though you need everything. My shoes may fit you. You look close to my size." I thought she was being generous by saying that I looked close to her size. She was young, thin, and taller than me.

A young, enslaved woman entered the room. She looked about the same age as Miss Woods. Dressed in a plain brown dress, with a white scarf to cover her chest, and her hair pulled back into a bun, she was beautiful and well put together. She placed a large pitcher of steaming water near a basin. "Anna will help you clean up, and I'll bring you something to wear."

"I can wash myself."

"Oh, nonsense. Anna enjoys helping," she said as she waved me off and left the room.

Enjoys helping. More like no choice but to help.

I looked at Anna sympathetically. "You really don't need to help me. I can do this by myself."

"Please, mistress. I can help."

"What if I refuse? What would happen?" I wanted to scream. She had no choice but to help me. She had no choice but to listen to do what Miss Woods tells her to do. "Apologies," I said as I put my right hand over my heart, in a signal of apology. "I will not ask for you to disobey Miss Woods, but I could ask for something to drink."

I felt terrible having her help me. That went against everything I believed in and held to be true. I couldn't ask her to disobey Miss Woods, but I thought sending her on a smaller task would somehow hold me less responsible for my participation in her oppression. It was a lie I told myself to get me through the night. The next day I would be on my way to Williamsburg, to Henry's house, where he didn't have enslaved people. I just had to keep my cool one night. I could do it at the Lovett's home, I could do it at Elizabeth's home.

As I got undressed, I tucked my notebook under the stack of dirty clothes. I cleaned up, dried with a linen towel, and wrapped myself in the blanket that was laid over the back of the chair. My hair was wet and wouldn't dry by the time we had supper, but I could pull it back in some sort of bun. I had been using a thin strip of leather to hold my hair back, but thought I might find something less rough, like a ribbon.

297

"Mistress Murray," Miss Woods announced as she entered the room. "I have a couple of dresses for you. You can take your pick." She handed me a shift that I slipped over my head. I felt so free and comfortable compared to the scratchy wool trousers I had worn for the past couple of weeks. I chose a soft blue satin dress, with lace trim, to wear. To my surprise, it fit like a glove. I must have lost some weight in my travels. If I was going to wear that for the evening, then I might as well go all out. I pulled on the silk stockings above my knees and tied a ribbon around each leg to keep them up. The entire ensemble was beautiful and heavy. In the past couple of weeks, I had forgotten the weight of the layers of clothing that women were required to wear. The shoes she offered to me to wear were slightly snug on my feet, but not enough to keep me from wearing them.

Elizabeth's green satin dress highlighted the tiny flecks of gold that highlighted her green eyes. With her fair skin, she looked as though she had never worked a hard day in her life. Poised, proper, and absolutely beautiful.

"I will have Anna help you with your hair. She does my hair so beautiful." She looked around the room and only then did she realize Anna hadn't been in there to help. "Where is Anna? She was supposed to help you."

"Oh, I asked her to bring me some tea." I tried to change the subject as quick as possible. "I was just going to pull it back in a bun or something simple. Is there is a ribbon that I could use? I've only had this worn-out piece of leather."

Elizabeth moved over to a small box that sat on the table. She rummaged through it, pulled out a ribbon and put it back. "You are going to have to tell me how you came to be with George. He is never here. Did you go on any adventures with him? What is he like as a commander of all those men?" She found a ribbon that she was happy with.

She was young enough to be my daughter, and she was the first woman that I met here that didn't make me feel always on edge. The fact that she looked like my dear friend Beth didn't hurt. I wondered if they were related. *They must be.* The family resemblance was uncanny.

"Oh, The French abducted me." I said, as though it happened every day.

"Did he rescue you from them?" She came over to help me pin my hair into place.

"No. Henry." I paused before continuing. "Captain Spencer did. I escaped the French, and he has helped take care of me ever since."

"He seems like he would be the romantic type," she said with a swoony look in her eyes.

I might have been on edge, but it was like having a conversation with Hannah. I needed to get off the men subject. "Who lives here with you? I would think a young woman would live with her parents or husband." *And straight back to the men holding the power. Great job, Amelia.*

"Father is a merchant and is always off at sea. Mother died after my birth. She came down with the birthing fever." She fidgeted with a ribbon between her delicate fingers.

"Oh, I'm so sorry to hear that." I knew during this time, many women died from infection during childbirth. It didn't make it any easier to deal with the aftermath.

"I am the mistress of the house and have Anna, Moses, and Mary to take care of my needs." A knock at the door interrupted our conversation. "If you would like, you may call me Elizabeth. I think we are friends now."

"And you may call me Amelia, if you would like."

"Miss Elizabeth," Anna had come to the door with my tea. "Captain Spencer has arrived for supper."

"Let us go have supper with the man that rescued you from the terrible French. I want to hear his brave story." Oh, geez. She laid it on thick. She might be good for some conversation, but if I was stuck in 1754, then I would need to find women my age to befriend.

"Thank you for my tea, Anna," I said apologetically. I didn't realize how long it would take her to bring me tea and the time we would have supper. "Please leave it on the table. I will drink it after supper." I was determined not to let her hard work go to waste and hoped the caffeine wouldn't keep me up all night. We were to leave for Williamsburg early in the morning.

As we descended the stairs, Henry stood at the bottom, waiting for us. He gave a sweeping bow.

"May I escort you to supper, my lady?" He said as he offered me his arm.

Oh, geez. Speaking of it being laid on thick. However cheesy as I thought it was, it made me blush. I gave a deep curtsy to mimic his bow.

"I would be honored, my lord." I looked up and gave him a smile. Elizabeth smirked and giggled.

As we walked to the table, he leaned over to me and whispered, "If I may be so bold, you look beautiful."

"I clean up nice. Don't I?" I gave him a teasing smile. "If I stay here much longer, I could get used to this. I hope you're rich enough to buy me dresses." *What was I saying?* I was inserting myself into his life, as if he didn't have a choice. *Whoa! I can be bold.*

He leaned close to my ear and whispered, "It would honor me to dress you."

I gulped and was desperate to look unaffected by his comment. The crimson blush that spread to my ears and down my chest gave me away. "I thought you mentioned something about getting me out of my clothes?" That time, I think I saw him blush.

We sat down at the formal set dining table. I panicked. If I thought I was out of my element before, I certainly was now. I took a deep breath and realized a couple of things. First, Elizabeth tied my stays a bit too snug for my liking. Second, I would just watch what Henry and Elizabeth did and imitate them. I was thankful it was just the three of us. I really needed to find a book on etiquette.

"Those wretched filthy clothes are the only clothes you own?" Elizabeth exclaimed. The look of shock on her face amused me. I almost shot the wine out of my nose from trying to hold in the laughter. "Am I missing something? Where are the rest of your clothes? Surely, Captain Spencer, you haven't left the lady without proper attire," she teased him.

"I have my dress, but it is in just as terrible a condition as the old uniform. The battlefield can make clothes a bit, um, dirty." Dirty clothes were the least of my concern during a battle. I had a feeling she wouldn't understand what it was like on a battlefield. Until a couple of months ago, I couldn't comprehend the chaos, and what we went through was only the beginning. "I lost all of my belongings in a fire."

"Is that how you lost your husband?" She looked down at my wedding ring. "In a fire?"

"My husband was killed, and I have nothing left." It was the truth. I needed to remember to be careful of the stories I tell in order to keep them straight. They killed my husband two hundred sixty-five years in the future, and I truly had nothing to my name in 1754. "And then, of course, I was held captive by the French." I looked over at Henry, who sat across the table from me. "Captain Spencer has been more than generous, but it is difficult to get clothes when we were constantly moving with the regiment. I'm sure when things settle down, we will figure out how to get me clean clothes."

"Oh, nonsense. I cannot let a friend staying in my house not have something proper to wear." She reached over the table, grabbed my hand, and gave it a squeeze. "I'll have Anna lay out clothes for you to take with you."

"That is most generous of you, Miss Woods." Henry interjected into the conversation. "I will, of course, compensate you for your generosity."

"I appreciate your generosity, however," Elizabeth had a determined look on her face. She went from playful to serious in a split second. "Instead of money, you can invite me to your wedding."

"Wedding?" I exclaimed and choked on my wine. "What wedding? Our wedding?" I shot a panicked look at Henry. "We're not getting married."

I looked at Henry in terror and confusion. He was a wonderful friend. I wanted to tease the idea of a relationship with him. But, married? We were nowhere near getting married. We hadn't even kissed.

"Oh, I beg your pardon," Elizabeth looked dejected. "I had assumed that you were engaged and to be married when you got to Williamsburg. I thought that was the reason for the expedited travel."

"I'm so sorry, Elizabeth." I grabbed her hand to ease the tension. "Henry, I mean Captain Spencer, and I are just really good friends. But if we get married, I will let you know." I gave her had a squeeze and took a drink of my wine.

I didn't know what else to say to ease the room. Henry sat there and drank a couple glasses of wine in the attempt to stifle his laughter and to hide the pink in his cheeks. I think he liked to see me squirm over the conversation of a relationship. I raised an eyebrow at him and smirked. *Laugh it up, jerk.*

We moved to the sitting room and had a couple of drinks after dinner. It was late, and we had an early departure. Henry retired to the inn, and Elizabeth and I went upstairs to look at the clothes Anna had set out for me.

A beautiful dark green petticoat and gown made of cotton, stays, a clean shift, bum roll, stockings, a pair of black shoes, and pockets. The cotton would be lightweight enough to help keep me cool during the heat of the day.

"You should take what you are wearing tonight. You will need something to meet Governor Dinwiddie." Elizabeth held up the dark green gown and glanced over to me. I gave her a confused look. I hadn't thought about what we were going to do when we got to Williamsburg. *Supper with the governor? Where is that book on etiquette?* "George mentioned meeting with the governor. I assumed he would have a ball or at least a supper to celebrate the battle."

"We lost. I'm not sure that is grounds for celebration." My eyebrows and nose scrunched in confusion.

"You will need it. Trust me. Every time I visit my friend Charlotte in Williamsburg, the governor is always hosting something. I'll have Anna bundle it for you in the morn."

"Thank you, truly."

CHAPTER FORTY-ONE

"Please tell me we are going to sleep at an inn or at a friend's house." I moaned, half-asleep to Henry. "Maybe a distant cousin twice removed?"

"Mayhap I should have left you with Elizabeth." Henry teased. "You could've shopped, do each other's hair, embroidered, or whatever else gentleladies do to occupy their time."

"You're a complete asshole." I elbowed him. "Do you know that?" I stroked Louis' neck. "Look, Louis wants a break from all of this riding." If I couldn't appeal to his good senses for my comfort, maybe I could appeal for Louis' comfort.

"I believe we overburden him with all your clothing." Henry looked back at the bundle strapped to the back of the saddle. We should have found a wagon or another horse before we left Fredericksburg. The men didn't want to bother with it for what they considered a quick ride. "Did you really need to take half her wardrobe?"

"I have my old dirty dress that I will eventually get

cleaned when we stay more than a day somewhere. I have what I'm wearing." To show it off, I flattened the front of my petticoat. The rest was in the usual tuck and fold to prevent chaffing from riding astride instead of sidesaddle. "I left the uniform for them to dispose of. We bundled the dress I wore last night. She said I would need it when I meet Governor Dinwiddie. I wasn't even sure that was going to happen, but she said he likes to show off his palace." I straightened the wide-brimmed hat I had procured from Elizabeth.

"He is the Lieutenant Governor, and it is the Governor's palace that he uses it as his own." He looked down at me. "I believe I left Mistress Amelia Murray in Fredericksburg. You must be an imposter."

I put my hands on my hips and scrunched my face in confusion. "What in the hell are you talking about?"

"Are you going to rattle on about clothes the entire trip? I think I liked it better when you talked about killing Bouchard. Not very ladylike, but it was a bit more interesting."

I could feel my entire body flush with embarrassment, anger, shock. My ears burned hot. I could've sworn that they whistled as steam radiated out of them.

"Listen here." I twisted and looked up at him. If I was going to cuss him out, I wanted to make sure he saw the fire in my eyes that were going to burn straight through him. "I have been through absolute hell and if I want to talk about being clean and wearing nice clothes and not some dead man's clothes, then that's what I'm going to do. Don't give me a hard..."

He smiled, put his hand on my chin, and stopped me mid-rant. "I would very much like to kiss you." With a kiss! I opened my mouth to answer but could only nod in response. He leaned down and planted the softest kiss on my lips. I kissed him back. *What are you doing, Amelia?*

Washington made an audible throat clear. "Will the two of you stop riling up the horses with all of your ranting and rutting?"

He had strong lips but was gentle with mine. I pulled away from him and looked ahead down the path. I lifted my hand to my own lips. My heart raced. The kiss left me breathless. And to Washington's pleasure, it left me quiet. My emotions went through me in five hundred directions. I stroked Louis' neck as I tried to figure out if it was just a kiss to shut me up or if he wanted more. I debated if it upset me that he used that tactic to get me to stop talking or if I would have done the same thing. *He asked, and I agreed. Oh, boy!*

Our first night on the road, we stopped at an inn. We secured a few rooms. The rest of the dozen men slept in a barn. We might have been able to play off the role of a married couple to share a room before, but after that kiss, that wouldn't be an option. It would mar my honor and get me labeled as a harlot. Washington had his reputation to protect as well. He didn't want prostitutes in his camp and after the last night at Fort Necessity and the free-flowing ale, wine, and whatever else was in the stores, he would limit the consumption of alcohol amongst his troops. He wouldn't stand for drunkenness or debauchery. Future soldiers of his would have me to thank for that.

Supposedly, I was to stay at Henry's house when we got to Williamsburg. I wasn't sure if that was going to happen now or not. It wasn't like we had to protect my virginity; I was a widow with a daughter, after all. Would he consider my reputation to protect? Perhaps he would rent me a room at an inn until I could find a place of my own. I wasn't sure how I could afford it. It's not like women could easily find jobs. In my old life, I was an author. I could write and sell my stories. I wasn't sure if it would work, but I had to learn to survive in 1754 and beyond.

We stayed out under the stars the next night. Henry didn't sleep near me. He kept his distance after dark. Our ride was quiet and uneventful. I wasn't sure if he thought the kiss was a mistake and was embarrassed to talk to me. It is difficult to ghost someone when they are sitting on a horse in front of you. It surprised me he continued to ride Louis with me.

The further south we traveled, the more humid it became. Mid-July on the Virginia coast was hot and humid. Bugs swarmed and they must have thought I would be a tasty meal. I smacked a mosquito that landed on my neck. Annoying little vampire better not give me malaria. The dark green fabric and the layers of clothing that I wore stifled me. The sweat trailed down my back and drenched my shift. I would wipe my face, but the sweat would creep into my eyes and sting as if I had squirted lemon juice in them. I wore the hat that Elizabeth had given me, having lost mine somewhere at Fort Necessity. It helped keep the sun off my face, but it was a boiling heat with a million percent humidity. Perhaps Henry didn't want to talk to me because I smelled like dirt and sweat. I washed up in a stream, but it wasn't as though I had soap with me. I should have thought of asking for some from Elizabeth.

The third night was a filling supper of fowl—I'm guessing chicken—potatoes and bread to sop up the juices at a tavern we stopped at for the night. Buying soap from the innkeeper, I felt better with a good wash of my cracks and crevices, but my clothes needed a good airing out. I made a mental list of items I would need if I were to stay in Williamsburg.

I pulled out my notebook. The pages were stuck together from caked on mud. Jumonville's blood stained through dates and locations I had written. It should have been burned a while ago, but it was the only thing I had to connect me to my old life. My clothes were destroyed. I never found my satchel at Necessity. It had been stolen or left behind. I had my wedding ring, but it was becoming too big. If I moved my left hand too quickly, it threatened to go flying off my finger like a frisbee. Maybe Henry could direct me to a jeweler to get the ring sized smaller? Or I could sell it to help pay my debts to Henry. I put the notebook next to my clothes, blew out my candle, and attempted to sleep. Who was I kidding? Sleep would play hide-and-seek from me. It was like being a child and trying to sleep on Christmas Eve. I would eventually fall asleep from pure exhaustion, only to wake up an hour later.

CHAPTER FORTY-TWO

Breakfast of johnnycakes, ham, and tea was to keep us fueled until our arrival in Williamsburg later in the day.

I leaned back in the saddle to speak so only Henry could hear me. "Will you eventually speak to me again?" One of us needed to break the ice. The silence drove me crazy.

In a low voice, he asked, "Are you still upset with me?"

"Who said I was upset?" My voice went up an octave, and I bolted tall in the saddle.

"I didn't treat you with the respect you deserve."

"What in the hell are you talking about? Do you mean the kiss?" It was a respectful kiss. A nice one, in fact. "Seriously? I know I must be out of practice, but I thought I kissed you back. Or am I... did I miss something?"

Henry smiled and let out a small laugh. "I am the one that must have missed something. I thought you were upset with me because I kissed you in public."

I sat back down, my excitement and anger subsided. "I mean,

to be honest, it was not romantic with our audience around us. Colonel Washington didn't look too pleased." I flicked my head toward the young colonel. "You will have to do better next time."

"Mayhap the colonel was not pleased." Henry chuckled at the thought of us getting caught. "He also suggested I propose to you to keep you an honorable woman."

The heat rushed through me. Either it was another blazing July day in Virginia, or my temper was about to flare again. "Why is everyone trying to get us married? Is that how it's done around here? You kiss a guy and then you get married? Besides, I'm not sure how honorable I am. I was married for thirteen years."

"Sometimes, the marriage comes before the kissing."

I wanted to change the subject away from marriage and kissing. I was a bit too modern to think about marrying someone after one kiss. "We need to talk about my lodging arrangements when we get to Williamsburg."

"What is there to discuss?" Henry sat straight in the saddle. "You will stay at my home."

"We are not married. If we thought people were giving us hell because of a kiss, imagine what they would say if I stayed at your place."

"Would it make you feel better to know that Colonel Washington will stay at least the first night? Governor Dinwiddie may ask him to stay after. He usually does, but he is to stay at my home tonight."

"Then it's settled. I will stay at your place tonight, in my own room. Don't get any naughty ideas, Lord Henry." I elbowed him. "The young colonel doesn't need any gossip." I quickly glanced at Washington, hoping he didn't hear me call him young or say that he would gossip. He seemed oblivious to our conversation.

I had visited the Historic Colonial Williamsburg when Hannah applied to the College of William and Mary. Many of the buildings were originals that were preserved or rebuilt to resemble the original building, and were used as shops, homes, or museums. Seeing these buildings again pulled me back to that visit. I missed Hannah. Certainly, she was worried about me.

Still mounted on our horses, Henry, Washington, and I approached a large red bricked, two-story house. There was a set of four brick steps leading to the front door. A smaller wooden building painted white sat to the right, which I assumed was the kitchen, and I thought I had seen gardens in the back. Henry dismounted Louis and helped me down. I stretched my arms out and over my head. I leaned to from side-to-side, front-to-back, in order to stretch out my tired back. Each individual vertebrae popped and cracked. Two weeks in the saddle, with not much for respite, took a toll on my back, hips, and legs.

"Will you excuse me?" Henry said to Washington as he walked up to the front door and opened it. Two men dressed in plain clothes ran out of the house and took the reins and led the horses to the back. Henry opened the door wide for us to enter and directed us to the room on the right.

I walked into the foyer. A black-and-white checkered oilcloth rug was on the floor. So much for originality. *Did Henry and Elizabeth shop from the same store?* The walls were a dark green. A set of stairs on the left led to the second floor. They showed us to the parlor on the right of the main hall foyer. The room had pale yellow walls, a red rug that covered the middle of the room, a chartreuse silk sofa, a variety of chairs, a small piano, a card table, and an enormous fireplace. Above the fireplace was a portrait of a young woman, mid-twenties, dark brown hair, brown eyes, wearing a chartreuse colored gown. I found her to be pretty. *Did he buy the sofa to match her dress?*

Loud, quick footsteps banged on the wood floor towards us. Henry came into the room where Washington and I waited. "If you please accept my apologies for not having my men prepared."

"If that is the worst of our troubles," Washington said as he sat back in the chair.

"Millie is upstairs finishing the preparations for your rooms. The men will bring your packs upstairs." Henry seemed uneasy. I don't think I had ever seen him lack that much confidence.

"We are doing great. Thank you for providing us a place to stay tonight." I tried to ease his tension. Washington seemed unnerved by it. All I was aware of was I was happy to not be on the road.

A young woman, not much older than Hannah, came down the stairs dressed in a dark brown gown, her hair pulled back in a bun. Small wisps of brown hair escaped around her ears. As she curtsied, I looked at the portrait. I was relieved to see that it was not the same woman. I wondered if the woman in the portrait was his late wife, Caroline.

"My Lord," she said, and curtsied again. "The rooms are ready for your guests."

Henry turned to us. "Let me show you to your rooms. Millie will bring up clean water for you to wash."

I followed Henry up the stairs. Washington behind me.

313

To the right was Henry's room. At the end of the large landing on the street side, my room was on the right and Washington to the left. The room was lovely, with a four-poster bed draped in floral print fabric and a matching bed cover. There was a gigantic fireplace flanked with a wingback chair and a smaller wood chair. They covered the walls in vertical striped fabric, possibly silk, in black and cream. In the corner sat a dressing table with a mirror, a wood chair, and a brush and comb. Pushed next to a door that led to a closet on the wall I shared with Henry was a tall set of drawers.

I had no time to settle in before there was a knock at my door. A man brought in my bundle that contained my pale blue gown, clean shift, stockings, shoes, petticoats, stays, and matching ribbons for stockings and hair. No sooner had I laid out the clothes on the bed, placed the ribbons on the dressing table, than there was another knock at the door. Millie was back with an ewer of clean water and linens draped over her arm.

"Thank you, Millie," I said. She didn't seem to want to look at me and left as quick as she had arrived. Odd.

We were to do a quick clean, come down for a few bites to eat, then Henry and Washington were to leave for Governor Dinwiddie's mansion. I remember visiting the mansion on my trip with Hannah; it was a short walk from Henry's house.

After a meal of slices of ham, rolls that were made in the morning, and cooked carrots, Henry and Washington prepared to leave for their meeting.

"Excuse us, Colonel." Henry said as he escorted me down the hall and to the room on the right. "Before I leave, I would like to show you the library. I can't have you wandering off looking for something to occupy your time."

We walked into the room with a wall full of books. There were a couple of wingback chairs by the fireplace, a matching red silk sofa, and dark green silk-covered walls.

"This is lovely," I squealed and clasped my hand over my mouth, when I realized that I might have shouted that for the entire house to hear. "Besides getting lost in a stack of books, is there anything else I should do or prepare or anything? I don't want to feel useless."

"Relax and enjoy yourself. Millie will bring you tea and biscuits later." Henry took my hand and brought it to his lips. "I won't be late."

My face was flushed, and my heart melted. I could get used to spending my days reading, eating biscuits, drinking tea, and being kissed by Henry.

I spun around to take in my new toy: a library filled with books. I found a set of *The Life and Strange, Surprising Adventures of Robinson Crusoe*. It may be an original print. I settled in one of the wingback chairs. When Millie entered the room with the tea service, it startled me awake. It was difficult to tell how long I slept. It was towards the end of July and didn't get dark until sometime around 9pm. Light continued to filter through the window.

"What time is it?" I asked Millie as she sat down the tea service on the nearby table.

"My lady?" She either didn't hear me or chose to not hear me.

"Never mind. Thank you for the tea." I sipped the tea, ate a biscuit, and looked out the window into the back garden. In the far back of the garden, I could see the stables.

After tea, I wanted to get some fresh air, stroll the garden, and visit Louis.

The occasional cool breeze that tickled across my skin interrupted the warm summer evening. I thought about going inside to grab my book and read in the garden, but the dark clouds rolled in. I was concerned that I would get stuck outside in a summer shower. With the dress I was wearing and the more formal one as my only clothes fit to wear, I didn't want to chance getting drenched and having nothing. I would have to save an evening read in the garden for another day.

Henry and Washington hadn't arrived home by the time I finished for the day. Leftovers from dinner made a great bedtime snack. I went upstairs to prepare for bed and plop down face first in the turned down bed. I found the clothes that I had left on the bed laid in the set of tall drawers. With my notebook safely placed in a drawer in the dressing table, I stripped down to my shift, wiped down my body with a linen towel, noted the chamber pot was behind a screen, and climbed into bed. The sheets were clean and crisp. They stuffed the mattress with straw to give it support and a feather mattress on top for added softness and comfort. Much like a pillow top mattress I had at home. Except, I had springs instead of straw, and memory foam instead of goose feathers. It was still more comfortable than the mattress from the inns or the hard ground.

I jerked awake by a loud clamor from downstairs. My heart raced. Cannon fire. No. *It was just a door, Amelia.* I could hear Henry and Washington stumble to their rooms. They must have celebrated with the governor. Boys. I laid back down to go to sleep. *I'll fuss at them in the morning for waking me up. Hopefully, they would be hungover and cranky, and I would torture them a bit to make them miserable.* It's the simple things in life that brought me joy.

There was a light rap on my door. I turned over to look at it but refused to answer. Whoever it was could wait until the morning. I could hear it creak open. "Amelia," an intoxicated Henry called out in a loud whisper. "Amelia, are you awake?"

Are you freaking kidding me? "I was asleep until your drunk and loudmouth came home." I peeked from under the blanket.

"I beg your pardon, my, my..." Henry hiccuped and stumbled over his words, "My lady. We shall attend the ball at the Governor's Palace tomorrow evening."

"Oh? Shall we?" I gave a sardonic reply. "Am I invited, or do I get to stay home alone again?"

"I shall escort the beautiful lady to the party." He swayed and grabbed hold of the door frame to brace himself. I refrained from laughing at the fool. "They are celebrating us as heroes."

I sat up and held the blanket against my chest. "They know we lost, right?"

"May I enter?"

"No, you may not. Get out and go to bed, you drunk fool." I was not about to put up with juvenile foolishness in the middle of the night. We weren't in college, he was not in his twenties, and I wasn't in the mood for any of his shenanigans. He closed the door. I laughed to myself and pulled the blanket back over my head. *Was Washington as drunk as Henry?* I shook off the thought of both men stumbling home and promptly fell back asleep.

CHAPTER FORTY-THREE

"You look and smell like horseshit." I looked at Henry and Washington with a snarled nose. Both men looked as though they had an eventful night. Henry, being the elder of the two, looked as though his recovery would take longer. They looked at each other and shrugged their shoulders. "Honestly, boys, you both smell like a tavern and look like someone pulled you out of a stable by your ears. After breakfast, you really should get cleaned up. If you can stomach it, eat and you'll feel better. Make sure you drink plenty of water."

Henry grunted a reply of some sort. "We need more wine." I was not sure what he thought he was going to prove with that tone. *Stay drunk? Was that his plan?*

"What is the plan?" I was getting frustrated with them.

"For what?"

"Are you still drunk?" I asked Henry. I looked over at Washington for an answer to my question. His head was in his hands, elbows on the dining table, and his eyes closed.

"Colonel Washington, did you pass out? What time do you have to meet with the governor?"

"Party." I got a one-word reply from Henry before he closed his eyes while he sat at the table. Plates of uneaten food sat in front of both men.

"Great. The both of you should grab your food and go sleep off your foolishness." I abruptly left the table and left my two hungover compatriots to wallow in their misery.

The heavy fog that crept through the garden told me it would be humid when the sun burned through the clouds. The garden was abuzz with bees moving from flower to flower. A squirrel skittered across the yard and twisted its way around and up the tree. One area of the garden had beautiful flowers of different colors and varieties. Most would grace tables in the house. Further back in the yard was a greenhouse and a vegetable garden. Directly behind the house, at the end of the path, was a plant covered domed outdoor room. Standing under it and looking up made me feel like I was looking at an upside-down interior of a ship's hull. The greenery covered it, making it a private room in the garden. It was peaceful and inviting.

I thought about what it would be like to live in this house permanently. Would I come out and tend to the garden? Would I read and write throughout the day? I might have to learn how to embroider. Women did that sort of thing during that time. It was silly to think about all of that, but I had to think of my future in 1754. I knew it would be difficult to make it on my own as a woman in the 18th century, and if I became the mistress of this house or any other house, I might lose my independence. He would allow me to stay if I asked. I just wasn't sure if that was what I wanted.

I had been thinking about getting home to my time, and then realized that couldn't happen. I wasn't sure how time travel worked, so just popping back home was out of the equation. Then I thought about Fredericksburg. Although that was my home, I wasn't sure if I wanted to stay there during this time. It wasn't the Fredericksburg that I had known. Williamsburg could be home. I would have a place to live and could live the rest of my life here. Would we get married? That was such a strange thought to me. I hadn't thought about marriage since Todd died. I had concluded that I would get cats, write books, travel, meet up with friends for breakfast or a hike, and just go about my life. Unattached. Independent. Tied to no one. My thoughts continued to race around my brain in a million different directions.

In 1754, my game plan might have to change. I had no income, limited rights as a woman, and the only woman friend I had was the very young Elizabeth. Henry would have to leave to fight in the war and leave me behind. What would happen in twenty years with the start of the Revolution? I would be sixty. There would be a great divide among the people that live here, and it would become dangerous for everyone. In Williamsburg, I couldn't escape it. I didn't know what I wanted. I needed to get out of the house to clear my mind and to see what I would have to deal with if I stayed here in Williamsburg or what my other options would be.

I noticed a couple of shops when we rode in the day prior and thought I could convince Henry to take me shopping. I needed dresses and shoes made, since I was going to be in

1754 for who knows how long. That would require me to drag him out of bed.

I knocked softly on Henry's bedroom door. "Hey sleepyhead, are you up?" No answer. Another tap on his door. "Henry? May I come in?" No answer. Something was wrong. He wouldn't have slept through the knocks. I opened the door and found his bed empty.

Millie closed the door from my room. "Oh, Mistress Murray, I beg your pardon." I gave her a quizzical look. I wondered what she was doing in my room. At that, she probably wondered what I was doing in Henry's room.

"Where is Lord Henry? I was looking for him and he's not in his room." I didn't want her to think I was in there with him, which I wasn't, but I needed no more gossip than I was sure was already happening.

"He mentioned he had appointments this afternoon. Mayhap I can be of service?" I was suspicious of what she was doing in my room and wanted to find a task for her so I could check for my notebook, the only thing I considered of value. Even though my wedding ring was loose on my finger, I still wore it. I hadn't been carrying the notebook in my pocket. I thought it would be safe in the room.

"Would you prepare me some tea and take it to the library? I will be down momentarily." I darted into my room and made a beeline it to the table. The notebook was still there. It didn't appear to have been moved, but I wouldn't have known if it had or hadn't. I was derelict in keeping it safe. I looked around the room to figure out what she was doing. The bed tidied, curtains opened, and the chamber pot cleaned. Suspicion level on high alert for no good reason. She was doing her job. I felt like an ass for suspecting her of being a snoop.

Shopping would have to wait until Henry returned. I headed to the library to see if I could find a book on etiquette. I needed to brush up before the governor's reception. Robinson Crusoe would wait.

Nothing. I found nothing in his library that was close to the type of book I sought. I would have to find it somewhere else. University? Book store? Did they have public libraries? Henry might help me find what I was looking for whenever he came back home. Washington had left for the Governor's Palace earlier and was expected to stay with Governor Dinwiddie for the remainder of his time in Williamsburg. Until Henry returned, I could read or head out for a walk. I spent the afternoon with Robinson Crusoe, after all.

"Amelia," Henry said as he walked into the library. I looked up from the book, slipped a ribbon in the book to hold my place, and sat up from my curled-up position on the sofa. "I beg your pardon for leaving you here alone today. There were a few appointments that I had to attend."

"Yes, Millie told me." I said lazily. From the heat of the day and from reading, I had almost fallen asleep. I stretched my arms up, a few audible pops from stretching my vertebrae pierced through the room like sniper shots. "Anything exciting?"

"One of my visits was to Matthew Hamill. He's a law professor. You'll meet him and his wife, Margaret, tonight at the governor's event." He pulled out a package he held under his arm and handed it to me.

I unwrapped the small brown paper-wrapped package. I opened the black leather-bound book to the first page. "The

Whole Duty of a Woman Or, an infallible Guide to the Fair Sex." I looked up to see his reaction. Henry wore a huge smile on his face, obviously quite proud of his find. "Containing, rules, directions, and observations, for the conduct and behavior, blah, blah, blah, and circumstances of life, good housewifery, rules, cookery."

"I thought it would be helpful for you to learn how to be a woman during this time." He looked like a dog that had done a good job digging up the garden. "Not that you're not a woman. That is to say..."

I held my hand up to keep him from inserting his foot any deeper into the bullshit. I opened to a random page in the book, ran my finger down the page, and read a few lines. "This basically says that I am to not be jealous of your improper behavior. It doesn't exactly say it, but I'm guessing I shouldn't be jealous of the things you do, to include infidelity. However, I need to remain faithful to you because you cannot control your jealousy. Does this sound about right to you?" I slammed the book shut. "What on earth made you think I would want a book on how to behave like a proper housewife? I wanted to know the protocol. When do I curtsy? When do I call you Lord Henry or Captain Henry or Asshole Henry? Do I call on someone? How do I introduce myself to people to make friends? You know, stuff like that. Not the importance of turning a blind eye to my husband's—not that I have a husband, mind you—infidelity."

He sat down next to me and took my hand. "Before you become upset with me, please hear me out." I lifted an eyebrow at him. Well, two eyebrows. I still couldn't figure out how to do the one eyebrow thing, even though I practiced while we traveled when Henry couldn't see my face. "I had asked Margaret for a book on etiquette and protocol. You were concerned about this evening's event. I've noticed your watchful eye when we've dined in Fredericksburg and here. You sought to learn. I wanted to help you get comfortable with your new world." He brought my hand to his lips and kissed my knuckles.

"I just don't want to look like a complete ass in social settings. I will have you know that whatever happens between the two of us," I said, pointing to the space between us. My emotions flared. "I will not be subservient. I have every intention of being jealous and kicking your ass to the curb if you even think about being with another woman."

"I am your humble servant, my lady." He took my hand again, kissed it, and slid closer next to me. "It would disappoint me if you were subservient. I quite enjoy your tenacity." He kissed my fingertips. "I should let you know. I don't want you thinking about being with another man."

He kissed my palm. I sucked in a quivered breath. I could feel my face flush and the goosebumps threatened to emerge over my body as he reached up and softly touched my cheek. "Oh, my. What are we going to do about this?" I let out in a breathy whisper.

"You'll stay here." He kissed my pulse point on my wrist and gave a light blow across it. Every goosebump on my body made their abrupt and pointed appearance.

"I know I'm not an expert about living in the eighteenth century and courtship, but I'm pretty sure I shouldn't be living with you." I gasp a breath.

He kissed the inside of my wrist again. He was smooth

and undeniably arousing. "You could stay here if we married."

"Whoa. Married?" I pulled my hand away. *Let's put the brakes on this for a moment.* "That's an enormous leap, don't you think?"

"As well as you are being here with me in seventeen fifty-four."

"Valid point."

"Will you, then?" He took my hand back to his lips.

"I may consider it under a couple of conditions."

Henry chuckled. "What are your conditions?"

"This is a partnership, and we respect each other. We are honest and take care of one another. We realize our upbringings are quite different. *Really* different." That was an understatement. "And we agree to work with our differences instead of against them. I will try to adapt to your time, but I need you to realize that I am not a meek wallflower."

"Agreed." He sat up straight. "Now, here are my conditions: friends first, love and respect always." I couldn't disagree with that proposal. "In public, there are certain etiquettes and protocols that are expected of the wife of a respected lord. I don't want you to deny who you are, but sometimes you need to understand your role. There will be times when we are in public where you will disagree with me and you will want to call me by my official title, Asshole Henry, but I will need for you to call me Lord Henry or Captain Spencer, dependent on the situation. We must maintain our reputations in order to get through the life we are going to lead together."

Together. He said a life together. That hit me like a ton

of bricks. "That sounds reasonable." I squeaked out and looked into his blue eyes to search for any reason for me to not to marry him. I couldn't find it. A deep breath helped cleanse my palate. "I may consider it, but there are no promises. I'm just not sure I'm ready to be married."

"I can make arrangements in the morn for the soonest potential date, if you decide it to be so. But for now, we need to get ready to go to the governor's palace."

CHAPTER FORTY-FOUR

Music and people spilled out of the governor's palace. The party was in full swing when we arrived. If I could've figured out what to do with my hair, we might have been there on time. Up, down, ribbon, no ribbon. I didn't know what I was doing, and Millie was of no help. The dress Elizabeth had given me was not as fancy as many other dresses with extra layers of lace and frills, but if I were dressed up more, I would have felt uncomfortable.

We went through the receiving line to greet Lieutenant Governor Robert Dinwiddie. He was a portly man of average height, with a powerful personality.

"Ah, Spencer, I didn't realize you were married." He attempted to sedate his Scottish accent as his voice pierced through the air. The excitement brought it out more than he had expected.

Henry bowed, and I gave a deep curtsy to Dinwiddie. "Your Excellency, I would like to introduce my betrothed Mistress Amelia Murray." I shot Henry a look. I hadn't agreed to be his wife, only that I would consider it. *Two can play at that game, my lord.*

"Is this the same Mistress Murray Colonel Washington spoke of? I heard all about the exploits of the French." Dinwiddie turned to a man standing next to him and nodded. "You fought bravely, Mistress Murray. Welcome to my palace."

I gave another curtsy. "Thank you, Your Excellency." I gave a small bow of my head. "I am honored to be here."

Henry escorted me to a quiet corner of the room. It was stifling in the packed room.

"How did I do? Was that right?" I looked behind me to see if Dinwiddie watched me and saw through my ruse. "Do you see why I need to learn protocol? I'm making this shit up as I go along."

"Stop with the worries." Henry brought my white gloved hand to his lips. "You handled yourself with beauty and grace."

"I wanted to throw up," I said with a forced smile, hoping no one could see the distress that was written in red paint across my face.

"Good thing you didn't. I'm sure His Excellency wouldn't appreciate having to change his shoes."

We mingled with his neighbors, friends, and other gentry that were invited to the party. It was all exciting and overwhelming at the same time. I wouldn't remember names, perhaps faces, but it felt as though I was trying to drink from a firehose.

The wine flowed like a rushing river. I was on my third or fourth glass—or was it my fifth?—trying to blend in with a group of women. Margaret Hamill was a young woman in her twenties, petite, with brown eyes and an unknown hair color since she wore a powdered wig. She wore a sunflower yellow silk dress over her milky white skin. She was vivacious and the center of attention amongst the other women. I felt plain standing next to her, but she brought me into the folds of her group with open arms.

"Mistress Murray," she said as she slid next to me. "I hear a wedding is in your future to the very eligible Lord Henry. You must tell us how you snared him." She gave a honey-soaked smile. "You might be the luckiest woman in Williamsburg."

I blushed. "He is quite a catch. He might feel the same way about me." I had no intention of these women thinking that I would self-deprecate. I looked over to where he stood in a new and clean uniform with a group of men, including Colonel Washington. Henry looked dignified in his uniform. He met my eyes. He caught me staring at my beautiful future-husband. *Nope, don't think like that, Amelia. You haven't said you'd marry him yet.* The many days on the road turned his skin a golden tan. I blushed and gave a shy smile. He said something to the men, and within a few strides, he was standing by my side.

"My humblest apologies. Might I steal Mistress Murray from you, ladies?" They couldn't say no to him. They curtsied as he whisked me away out to the garden. He left my glass of wine with the servant. I think I heard them giggle like schoolgirls as we flew out the back door.

The night air was cool and refreshed me. There were fire baskets illuminating the paths around the garden with puddles of light every few meters. "Thanks for rescuing me from the ladies. If I had to hear the singing of your praises anymore, I was going to fake being ill and collapse on the floor."

He snorted a laugh. "Not that terrible, was it?"

"Apparently, I might have placed a spell on the most eligible bachelor in all of Virginia in order to get you to marry me." I shook my head and laughed.

Frogs chirped and croaked songs at each other in the summer night. Maybe they were the ones spreading the gossip? An underground frog gossip circle. "News travels fast through the whispers of Williamsburg." We continued walking through the garden and made our way near the back.

"Henry," I stopped and looked up at him. "Are you sure you want to marry me and not one of the young women?" I looked back towards the house. "You realize I will not give you children. I'm too old for that madness."

He stopped and turned to look at me. He took my face in his hands, leaned down, and gave me a soft kiss on my lips. I lost my breath and my knees buckled. "If I wanted an insufferable brood mare, I would have already bedded one. I want you, Amelia Murray, and only you."

"Yeah, well, that's a good thing," I said as I rubbed my gloved fingers across the buttons on his waistcoat. "All I want is you, Henry Spencer." He grabbed me around my waist, and we sunk into a deep kiss. It was completely disreputable to make out in the garden and neither one of us cared.

His voice was deep and seductive, "Are you ready to leave?" He traced the edge of my gown across the top of my breasts. I gasped.

"Can we sneak out the back and avoid everyone?" I

wanted to run back to the house with him and jump into his bed. I felt alive, tipsy from the wine, young, indestructible, and, above all, happy and in love. *Could I admit it to myself that I was truly happy and in love with that man?* I wasn't sure I was ready to admit it to myself or to him.

We had walked around the side of the house and found Josiah, one of Henry's men, with the carriage. It was a short distance from the house. We could've walked but had to arrive in a carriage for all the pomp and circumstances which was required of the gentry.

He helped me out of the carriage, into the house, and we started up the stairs. We couldn't keep our hands to ourselves. Candles lit the foyer and up the stairs. At the top of the stairs, he gave me a long, deep kiss. I melted into a puddle—a big messy puddle.

"Stay with me, in my bed," he said as he fumbled with the pins on my gown, "tonight."

"Give me a couple of minutes to freshen up." Truth be told, I had to pee. Five—or was it six or seven—glasses of wine would do that to a person. "I'll be right back."

I stumbled towards my room. As I grasped the doorknob, I looked down and noticed a button. Or was it a coin? Where did this come from? Someone must have dropped it. I reached down to grab it. I couldn't see what was on it. It was too dark in front of my room, and I was too intoxicated. Shadows cast along the corner. I would have to look at it next to a light. I opened the door and could smell the scent of burning cherry wood. A bright light emerged from the darkness of my room. *Did Millie light a fire for me?* I felt as though I was being pulled into the room. The lights swirled around me. I remembered this feeling. It was the same feeling I had when I had gone to Fort Ashby and slipped through time. The force of the pull was too great for me to resist. I could only call out to Henry, but my voice didn't seem to make a sound over the swoosh of the wind. No. I wasn't ready to leave. I wanted to stay.

   It all went dark.

CHAPTER FORTY-FIVE

"Excuse me, ma'am. Are you alright?" I fought to open my eyes. I was exhausted, hungry, and needed to find a chamber pot. "Do you need me to call an ambulance?"

"What?" I croaked out. My throat felt as though I had swallowed the Mojave Desert.

"Do you need an ambulance?" There was a young woman standing over me. She was wearing colonial attire. She had blond hair, blue eyes, and a fake tan. *But did she say ambulance?*

"No, I don't think so. Where am I?" I propped myself up on my elbows and looked around the room. It was the same setup as my room at Henry's house, but the fabrics were all wrong. The table was in the wrong corner. I was confused. I squeezed my eyes tight and rubbed my temples. My head held onto a hangover.

The young woman reached for my shoulder. "You're in the Spencer House and Museum. What are you doing in here?"

"Spencer House?" My eyes sprung open. "Museum?" I shot into a seated position.

"I believe you went to the wrong house. I am the opener for today."

"Today? What day is it?" I was confused. The last thing I remembered was walking into my room to freshen up before I was to spend the night with Henry. "Where is Henry?"

"Henry?" She looked at me as confused as I felt. "Ma'am?"

"You know, Lord Henry Spencer. Where is he? I need to talk to him. And who are you? Are you a bondservant? No." I shook my head. "You're dressed too nice to be a servant. Long-lost sister?"

"I think Tom will arrive later. His shift starts at ten o'clock." She squinted her eyes, questioning what I was asking. "Do you need help up?"

"Who is Tom?" I was getting agitated. *Why couldn't she just give me a straight answer?*

"Tom Miller. He plays Henry Spencer during the week."

"Oh, no." I felt as though a ton of bricks dropped on my stomach. My heart ached. I knew what the answer was going to be, but I had to ask. "What is today's date?"

"July nineteenth." The morning after the party. I must have slept throughout the night.

"I know this is going to sound strange, but what year is it?"

She had a concerned look on her face as she told me the year. "Are you sure you don't need me to call you an ambulance?"

"No." I shook my head and tried to wipe the tears from my eyes. I couldn't control the water works. She helped me stand up, and I ran over to the desk. My notebook was missing. "Where is the notebook that was here?"

"If you are talking about the brown leather notebook, we keep that in the case in the study. I only got to see it opened once when the archaeologist came to do a preservation analysis."

I flew down the stairs, the young woman not far behind. I headed directly to the study. The house was decorated a bit differently than I remembered it. For me, it had only been yesterday. For the preservationists, it had been over two hundred and sixty years. There was my notebook, encased in a glass box. The caked-on mud was cleaned off it. I held my breath and closed my eyes. This wasn't happening. "I'm sorry, I should have introduced myself. I'm Amelia. May I borrow your phone? I seem to have lost mine." I patted my hips as though I looked for a phone hidden in my pockets.

"Sure," she said as she dug into her pockets and pulled out her cellphone. "I'm Paige, by the way. I started a couple of weeks ago and I'm still meeting everyone. Sorry I hadn't met you sooner. I love your dress, by the way. That looks so authentic."

I looked down at what I was wearing. It was my pale blue dress that I had worn the night of the party. It looked authentic, because it was authentic colonial attire. "Hannah, it's your mom." Hannah and I both started to cry. I was so happy to hear her voice.

"Where are you? You've been missing for months. We've been looking for you. The police tried to arrest Kyle for your disappearance. We thought he killed you."

"Slow down. Come get me. I'm in Williamsburg at the

Spencer House and Museum. Oh, and bring me food. I'm starved."

"I'll be there in fifteen minutes, tops." I could hear her grab her keys and slam her apartment door shut.

I handed Paige her phone. "Thanks. Do you mind if I look around for a few minutes?"

I wiped my wet cheeks with the back of my hand. I ran my hand across the desk. Henry's desk. I wandered into the parlor. The sofa had a chartreuse silk, but it wasn't the same as the one I sat on a couple of days ago. Above the fireplace was the portrait of Henry's first wife. "We found it in the attic. She's beautiful." Paige said behind me.

"She is." I stared at the portrait of Caroline. "Is there a portrait of Lord Henry?"

"In the library."

I nearly knocked her over as I sprinted to the library. I ran in and on the wall was a portrait of Henry in his uniform. My Henry. Young. Handsome. Just as I remembered him.

"Are there any other portraits of women?" I had hoped he had one painted to remind him of me. I worried about him. He would have looked for me. Maybe he thought I left him under the pressure of marriage. Maybe he met someone else and married her. Perhaps I would find her portrait on the wall. I might have lied to myself when I told myself I wouldn't be jealous.

"His wife's portrait is at the art restorer's shop. Some crazy guy came in a couple of months ago and threw a knife at it."

There was a knock at the front door. Hannah's voice rang through the house. Within a few strides, I was in the foyer, face-to-face with my daughter. We ran to each other. I didn't want to let her go. I wiped my tears. Then I wiped her tears. We were an absolute mess. A beautiful, happy mess.

"We've got to go to the police. What are you wearing?" She held out my arms and looked down at my gown.

I turned to Paige. "Thank you for all of your help."

"The portrait is supposed to come back next week if you want to see it. I think she looks just like you," Paige said as we left the house.

"Did she say the portrait looks like you?" Hannah said as we walked down the front steps.

"Did you bring me something to eat? Where are you parked?"

"This way." I could see the parking lot behind homes and across a field. "You've lost a lot of weight, mom. We should get you checked out."

"I'm fine. Just hungry, tired, and I really got to find a bathroom." I looked around the area for a restroom. I should have asked Paige before I left, but I was more concerned about Hannah than my bladder.

"What about the police? I called Detective Perez and told him you were here." She wrapped her arm around my waist. I needed all the support I could muster. Time travel took the energy out of me.

"Who?"

"You know, Detective Perez, Fredericksburg police detective." Hannah put the back of her hand on my forehead. "I'm taking you to the hospital."

"Hannah, stop." I stopped in my tracks and held her hand. "I promise you, I'm fine and will tell you what happened."

"Promise?"

"I promise you. Trust me." I gave her hand a squeeze and caressed her face. My beautiful daughter. I thought I would never see her again. "I will explain everything to you, but I need to use a bathroom, eat everything on *Betsy's* menu, and get a week's worth of sleep."

We continued walking towards the parking lot across the street and down the block. "You need to call Beth. She has been worried sick about you. Mom, we all have. We thought Kyle killed you. You just disappeared."

"Why would you think Kyle killed me?" A flash of thinking I had seen Kyle at *Betsy's* and Fort Ashby crossed through my memory. "He's weird, yeah. A bit of a stalker? Sure. But murderer?"

"They originally arrested him on vandalism charges."

It was early, and the streets were empty of the tourists that would flock in later. "Where?"

"At that museum. Detective Perez told me. He took a knife to a portrait. Then, when they were doing more investigating, they discovered he had dated missing author Amelia Murray. And they did a GPS tracking thing on him and found out that he followed you to Fort Ashby. Your cellphone's last ping was at a nearby tower and so was his." We reached the car. I had a lot of dress to fit in her small two door Honda Civic. "I think you're going to need to remove some layers. You are wearing something under that, aren't you?"

"I can remove my gown and petticoats." I unbuttoned my gown and laid it in the back seat. Thankfully, it was summer, which meant I wore only one petticoat. I tossed my bum roll and pockets on top of the clothes. I left on my stays and shift.

"Wow, corset and all, huh?"

"Actually, they're stays. It doesn't matter." I flittered my hand. "I'm just so happy to see you."

We drove north towards Fredericksburg. We went through McDonald's drive thru and picked me up a breakfast sandwich to hold me over until I could get changed and to *Betsy's* for the lunch menu. It took me four days to get to Williamsburg from Fredericksburg. It only took two and a half hours to get back.

She wanted to know what happened to me over the past few months. While she drove her little car 75 miles per hour up Interstate 95, I was hesitant to tell her. I didn't need the shock of hearing that I traveled through time to make her veer off the road. I didn't travel two hundred sixty-five years back to end up in a ditch.

CHAPTER FORTY-SIX

Beth was on her way to join us for lunch at *Betsy's*. She had recently moved to Williamsburg to settle in before the fall term. I remember the day I left. She said she was going to move. Everyone's life continued without me. I wanted to invite Maggie to lunch. She said she wasn't sure she could stay, but she would stop by. I spent most of the car ride thinking about what I was going to tell everyone and if they were going to commit me to a psych ward, if I told them the truth. They needed to know I was safe and alive. I would give the details in a small dose.

We pulled into the driveway at my house. I could smell the fresh cut grass. The gardener must have just left. I wanted to touch it all. It was a dream to be home. Hannah unlocked the door. The house needed airing out.

"Quick shower and change. I'll be right back."

First stop, the toilet. Again! My bladder felt as though it would burst. No chamber pot, no outdoor privy, but a flushing toilet and soft toilet paper. Bliss! Next stop, a shower. The hot running water cascaded down my body. I could stand in the shower forever. I missed flushing toilets and hot showers. Teeth brushed, hair brushed and put in a bun, and the struggle to find clothes that fit. Everything was a couple of sizes too big. I hopped on the bathroom scale. 139 flashed on the screen. I lost twenty-seven pounds. Until I could rebuild my wardrobe, I would have to pick up a few outfits. I slipped a light green sundress on over my head and a pair of sandals. The dress was oversized but would make do. It felt odd to wear underwear again.

"Beth is almost at *Betsy's*." Hannah said as she knocked on the door to my room. "Are you ready?"

Hannah and I met Beth in front of *Betsy's Biscuits* in downtown Fredericksburg. We found a table in the corner and sat down with our menus. "Is Maggie coming?" No sooner had I asked, but Maggie's voice trilled across the room, causing everyone in the restaurant to turn their head and look at her.

"Amelia," she squealed from the front door. She ran over and slid onto the bench next to Hannah, giving me a hug along the way. "I can't stay long. I must get back to the bookstore. Now that you're back, I wanted to see you. Come, say hi to Pom and Fritz when you get a chance. Hugs and kisses." With that, she flittered out the door.

"I don't think she took a breath that entire time." Beth said as we laughed. The waitress took our order.

"Tell me what's been going on since I've been gone." I wanted to break the ice without delving into my whereabouts.

Hannah and Beth took turns tell me the story of what

happened when I disappeared. Hannah had gone to the hotel in Winchester to meet up with me like we had planned. I had never checked in. They found my SUV in the Fort Ashby parking lot, but I was nowhere to be found.

A few days later, in Williamsburg, Kyle was arrested for vandalism. He had taken a knife to a portrait in the Henry Spencer House. One of the historic interpreters tackled him on the way out and the police took him in for questioning. They discovered he knew me and was a person of interest in my disappearance. They searched phone records and found out that he was at Fort Ashby at the same time I was supposed to be there. He couldn't explain what had happened to me, so they monitored him as a suspect in my disappearance. They believed he kidnapped me and could've murdered me. With no concrete evidence or confession, they couldn't hold him. I should start a new series of crime fiction based on my crazy life. They had dogs out in the area looking for me, but there was no sign of me. The story was juicy.

"Now that you know what has been going on here," Beth began. "We would like to know where you were. You had us worried."

"I've talked to Detective Perez while you were in the shower," Hannah interjected. "I told him you were fine and didn't want to talk to anyone right now. He said you can come in next week to give your statement. He also recommended that we take you to the hospital for a health and wellness check."

"I will call him after lunch, no problem. To be honest, I'm not sure what to tell him." I stopped talking when the waitress brought our food out to us. She sat down my order of barbecue chicken salad with extra greens. I missed the taste of tomatoes. While in 1754, people were still under the belief that tomatoes were deadly. I devoured the greens and extra tomatoes. I took a sip of my soft drink. My eyes were getting heavy. I needed to get through this meal and crawl into bed.

"Did you need time for yourself? Was the research too much to handle?" Beth took my hand. I stopped mid-bite and put my fork down. "We were worried about you."

I took a deep breath. "The reason I'm not sure what to tell him is... well... I can't tell him the truth."

Hannah shot daggers from her eyes at me. Beth squeezed my hand. "You can tell us the truth."

"I... you see..." I hesitated to gather my thoughts. Then, like a fountain, it all started coming out of me. So much for giving it to them in small, measured doses. I explained how I slipped through time, kidnapped by the French, and my escape. Hannah looked at me like I had two heads. Beth just sat there and listened.

"I met Captain Lord Henry Spencer. Yes, the same Henry Spencer whose home I was in this morning in Williamsburg."

Hannah threw her hands in the air. "This is unbelievable. Please, mother, tell us the truth."

"I am." Her accusations hurt me. "Jumonville had my notebook and was going to use the information in it to find out where Washington would be and attack him. He thought it would bring glory to his mediocre career."

I told them the story about taking the child to Tanaghrisson's people and the skirmish at Jumonville Glen. Tanaghrisson killed Jumonville to keep my secret and get my notebook back. If it wasn't for his actions, the French could've killed Washington.

The defeat at Fort Necessity brought me, Henry, Washington, and a few others down to Williamsburg.

"Are you going to eat those fries?" I pointed across the table at Hannah's plate. She slid her plate over to me. "Beth, I met one of your ancestors." I shoved a fry into my mouth. "She had to be your ancestor. Her name was Elizabeth Woods, and her house was still standing here in Fredericksburg. I met Hector's ancestor as well, a young Lieutenant Hector Bennet." I grabbed another lukewarm fry. "Hubba-hubba. He was a cutie." I wiggled my eyebrows at her and shoved the fry in my mouth. "I last saw him taking the troops to Alexandria to restock supplies while we headed down to Williamsburg."

"Really?" Beth seemed more interested, rather than doubtful. It was refreshing to be believed.

"Last night, we went to a celebration at the governor's palace. Henry and I were joking about saying we were engaged. We were going to spend the night together. I had gone to my room to freshen up, and I woke up this morning and you know the rest."

"You're trying to tell us you time traveled two hundred sixty-five-ish years into the past, got kidnapped, escaped, found a baby and gave it to a guy called Tanaghrisson, got a man scalped by the same guy you gave some random baby to, started a war between England and France over territory boundaries, met George Washington, met Beth and Hector's ancestors, got engaged to a Lord who is also a Captain, and then you just traveled back through time to now?" Hannah was upset. I understood why she was so angry. The truth sounded like the biggest fantasy of all time.

"That's exactly what I'm saying." I grabbed another fry. "And that is why I can't tell Detective Perez the truth. He will look at me like I'm crazy, worse than you are looking at me right now. You believe me, don't you, Beth?" I searched for sympathy and understanding from my friend. Hannah wouldn't give it to me, and I needed someone on my side.

"Actually, I do. It all sounds so farfetched, but I believe you." Beth seemed amused with revelation. "In fact, it is like I remember meeting you in seventeen fifty-four, but I couldn't have, obviously. Like we've always known each other. It must be a family memory passed down somehow. It just all makes sense to me."

"You both are crazy." Hannah threw her napkin on the table. "I think they should commit you both to a psych ward."

"Hannah, please, give me some time to prove it to you before you commit either of us."

After lunch, we drove by the house where I met 1754 Elizabeth Woods on the way to the police station so I could give a statement to Detective Perez. I told him I had lost my phone and ended up staying in a cabin for the past few months while I worked on my book. A writer's retreat. He only half-believed me. He warned me that there was something strange about Kyle, and that he would recommend, as a friend, for me to stay clear of him. I agreed.

Beth planned to take me to her house in Williamsburg for a few days so I could figure out what would happen next for me. We stopped by my house, picked up my gown and a few extra clothes. I would have to come back to

Fredericksburg to get my car and my belongings out of police custody. Here I was, again, dependent on someone else for my wellbeing and transportation. I had become so independent since Todd died. I had forgotten what it was like to put my trust in people. First Henry, and now Beth. Both proved to be good friends that I could rely on.

CHAPTER FORTY-SEVEN

"Please, Hannah," I begged into the phone. "Come explore with us."

"Okay, mom," she grumbled. "I'll meet you there."

I spent the weekend sleeping and eating. The strange thing about time travel is the amount of eating and sleeping I want to do afterwards. It drained my energy. It is like it needs to absorb my energy to hurl me back-and-forth through time. I had little energy or time to go shopping, so I ended up throwing on my sundress for the third day in a row. The middle of July in coastal Southern Virginia wouldn't require much more than what I wore. The heat and humidity would kick in before noon. I made a mental note that I would have to get to the store later this week.

Hannah met me and Beth in front of Henry's house. I hugged her and kept my arm around her waist as we looked at the front of the bricked house. Memories of my time with Henry and Washington flooded back like someone opened the Hoover Dam.

"What was Washington like?" Beth asked as we waited for the museum to open.

"Determined." I laughed. "Determined to make a name for himself. Determined to do things right, even if he was completely wrong." I took a moment to think about the young leader. "And young. He was only twenty-two, and he was leading the Virginia Regiment. Also, he was pretty ticked off at me when they scalped Jumonville. He blamed me for it." I snorted out a laugh. Good times.

A man dressed in colonial attire opened the gate to the museum. "Greetings, ladies. Welcome to the Henry Spencer House. Please have your tickets available."

Beth showed him our e-tickets on her phone. Later in the day, we were going to pick me up a new phone. I buried my old one under some tree in West Virginia.

We started the tour through the backyard, in through the back door, and into the parlor. "They restored each room to its true original design. This is Henry Spencer's first wife, Lady Caroline," the historic interpreter said. "She died in England, and he brought her portrait with him as he journeyed across the ocean to settle in the Colonies."

"It's almost right," I leaned over to Beth and Hannah. "There was a red rug in here and the fabric is all wrong on the sofa. It was closer to the color of her dress." Hannah shot me a disapproving look. It would take more than pointing out the sofa was a different color for her to believe me.

"The dining room is across the hall."

We entered the room. There were pieces missing, and the table was all wrong. I held my tongue after the look Hannah had given me in the parlor. With my arms crossed, I gave a slight nod.

THE TIME WRITER AND THE NOTEBOOK

We went down the hall to the study. Henry's office.

"This is Lord Henry Spencer's office. The most notable item we found is this notebook. It was found in the back of a drawer and covered in mud and blood. The pages were too fragile to flip through, so we don't know what they wrote in it. We believe he carried the notebook with him to the battles during the French and Indian War. Oh, to know what he found noteworthy."

Hannah gasped and quickly covered her mouth. "That looks like your notebook."

"It *is* my notebook. That is Jumonville's blood on there." I said as I raised my eyebrows in an "I told you so" kind of way.

"We will move on to the library across the hall."

We crossed the hall to the library. One of my favorite rooms in the house. Paige came bounding down the stairs. "Oh, you're back. I'm so happy you came back. I've got something to show you in the library."

"That's where we're headed now." Our tour guide informed Paige.

Next was the library. The first portrait we saw was of Henry. I stood there and stared at him. It was only days ago when I last saw him. The portrait was the only thing I had left to remember him by.

"Mom, is that him?"

"It is." I stood there with a stupid grin on my face. I missed my friend. "Snap a pic, will you?"

"No photography in the museum, ma'am." The man held up his hand to stop Hannah.

"Take it when he's not looking," I whispered to her. "Send me a copy."

349

"I wanted to show this lady," Paige began and was abruptly interrupted by the fun police. She had distracted him long enough for Hannah to snap a pic of Henry's portrait.

"Let me finish my tour," the man hushed Paige. I gave her a sympathetic look.

"Lord Henry Spencer was a captain in the Virginia Regiment, serving under George Washington. We are not sure of the date, but we know he married his second wife during that time. We had an attack on it a few months ago and received her portrait back from the restorer this morning. If you turn to look behind you, you will find the portrait of Lady Amelia Spencer."

Beth and Hannah looked at me, and simultaneously, we all turned to look at the portrait.

"Amelia," Beth gasped. "It's you."

I stared at the portrait. Tears flowed down my cheeks. Hannah wrapped her arm around my waist. Beth took my hand. My knees weakened.

"It must be one of your ancestors, ma'am." The man said, his voice was becoming a blur to me. I could only focus on the portrait of myself. "The family resemblance is uncanny."

"It's me." I whispered to Hannah and Beth. "How?"

"It is you," Hannah said. "I believe you. I don't know how it could be possible, but I believe you."

"That's what I wanted to show you," squeaked Paige. "When I saw you that morning, I knew you looked familiar. I thought you were one of the new employees. Then you mentioned your name, and I remembered the painting. I figured she must have been your great-great-great—well, I wasn't sure how many greats—grandmother."

"It's something like that," I smiled. "Can you give me a moment with my daughter and friend?"

"We can't leave you alone in the rooms," the man started.

"Please," I snapped. I took a deep breath and let it out slowly through my nose. "I just need a moment."

"We'll give you time," Paige said as she pulled the man out of the room. He moaned something about protocol.

"I don't understand. I certainly didn't sit for a portrait. We didn't get married. I came back before that could happen." My head spun. I could feel all the blood drain from my face. "I sat over there on the sofa and would read. That is where Henry proposed." I looked around the room, trying to make sense of it all. "But I'm here. Now. I didn't tell him I would marry him. We didn't get married."

"You must have gotten married. Why else would they say that?"

"We didn't." I looked at my portrait for a few moments as I raced through my memories of the past few months. I spun around and looked at Henry's portrait. My heart ached for him.

I looked at Hannah and Beth. I stared at Henry's portrait. My heart tried thumping out of my chest. I wanted to run up the stairs and collapse onto his bed. Dramatic, but my pent-up emotions wanted to take over.

"What are you going to do?" Beth asked. She could tell wild thoughts were spinning around my head.

"I've got to go back."

"How?" Asked Hannah.

"I have no clue how any of this works." My eyes made their way back to Henry's portrait. I took hold of Hannah and Beth's hands. "All I know is I left half my heart in seventeen fifty-four. How do I continue without him? I know it somehow happens; the portraits are proof. I don't know how I did it. I must find a way back to seventeen fifty-four. Back to Henry."

The adventure continues with
The Time Writer and The March

Thank you for joining me on this adventure. Join my newsletter, *The Chrononaut*, to download the prequel,
The Time Writer and The Cloak
(ebook and audiobook available), and to keep up to date with my shenanigans and new releases.
https://bit.ly/CloakNB

Reviews and ratings help readers discover books you love. Please consider leaving a review or rating wherever you purchased this book.

NOTE TO READERS

History and fiction take a wild entwining ride in this Historical Time Travel Adventure. This novel shouldn't be confused with a history book or a historical fiction book for the purists. I wanted to explore historical events from the view of a modern woman and add my own set of twists and turns. The actual history is more convoluted and detailed than represented in this novel. Years of research were undertaken to create this story, but it shouldn't be considered anywhere near an exact historical representation of the time or situation. The reasoning behind the historical anachronism of the story has nothing to do with the experts, but with me wanting to present the story the way I wanted to tell it, hoping you will enjoy it.

I make stuff up!
The words and speech of our characters are remembered through a modern woman (and terrible historian!), and you will find anachronistic words throughout the dialog and story. This was not meant to be a history book, but a look at history and time travel

NOTE TO READERS

through a sassy, crass, and outspoken twenty-first century woman. She's been through a lot of trauma, and she behaves the way she needs to in order to mentally and physically survive.

A few notes on what is fact and what is fiction in this book. The major events and the end results happened the way they were told in the story. Lieutenant Governor Robert Dinwiddie sent soldiers to build Fort Prince George at the location of William Trent's trading post on the confluence of the Allegheny and Monongahela Rivers. Captain Trent was at Wills Creek for a conference and Lieutenant John Fraser was at his plantation, leaving Ensign Edward Ward to command the building of the fort. A group of five hundred or more French soldiers confiscated the fort from the small group of Virginian soldiers, led by Ensign Ward. Ensign Joseph Coulon de Villiers, Sieur de Jumonville, was a French-Canadian military officer, and was said to be present at the confiscation of the fort that would later become Fort Duquesne, in modern day Pittsburgh, Pennsylvania.

Jumonville and a group of thirty-five soldiers were ambushed in an early morning attack by Lieutenant Colonel George Washington, forty soldiers, and a group of approximately twelve Seneca, led by Tanaghrisson. The location of the attack, Jumonville Glen, is approximately five miles from a location called Great Meadows, now Fort Necessity. There has been controversy over the reason for the movement of the French troops into the territory. One claim was for ambassadorial purposes, as Jumonville had diplomatic papers on him at the time of his death. Some believe that the papers were standard in case of being found in British territory. Jumonville and his men had spent many

NOTE TO READERS

days in the area, and it was believed that he was there on a scouting mission to expand the border of French territory.

Tanaghrisson killed and scalped Jumonville. Eyewitness accounts state that as a fact. Again, there have been multiple theories why. For the sake of *The Time Writer and The Notebook*, I used controversy as a smokescreen and assigned the reason for retrieving a notebook for his death.

Amelia and Henry's meeting with Tanaghrisson, the Seneca adopting the found baby, and the need for the retrieval of the notebook came from my vivid imagination. Our baddies: Jumonville's actions and the character Bouchard are fictitious.

The battle at **Fort Necessity** happened close to the way I represented it in this story. George Washington signed the terms of surrender, stated that he had Jumonville assassinated. Washington stated the translation of the terms, stated Jumonville was killed, not assassinated. *The Articles of Capitulation*, and the account by George Washington and James Mackay on the Capitulation of Fort Necessity on the National Archives, Founders Online, make for an interesting read on the history of the battle.

Let's discuss horses, saddles, and the second rider. I'll try to make this brief and not write another novel to discuss the intricacies of horses and horseback riding in Colonial America. In the 18th century, riders would work or ride their horses into the grave, if they weren't careful. And they weren't! Washington rode many horses to an early grave. We put quite the working on Louis; however, he was not ridden hard day-after-day, week-after-week with two riders. There were times when Amelia or Henry or both would walk instead of ride. I showed an example of this in Chapter 26, when Amelia, Henry, and Tamhas were on their way to visit Tanaghrisson. Stopping throughout the trip for water, food, and rest breaks were common, and one of the many reasons why travel took quite a while. Most saddles did not have the same type of pommels of today, if any, during this time period. In fact, some saddles were little more than a piece of leather to help prevent chaffing. Riding two to a horse, one in the saddle, the other behind the saddle was possible, but not preferred. I never said they were comfortable up there! Their travel time was to get them to their next location, build their friendship, and discuss the events surrounding both of their missions, and sometimes having them on a horse together just made more sense.

Most of the other characters, their personalities, and actions, are fictitious. Many locations are fictitious, but there was inspiration found through actual locations. Fredericksburg and Williamsburg, Virginia, are both rich in colonial history and worth the visit. I used locations in both cities as an inspiration throughout the book. Fort Ashby, West Virginia, offered Amelia her gateway to the past. Jane Ashby was a young woman (and by young, I mean, she was fourteen when she married John Ashby) that existed and was there during the construction of Fort Ashby in 1755. Washington wrote to her husband, Captain John Ashby, to get her under control because of the sedition and mutiny caused by her and rum selling by her brother at the fort. She seemed liked quite the firecracker, and I hope to explore more of her story in the upcoming book, *The Time Writer and The Hunt*.

Future books will delve into more historical events, relationships, and characters.

NOTE TO READERS

Yes, my friends, this novel takes a liberal dose of fiction and sprinkles some history throughout.

If you are interested in an in-depth writing on the history and politics of the French and Indian War, I recommend reading **Crucible of War** by Fred Anderson.

ACKNOWLEDGMENTS

The Time Writer and The Notebook, A Historical Time Travel Adventure, couldn't have been possible without the assistance and support of my family, friends, and experts.

Thank you to my editors, beta, sensitivity, and ARC readers.

I want to call out a few people on my awesome support team:

Roland DeLeon: My bestie and awesomest supporter. You've answered questions about military strategy, my partner in crime when visiting locations, my bouncer of ideas, and my inspiration for everything. Whenever I had a crazy idea, you were always by my side to help figure it out. With all I can muster from my goofy little heart, thank you. YOU ARE AMAZING!

Lars D.H. Hedbor: My friend and the most prolific novelist of the American Revolution. You're awesome, don't let it get to your head. Thanks for nerding with me, running around Las Vegas and Philadelphia, discussing history, and visiting museums. https://larsdhhedbor.com

Criss Velazquez: You gave me the push to the tools and support groups for writing a book. Thank you. I'm still waiting for you to write your next one!

Special Thanks to:

The team at **Spilled Red Ink**, whose patience through

the many rounds of edits and my pickiness for the cover art, has my eternal gratitude and love. I love the door. I love the coin. I love the map in the Time Writer logo. I love the shape of the woman. I love it all! Thank you! spilledredink.com

Fort Ashby, West Virginia: The historical experts, especially **Barbara Crane**, who answered a million and one questions from me. Visit www.fortashby.org

The Maryland Forces reenactors: Thank you for spending hours discussing camp and military life with me while you were at Fort Ashby.

Colonial Williamsburg: George Wythe House, the inspiration for Henry Spencer's house; Governor's Mansion; and the rest of Colonial Williamsburg. Visit www.colonial-williamsburg.org

Fredericksburg, Virginia, and Stafford County: Ferry Farm, the location of George Washington's childhood home; Kenmore Plantation; and Historic Fredericksburg. Visit kenmore.org

Fort Necessity and Jumonville Glen, Pennsylvania; National Park Service: Walking the same grounds and terrain gave me a better understanding of what life would have been like and how the battles played out. The impact of boots on the ground allowed me to understand the difficulties the soldiers and their supporters experienced. Thank you. Visit www.nps.gov/fone/index.htm

Museum of the American Revolution, Philadelphia, Pennsylvania: The Don Troiani display and paintings were inspiring. Visit www.amrevmuseum.org

ABOUT THE AUTHOR

Alex R. Crawford is the author of *The Time Writer*, A Historical Time Travel Adventure series. Alex grew up in Southern California and traveled the world with her military husband and daughters. She has lived in California, Texas, Georgia, Missouri, Virginia, and over six years in Germany. Crawford now calls the history-rich Washington D.C. area home.

Alex obtained a Bachelor of Science in Marketing and International Business and was one class short of having a minor in History. She regrets not completing the history minor (she loves history!). She doesn't regret not completing the two master's degrees she started in International Relations and Human Relations.

Once upon a time, she worked for the United States Federal Government as a writer, copyeditor, social media manager, and webmaster. Prior to working in public affairs, Crawford worked for the U.S. Marine Corps and U.S. Army in managing various outreach programs supporting service members and their families. Now, she is a full-time novelist, avid reader, and dog and cat wrangler.

When her nose isn't in a book or fingers typing away, she enjoys visiting historical points-of-interest and museums.

Stay in touch! Join Alex's monthly newsletter for updates on upcoming books, adventures in research, and more shenanigans. Your information is not shared, nor will you be spammed. If you like SPAM®, then Alex recommends her favorite SPAM® recipe, SPAM® fried rice.

Visit Alex's website to receive the prequel *The Time Writer and The Cloak* ebook for FREE:

https://bit.ly/CloakNB

Did you find a typo? I wouldn't be surprised. My proofreader hands me a perfectly proofread manuscript and I start changing things, because I can't leave well enough alone. Mistakes, typos, and whatnot happen. If you find an example of my disruptive behavior (typo, missing word, whatever...), please reach out to: editor@spilledredink.com and they will make updates to the book as necessary.

I stink at social media, but I'm getting better! Join me on: Facebook and Instagram @AlexRCrawfordAuthor

facebook.com/AlexRCrawfordAuthor
instagram.com/alexrcrawfordauthor

MORE ADVENTURES

The Time Writer Series:

Prequel: *The Time Writer and The Cloak*

ebook and audiobook available for FREE download to newsletter subscribers

https://bit.ly/CloakNB

Season 1: 1750s Virginia - French & Indian War

Book 1: *The Time Writer and The Notebook*

Book 2: *The Time Writer and The March*

Book 3: *The Time Writer and The Hunt*

Season 2: 1690s - The Golden Age of Piracy

Book 4: *The Time Writer and The Escape*

Book 5: *The Time Writer and The Chase*

Book 6: *The Time Writer and The Surrender*

Visit my website for early releases, special offers, and to purchase ebooks, audiobooks, signed paperbacks, and exclusive merchandise.

alexrcrawford.com